BY ELISE KOVA

Arcana Academy
Arcana Academy
Arcana Academy Book Two

Dragon Cursed
Dragon Cursed
Dragon Cursed Book Two

Married to Magic Novels
A Deal with the Elf King
A Dance with the Fae Prince
A Duel with the Vampire Lord
A Duet with the Siren Duke
A Dawn with the Wolf Knight

Air Awakens Universe

Air Awakens Series
Air Awakens
Fire Falling
Earth's End
Water's Wrath
Crystal Crowned

Vortex Chronicles
Vortex Visions
Chosen Champion
Failed Future
Sovereign Sacrifice
Crystal Caged

Golden Guard Trilogy
The Crown's Dog
The Prince's Rogue
The Farmer's War

A Trial of Sorcerers
A Trial of Sorcerers
A Hunt of Shadows
A Tournament of Crowns
An Heir of Frost
A Queen of Ice

The Loom Saga
The Alchemists of Loom
The Dragons of Nova
The Rebels of Gold

ARCANA ACADEMY

ARCANA ACADEMY

BOOK ONE OF THE
ARCANA ACADEMY SERIES

ELISE KOVA

NEW YORK

Copyright © 2025 by Elise Kova

Penguin Random House values and supports copyright. Copyright fuels creativity, encourages diverse voices, promotes free speech, and creates a vibrant culture. Thank you for buying an authorized edition of this book and for complying with copyright laws by not reproducing, scanning, or distributing any part of it in any form without permission. You are supporting writers and allowing Penguin Random House to continue to publish books for every reader. Please note that no part of this book may be used or reproduced in any manner for the purpose of training artificial intelligence technologies or systems.

All rights reserved.

Published in the United States by Del Rey, an imprint of Random House, a division of Penguin Random House LLC, New York.

DEL REY and the CIRCLE colophon are registered trademarks of Penguin Random House LLC.

Hardback ISBN 978-0-593-72634-1
Ebook ISBN 978-0-593-72635-8
International ISBN 979-8-217-09124-9

Printed in China on acid-free paper

randomhousebooks.com

2 4 6 8 9 7 5 3 1

First Edition

Maps by Diana Dworak
Book design by Elizabeth A. D. Eno

For Jenny
Thank you for believing in me.

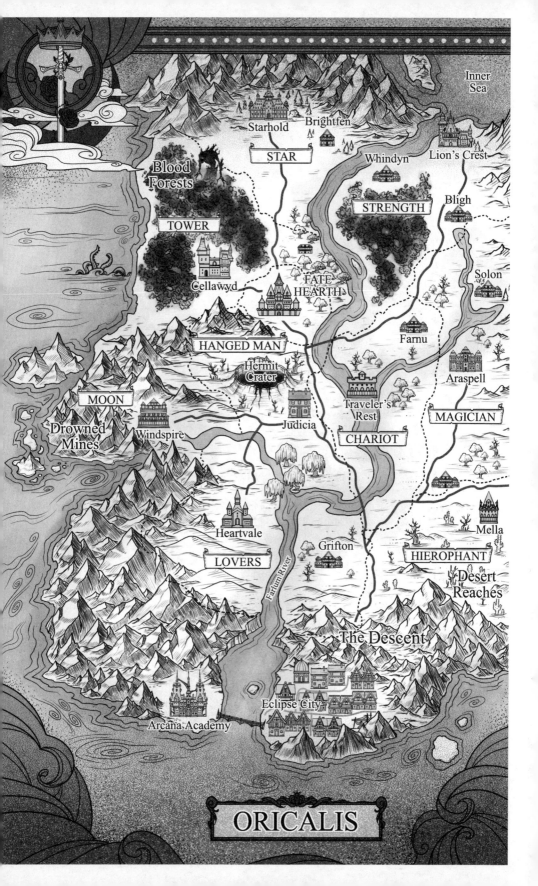

ARCANA ACADEMY

CHAPTER 1

Break or die. It's one or the other in Halazar Prison. I refuse to do either.

Two guards approach my cell. The man in front is carrying an annoyingly efficient lantern. After nearly a year of not seeing the sun, I'm blinded by mere lamplight.

It's too soon for them to be coming for me again. I expect them to pass, but they stop at my door. I don't recognize either guard, but Warden Glavstone is always rotating them out—anyone who sticks around for too long might learn too much.

"Clara Graysword?" *Graysword:* the name given to all orphaned and unwanted children in Eclipse City. The name I gave when I was captured. The name that told the world I had no family to take down with me.

I lift my chin in answer.

"You're requested for an audience." The man raises his lantern higher as if trying to get a better look at me through the bars. Unfortunate for him, as I've been left to rot, and my visage reflects it.

"Sounds formal." My voice cracks, my throat drier than yew ash. "With whom?" The guards don't answer and instead slip a key into the heavy padlock on my door.

Usually, that lock is undone once per week, and they already came for me three days ago. I'm let out only to be taken to a hidden and cramped closet in Warden Glavstone's office, where I ink tarot cards for him in exchange for what little comforts can be found in this tomb. But I would've done the work even without bartering. It has kept my mind sharp and hands skilled for when I get out of here.

Because, whether by my own skill or from my family coming for me, I am getting out. *I refuse to die here.*

The men step aside, and I slip into the space between them. Once my eyes adjust to the lamplight, I can see the place of my captivity with more clarity than ever before—more than I'd like, frankly.

By the Twenty Major Arcana, Halazar truly is horrendous.

The walls are thick with grime and blood and other substances I have willed myself not to think about. I can only imagine the stink that clouds the air—my nose has been so overwhelmed for so long that I can't smell anything anymore.

My fellow prisoners hiss at us, then shrink away from the harsh glow of the lantern and back into the safety of their shadows. Reduced to animals, their clothes in tatters like mine, they crawl over the filth on hands and knees.

The minds and bodies of the incarcerated wither away in the darkness. This is the bleakest prison in the entirety of the Oricalis Kingdom, the place where the worst of the worst go. Murderers, rapists, abusers of innocents, and those like me . . . who would *dare* to use the arcana without being under the crown's control.

I'm escorted down a passage I'm not familiar with and up a narrow flight of stairs. The guard behind me rests his hand on the pommel of his sword but doesn't bother unsheathing it. There's no need for overt threats. *Where could you go?* is the unasked question.

From a slit in the wall at the top of the stairs, a gust of icy wind batters my face. Through it I stare out at the churning river. It's dusk, or perhaps dawn; it's hard to tell, overcast as it is. Either way I can't help but squint. All I see are mountains; we're facing west, away from the city.

I inhale air so crisp that it burns my lungs. I've been reduced to a creature of squalor who doesn't even know how to breathe clean air.

"Keep it moving." The guard at my back shoves me. I stumble and grip the wall, snapping one of my brittle nails down to the bed. But my body has already suffered so many other abuses that the pain hardly registers.

We halt before an unfamiliar door. On it is carved a single sword emerging from a field of clouds. A crown caps its tip, and rose vines trellis down and around the blade.

The iconography is unmistakable—the Ace of Swords. First of the suit. Symbol of the royal family of Oricalis. Standing on either side of the door are two knights in silvered plate. Not city enforcers, or prison guards, but *royal knights*. Stellis, they're called. An elite organization of the best of the best fighters in the kingdom, sworn to protect the crown and uphold its laws. The only thing that's said to outmatch their skill and strength is their brutality. Dove-white and raven-black plumes extend from behind decorative fans of tiny swords carved into their helmets over their ears.

For a moment, I'm no longer in Halazar but back to my last hours in Eclipse City, when Stellis adorned in identical plate held me down before a judge from Clan Hanged Man. I remember the cold floor against my cheek. It contrasted with the searing heat of my shame— I'd been warned I was walking into a trap, and I did it anyway.

It takes every scrap of strength I have to remain calm. To keep my hands from shaking. To stay present even as the judge's words echo in my mind: *By decree of the crown, you are sentenced to life in Halazar.*

"Your highness, we have the prisoner," the Stellis knight calls through the door.

Highness? No. No, no, no. The urge to run nearly overwhelms me.

"Bring her in," demands a voice that is little more than a whisper of shadow, and no warmer than the darkest night of winter.

The door swings open, revealing a lavish room that should have no place in Halazar. On either side of the door are four cabinets made of yew—it's a mark of luxury to use that wood for furniture rather than burn it for inking powder. Heavy velvet curtains ward against the chill, barely letting in slivers of light.

The sheer opulence is jarring. A man dressed entirely in comparable finery dyed as black as pitch reclines in one of the two wingback chairs, his feet propped on the back of Warden Glavstone himself.

The warden's muscular arms tremble under the weight of the other man's heels—and from a thousand cuts covering his body. The pallor of his skin is in striking contrast to the blood, highlighting the brutality.

I would smile with delight at seeing the warden reduced to such a state if my every hair weren't now standing on end. *Danger*, the very air around the man in the wingback seems to whisper. Even the light seems to fear him.

Prince Kaelis, second of three sons of the Kingdom of Oricalis, reverse wielder, and headmaster of Arcana Academy. The prince who reduced an entire noble clan to rubble. A man whose name is synonymous in Oricalis with despair. Who I have every reason to believe killed my mother . . . And the man who put me in Halazar Prison.

"Clara Graysword." He speaks slowly, as if it's somehow painful to pronounce. If "Graysword" annoys him, I'd love to see him pronounce my birth name. But my true name is one of my most closely guarded secrets.

"Your royal highness." I force my tone to be dull, bored, even. To pretend I haven't spent every month of the past year cursing his name and plotting my revenge against him.

"Sit." A smirk plays on his lips.

I want to spit in his face. But I do as I'm told, stepping into the room and around the puddle of blood under the warden. As I pass, I get a clearer picture of the warden's wounds. Each of the hundreds of cuts results from a perfect slice—and each one is clean, penetrating even the warden's thick leather jacket. I've heard about the destruction the Knight of Swords card can reap in the hands of a skilled Arcanist. But I've never seen its effects in person—and I've never hated anyone enough to want to use it against them.

That is, before I met Kaelis.

Seated opposite the prince, I assess him as openly as he does me.

Everything about Prince Kaelis is severe, as if an artist were challenged to render the most brutal interpretation of masculinity one could imagine. His black patent leather boots shine with a near-mirror finish. Fitted trousers skim his strong thighs. A collared black shirt is barely visible underneath an oversized coat that's intricately embroidered with a thousand swords in silver threads. And from a chain around his neck, crafted out of a dark, flat gray steel hangs a sword with a crown on its pommel. Deep purple, nearly black hair falls around his face in messy waves, casting his eyes in perpetual shadow.

He exudes power and poise, a stark contrast to my own state: My bones protrude underneath my thin skin. My hair has never been particularly noteworthy in either texture or shade of dark brown, and now it's been roughly chopped to my ears—it was impossible to keep untangled in the depths of Halazar. My prison uniform looks as if I've worn it since the day I arrived, which I have.

"If you know who I am, then you must suspect why I'm here." Steepling his fingers, he presses them against his thin lips.

"I have my suspicions, your highness." His title tastes bitter.

"Good. Even better that you're still able to hold a conversation. Halazar has a way of making people . . . quiet," he murmurs.

Quiet? He means broken. Shattered. Not that I have much sympathy for the majority of those in these accursed halls. But there are a good few, like me, who were punished for nothing more than daring to try to make a better life for themselves and those they loved.

Kaelis reaches into his coat and retrieves a deck of cards, each one hand-painted in breathtaking detail. The colors, the symbols. Every brushstroke is immaculate. The deck fits perfectly in his long, elegant fingers. A tarot befitting a prince. It's unbearable to think that a man like him can create such beauty.

What I wouldn't give to see every card up close. Even with a man bleeding out before me and my worst enemy opposite me, all I can focus on is the stunning artistry. My hands twitch as he shuffles, drawing a card with a dramatic flourish rather than summoning it from the deck by magic.

"I've a few questions for you, Clara. And, while I'm sure you would be the image of honesty, I'm afraid I simply won't be able to take a convict at her word." He places the selected card on his palm.

The Nine of Swords. A woman lies in bed half-covered by a sheet, nine blades pin her to the mattress, her face twisted in agony.

This card must've taken nearly an entire day to ink. The level of detail—and thus the power imbued in the card—is incredible. But horror competes with my amazement. Because I know what this card means, and I know what is about to come. I was surprised it wasn't used on me at my trial. Though I'd always assumed it was because my fate had been sealed well before the trial even began. Why would they waste a card on the likes of me?

"If you please," he says. As if I have a choice to do anything but brace myself and lay my hand atop the Nine of Swords.

A flash of silver—then cold white flames incinerate the card. The fire transforms into nine skewers of light and shadow that painlessly impale my hand and his, connecting us palm to palm. Intensity overtakes the prince's eyes.

A shiver rips through me, and I briefly lose myself as the magic takes hold. The tension in my neglected and abused body ebbs from my shoulders. *Relax,* the magic of the card whispers, *give in . . .*

"Your name?"

"Clara," I answer. Even though he already knew that. One of the nine glimmering swords vanishes.

"And why are you here, Clara?" He's toying with me.

"For illegally inking, selling, and using tarot cards without first graduating Arcana Academy and being placed with a clan," I answer. The words don't feel like my own. It's as if they were forced from me by invisible threads moving in my throat.

Another sword is gone.

I refrain from adding that if it weren't for him and his family and their laws controlling the teaching and use of arcana, people like me, people without money and access, wouldn't be forced to such measures. And that it's only because of illegal inkers like me that the common folk of the kingdom can even see how the arcana could change their lives for the better.

"Illegally inking tarot got you into Halazar." He clicks his tongue. "And then what did you do once imprisoned for these crimes?"

"I inked cards at the command of Warden Glavstone." The third sword vanishes.

"You bitch," the warden snarls, yellow eyes darting to me as if *I've* somehow betrayed *him*.

"I guess I am," I answer him casually. I think I hear a snicker from the prince.

But he quickly dismisses any amusement with a shake of his head. "How many cards did you ink for the warden in the past year?"

"Hundreds, maybe almost a thousand." The answer is vague but honest. I hardly kept track . . . "It was often hours a day." The fourth sword disappears.

"From what suits?"

"Every Minor suit." *Fifth.*

"Any Major Arcana?"

"I don't know how to ink a Major Arcana; no one does," I answer plainly. *Sixth.* That magic has long since been lost—if it ever existed at all—and is now relegated to folklore.

A smirk twitches his lips. "Would you have inked a Major Arcana, if you knew how?"

"I would've tried," I admit. Mother, my arcana teacher, told me never to even attempt it—that no one had ever succeeded in doing it and my talents were better focused elsewhere. And that, even if I were to succeed, such a thing would lead only to misfortune. But I always struggled a bit with following instructions when opportunity presents itself. If I'd had an inkling of where to start, I know I would've tried.

Two swords remain.

Prince Kaelis tilts his head, studying me as though I am some kind of little animal.

"Well, then, it seems you didn't learn your lesson while here," he says gravely. "People like you—who risk the careful order of the arcana, who are a danger to our society by putting power in the hands of those untrained to use it . . . and who cannot learn from the error of their ways—must be dealt with. How do you think I should deal with you?"

"Mercifully." Even I can't help the slightest quirk of a grin when I say it.

He snorts, and the sly smile he's been wearing—like that of a cat about to pounce—widens into a full, predatory grin. One sword remains, one more question. I fear he's saved the worst for last. I brace myself.

"Who was it?"

"Who was what?" Pain rips through my hand and races up my arm. The cost of not answering.

"Who in Arcana Academy gave you and the little operation you were a part of access to my resources?"

I clench my jaw so tightly it pops. My teeth ache. *No. No!* I insist to myself. I will not say her name. Not even when it feels as if an invisible knife is slowly flaying the skin off my arm from wrist to shoulder.

"I . . . I . . ." I try to deflect from the question. The pain is making my thoughts hazy. My arm feels as if it's been dipped in boiling acid.

Kaelis pulls his feet off Glavstone's back and leans toward me. The light of the magic skewering our hands turns the pale edges of his face ghostly and deepens the shadows in the wells of his cheeks and underneath his eyes.

Looking at him, it's easy to wonder if the rumors are true that he is void-born—a wielder of the reversed arcana, an abomination that has only ever lived in folklore. And that with the twisted magic of one of those cards he ended Clan Hermit, reducing it to nothing but a memory.

"Tell me."

I clench my jaw and keep silent. I took the fall so no one else I loved would have to. I'm not losing another person who's precious to me. Not to *him*.

"I admit, I'm impressed you're able to endure this much pain, given the pathetic state you're in."

I bare my teeth at him. The swords beneath my skin have reached my chest. They're routing out my lungs.

"But you know the pain will only get worse. So, tell me, Clara . . . Who stole the resources from Arcana Academy?"

"A . . . student . . ." There's a brief second of respite, but the glowing sword skewering my hand doesn't disappear, and neither does the pain.

For some reason, my stubbornness sparks amusement in his eyes. And yet he persists. "A name, you know I want a *name*."

"Clara is a name." I struggle to think of clever ways to avoid answering. My throat aches as I dodge the truth the magic knows he wants. A thousand knives gouge into my muscles; stars explode across my vision. I'm so weak that the pain nearly makes me pass out.

His fingers tighten around mine and our hands quiver. It's as if he's physically lashing my fading consciousness to my body. "What was the name of the student, or students, who gave you access to inking tools reserved only for the academy?" he growls.

"Arina." The name escapes from me like an arrow from a bowstring. It soars all the way from Halazar Prison, across the river, to the fortress of the academy. To where my little sister—my only living blood relation—still studies. But probably not for long. My weakness has just condemned her to death. Cold horror sweeps across me, more vicious than the most brutal winters.

"Good. I'd been wondering." The prince removes his hand, and the silvery light fades. The pain vanishes, but the weight of the world crashes down on me. It takes all my strength to keep myself from collapsing back into the chair.

He stands, looming over me. "Now there's only one thing left for you."

As I look up at him, I do not even try to conceal the hate in my eyes. But my loathing only excites him more. *Twisted bastard.*

"I sentence you to death at sunset, Clara Graysword." The declaration clearly brings him immense joy.

"What?" Shock softens my voice. I'd been condemned to die here... but I was still breathing. I had been plotting my escape. However slim my chances were, there was hope.

Kaelis starts for the door, snapping toward the Stellis, who collect Glavstone and carry him out of the room.

He glances over his shoulder. "Enjoy your last hour alive, arcana traitor."

The door slams, bolting shut behind him.

CHAPTER 2

An hour. Not a lot of time. But enough to collect myself and plan my next moves.

I swallow thickly and lean back into the chair. Panic is only going to waste precious minutes on careless actions. Arina needs me to be collected and strategic. Getting out and warning her might be the only thing standing between her and a horrible death at Kaelis's hands or, worse, being Marked and sent to the mills.

I move first to the cabinets. They're locked, of course, but the locks are so flimsy they're almost merely decorative. Returning to the chairs, I pry out an upholstery nail from the satin. It's just long enough to reach the simple locking mechanism on the cabinet door. With the nail and some brute force, the lock breaks and the door opens.

In the first cabinet are rows of wine bottles covered in dust. I move on to the next cabinet. It's full of books on arcana that I have to stop myself from immediately leafing through.

Well, if I'm going to die anyway, I'm going out with a good book in hand and drunk halfway to a stupor.

On to cabinet three . . .

"Victory." I'm instantly beaming from ear to ear as the third cabinet swings open. It's been so long since I really smiled that it actually hurts. "Kaelis, you fucking idiot." Arina always griped that the prince overlooked nothing, making her plotting in the academy difficult. Based on the evidence before me, I'd beg to differ.

Unless . . . he *wanted* me to find this, and this is why he's left me here unattended. It's a possibility. But, even if he did, that won't change my actions when the alternative is certain death. I'm taking my chance when I have it.

The cabinet is filled with inking tools: Human-hair paintbrushes in all sizes. Canisters of rare pigment and bottles of oil, ready to be mixed with a palette knife. And my favorite of all . . . inkwells and pens.

Taking up an entire shelf are blank cards. I run my thumb along their edges, savoring the feel of the paper. It's an inker's dream.

I don't bother trying to cover my tracks. There's no time. My only chance is to get as far away from Halazar as I can, as quickly as possible.

Inking one card—even a simple, bare-minimum design—will take me nearly ten minutes. As I lay out the supplies on the floor, I think about which cards I have the greatest skill with. *I have time to ink three*, I decide, and set to work.

I pull out two canisters of powder, one for Coins and one for Cups. But they're both empty. Cursing, I grab for a third, Wands, also empty. The only one to have any inking powder is the fourth. I stare at the iridescent obsidian powder. Swords . . . useless for what I need to do.

But I'll make it work, even though it shouldn't.

Each suit requires its own unique pigment. Every other Arcanist I've ever met can ink Swords only with the dust of falcon feathers from the Barren Mountains, Coins with the dried and crushed berries from the Desert Reaches, Wands with the ash of yew trees from the monster-infested Blood Forests, or Cups with crushed crystal from the depths of the Drowned Mines. Being able to ink any suit with any powder is a gift, as Mother would say. Not even she could do the same.

No matter how hard I tried, it was a skill I've never been able to pass on to anyone else.

I scoop the powder into two inkwells and then mix it with a few drops of water from a bottle also in the cabinet. Then I dig a fountain pen into my fingertip. A drop of blood bubbles around the nib. I hold my finger over the inkwell, dripping blood into the ink.

Blood isn't a necessary part of the process for Arcanists, but it's the only way I know how to use a pigment designed for one suit to ink another. Mother taught me to let the magic flow organically and allow the cards to be an extension of me. Discovering this approach for pigment blending was a lucky break.

The ink charged with my power, I set to drawing. Even with a clock ticking in the back of my mind, my hand is steady. I've done this so many times it's second nature. Before I could even read, I was drawing.

Inking cards became my lifeline. The first time I was ever alone and hungry, at thirteen, Arina's hand in mine, our father long gone and our mother dead . . . I realized that I could turn my skill into food and protection. Arina followed my lead, the capricious little rebel.

As soon as the three cards are finished, I tuck two into the binding around my breasts. The third I press into my chest, and with a burst of emerald light, the card sinks into me. Magic floods my body, filling it, fueling it.

The Page of Coins grants expertise in a task for one day. And, right now, I need to be an expert in climbing. What I lack the strength for, I'll make up in skill.

I throw back the curtains, blinking into the gray light. In the distance I can see the glittering silhouette of Eclipse City. The city is close enough to swim to, but just far enough that only fools would dare to brave the eternal white water where the Farlum River meets the sea.

Today, I'm one of those fools.

I open one of the other windows, stare down at the sheer prison wall, and swallow hard. The water below seems to stretch farther and farther away the longer I stare at it. It's much too far to jump.

As I swing my leg over, I think—even with my abnormally good luck—*this is suicide.* But I'm out of options and desperate. Even if I'm playing right into the prince's game, I'll take my chances and go out fighting.

I can feel the magic from the Page of Coins surging through me as I begin to climb down. The frigid rock numbs my fingers, and still I hold fast. My toes find purchase in the cracked and wind-battered stone. Thanks to the card, I know just how to shift my weight and lock my trembling muscles to make up for the strength I've lost. I progress little by little.

But then the wind whips up the side of the building and the wall crumbles beneath my foot. Off-balance, I swing. A scream rips up my throat and I swallow it. The world spins as I look down and realize just how high I still am and just how far away the jagged rocks and river are. I strain, slamming my body back to the wall. My nose explodes with blood. But it's still better than the alternative.

Had I not possessed the skills to feed Arina and myself by illegally inking cards, as the oldest in our household I would've been climbing like this, scrambling up and down the giant chasm known as the Descent to collect the feathers of the rare falcons that roost there, to be turned into ink. Climbing until my nails fell off and my toes broke. Until my fingers gave out and I fell into the canyon, my name and face lost to the mists of the Descent's abyss forever.

That was Mother's fate, or so the enforcers told me—a lie I've never believed. *She was murdered.* Her rope was cut. But by who, and why? I still don't know. Even though trying to uncover the truth and exact my vengeance is what got me into this mess.

I continue my descent, trusting in the Page of Coins, in my own magic and strength. And as my muscles quiver and threaten to give out, I think of all the ways Kaelis could harm Arina. Even if I know my headstrong little sister would never admit it, Arina needs me.

At long last, I reach the bottom of the wall. All I want to do is collapse and catch my breath, but I force myself to keep moving. I guess I'm about forty-five minutes into my hour, and Prince Kaelis is the sort of man who would come to gather me early. If I'm on Halazar Prison Isle when he realizes I've fled, I'm dead within minutes. My only hope is to get into the river before he knows I'm gone.

Not far away, I spy a boat. The one the prince arrived on, perhaps? It's small enough that I could possibly row it solo, and I don't see anyone nearby. I'm about to make my way to it, thanking my lucky break, but then I stop: *It's too easy.* If he's toying with me, it's a trap. Even if he's not, a boat will make me too noticeable.

Swimming is insanity in my weakened state, and yet somehow safer.

I reach for one of the two remaining cards, pulling forth the Ace of Cups. Resting the card on the surface of the water, I touch it lightly. Droplets rise and arc around me, enveloping me with raw power. My eyes flutter closed as I inhale the ancient magic of the Ace of Cups, the first card in the suit. Its power gives me dominion over water.

Each Minor Arcana is governed by an element. Wands are fire, Swords air, Coins earth, and Cups water. The cards Two all the way through King of each suit have their own unique properties . . . but the Ace? That's the beginning. The primordial essence of the suit.

Taking a bracing breath and exhaling with a mantra, "Luck is on my side," I jump in.

The water is like ice and knocks the wind from my lungs. Yet, I kick my feet and fight to keep my head above the surface. Exertion warms me just enough. With the power of the Ace giving me a slight control over the element of water, I can cut through the smaller waves effortlessly. But the larger ones still overpower me.

I lose track of time. Surely, Prince Kaelis knows I'm gone by now. He's looking for me. He'll see the evidence and he'll assume what I've done, if he isn't tracking me already.

Keep. Swimming, I order myself with every gasp. My strength is leaving me, and the magic with it. The current is threatening to pull me under. And the city is still so far away . . .

Memories of the Starcrossed Club and all its comforts give me strength. *My friends. No, my family.* Bristara took Arina and me in, gave us hope. Even on the darkest of days in Halazar, my thoughts went to Arina, Gregor, Ren, Jura, Twino, Bristara . . . Even when my mind said they'd given up on me, my heart refused to believe it. *They're waiting for me. Counting on me.*

A wave crushes me. I'm pulled under to a place where only cold, oppressive darkness awaits. There in the swirling waters my nightmares lurk and become reality, threatening to rip the last breath from my lungs.

But no matter how dark the night, I refuse to give up hope of the dawn.

I touch my breast where the final card is waiting. My most popular inking. By now I must have done thousands of this one card. Nine of Cups—the wish card, a chance to make a small alteration to your fate.

Save me.

The Nine of Cups mixes with the last of the power from the Ace. The water parts, and I surface once more with a flash of purple-blue magic. I inhale deeply, catching my breath, and keep kicking. The shore isn't so far away anymore, and if I keep my head above water, I can make it. It's *so close.*

And that's when I feel the *zing* of magic from across the waves, hear a hull cutting through the water, and see the grim light fleeing from the creature that it cannot bear. My luck was bound to run out, eventually . . .

It's my worst fear proved true. *The bastard knew I would escape.* I bet he knew he'd kill me from the day of my trial and just let me rot in Halazar because he could. Everything Arina ever said about him was right.

My life is nothing but a game to him is my last thought before a snap of magic strikes me and, with a surge of agony, my muscles seize, a wave overtakes me, and the world goes dark.

CHAPTER 3

I'm kept unconscious. Every time awareness creeps back to me, someone shoos it away again by both draughts forced down my throat and ripples of magic cast across my body. Slivers of light shine into the room, and I open my cracked, dry eyelids only for them to be closed again by gentle fingers. Voices fade in and out, but none are distinguishable.

When consciousness finally settles upon me, I jolt awake, trying to capture it before it can flee again. Before they—whoever "they" are—can take it from me again.

"There, there," an elderly woman soothes. "You've been through a lot. Rest."

The room around me is nowhere I've ever been before. I'd remember somewhere this . . . *obnoxiously ostentatious.*

Every piece of furniture and framed painting is embellished with silver. On each side of the room stand ten black marble pillars. There are two sitting areas, one at the foot of the bed I lie in and one before a distant hearth large enough to roast an entire bear in. Chandeliers cast soft candlelight across the excessively dark space. The light illuminates every oddity and curio that cram the walls so extravagantly that the effect would be claustrophobic were the room not so large. However, thanks to the size of the space, the number of curiosities just makes the room feel almost . . . museum-like. Cold. Far more sterile than a typical bedroom.

And despite its size, I do presume it is a bedroom. I'm dwarfed by a four-poster bed the size of a small apartment. It's made of black stone and lined with heavy curtains. An endless ocean of quilted velvet with islands of fur at my feet drowns a vast expanse of silken sheets.

"Where in the four suits am I?" I demand, glaring at the woman and wishing I had some kind of weapon. Unfortunately, I have nothing. Not even my tattered clothing from the prison. I've been dressed in a chiffon nightgown by hands that I hope were hers.

"Arcana Academy," she answers easily, though I'd half expected her to play coy. "I'm Rewina, his highness's maid."

A maid? Not a butler? How odd . . . But the prince's unorthodox staffing is the least of my concerns.

"Why am I in the academy?" Beyond the windows that are framed in—unsurprisingly—*more* heavy velvet drapes, Eclipse City glows in the distance on the other side of the mouth of the Farlum River. An imposing wall barricades where the river meets the sea. It serves both as the bridge that connects city and academy and as a means for the royal family to control all trade to the kingdom and territories beyond.

"The prince will tell you, I presume." Is that her deferring to Kaelis's authority? Or does she not know why I'm here, either? The truth is hidden behind a seemingly warm smile, crinkling eyes, and wispy gray-and-white hair. Rewina reminds me vaguely of Bristara, though she's older than the matron of the Starcrossed Club. "Speaking of, he will want to know you're awake. Please excuse me," she says, as if I have any power here to excuse anyone.

The maid leaves, and I am alone.

Instantly, I throw aside the covers and swing my feet off the bed. It feels like it's two stories high, and my knees pop as I push myself off.

Every bit of me aches and creaks. My legs wobble. My stomach is hollow against my ribs. I somehow feel *worse* than when I left my cell. *How long was I unconscious for?*

I might be a mere twenty years old—maybe even twenty-one by now, depending on the date—but regardless, I feel three times my age.

First things first: *weapon.* I head directly for the fireplace, fighting the distractions of the view of the city out the window and the curiosities that line the walls. I grab the fire poker. The hook at the end would be a nasty thing to sink into a skull. Though I struggle to lift it in my current state, it's better than nothing.

Now to investigate the shelves for something more practical, perhaps concealable. Cards, ideally . . . and then—

"Are you going to attack me with *that*?" Kaelis's voice shivers over my skin. He makes me aware of just how naked I am under the paper-thin nightgown barely covering me.

"I was considering it." I turn, not allowing him to see my discomfort. Kaelis leans against one of the posters of the bed and shuffles his deck nonchalantly. The cards fly as effortlessly as the threats he doesn't need to speak.

"I'm glad to see you've recovered enough to be your wretched little self again."

I don't rise to his insults. "Why am I here?"

"You're in no position to make demands of me."

"Just fucking tell me." My fingers tighten against the iron. I can't shake the sense that I'm staring into the face of my mother's killer. Was it really Kaelis who ordered her rope cut? He oversees all Arcanists and laws binding them.

"Language, *language,* Clara. That's no way to speak to a prince. You'll have to work on that."

"You're going to kill me anyway, what does it matter?" I shrug, as if my own mortality is little more than a trivial matter. "At least I'll die without playing into your hands."

"Haven't you already?" He's referring to my escape attempt. *Damn it.* My suspicions were right. But even if I'd *known* for sure and not just suspected, I still would have tried my luck and attempted to escape.

"I have too much dignity to do it again," I say, goading him into telling me his plan. Because if he'd wanted it, I would already be dead.

"Dignity? The woman who was crawling through mountain tunnels and scavenging in back alleys claims to have *dignity*?" He scoffs. "Forgive me, I didn't know I was talking to the queen of the rats."

"I'd rather be queen of the rats than king of the snakes," I jab. All my life, I've heard stories of the Oricalis family. I have seen how they have ruled the Kingdom of Oricalis. I have seen the glittering spires of the rich neighborhoods of Eclipse City and the poorest shacks that lie in their shadows, filled with people hungry, cold, and desperate for a moment's compassion.

He hums. "Then, by that logic, we are well matched indeed, as you are my most perfect prey."

I grip the iron tighter, willfully ignoring the involuntary quivering in my muscles that I don't possess the strength to stop. I've no cards and no power against him. Nothing to defend myself with other than my fading strength and a poker. Meanwhile, if he wanted to, he could flay the meat from my bones with one flick of his fingers.

"Fine." I drop the poker with a clatter and hold out my empty palms in a gesture of surrender. "Why am I still alive?"

"Now you're asking the right questions." He pushes away from the poster, pockets his deck, and approaches me. As Prince Kaelis grows near, I briefly think of hooking the poker with my toes and seeing if I have enough strength to shove it right through his breastbone. I suspect I do not. And I know that with a thought he could magically summon a card from his pocket; my safety is an illusion. But it'd be a satisfying experiment. "I need you."

"You? Need *me*?" I snort.

"Why else do you think I liberated you from that prison? That I didn't let you die there?" A glint in his eyes tells me he's not lying. *A prison* you *put me in,* I want to say. The prince takes another step closer, and so I take a step back. I hit the wall by the fire. "What do you know of the twenty-first tarot card?"

Twenty-first tarot card? There are fifty-six cards in the Minor Arcana, fourteen of each suit, and twenty in the Major Arcana, not counting the illustrious Fool—the start of it all and so numbered at zero . . . Unless . . .

"The twenty-first tarot is nothing more than a myth." Mother would tell us legends of the twenty-first tarot, the World. The stories say it gives the wielder the power to change anything—*everything*. It's like the Nine of Cups but infinitely more powerful. One card so mighty it can bend reality and change the world itself. But a card like that is a dream . . .

"I assure you, it's not." He looms over me. "Think about what you could do, if the World was in your hands."

I do. Before I can stop myself, I'm imagining how a carefully worded wish and the mysterious card known as the World could make me the most powerful Arcanist to ever exist. I could own all of Eclipse City—the entire kingdom. I'd end Kaelis and his family. I could bring my mother back to life, and no one would ever hurt me or anyone I loved ever again.

Kaelis appraises me with intent, eyes shining in the flickering firelight, as if he can see all my thoughts, even the ones involving his demise. Yet, the more I fight him, the more it seems to delight him.

"Do you want it?" His voice has dropped to a whisper, heavy with purpose.

"It doesn't exist."

"It does. And you, Clara, are the final key to getting it."

"What?" This man has lost his mind.

"You look surprised." The arrogant little smirk he's been wearing widens. "Are you not the master thief who was rumored to be able to acquire anything? The woman who stole ancient inking brushes from the grand museum of Oricalis? Who would smuggle Unmarked Arcanists and illegal tarot throughout Eclipse City and beyond? All before she even reached the age of twenty?"

"I see my reputation precedes me," I manage to quip, despite my throat being as dry as the vast desert in the east of the kingdom.

But he continues as if my voice had been swallowed by the encroaching shadows. "The same woman . . ." With a slow, deliberate movement, Kaelis rests his hand on the wall by my head, a mere whisper from my short-cropped hair, and leans even closer, until there's not enough air in the room for me to breathe. There's only him, igniting every inch of me with the heightened awareness of his shape.

"The same woman who is said to be able to ink any card with *anything*? A feat so impossible it's already becoming legend in the underbelly of Eclipse City. Tell me, Clara, in Halazar, how did you manage to ink Coins and Cups cards for your escape with powder for Swords alone?"

"You . . . you made sure there was only powder for Swords there," I realize.

His eyes threaten to consume me whole. Waves of hair partially obscure the fire smoldering in his gaze. I had been used. *Tested.* My escape . . . no, even before that. The warden had me ink all manner of cards with practically nothing. *Kaelis could've killed me from the start, if he wanted to.* Perhaps my whole imprisonment was a test, all the way back to the night I was captured.

"What do you want with me?" I return to my earlier question.

"I wanted to know if you were the real deal, Clara." He scrutinizes me through his long lashes. "I wanted to see if you had not only the skill, but the *grit* to survive what comes next. To give me the World."

"I will *never* help you," I say, seething.

"Thrive in my world or die in yours. Help me and be rewarded. Fight me and everything—and everyone—precious to you will be annihilated in ways beyond your worst imagining." It is a promise, not a threat.

Arina flashes before my eyes. She's right here at the academy, under his control. I think, too, of my crew at the club, which I must assume he also knows about.

My hand flies for his throat like a viper. I press wells into his ghostly skin. Even after almost a year of not seeing the sun in Halazar, my skin is still slightly tanner than his. Kaelis's lips split into an all-out grin.

"Don't you dare." Even as my fingers tighten, they quiver. He can feel just how weak I am. Was putting me in this state part of his plan, too?

"Then do exactly as I say." He speaks with ease, despite my pathetic attempt at choking him. I don't even have the strength to reduce his words to a wheeze.

I want to break him. I want to squeeze until his eyes bulge. I don't care what it means for me: My life is forfeit anyway. That much has become apparent. Prince Kaelis is known for breaking his toys.

Without warning, the door slams open with such force it rattles the windows. There's a burst of light and the fizzle of magic from a card that, judging from the deep gouges it left in the doorframe, I can only guess was some kind of Sword.

In the doorway stands another man. He has dark hair and black eyes like Kaelis, the same shade of skin, and the same arrogant aura.

But the two are opposite in every other way: This man wears a finely tailored coat of gold with a white shirt and white trousers. His boots are a warm, honeyed color. Even the sword pendant at his neck is different. It's made of a brilliant silver that shines so brightly even in the low light that I can see it from here.

I let go of Kaelis with a shock as I realize I'm beholding Prince Ravin, heir to the Oricalis throne and regent of Eclipse City.

Kaelis leans away from me, still nonchalant, as if I hadn't just nearly tried to choke the life from him. "Hello, brother. Have you ever heard of knocking?"

"As if you'd unlock the door for me." Ravin's eyes dart between us. "What do you think you're doing?"

I'm not sure who the question is intended for, so I keep my mouth shut. Especially since I don't know if Ravin saw me with my hand at his brother's throat.

"I could ask you the same." Judging from Kaelis's tone, there is no warmth between the brothers.

"I was coming to inform you that I just received word from Glavstone that Halazar has an escapee."

My blood freezes over. Especially when Ravin's gaze settles on me.

"And that is my concern *because*?" Kaelis draws out the question, somehow managing to sound both annoyed and bored.

"It was an illegal Arcanist. Cell two hundred and five." *My cell number.* "This matter must be taken seriously and investigated to the fullest extent of the law."

"Of course it will be. I'm sure Glavstone has the matter covered."

"Indeed. I've granted Halazar guards leave to sweep Eclipse City."

"Good of you." Condescension is thick in Kaelis's voice.

"They will come here next."

"Exceptional." Kaelis shrugs.

Ravin's agitation rises at his younger brother's performative ease. "I assume you will grant them access to conduct a search, since the academy doors are open tonight."

"Yes, of course." Kaelis shifts his attention pointedly back to me. A mix of shock and fear freezes me. I'm not sure where to look. And I wish I had something more than a slip of a nightgown to protect me. "Now, if you don't mind, I'm busy."

"With what?" Ravin's attention is harsher than the lamplight in the depths of Halazar.

"I'm informing the latest applicant to the academy what will be expected of her in the upcoming Fire Festival tonight."

That's tonight? Then that means today is the first day of Wands, my birthday. *Worst birthday ever.*

"Applicant?" Ravin and I say in near unison.

"Has she not aged out of being an applicant?" Ravin asks.

"You make me sound ancient," I mutter under my breath, indignant. I turned twenty-one today. Though after Halazar I probably look eighty.

Still, twenty-one is *technically* outside the limit . . . All Arcanists in Oricalis are required to join the academy in the year after they turn twenty. The timing mirrors the twenty Major tarot, one year for each Major, with the belief that an Arcanist's skills can't mature until they've had enough time to live a year for every Major.

Those who refuse to enter the academy, or are discovered afterward by enforcers as Arcanists in hiding, are automatically Marked and sent to the powder mills. The academy offers a chance at a better life, *if* you succeed in getting in. Though . . . most fail the year one tests, or die trying.

"Her birthday is today." A slimy sensation coats my flesh at Kaelis's remark. He's clearly done his research on me.

"Then she should have joined last year. I'm not sure what entertainment she is to you, but your amusement isn't above the law."

"I disagree," Kaelis japes. His playfulness sends a vein in Ravin's temple bulging.

"Mark her and send her to a mill. Or kill her. Either way, be done." Ravin's eyes flick to me, and a frown tugs on his lips.

"Exceptions are made for nobles," Kaelis counters. "It wouldn't be the first time a nobleman's son or daughter joined the academy a *bit* late so they could finish their other tutelage."

"She's not a noble." Ravin is far too certain of that fact for my comfort.

"But she is." Kaelis reaches into his coat and withdraws a folded paper. It's yellowed and frayed at its edges. The prince crosses to his brother. "You see, I've been doing some digging. You know how . . . plagued with guilt I've been these past five years." The words fill the air with the heaviness of what's left unsaid.

Five years ago . . . No one knows the truth of what happened the day Clan Hermit was destroyed. The official statement is that the noble clan revolted against the crown and so Kaelis annihilated them all with inexplicable power. Innocent people. Countless lives. *Gone.* All by Kaelis wielding unknown magic so far-reaching and fearsome that it sparked rumors that the only thing it could have been was a reversed card. An unnatural force that is said not to exist. *But what else could it have been?* the rumors and whispers ask.

"*You* looked up something regarding Clan Hermit?" Ravin is a mix of shock and doubt.

"I wondered if, perhaps, someone survived." Kaelis hands his brother the paper. I can't read it from here, but what he says next fills in enough of the blanks. "As you can plainly see, this is Clara Redwin, the multiple-times-removed niece of High Lady Hannah Tymespun—watering down the bloodline just enough to spare her on that fateful day and making her the last surviving heiress of Clan Hermit."

What in the Twenty is he talking about? When I was captured, the last name I went by was Graysword. Before that, Mother told Arina and me to say our name was Daygar. Redwin is completely new.

As Kaelis walks back to me, I'm too stunned to speak. His dark eyes shine the way they did before he left the room in Halazar. Then he stands a bit taller, brushes the hair from his face, and laces his fingers with mine. It's oddly intimate, and the only thing that keeps me from shoving him away is the pure, full-body shock at what he says next: "Which means, as a noble and future High Lady of a clan, she is more than eligible not only to join the academy late, but also to be my future bride."

CHAPTER 4

It's rare that I'm too stunned to speak, but Kaelis has succeeded in that. I must have heard him wrong. I—

"*What?*" Ravin steals my question.

"—are you talking about?" I add, snarling under my breath.

"Father has been relentless ever since I turned twenty that it is improper for a man of my age to not have any prospects. I can only bear his griping for so many years. And, should something happen to you and your beloved Leigh—or any offspring you might someday get around to siring—the crown would fall to me." Even though Kaelis speaks matter-of-factly, a shadow crosses over Ravin at the mention of "something happening" to him and his wife. "So it's well past time I do my duty as the second-born prince. And what better way than to mend old wounds by taking the last surviving member of the clan that I destroyed by my own hand as my bride?"

"Enough of this game," Ravin snaps, discarding the parchment.

"It's not a game," Kaelis says solemnly. "I have asked her to swear upon the Four of Wands to marry me. She said yes and did so. It is done." None of that happened, but I keep my mouth shut.

Do I want to be engaged to the prince? Four suits and every Major, *no*. But I want to be Marked or sent back to Halazar much less. So I keep my fingers laced with his and ignore the taste of vomit in the back of my throat. "The only one playing a game, I think, is you. As you continue to regularly trespass into my academy without my invitation."

Ravin crosses the room in a few wide strides. Kaelis's fingers tighten, as if he's trying to keep me from running away. The elder prince comes to a stop, glaring.

This close, I pick up on differences between the brothers. They're nearly the same height—it would be impossible to tell who's taller without looking at them back-to-back—but Ravin is more muscular. His lips are slightly fuller, even when pressed into a scowl. His eyes are a very dark brown, instead of black like Kaelis's. And his hair is the shade of a flat black ink. Kaelis's is more of a deep midnight purple, like the falcon feathers harvested for pigment—a prismatic shadow of night.

"I *know* you're lying," Ravin growls.

Kaelis merely smirks at his brother's agitation. "What proof do you have?"

"Abandon this foolishness before I get Father involved."

"Before you get Father involved," Kaelis repeats with a mocking sneer. Then his voice drops to a whisper. "*Do it.* Get him involved. Try to prove wrong my claim of her lineage with or without his help. But, while you undertake your investigation, she's under my control and protection, especially after tonight."

Ravin clenches his jaw, and the muscles in his cheek bulge. His eyes dart to me. For a second, I think he'll address me directly. Though I've no idea of what he'd say. Ultimately, the firstborn prince lets out a noise of disgust. He leaves without another word, slamming the doors behind him with such force that I nearly feel the ancient foundations of Arcana Academy tremble.

The instant that we don't have an audience, Kaelis eagerly releases me. At least mutual disgust is one thing we can agree on.

"We need to get you formally enrolled as an initiate as quickly as possible and solidify your new name with the other nobles." Kaelis takes out a kerchief and wipes his fingers with it, as though he's trying to expunge my essence from him. "Before guards or enforcers arrive, or Ravin comes up with some idea to meddle in my academy, yet again."

I lock eyes with the prince. "I can't say that *he's* the one I'm worried about."

"Now, why would I harm my bride-to-be?" Kaelis flashes me a smile that only puts me more on edge.

"You can't be serious about any of this," I say flatly. It's ludicrous.

"Oh? Would you like to be Marked and sent to a mill?"

"Of course not." For most, that's a fate worse than death.

"Do you want to go back to Halazar instead?" He arches his brows, and I purse my lips in response. "I didn't think so." Kaelis shifts to face me. "I'm the only thing keeping you from going back to the lowest pit of Halazar and rotting away for the rest of what is sure to be a pathetically short life."

The "lowest pit" means one thing: the dungeons. A forsaken place solely in Glavstone's control. Somewhere that not even most guards of Halazar know about. Fear rips through me with a force I can't stop. I had to endure the forgotten lower levels of Halazar for only a brief time—after the one instance I ever dared to speak back to Warden Glavstone. The dungeons quickly taught me the lesson that he was not to be questioned: They are void of all light, warmth, and kindness. They are the place that the world forgot, where not even screams can escape.

I search Kaelis's face for the hint of a lie. For some sign that somewhere in those two voids he calls eyes there is a spark of compassion. That maybe, just maybe, he is not as horrible as the stories say.

But there is neither friend nor safety to be found in Prince Kaelis.

His threats against those I love still weigh on me. Kaelis had already maneuvered me into his clutches once, when he captured me the first time. He did it again as I tried to escape. The man is clever, scheming, and dangerous. Arina and the Starcrossed Club are all at risk thanks to me.

"And what do you want in exchange for this . . . *freedom*"—I nearly choke on the word—"you're offering me?"

"I already told you." His eyes shine in the firelight with amusement tainted with malice.

"The World," I finish for him.

He nods.

"And how am I supposed to get that for you?" If I could access that kind of power, I would have a long, long time ago. Arina and I would've brought back our mother and ended Oricalis.

"I'll go over the details, in time. For now we need to focus on getting you to, and through, the Fire Festival. You look like you can barely walk, much less fight your fate in the festival." Kaelis starts for one of the doors that line the room.

"Well, whose fault is my current state?" Kaelis pretends to ignore my remark. "What comes after?"

He pauses to shoot me a confused look. "Then you will be an initiate in the academy, and you will succeed in your tests and trials to become a student . . . or you will die."

"No." That much was clear to me. "What happens after I get you the World?"

"You think you have a right to know?"

"I do if you want my help."

"Oh, Clara . . ." He chuckles darkly. "You're not in any position to negotiate." I know the bastard's right. "Now, clean up, gather your strength, and make yourself presentable as the long-lost noble you'll claim to be—and as my one-day bride. The last thing I want is for you to embarrass me." Kaelis departs, and silence rings in my ears.

My gaze drifts out the windows and to Eclipse City beyond. Where my home is. The only home I've ever known. Where the people I must get back to are. And now that I'm out of Halazar, there is a chance I can reunite with them. Arina is in the academy. She knew of a secret passage out of the school that she can show me. This "engagement" is only temporary. My luck hasn't left me yet.

Just when I'm about to resume my search for cards—or anything else that might be of use—another door opens and Rewina enters with a bundle of dark fabrics burdening her grasp. "M'lady, his highness has prepared some options for you."

"Lovely." I don't even bother expunging the sarcasm from my tone. "Let's see what he thinks will suit me."

The prince has impeccable taste, and I think I hate him even more for it. Rewina hands me an ink-black leather coat. Its high collar grazes my chin, nearly reaching the ends of my hair. Rewina tried to style it, but she could do only so much with that Halazar hack job and me struggling to resist, flinching every time she drew close with the shears. The coat's long sleeves skim my arms with perfectly tailored precision after Rewina used the Three of Coins to tighten the seams on the supple leather. With all the layers of fabric, it's harder to tell I'm all skin and bones. A tactical choice, I assume.

Rewina attempts to remedy the latter as best she can. She brings me food that I force myself to eat slowly or else be sick. It's simple fare but heartier than anything I've eaten in almost a year. She further fortifies me with the aid of a few cards. Eventually, she steps back, admiring her handiwork. I feel like a shattered vase pasted back together. The cracks are still there, but only if you look closely.

My fingers settle on the broach pinned over my left breast. It's an intricately detailed silver pin of a fist clasping the handle of a lantern. The symbol of Clan Hermit, the once keepers of the knowledge and histories of the Oricalis Kingdom and beyond.

Every noble clan is a family that controls a small domain under the rule of the crown. The head lord or lady of the clan oversees the family, lands, and other wards on behalf of Oricalis. Clan Hermit was one of the ten major clans still standing at the end of the brutal Clan Culling, a war that narrowed the clans down from the original twenty—one clan for each Major Arcana, said to have been founded by the original acolytes of the Fool. Clan Hermit had survived countless ups and downs throughout the history of Oricalis.

But they couldn't survive Kaelis.

"The prince, did he really destroy Clan Hermit?" I ask softly.

Rewina purses her lips, and I already have my answer. "The prince does not delight in speaking of Clan Hermit. So I would avoid it if I were you. And should you seek out information, I'd do it privately." It's part advice and part warning.

"Isn't that what I'm doing by asking you?" I counter. I think I almost see a smile quirking her lips.

"Focus on what you must do to prepare for the Fire Festival."

I grew up in the slums. I don't know the first thing about being a noble, much less about Clan Hermit specifically, and least of all about how to be engaged to a prince. Especially if the ways of the clan are something that Kaelis isn't going to give me much information on.

Rewina escorts me out of the same doors that Ravin smashed in no more than an hour ago. They've already been magically repaired. A sparsely decorated receiving room awaits me, with four doors and a central table with a variety of swords stabbed into its center as some odd, macabre art piece. Kaelis and a Stellis knight talk at its side.

". . . cannot keep letting him in," Kaelis scolds, low and harsh. He's talking about Ravin, I assume.

"Yes, your highness. We'll find out who was stationed at the main entrance. And when the guards from Halazar arrive?"

"Stall them. The academy's traditions come first, and the Fire Festival parade has already begun."

The Stellis bows his feathered helmet and slips out the double doors opposite. I stare at where he just stood. All my life I was taught to fear the Stellis, and now I suddenly find myself surrounded by them.

Kaelis's attention turns to me.

"You do not look pleased." It's hard to miss my scowl when my lips are painted blood red. The deeper my displeasure, the more amused he becomes. Kaelis's voice drops—so the knights on the other side of the door don't hear our conversation, I presume. "If you'd like, I can put you back in your rags and return you to Halazar?"

"That threat is already tired, highness. You have my full compliance." I tug on the points of the sleeves that run over the backs of my hands. As I walk, the open flaps of the coat below my waist shift, revealing skintight leggings stained oxblood and tucked into boots polished to a mirror-shine finish that match his. More than a coincidence, I suspect. At least the red accents complement my carmine eyes.

"Then I suggest you tell your face as much." Kaelis blocks my path, not that I have any idea where I would go. The academy is a mazelike building that is constantly built and rebuilt by magic. From what Arina told me, it's a playground for the kingdom's most talented Arcanists—the one place where their powers are allowed to run rampant, under only the loose oversight of the sinister headmaster, who's standing right before me.

I force a smile for him and say, through clenched teeth, "Better?"

His arm snakes around my waist, and I fight a flinch as it glides over the wide belt that cinches all the heavy fabrics together. The belt is detailed with silver embellishments that mirror the lacelike metal of the decorative pauldrons that cap my shoulders. The pauldrons match similar shoulder detailing sewn onto Kaelis's shirt and the clasps that run the length of his strong torso at perfect intervals.

Kaelis is a gilded shadow, and through his clothing alone he has communicated that I am now within his gloam.

"Mildly." He's honest about how my grimace is lacking. A fair critique. "You know, there are women who would kill to be engaged to me."

The way he speaks almost has me wondering if he has ever organized such a challenge for would-be paramours. "Why haven't you made one of them swoon, then?"

"Too easy. Boring." With his fingers splayed over my hip possessively, he escorts me across the room.

I continue suppressing the urge to push him away in disgust. So far, Kaelis has been everything I imagined him to be—pompous, cruel, cunning. It's hardly surprising to hear he would prefer a courtship with a less-eager partner over a ready and willing one.

Kaelis's tone shifts, becoming serious. "I trust the little web of spies you were a part of gave you detailed information about the Fire Festival."

"I know enough." The Fire Festival is the annual opening ceremony of Arcana Academy—an extension of the summertime solstice tradition of lighting the lanterns in honor of the suit of Wands.

"Good, then you're not going in blind."

Kaelis pauses before the heavy oaken doors that the Stellis departed through. They, too, bear the sword sigil of the Oricalis family.

"So many royal motifs . . . Are you worried about forgetting what family you belong to?" I ask dryly.

Kaelis stiffens slightly. I would've missed it if our sides weren't brushing together. If his hand weren't heavy on my hip.

Interesting. He hardly seemed to get along with his brother. And the way he spoke of his father didn't seem any warmer . . . I'm already wondering if, or how, I could use this information to my advantage.

"I'm more interested in ensuring no one else forgets." His eyes dart to mine. "The rabble must remember who owns them."

He's speaking to me. *Owns.* Prince Kaelis oversees all the Arcanists of the realm, by the blessing of his father, the king. I swallow down my pride and bring my gaze forward. *Play along,* I instruct myself. He holds all the cards—all the power. My clothing might be as sharp as a dagger, but looks alone can't kill. Until I'm in a position to fight back, I need to stand down. As bloody painful as that is.

Kaelis opens the door, and I am instantly greeted by the grandeur of Arcana Academy.

Silver moonlight drenches the colossal structure, and for a moment I am left breathless. A long and narrow bridge connects the tower of Prince Kaelis's apartments to the main structure. The fortress of the academy is a titan even in silhouette, gleaming black against the last of the fading light. Spires connected by arching bridges stretch up like the hand of a fallen god, reaching as if to spite the very sky. My heart quickens, each fluttering beat sending waves of fear and thrill through me.

For years, I have stared up at this fortress from across the Farlum River. For years, this monolith was as much a legend as it was a ruin. A mystery. A danger. A pilgrimage site for Arcanists. An academy. Now I'm here. Privy to both the privilege and the peril of this illustrious institution.

Never step foot in the fortress. Never partake in the profane rituals that happen there, comes my mother's cautioning from beyond the grave.

At the same time, Kaelis leans toward me, lips by my ear. He whispers, as if to drown out the warning, "Welcome to Arcana Academy."

CHAPTER 5

We move past the two Stellis who flank the main entry of his apartments, and they close the doors behind us.

Beside me, Kaelis is a living shadow, the night clinging to the inky folds of his clothing and his every movement fluid and graceful. He holds me close, his hand on my hip, as he guides me into the heart of his dominion.

We glide across the narrow bridge and under an archway, plunging into unlit passages. The halls yawn, wide and endless. Unlit lanterns wait for the festival of light to rekindle them. A palpable energy hangs in the air, an anticipation that slithers under my leather coat sleeves. It's hard to tell if it's my nerves or the ancient magic of this place.

To collect myself, I recount every bit of knowledge I've ever been given about this strange fortress.

Arcana Academy predates the Oricalis Castle in Fate Hearth far to the north of Eclipse City and is rumored to be a remnant of the ancient Revisan Kingdom. Its ties to the long-ago kingdom made it forbidden ground, the crown punishing any who were found entering.

But in a surprising reversal of historical precedent, King Naethor Oricalis put Kaelis in control of the fortress and allowed him to found the academy within around his eighteenth birthday—a scandalously young age. Two years younger than the first crop of students he would be inducting.

But, Prince Kaelis has always been a legendary wielder of tarot. And in the year after he annihilated a clan, very few would dare utter anything but support for the prince. In the four years since its founding, he's used the academy as an institution to harness the power of every Arcanist for the crown, as a fortress to defend the kingdom, as a bottleneck to control all trade through the Farlum River, and as a means of intimidation against any who would even *think* of acting against the crown.

If I'm being objective, what Kaelis has accomplished as someone just shy of twenty-three years is impressive. But I can't be objective when it comes to him. Not when his accomplishments are steeped in the suffering of others. While he was founding the academy with all its power and opulence, I was living in squalor just across the bridge.

Kaelis's aura only lends more credence to the impossible stories about him: An esteemed scholar and a ruthless general. An exacting teacher and a tortured genius whose cruelty is only outmatched by his brilliance.

As we walk, I get little more than night-coated glimpses of the splendor of this place. Each room we pass is filled with mystery. We walk around a cloistered courtyard. Glass fills every archway, creating a greenhouse, its humidity beading the windows and obscuring the viridian domain. As we pass it, the air is heavy with the perfume of flowers and peat.

Our path then brings us to a vast library. Heavy tomes wait to aid quiet study, lining the shelves that span three floors. I nearly stop in my tracks and beg for a moment to savor the ink-laden pages. Books on arcane magics are forbidden to anyone outside of the academy and the clans. Mere possession of these texts is punished by amputation of a hand or eye.

A deserted lecture hall is silent in anticipation of the students' return, the podium at the front of the room standing tall and expectant. Every velvet-tufted seat holds the echo of knowledge once imparted to students, and possibly long forgotten.

Stairways spiral toward the heavens. Doors are inexplicably locked and barred. Others are temptingly ajar. The path we take plunges deeper, passing windowsills turned silver with dust and statues clothed in cobwebs. Kaelis, of course, offers no explanation for anything we pass, and I'm much too proud to ask.

Our walk concludes in a long hall with a beacon of orange light at the end. The light flickers defiantly against the near abyss of darkness the entire academy is shrouded in. At first, I think my eyes are tricking me after straining to see with nothing more than moonlight for so long. But, sure enough, just like the lamplight that brightened my cell, the light that streams through a crack in a door is no illusion.

Kaelis's hand is still on my hip. It anchors me in place as we slow to a stop. The entire time, I've been fighting unease at his touch—at his proximity to me. The orange glow outlines his face. Our gazes lock. I jut out my chin in a silent challenge. He dips his. A shiver runs down my spine at just how hot his proximity feels in the cool darkness.

"What?" The atmosphere compels me to whisper.

He's surprisingly forthright after being silent for so long. "The procession marches through that passage. If you join now, you'll be somewhere in the middle. It'll be impossible for any guards to notice or pluck you out if you keep your head down. You will split and go off with the other applicants and will ultimately be called to the chamber of the Arcanum Chalice. There you will—"

"Expand my powers as an Arcanist and fight for my place as an initiate in the academy." I fight a sly smirk. "So that way the four houses of Arcana Academy can see my mettle and pass their judgment on if I am 'worthy' of being counted among their ranks."

The dark pools of his eyes search mine, threatening to drown me in that endless stare. But he's probably just annoyed I interrupted him.

My amusement breaks free, curling the corners of my lips. I jape, "Worried about your bride?"

He laughs, low and ominous. "Worried? About *you?*" Kaelis pulls me closer. For a moment, I think he will kiss me, and the idea sours my stomach. But his head turns, his cheek nearly grazing mine. I'm consumed by the scent of him—the richness of oiled leather, the earthiness of dry ink, a cologne of cedar and frankincense. *Four suits, he even* smells *fabulously wealthy.* The prince shifts to whisper in my ear.

"Not about you. Never you. Luck is on your side, after all."

Kaelis releases me and leaves without another word. Even though I feel lighter without his contact, I'm left staring at his back as the night consumes him whole, the sound of his footsteps fading with the outline of his visage.

Luck is on my side . . . The closest thing I've yet felt to pure, unyielding terror dizzies my thoughts.

He knows me.

How many times did I say that phrase at the Starcrossed Club before I did something particularly risky or stupid? He had—maybe even still has—someone on the inside. As horrifying as it is, that's the only logical explanation. And it's not the first time I thought our den of safety had been compromised, either.

I think of the last job I did before I was captured. That man, Griv, who came to me in search of a way out of Eclipse City as an Unmarked Arcanist but offered more information than he should've known. He'd offered not only inking supplies . . . but details about my mother's death. It's because of him I was captured—he led me into Prince Kaelis's trap. If Griv knew enough about me to get me to trust him, then Kaelis must have known as much or more.

My hands ball into fists. I turn, push open the door with purpose, and find myself immediately caught in a flow of people, just as Kaelis predicted. I fall into step, ignoring the whispers of those around me about the person who entered the procession late.

Am I honestly going through with this? Every step is harder than the last. I scan left and right for another door or side hall. Trying to make a run for it now would be difficult, if not impossible. But the crowd consumes me.

Glancing over my shoulder as inconspicuously as possible, I spy about a hundred people marching behind me, but there are only a few dozen ahead. I'm somewhere toward the start of the pack. People step closer, pushing me toward the center. I can't tell if it's intentional, but I wouldn't put it past Kaelis to have others in the academy ensuring I end up right where he wants me.

That's when I see them: Halazar guards. I'd know their drab uniforms anywhere. They're coming up from the back.

I swivel my head forward again, take a deep breath, and still my racing thoughts. I will be of use to no one—myself included—if I panic. Arina went through this, and she survived. My best chance of ensuring she's all right and reuniting with those I love is if I go through the Fire Festival.

My gaze sweeps across the crowd anew, this time searching for my sister, but with the torchbearers in the front, it's hard to discern faces in the darkness.

The people around me are dressed in all manner of garb. But it's easy enough to tell who are the applicants that will go through the trial by arcane fire and who are already full-fledged students. The Arcanum Chalice demands a fight only in a student's first year; later sacrifices to the Chalice are easier, so I assume the ones dressed in yards of silk and velvet are already students. Their suits and gowns look like they were designed for no more than standing, sitting, and *maybe* drinking and eating. And their corsets are laced up so tightly and their trousers are so constricting I'm not even sure of that last part.

Those whom I pin as applicants are in much more practical, battle-ready clothing that, like mine, can be moved in—though theirs is admittedly less fine.

Some of the applicants whisper eagerly to one another. They're *excited* for the ceremony—they're ready to uncover the mysteries of Arcana Academy. Poor souls. *The Arcanum Chalice is a cursed ritual,* Mother told me once when I'd asked her about the pilgrimage many would make to the fortress in search of power, before it was the academy.

Since Kaelis took over, access to the fortress is limited to only applicants, initiates, students, faculty, and staff. The rituals and teachings of the academy are supposed to be closely guarded secrets. But, like any secret, they're well known among those in power. The nobility of Oricalis trade in secrets as readily as they do tarot or shining regill coins and notes. The only reason I know as much as I do is because of my work in the Starcrossed Club.

I try to focus on those whom I assume are students. Arina would be a second year now. Hard to imagine that she'll be my senior at the school after spending my whole life trying to look after my wild little sister. She's only a year younger—having lied about her age to enter at nineteen—but she always seemed even younger than that to me.

I've no idea what clothing she might be wearing to fit in with her peers of the academy. And fashion choices like high collars, hoods, and intricate hair designs make it even more difficult in the low light to tell one student from another.

So instead I focus on the wrists of the women. Before Arina left for the academy, I gave her a silver bracelet—simple, but something I'd recognize anywhere. On the inside of a circular disk are engraved the letters sXc, for the Starcrossed Club, so she'd never forget where she came from. I don't see anyone wearing a bracelet anything like hers.

But the space is very cramped and there are a lot of long sleeves . . . I reassure myself. *I'll find her once I'm through. Or she'll see me in the Chalice challenge and seek me out.* Even though I know I look different from the tortures of Halazar, I've no doubt my sister would recognize me no matter what. Just as I would her.

Ahead is a sign on the wall directing applicants to the right and fully enrolled students to the left. I head right, descending with the others toward the ritual of power and sacrifice that awaits us.

CHAPTER 6

I've correctly pinned most of the people as student or initiate, but a few who head right surprise me. I follow down a gracefully arcing staircase behind a woman in a strapless gown with full skirts and a breathless-looking bodice, who'd better hope her trial doesn't involve a lot of movement.

Our march comes to an end in a large room lined with wooden benches and nothing else. A woman who is the human embodiment of a rapier stands in front of a door opposite the entrance like she's guarding it. Her long, silver-white hair is slicked back into a high ponytail. Her body is lithe and rigid, her eyes cold and narrowed.

Two horizontal lines of thin window slits stretch along either side of the door she guards near the ceiling. The windows glow with an unnatural blue haze. The applicants are drawn to them, bypassing the rows of benches.

"You will all wait for your turn," she instructs, her tone indifferent but her gaze cold. "Your name will be called when it's your turn to stand before the Chalice."

Even though I know what awaits me, I join the rest of the applicants in peering through the windows. Arina had described the logistics of the academy's first test but not the room itself.

The Sanctum of the Chalice is more of an arena than I was expecting. Set into a massive wall are stands that are veiled in shadow. Giant marble columns form the skeleton of the hall and support a ceiling set so high it's impossible to see from my vantage in the partially subterranean room. The numbers one through ten trellis down each pillar among intricate carvings of the court cards of the Minor Arcana—one of each for each unique suit.

But what commands my attention is the legendary Arcanum Chalice. It's a cauldron-like structure set on an alabaster pedestal. I'm too far away to make out any more details than that. Kaelis stands beside it, bathed in its pulsing glow.

One by one, students walk up and select three cards from the deck, which Kaelis lays on the edge of the pedestal the chalice is upon. They choose one and throw it into the Chalice. It flares brighter, cold flames consuming the card, and the shifting glow envelops the student briefly. But they emerge unharmed.

"What's happening?" a woman with short red hair asks.

"I don't know any more than you do." The same woman whose skirts I was pitying minutes ago shakes her head.

"Right now, the second and third years are making a new sacrifice to the Chalice so they can unlock the ability to ink and wield more advanced cards. Since they've fed the Chalice once, it goes quickly because they're already connected to it. Unlike us." I sound like a textbook. The two look back at me, startled. Others are glancing over their shoulders as I speak.

The Arcanum Chalice is one of the legendary relics of Oricalis. Before the days of the academy, noble and rogue Arcanists alike would make a forbidden pilgrimage to the fortress to sneak in and stand before the Chalice. Then, they'd make their sacrifice, by which unlocking a deeper power that allowed them to make and cast more advanced cards instantly. In the years following the opening of Arcana

Academy, the royals have spread that it is the *only* way for Arcanists to use more advanced cards—you gain your reward through sacrifice. Another reason for why *all* Arcanists must walk through these doors.

But, even if the royals forbid talking about it, finding power without the Chalice is possible. It's just harder, takes longer, and is not *guaranteed* to work, since every Arcanist possesses different innate abilities. As much as I hate the academy, even I must admit it's an impressive process that ensures every Arcanist in Oricalis's arsenal is as strong as they can be.

"When the students are done," I continue, "it'll be our turn. When they call your name, you'll go before the Arcanum Chalice and they'll give you a simple three-card spread, with each card representing a different aspect of your future. Then, you'll pick what part of your future to give up."

"Give up?" Skirts echoes, leaning back. Her brow furrows. "What . . . what do you mean?" She has a soft voice and kind eyes. Neither is going to help her much here.

I lock eyes with her. "This is Arcana Academy. Your future is your tuition."

The words have a weight that settles on her shoulders and pulls her down. She opens and closes her mouth, and the lines in her brow deepen.

Is it crueler for her to know what's to come and be forced to sit with the weight of that knowledge? Or would it have been worse to leave her ignorant?

"And it's just . . . gone?" her friend asks.

I nod. "Whatever card you select to surrender to the Chalice will never come true. That part of who you are—or could have been—is removed."

"Forever?" someone else whispers.

"Forever. That's the bare minimum tithe you pay just to walk through these doors." Which is so much for very little.

"Once we make our sacrifice, then we'll be initiates?" Skirts rightfully asks. I let out a low chuckle, and her expression sinks further.

"No. Then you'll be forced to fight and kill that future while everyone in the academy watches you . . . and judges your innate prowess with the cards. Succeed, and then you'll be an initiate. Fail, and it's a hot branding iron and a one-way trip to the powder mills." I step back, beckoning Skirts. Her friend had the much better sense to wear well-fitted trousers. "Which, speaking of . . . let me see you."

"Me?" The young woman blinks. I know she must be twenty, given the academy's age requirements. Unless she's lying like Arina did. She looks so much younger to me, so it could be possible. Perhaps it's the roundness of her cheeks, or their faint blush. Perhaps it's that the skin under her eyes is still bright, where mine is all dark shadows. Perhaps . . . it's how the little tufts of brown hair at the nape of her neck remind me achingly of Arina.

"Yes. You . . ."

"Luren," she says, stepping to meet me, clearly confused.

"I don't have a change of clothes for you, so we're working with what we've got." I reach forward and gather her skirts, pulling the hem to her knees and gathering the additional fabric.

"Excuse you!" She swats harmlessly at my hands. I hope her wielding of tarot is more fearsome.

"I'm not assaulting your modesty. In fact, it's the opposite. This goes through your legs." I allow her to assist with pulling the skirts through her legs, even if she looks terribly confused about what we're doing.

Once we've gathered the bulk of the fabric at the small of her back, I split the bundle and tie it at her waist. It's a bit comical looking, but it does the trick. "There, now you can move. Take off those heels and you'll be able to face whatever the Chalice throws at you. So long as your bodice is tailored as tightly as it looks, that is."

"I . . . I can't go out there like this," she whispers, then quickly begins untying my knot. "I look ridiculous. They'll all laugh at me."

I shrug. "Suit yourself, but remember how it's done in case you need it."

Luren doesn't have a chance to reply. The proctor calls the first name. We all watch as the first applicant leaves the holding room through the door behind the proctor and up a short staircase that connects to the arena partially above us. Everyone presses tighter against the windows as he crosses to Kaelis. I don't know the applicant—never seen him before in my life—but my heart is in my throat for him. Even if he heard my warning about what was to come, he can't truly know what he's walking into. Arina knew all she could about the ceremony before coming to the academy, and even so, something changed inside her after this first trial. It left her with a hollowness to her gaze that sometimes not even I could fully comprehend.

Kaelis speaks as he draws three cards, though his words are lost in the vast room. After placing the cards before the Chalice, the prince leaves the man to choose one from the spread. After a tense minute, the applicant throws one into the Chalice. It explodes with light, enveloping the arena and blinding all.

When the light fades and our eyes adjust, it's to a chorus of gasps.

The arena is gone. In its place is a wide field, a quaint cottage at one end. The applicant stands in the center of the field, looking around, bewildered.

"What happened?" Luren whispers.

"It's the future he chose to give up." I can't tear my eyes away as the man steps forward toward the cottage, movements jerky, hands shaking. Whatever this place is . . . it meant something to him.

The door opens, and a woman goes to greet him with open arms. He rushes into her embrace and is crushed against her. Even though we can't hear anything from halfway underground and behind the thick windows, I can see him sobbing.

Poor man . . . he gave up a reunion he clearly yearned for. Unfortunately for him, he's going to lose a lot more than that. He doesn't even fight. He doesn't push the woman of the vision away. He gives in completely to her, staying in her arms until everything fades into a hazy blue light that dissipates into the air, leaving him falling to his knees, arms outstretched, as if begging for mercy from a cruel and mocking god.

Two city enforcers march from the far archway. The applicant hasn't seen them. He continues to stare upward with tear-filled eyes and a mouth that is slightly agape with soundless begging.

One of the enforcers grabs his left arm. The other, wielding a red-hot brand, presses the iron to the soft flesh of the inside of his wrist. He screams and writhes, but the first holds him steady as the Mark is made.

The Marking is an A for Arcanist. It's done on the inside of the wrist to make it nearly impossible to cut off. All other neighboring kingdoms will send back any rogue Arcanists who attempt to escape Oricalis, or risk Oricalis halting their access to tarot resources.

Pain brings the man back to reality; the trance the vision left him in is broken. He suddenly writhes against his captors. They clearly weren't expecting him to resist, as their hold on him breaks. The man scrambles, swiping the deck that had been left out by the Chalice for him to use to fight his vision. He fumbles for a card.

There's a flash of light, but it's not from the Marked Arcanist. Blood dribbles from his chin, a sword of writhing shadow and light impaled through him. The other applicants gasp, jaws slack in collective horror. Meanwhile, my teeth are clenched so tightly they ache.

A shadow emerges from the darkness behind the Chalice: Kaelis.

He nonchalantly pockets the deck and gives a nod to the enforcers as the man falls to the floor, lifeless. The two enforcers drag the body away unceremoniously. I doubt his family will even be given a chance to mourn.

He came here dreaming of a better life. Hoping for an opportunity to improve his standing—even if he had to give up his very future for it. It was better than the alternative. Than this . . .

The crown eagerly took everything he had and left nothing but suffering. As the crown always does.

Kaelis's eyes drift toward the windows all the applicants are pressed against. Somehow, it's like he knows *exactly* where I am. As if he can feel my palpitating hatred toward him.

"Luren," the proctor calls.

Panic fills her eyes. *Good. That's the right emotion.*

"Good luck." That's all I can offer her.

"You can do this," her red-haired friend reassures her. The confidence doesn't quite reach her eyes.

Skirts back down by her ankles, Luren is gone.

I turn away from the windows and walk over to one of the benches, resting my elbows on my knees and folding my hands to make a shelf for my forehead. I can see the flash of light, but I don't watch Luren's test. I don't watch any of the others. The only thing I catch a glimpse of is a dark-haired woman tying up her skirt before she ascends the stairs.

At least someone took my advice . . . whatever little good it might do.

My fingers tighten to the point that I'm shaking. I tap my feet. I rock. But I can't find an outlet for this restless energy as the names get called one after the other. This cruelty that we are forced to endure makes my stomach churn and my saliva turn to bile.

I'm the last one. Not that I'm surprised. I would've been added to the list at the last minute.

"Clara Redwin, of Clan . . . Hermit." The proctor watches my every step, her stormy eyes cold as winter.

For a second, we hold each other's gaze. But only for a second. She's not about to wish me luck. If anything, she looks like she's ready to kill me.

Alone, I ascend the dark, narrow staircase and then step into the light.

CHAPTER 7

I emerge from an opening in the wall that rings the lower floor and supports the stands looming above. In the shadows, indistinct figures—the academy's student body, staff, and faculty—whisper, but the words are too faint to comprehend, along with the details of their appearance. The weight of their collective gaze, heavy with scrutiny, settles on me.

From this vantage, my eyes can follow the sculpted columns up to the massive domed ceiling. Leaded glass creates the outlines of the four suits of tarot along the lower edge of the dome. At its apex, the glass portrays a man mid-step, forever embarking on an unknown journey: the Fool. The trials and triumphs of his adventure are depicted by the Major Arcana that adorn the archways between the upper pillars.

Kaelis waits beside the Chalice, bathed in its pulsing glow. The vastness of the room swallows the echoes of my footsteps as I make my way to him.

"Welcome, Clara Redwin of Clan Hermit." Murmurs ripple

through the crowd at that proclamation, nearly drowning out what Kaelis says next. "My betrothed, future princess of Oricalis."

Outright gasps. Kaelis pauses for dramatic effect, allowing the shock to rip through the students and faculty.

"Smile like this is the best day of your life," Kaelis mumbles, barely moving his lips.

I force a smile, grateful everyone else is too far away to see the murderous glint in my eyes.

Kaelis continues as the noise dies down, "Welcome to the sacred and secret halls of Arcana Academy. As headmaster of the academy, and second prince of the Oricalis Kingdom, I welcome you into the illustrious ranks of the Arcanists. In the past few years, you have heard the call of the cards and your noble lineage. Now it is time to realize your potential, however great or small it might be."

In the past few years. I snort softly at that. Mother was teaching me how to ink from the moment I could hold a pen. I knew how to read cards before I could read words. While most Arcanists don't begin showing even the rough edges of an affinity toward tarot until the age of eighteen or nineteen, my skills appeared much, *much* earlier—a fact I suspect Kaelis is well aware of.

"All Arcanists are required to offer their power to the Chalice in exchange for even greater skill. When you make your sacrifice, you will be forced to fight what was once your fate. Should you triumph over destiny, you will be granted more time within these hallowed halls. Lose, and you will be Marked and cast out." He sets the deck he's holding on the pedestal and fans it out. "For yourself, for your kingdom, it is time to pay the price for the knowledge we protect here. Select three."

I stare at the cards. *Here I am, where I never thought I'd be . . .* Where I'd hoped to—been outright told to—avoid. Taking a breath, I flutter my eyes closed and hold out my hand, moving it left and right over the cards. My fingertips lightly touch the corner of one, drawn by a tingling in my palm, and I slide the card upward. I repeat the process two more times before opening my eyes.

Three cards for me and me alone. My destiny. My future.

Kaelis puts the rest of the cards to the side. One by one, he flips the three I've drawn and announces them to the room.

"The Ten of Coins."

A beautiful card. Ten golden coins shine like suns above a joyous family, every generation as happy as the last. The Ten of Coins symbolizes wealth and joy and reaping the rewards of one's work. In the image of the people painted on the card, I see the Starcrossed Club gathered around a table for an All Coins Day feast.

The next card is the Five of Swords. A woman stands facing a bloodied battlefield, two swords in each hand. Three men are positioned behind her, prepared to drive their own blades through her back. It's a card of conflict and loss. Of battles that might be ultimately won, but, if so, just barely . . . and that victory achieved at a great cost.

The crowd murmurs with excitement as Kaelis announces the Five of Swords. They suspect this will be the one I throw into the Chalice, and it would undoubtedly make for a good show for all of them to watch. But I have one more card left to read . . .

As Kaelis flips the final card, his movements halt in midair. We both have barely a glimpse of the image painted on its front. But it's unmistakable—a noteworthy card that *everyone* knows.

"The Two of Cups." His voice doesn't waver, but when his eyes, swirling with the colors cast by the Chalice, drift toward mine, I can see a full array of emotions in them. His mouth presses into a hard line, as if he's physically trying to hold back the unspoken threat that I can practically hear him screaming in his mind.

The Two of Cups. A romance card. A man and woman stand facing each other, both toasting full goblets. Their expressions are relaxed—and yet tinged with apprehension and excitement. Their lips are parted as if frozen on an inhale. Ribbons swirl up and around their hands, linking them together and then gathering in the shape of a dove.

It is the card of fated meetings, of new unions rooted in harmony and balance. The card of falling in love.

"Choose one to cast into the Chalice—choose which future to kill."

Kaelis steps away, but our eyes remain fixed like two rams locking horns. With a sharp turn, he strides away, and I wait to make my choice until I see him high on the risers above. He's easy to spot. As the headmaster, he has his own balcony.

Three faculty stand with him, and one man makes his way directly to Kaelis. He's a broad-shouldered fellow with dark brown hair. But his eyes are so brilliantly green they stand out as they dart my way. I can feel disapproval of me radiating off him, as if he already knows I'm not who I claim to be. *An adviser, or a lackey?* A question for my future self to answer.

I turn back to the cards. There's no question which I will choose. The Ten of Coins is my friends and family. The future that I have always dreamed of for myself. The Five of Swords is hardship . . . but I have always known struggle. I will always be moving from one battle to the next, constantly watching my back.

My fingers come to a stop over the Two of Cups. The relationship card. I look back to Kaelis and can feel the weight of his stare.

"I am not your plaything," I murmur. He said he likes a challenge. Well, I'll give him one. I will show him, and his entire academy, that I will not be quiet or subservient.

The students immediately go wild. They're shocked and confused. It makes no sense why someone would willingly throw away an opportunity at a smart match. Especially when there's the obvious choice of the Five of Swords. *Especially* when the person throwing away the fated meeting is engaged to a prince.

But, within their shock, I hear something far more telling. Far more expected. Amusement. Entertainment. They're ready to bear witness to what awaits me and how I conduct myself in the trial to come.

With a flick of my fingers, I cast the card into the aura of the Chalice like I'm throwing down a gauntlet. The card explodes with a cavalcade of stardust and shimmering motes of silver light.

An unseen force wrenches at me, grabbing at the essence of my soul and pulling magic from my depths. A gasp escapes me, and I'm left breathless. I stagger forward, every muscle shaking. It feels like a light within me is growing dim. A star flickering and then winking completely out of existence. Forever lost.

I grip the pedestal to keep my balance. The crowd is ravenous. They know what is to come, and even though I am the last of nearly four dozen applicants . . . they want more. They want a grand finale.

The aura of the Chalice has enveloped me now. It pushes me down, forces my breath to become shallow, my heart to quiver. I close my eyes, but behind them is nothing but flashes of light and incoherent visions. I am trapped between the real world and the world of the future I must destroy. Not quite in one nor in the other—neither what is nor what could've been.

With every pulse of these worlds—dream, vision, future, reality—I try to focus on a single point: the deck that Kaelis left on the pedestal. Moving my arm toward the cards requires a titanic amount of effort. Yet when my hand settles upon them, I heave a sigh of relief as I instantly sense the magic of every inked card in the stack. Arcanists can't summon cards from an unfamiliar deck. Fortunately, to know a deck requires only a single touch.

The ones who have the hardest time in the festival are those who forget to grab the deck early, Arina told me when she regaled me with her tale at the first opportunity she found to sneak out of the academy. *If you have to waste time trying to find it in the future world, you're done for.*

Little did she know she was preparing me for my own Chalice trial. I hope she's watching now with pride.

I push away from the pedestal and shove the deck in my pocket. The aura of the Chalice has amplified now. It's in and around me. There's no difference between the blinding images behind my eyelids and the glow solidifying before me.

Swallowed whole by the Chalice's overwhelming light, I inhale sharply. I blink one final time, and when I open my eyes again, I find myself standing in a brightly lit dance hall.

Face-to-face with the last man I wanted, or expected, to ever see again.

CHAPTER 8

I stand at the edge of the dance floor in an opulent ballroom. *I know this place.* From the crystal chandeliers cascading from the ceiling like suspended raindrops to the polished marble that gleams beneath the gem-studded shoes of the patrons on the dance floor.

The Fatefinders Club. The oldest establishment in Eclipse City for entertainment and revelry. Operated by Clan Lovers and authorized to use tarot because of their clan backing.

As the elite of the city twirl and laugh, their faces blur like paints left in the rain. Nothing seems solid. Real. This place is both familiar and foreign, past and future condensing into a watercolor present. The last time I was at the Fatefinders Club was for a job. And that was when I saw . . .

Him.

Everything comes into focus on a single point: his face. His deep sapphire eyes are still as vibrant as a cloudless sky. His chiseled jaw and the dip in his chin are accented by the hint of stubble. A tailored suit clings to his broad physique, a body honed by laboring at the forge in his family's business. That was the job he held until his magic appeared and he left for the academy just before his twentieth birthday.

"Clara?" His voice, deep and familiar, slices through my daze like a honed knife. As if it's the only thing that's *real*. I cling to it like a lifeline.

"Liam?" I breathe. *Not here. Not now. Not like this . . .*

"Is it really you?" His hair, the color of wet sand, is longer than I remember and falls gracefully over his forehead, brushing his neck just above his shoulders. "I didn't expect to see you here."

"I didn't, either." The words come from my mouth, but they don't feel like my own. Inside I'm screaming. Screaming at the pain he caused me. And at the audacity of him to be so nonchalant after what he did to me.

He runs a hand through his hair, an old habit he always returns to when he's deep in thought or nervous. "After I left for Arcana Academy, I thought our paths might never cross again—that I might never see you again."

As he speaks, stolen moments rush back to me: A whirlwind of laughter and hasty kisses. Of shared dreams and secrets known only to us and the stars.

He doesn't know, I realize. He doesn't know that while he hasn't seen me in years, I've seen him. It was here, in this place, not long ago. Or, perhaps, a very long time ago. My mind has become so hazy. But I can remember a moment, two years ago, with aching sharpness. I was doing a job at this very club. It was his second year in the academy, I hadn't heard from him since he entered, and his arms were wrapped tightly around another woman—a woman from Clan Star. And that shining brightly on her finger was an engagement ring.

I shift back slightly. He catches the movement. His brow furrows.

"You could have visited me," I say.

"You know the academy only has two breaks in the year, and they were always busy for me. My family wanted me back in the winter. Then there was Clan Star . . . which meant I was even busier, and, come spring, I was assigned to report to the clan early, with—"

"Another woman?" A hurt that's never quite healed sharpens my words.

"Wha—"

I won't even let him finish the objection. "I saw you with her. Right here."

"I tried to speak with you about it. After I graduated, I looked for you, even."

"Lies." I glance away, unable to handle his face for a moment. My attention returns just in time to catch a glimpse of a pained expression that briefly twists his handsome features.

"I can't change the past . . . but I can mend the present. Dance with me."

I take a full step back.

Liam extends his hand across the gap between us, an earnest invitation. "Dance with me, Clara, please," he implores softly. "For old times' sake, if nothing else."

It is tempting to refuse. The need to protect the fragile remains of my heart from further damage is strong.

"You left me." The words tremble. *Like Mother . . .*

"The one unforgivable sin," he agrees, knowing me too well. "But I'm here now. Please, I'll tell you everything. I won't leave again."

Deeper than the hurt is a part of me that aches to reclaim what we lost. With a breath that feels like a surrender, I place my hand in his. Liam guides us onto the dance floor.

The room, the dance, the colors, everything spins into a blur once more. It loses clarity again, growing less real by the second. Is this a memory? Is this what is, or what could have been? The only thing that's anchoring me in the present is Liam and my feelings for him. Those emotions still have their hooks deep in my marrow.

As we find our rhythm, his voice is like a caress, as sweet as the memories from days long gone. "I'm sorry, Clara, for all of it."

"Tell me what happened," I demand. Petty hatred for its own sake will do these old wounds little good.

His hold on me tightens, his eyes searching mine. "In my first year,

I found out I would be placed with Clan Star as one of their Arcanists. They saw potential in me and selected me early, usually it's not until year two. That spring break, I went to them—it was purely business. I tried to get word to you . . .

"But then it all happened so fast. One of the lower nobles liked the idea of an Arcanist marrying his daughter, thought it could put some magic in his family's bloodline, and suddenly, there was talk of marriage. You know how those zealots can be. They think blood and family lines can impact whether magical ability manifests in a child."

Being born an Arcanist is as random as whether you come out with a cock. It's a well-known fact. But there are some on the fringe who treat the tarot like a religion . . . and as a result they hold odd beliefs.

"The marriage was arranged, and we had little say in it. Which meant it had little chance of working out." A rueful smile plays on his lips. "When it ended, I wanted to find you . . . But, by the time I felt like I could look you in the eyes again, I didn't know where you were."

"When did it end?"

"Weeks ago."

The revelation has my heart skipping a beat. Possibilities I'd thought long dead can suddenly be entertained again. Futures I'd thought were lost . . .

Lost futures . . . My brow furrows in confusion. Pain sears between my temples. There's something there. Something I should be . . . doing?

Liam pulls me closer, as if sensing both my turmoil and my renewed hope. The warmth of his body melds with mine. It's still there—the need that pulses between us as heavy as the music. Wrapping us so tightly together that I can hardly breathe without my chest swelling against his.

"Clara." His voice is heavy, almost drunken. "All this time . . . I thought of you. It was you I wanted. Only you . . ."

The words dissolve into nothing more than breathy kisses on my neck as his mouth finds the sensitive skin there. I clutch his jacket, acutely aware of his strong, muscular form. We turn, his knee slips between mine, his thigh gliding all the way up, and I'm lost in the sensation.

My eyes flutter closed, my defenses reduced to cinders. I let out a soft sigh.

Liam encourages me with the gentlest plea in my ear. "Let go, Clara. Never push me away, not now, not ever."

For a fleeting moment, I do let go. I am ready to surrender to the fantasy. To the idea of us. To finally getting someone back in my arms again after losing them.

"Luck is on our side, after all."

That's mine to say. The moment the thought crosses my mind, it's followed by the realization that he is not the first man to steal my expression. A flare of anger lacks a target until the outline of a particularly arrogant man flashes across my memory. *Kaelis.*

My eyelids flutter open. The room is painfully bright, a mockery of reality. Even though I cannot see beyond the half-real illusion before me, I know that the entirety of the academy can still see me. The thought has me hot with nausea.

"Don't end this." Liam's lips trace a path along my jaw. Pleading. "Let yourself have it."

Awareness is a cold wave crashing over me. I jerk away, gasping for air with the same desperation as when I escaped from Halazar. Every dull ache and sharp pain is back in my body. I'm in not a ball gown, but tight leathers.

The spell is broken and the fantasy shattered. To think . . . I'd almost let myself have it—let fate win by giving in to the illusion rather than killing it as I should have been doing all along.

"I can't." My voice trembles as my heart screams for me to reconsider my decision. "I'm so sorry, Liam."

The space between us is back, as vast and insurmountable as it has been for years. Tears threaten to well in my eyes as I slowly beckon cards from the deck in my pocket. The cards hover in midair, shimmering with the magic grip I still keep on them.

I know each card without seeing them—even if their inking is a bit strange to me. Before I had friends, I had the cards. I knew the faces of the royal suits better than the faces of my neighbors.

Sword cards crack and snap like heat lightning near the mountaintops on a summer day. Wands crackle like fire, their warmth shooting into my elbow. Cups douse the sensation with a rush of cool water through my veins. And Coins are as heavy as rocks despite being made of nothing more than paper and pigment like the rest.

Every suit in the deck is missing its later cards, ending at fives. First years are supposed to be able to use only the first five cards in each suit and are limited thusly. The expectation is that first years have no real training with tarot before their entry, despite nobles getting a clear advantage by early exposure within their families. Additionally, a first year's magic is too "immature" to handle more than the first five in a suit without the card reversing and becoming dangerous, twisted, and uncontrolled power. The mere suggestion of anything more being possible is forbidden.

Liam's eyes widen. Then his brow furrows, almost angry. "Still hiding behind tarot when you're scared, I see." Then, everything about him softens once more. "Don't do this, please."

I didn't know that *this* was what I would be sacrificing when I threw that card into the Arcanum Chalice. I thought that I would be destroying any chance of Kaelis thinking there could be a peaceful future between us. Not a second chance with the first man I ever truly loved.

"I must do this," I say, more to myself than to him. He's not real. None of this ever will be. What I'm about to do is akin to cutting off my own arm. Fate must be killed with force.

As I swing my hand, the Five of Swords magically lifts from among the cards that hover around me. I catch it with two fingers and move it across me. There's a rush of wind. The card is enveloped by a silvery glow that hardens into a rapier; the light vanishes as I grip the sword's hilt. The second my hand closes around it, in the back of my mind, the weapon screams for blood.

Rapier in hand, I lunge for Liam. Reality bends and twists with a nauseating tilt. The room distorts like wax figures left out in the sun.

Liam's expression contorts as well. The specter who's taken the shape of the man I once knew shows his true form. A smile too wicked. Eyes too sharp. This is not Liam but a shade of him created by the Chalice. The monstrosity lifts a hand and calls upon his own card from his jacket pocket.

The Ace of Wands. The card summons a wall of fire from his feet. I reel, stumbling and falling to the ground. The flames lick at my exposed hands and lap at the side of my face as I fall. I drop the sword with a clatter, and a deeper, sharper agony than the burns shoots through my body. The Five of Swords is a weapon that demands bloodshed, and if not heeded, it will exact that price of its own accord from its caster.

Before I can get to the rapier again, Liam follows up with the Six of Swords.

"Listen to me." His magically enhanced voice soothes the furrow of my brow. It's a balm to the stinging ache of my heart and the growing pain from my abandoned rapier. "Give up this crusade and let go of your hurt. Together we can achieve great things. We will be happy."

For a moment, I falter. The Six of Swords and its magical ability to smooth over the heart's pains overtakes me. The strength in his voice, the love that's so apparent in his eyes . . . it nearly sways me. And there's the ghostly memories of his body on mine. Visions of nights that I have never experienced—that I might experience if I make a different decision—dance across my mind. Every hasty kiss. The feeling of his mouth on mine, my nails in his flesh. All the words I could possibly say reduced to one: *more*.

My fingers close around the sword I'd called upon, and the pain abates as the cry for blood returns. "I will not give in."

I push myself off the ground and almost collapse again. I'm exhausted. My muscles are already spent. Even my magic falters.

But my will doesn't. I have one more card in me. One more attack before I'm spent physically and magically. I must make it count.

I grit my teeth and steel myself. A flick of my wrist, and the Ace of Swords sends a gust of wind that leaves him reeling. It's my one window of opportunity. I lunge.

My blade meets its mark, plunging straight through his chest. Our bodies crash into each other. My grip goes slack on the rapier and it vanishes, finally getting the blood it was so hungry for.

"I would've loved you well, Clara," Liam murmurs, blood dribbling from the corner of his mouth.

"I know," I whisper back as I grip him tightly. The bright lights of the chandeliers go dark. One by one.

We collapse to the polished marble floor of the Fatefinders Club. It cracks under our weight. I pull him to me as he goes limp.

Ripping my future—my once destiny—from the fabric of my soul was never going to be easy. And somewhere beyond the realm of my perception in this fabricated reality, all the students and faculty of the academy are watching. Including Kaelis himself.

The room fades as the light leaves his eyes. Dancing figures evaporate like mist on the morning's light. The final chandelier goes dark. Liam is the last to vanish, from my arms.

I am alone, kneeling before the Arcanum Chalice. The vast room is as silent as a grave.

CHAPTER 9

I work to compose myself, inhaling slowly through my mouth followed by quivering exhales through my nose. The deep breaths slow my heart, though they do little for the bone-deep aches in my body.

The deck is scattered beneath me. The cards, the burns on my hands, and my face stinging are the only signs that what just happened was at all real—real enough to cause injury and completely exhaust my magic. I was so much stronger than this, *should be* so much stronger. I hardly recognize the trembling woman I've been reduced to.

But I'm determined not to let them know just how worn out I feel. I push myself off the floor and stand tall like the victor I am. No matter what, that future was forfeit the moment I cast it into the Chalice. At least I didn't fail in defeating it so I can claim a place in the academy as an initiate.

My gaze sweeps across the stands. The students are in a silent thrall. Their faces are too blurred by the dimness of the hall to make out whatever emotions they might be feeling. My eyes meet Kaelis's, and as my focus narrows to him, the rest of the room falls away. I can't make out his expression. But I can *feel* the disapproval radiating off him.

No, it's something more intense than disapproval. It's hatred. *Yes, you hate me. You loathe me—as much as I loathe you.*

I manage to sink into a bow without falling flat on my face, adding a flourish by outstretching a hand. Straightening, I cross the length of the circular hall and step around the Arcanum Chalice. The student body finally begins murmuring, and I can only imagine what they're saying after that display.

Plunged once more into near-total darkness, I ascend a staircase. There's a fork in the road, but the path to the right is barred. I can make out the shadow of an enforcer farther down, and a chill runs its nail down my spine. That must be the path for those who failed.

I continue ascending into a beautiful parlor. That beauty only further accentuates the anger welling up within me: We've been afforded such comforts while others have been Marked and marched to what will be their death. This year's round of initiates is twenty-five, by my count. I'm not sure if this is a lot of people or a few, but given that we started with more than forty, it doesn't seem like nearly enough.

Instantly, I know that all those sitting in the far corner, chatting exclusively amongst themselves, are the nobles. They have an air of familiarity with one another that wards away any who isn't already "among them."

I suspect that the handful of others milling about who seem taken with the silks and tufted velvets are from humbler backgrounds, like me. I'm surprised, yet pleased, to find that we outnumber the nobles nearly two to one.

My eyes meet a familiar cerulean set. "Luren?"

She grins up at me from the ottoman she sits upon, waving me over. Her gaze is a bit more shadowed than before the sacrificing. Her carefully pinned hair has come loose and now falls half down in waves. Her red-haired friend is still at her side.

"Glad to see you made it, too," Luren says as I approach. Her apparent sincerity catches me off guard.

"Thanks." I'm not sure what else to say.

She notices the burns. "Oh, you're injured."

"It's superficial, I'm fine." I tousle my hair a bit, trying to hide the burns on my cheeks.

"Who would've thought a vision could have bite?" her friend murmurs as she massages her right hand. Bruises coat her arm up to her elbow.

"The Chalice is ancient magic." I sit on the edge of the sofa, in the farthest spot from the group of women and men whose company they keep. "Knowledge of it is fairly limited."

"Oh really? You seemed to know a lot about it all before the trial, for an applicant." Red Hair seems a bit skeptical of me. Not that I blame her.

I shrug.

"*Be nice.* My rather brisk friend here is Kel," Luren says.

"You don't have to tell everyone our names," Kel mutters, swooping bright-red bangs out of her eyes.

"We're all going to be initiates together; people will find out." Luren seems unbothered by her friend's innate skepticism. Between the two, I think Kel has the right approach for the academy.

"Your knowledge came in handy," a dark-haired and fair-skinned woman says to me. I recognize her as the one who followed my instruction with her skirts. "The dress trick was worth knowing. Thanks." Her skirts are untied now but still wrinkled.

"Happy to help," I say.

"Unusual to see someone helping others here," one of the men says. His expression is unreadable, made harder by the shaggy mass of brown hair that shadows his pale eyes set against light skin.

"We don't know yet how many spaces the houses have to accept students." I know what he's getting at, even if he assumes I don't. The man has the energy of a lordling. Doubtless he considers himself to have an advantage over those of us with humbler backgrounds who don't have the privilege of already knowing the workings of the academy. "We could all be walking to a spot in a house."

He snorts. "Unlikely."

"Do you know how many spots the houses have, Farom?" a dark-skinned and spectacled man asks. He has a surprisingly deep voice for such a boyish face. I suspect the neatly trimmed shadow of stubble is to further emphasize his more adult features.

"I know she's probably wrong, Dristin," Farom says.

"So you don't know at all, then." The spectacled man—Dristin—shrugs.

Farom stands in a huff, muttering to himself as he heads toward the other nobles in the corner, "A long-lost noble? Can hardly expect her to be educated . . ."

The third man, who had yet to say anything, follows Farom, rather than remaining.

They both go to sit near a man who lounges in the back corner with the other nobles. His eyes are an almost luminescent yellow and deeply sunken into the shadows beneath his brows. Silver-white hair, short and wild, sits above a face more angular than a dagger point. His eyes lock with mine, and his lips curl slightly in a manner both smug and sinister.

Dristin rolls his eyes, shifting his body back to the group and away from the other nobles. The movement pulls my attention from the pale-haired man, but I can still feel his piercing eyes on me. "I'm afraid I didn't catch your name."

"Clara Redwin," I reply, still trying on my latest fake name.

His eyes drop to my chest. For a moment I'd forgotten about the pin. But his shocked expression brings Kaelis's deceit and my ruse rushing back. "Clan Hermit." The words are more of a gasp. "But . . . you're all dead."

"I guess not." I shrug. "I found out about my distant lineage recently. I'm barely a Hermit by blood, and wasn't by name . . . probably what spared me from the clan killing." The only benefit to this whole charade is that I can claim it's new to me as well. Meaning, it's all right if I'm at least a *little bit* in the dark about my clan and the school. I hope.

"Really? But you already know so much about the academy." Luren's surprise is genuine.

"I'm a fast study."

"As is to be expected of Clan Hermit." Dristin gives what seems like a sincere and encouraging smile. I try to mirror the expression politely, despite having to resist squirming uncomfortably at being associated with the nobility I've spent my life despising.

"I'm Sorza, by the way." The dark-haired woman adds the final name I was missing from the group.

"Nice to meet you all." I try to commit their names to their faces.

"I agree with Luren on this. It's nice that it doesn't feel futile to learn each other's names. I didn't expect them to brand people the second they failed." Sorza leans back on the sofa, rubbing the inside of her wrist.

"Any of you ever met a Marked Arcanist?" Dristin asks. Once an Arcanist is Marked, they're relegated to the mills and nothing more. Forever. Despite their power, they're pariahs.

"No," Sorza answers.

"Me, neither," Luren says.

For a second, the room fades, and I'm focused on a memory: a blood-drenched floor, a dagger, a shaky hand, and a shredded wrist. Mother's panicked voice as she demanded I leave and go home to Arina. To put the candle in the window that would signal to her friends.

"Clara? What about you?" Dristin brings me back to reality, brushing short, thick locs away from his eyebrows.

"Once or twice." I wrench myself from the past. The Arcanist that night didn't bleed out from their clumsy attempt to remove the Mark, Mother told me later. But I never knew what happened to them. *They're safe with friends*, she whispered as she tucked me into bed. Later, I suspected they were taken through the mountain passages she showed me when I was older.

Since then, I've helped nine people with that brand escape Eclipse City through Mother's passages in the eastern ridge, and they all told me the horrors of receiving it. I helped fifteen more Arcanists who had yet to receive it get out before they were forced to come through the academy—fifteen individuals who would rather chance escaping than face the Chalice, the academy, and placement within a clan.

There are only two paths for an Arcanist in Oricalis: graduate the academy and be placed in the service of a noble clan, or be Marked with the brand and sent to a powder mill to work until a swift death. Magic is a rare commodity that requires even rarer resources to perform, making it highly controlled by the crown. Those who can wield it are never safe, and never free. Not really.

"You've managed to speak with one?" Dristin sounds surprised.

"They're still people." I assess him again. His clothes are a little too fine for him to have come from the lower rungs of society. Perhaps he's a noble offshoot?

Status in the noble clans is mostly hereditary. The closer you are in blood, then marriage, to the High Lord or Lady, the higher status you have. The further you are, the less connection you have . . . until it dissolves entirely. In rare cases, a High Lord or Lady can ascend someone to status within their clan regardless of relation. But, given that the power of individuals within a clan comes from their exclusivity, it's rare to see.

Dristin strikes me as someone who's far enough down a clan's family tree that he's not of the inner circles. But he's also someone who's had one too many comforts to know what the streets are like.

"After the Marked are sent to the mills, they never leave." Dristin uses the words "never leave," but what I hear is "die." Only Arcanists can work the mills, due to the magic required to process powders. So they're worked until they cannot any longer. Which is why Mother always said we had to help other Arcanists in hiding, Marked and Unmarked like us.

A new presence interrupts our conversation.

"Welcome, initiates." A man emerges from the doorway on the opposite side from where we entered. "I am Lord Vaduin Thornbrow, and you may all call me Professor Thornbrow, Lord Thornbrow, or Head Professor. As I am the department head for wielding."

He certainly sounds full of himself. The professor's tone alone suggests that he has very strong opinions about the "respect" we're supposed to give him. The tiny hairs on the back of my neck instantly rise as I get my first real look at the man. He's of moderate height and build with black hair and light tan skin, the sort that keeps its color no matter how much exposure to the sun. Those striking green eyes are impossible to miss, or to mistake. It's the same man who spoke to Kaelis on the balcony. His broad shoulders and perpetually furrowed brow give him an imposing appearance, despite not looking much older than a third-year student. His dark hair has been carefully coiffed on the sides but kept long on top. As his attention sweeps the room, I don't think I imagine it snagging on me for a breath.

"If you will all please follow me, I shall escort you to the Fire Feast. There we shall celebrate your victory, and you shall learn more about what is to come in your first—and for some of you, perhaps only—year at the academy." Nothing in his tone sounds remotely celebratory. Vaduin turns on his heel and strides through the doors and up the stairs beyond, back as rigid as a Stellis.

The other initiates are abuzz. It's settling in to everyone that they are no longer mere applicants. They now formally stand as initiates. Their smiles would suggest the hard part is over, but I know our trials have only just begun.

Once more, I'm led through the corridors of Arcana Academy. But this time there are two key differences: The first is that we are taking a much more direct route through the school, with fewer shortcuts through rooms, going through a passage that seems to have been designed for the purpose of getting initiates to wherever it is we're being taken. The second difference is that, this time, I can more clearly see where I'm going.

The lanterns have now been lit, and in their glow the stone walls uncoil before me like an ancient serpent. The spheres of warm, inviting light guide us up and up and up farther still, and now that they're alight, the previously grim corridors are an enchanted spectacle. Extravagant carvings and tapestries catch the eye. Oil portraits so realistic that the eyes seem to follow us line the walls. Judging from the quantity, and the names beneath them, the portraits are of past house royals of every suit, every Page, Knight, Queen, and King.

Finally, one passage merges with another, dropping us all into a half-moon-shaped room, as if this room is where every corridor in the academy leads. Vaduin pauses before two metal doors that are twice his height and three times as wide. He puts his back to them, facing us, and outstretches his arms.

A lash of fire blazes along the outlines of the doors, trailing over the carvings of each of the four suits. At the same time, magic pops on the other side. The doors swing open, and, for the first time, we are ushered into the main hall of Arcana Academy, where we get our first real look at the students and faculty who will decide our fates.

CHAPTER 10

It occurs to me that, out of everything I asked Arina about the academy, I never asked for too many specifics about its decor. I didn't need to know. Perhaps I didn't *want* to know. Part of me knew that whatever the answer would be, it'd be rage-inducing. The opulence. The hoarded and wasted wealth.

And there's certainly that. The main hall is as opulent as the rest, filled with feasting tables laden with more food than the hundred and fifty or so who occupy the room could consume. Though the way my stomach growls, it certainly wants to try. What meager food I managed to eat while getting ready has done me little good.

The hall isn't an oppressive castle atrium like the Sanctum of the Chalice but more of a conservatory perched at the edge of the fortress, offering views of Eclipse City and the eastern mountain ridge beyond. A birdcage of metal and glass blocks against the biting winds from the sheer cliffs that frame the mouth of the Farlum River. Smokeless bonfires line the outer edge of the room, interspersed between exotic trees.

Somehow, it had never entered my mind just how *magical* this place might be.

Yes, Arcana Academy is run by the worst man in the world. It represents everything I loathe about the laws surrounding Arcanists. It is a haven for those who have and a false aspiration for those who do not. But it's also . . . beautiful. It *feels* like a place steeped in ancient power, a remnant of an age long gone, hiding possibilities that seemed impossible in Eclipse City, just on the other side of the bridge.

Each house has its place at one of four L-shaped tables that form a large square. The tablecloths denote which is which—vibrant red for Wands, shimmering gold for Coins, bright cerulean for Cups, and a slate gray for Swords. On the front of each tablecloth is the signet of that house. At the center of the square are two parallel tables, lined with twenty-five empty seats. The far back wall of the room arcs around a semicircle-shaped table where all the stern-faced faculty of the academy sit.

With Kaelis at their apex.

The moment our eyes meet, an undeniable spark of tension rips through the air. My chest tightens, squeezing the breath from my lungs. A shadow passes across his face right before he stands to speak. But it's gone by the time he opens his mouth.

"Welcome, initiates, to the hallowed halls of Arcana Academy, a bastion of learning, and the seat of tarot magic itself. You have done well, making it through your initial trial. However, your tests have only just begun.

"A full tenure at Arcana Academy spans three years, each representing a position in the traditional three-card spread—the past, the present, and the future. In year one, you will shed your past to earn the knowledge that we have to impart. The future you thought you had is now behind you, as is your family and all you once thought you held dear before you joined our ranks. To truly become one of us, you must sacrifice all you once were." His eyes flick to me like a challenge, or a command.

The prince is downright delusional if he thinks for a second I'm going to cast aside my past anytime soon or forget about all the people in it. The memories of the club and my sister—the belief I could get back to them, help them, be with them—were the only things that got me through Halazar. And I'm especially not about to forget about the past that involves him throwing me in prison for a year so he could turn me into his plaything for whatever game he's designed.

"Starting tonight, those already among the houses of this academy—the new families you seek to join—will be observing you. Each student has one coin they *can* give, but not *must* give. At the closing ceremony of All Coins Day in the fall, students will present the initiates they deem worthy with a coin of their house. Those who are not given a coin will not proceed further in their studies at the academy."

The other initiates murmur in surprise. They had no idea what they were walking into. Just how few of us will make it.

"Those who stay will prove themselves during the Three of Swords Trials in the winter. All who do not pass two of the three trials—and it is possible for half, or more, of all initiates to fail—will not proceed further in their studies at the academy."

The murmurs are punctuated by outright gasps.

"If you make it through All Coins Day and the Three of Swords Trials, you will be able to bid for any house that has gifted you a coin. The house will have the final say on if you are accepted or not.

"Those who remain—who are deemed worthy by their peers to be accepted into houses—will become full-fledged students. They will finish their first year in the spring and celebrate at the Feast of Cups gala.

"You may not bid for a house that has not gifted you a single coin." Kaelis leans forward slightly, eyes darting over the twenty-five people gathered. "You do not simply have something to prove only to yourself, or to your professors . . . you must also prove something to your peers. Fail, and you will be cast out and Marked. Succeed, and you will see your next two years here and all that awaits you as an Arcanist in service to Oricalis."

A wave of hushed yet panicked conversations crashes down around me from about half of the initiates. The other half look as unsurprised as I am. Nobles already knew this was coming. They also know that they have nothing to fear, since they made it this far. A house will accept them regardless of how skilled they are with magic. They have already built the relationships with their peers that Kaelis is alluding to. And for the Three of Swords Trials, they've had tutors prepping them with information on what's to come before they ever stepped foot through the main entry. For them, the rituals and trials of the first year are but a formality; their sole challenge was making it through the Arcanum Chalice. They can relax and focus on their studies. The common-born are fighting for what little hope remains to avoid a Mark and a future at the mills.

"Oh, and one more thing . . ." There's a spark to Kaelis's eyes that my gut instantly dislikes. A sort of smug, I-have-all-the-control glint that makes me want to punch him square in the nose. "The academy is only so large. Just like we cannot accept everyone who applies into the initiates' dorm, every suit's house also has only so much room. They can only accept as many as are leaving at the end of the year. Kings, if you please." The prince gestures with an open palm.

Unsurprisingly, a man immediately shoots up from the corner of the Wands table. *It would be Wands that'd move first . . .* He's a towering individual with a build that reminds me uncomfortably of Liam. Brown hair is trimmed and coiffed into a short, neat haircut with streaks of lighter blond that come alive in the firelight.

"House Wands has five among us graduating this year; therefore, we will be able to accept five initiates," he announces with a booming voice. "We will be looking for those who burn with passion in all they do, creative spirits willing to push the boundaries of the normal. The freethinkers who are fiery, bold, energetic."

A woman with a particularly youthful appearance stands for Coins. A mass of auburn curls tumbles over her shoulders. Her porcelain skin is near flawless, and her revealing gown puts it on display along with her curves.

"House Coins may graciously accept six initiates," she says in a low and even manner. "We will be seeking the pragmatic—those who know that without stability it is impossible to achieve greatness. And with that knowledge are those who will invest in their health, wealth, and family. Nurturing, grounded, and levelheaded."

With fluid grace, another man rises from the table of Cups. His wavy black hair is kept messy to his ears. The rich brown of his skin accents the muscles of his arms—as on display as the curves of the woman from House Coin—and offsets his dazzling smile.

"House Cups would gladly welcome five initiates, much like our friends in Wands," he says warmly. "To be counted among us, you must come with an open heart. Be someone who is unafraid of allowing fate to carry you along its uncharted waters. A person who finds strength in the depths of their emotions. Thoughtful, caring, easygoing."

The last woman to stand does so almost reluctantly. She rises like a sword unsheathing, elegant and deadly. Her sharp, angular features are softened by two long strands of platinum hair. Her skin is a similar shade to mine, not brown nor overly fair—the sort that will readily darken with the sun. Her eyes are light brown, and, for some reason, out of everyone, they find me.

"House Swords will only welcome *two* initiates." Even though her voice is soft, it carries. "We search for those with the sharpest wit and even sharper intellect. Those who are unafraid to wield power but understand the responsibility with which it comes. Clever, powerful, intelligent."

More murmuring around me. At first it's because of the surprisingly small number of initiates that House Swords can accept. But that leads to other realizations. Five in Wands, six in Coins, five in Cups, and two in Swords. That's just eighteen spaces for twenty-five initiates.

No matter what, some of us will be Marked before the year has made its turn . . . And judging from the wary looks the non-nobles are giving one another, they're realizing the number of available openings is even smaller for all of us who don't have guaranteed placements. By my estimation, at least ten of the initiates are of noble birth. Meaning . . .

Of the eighteen spots across the houses that are available, with ten practically promised to nobles, that leaves just eight spots for the remaining fifteen of us to war over.

My hand balls into a fist, and I look back to Kaelis. His attention was already on me, a slight smirk on his lips, as though he were waiting with bated breath for me to come to this realization. I can almost hear him in the back of my mind: *See, Clara, you need me. Only I can ensure your safety here.*

It makes me want to spit in his goblet.

"Now, with that out of the way, please enjoy your Fire Feast. Mingle with the students of Arcana Academy. Because tomorrow, class will be in session."

CHAPTER 11

The moment we sit, I waste no time heaping my plate. I need to regain my strength and build my body back if I'm going to survive here and have any chance of escaping.

It's a monumental effort not to lift my plate and quite literally shovel the food into my mouth. But I force myself to take small bites. I'm no stranger to starvation. After Mother died, Arina and I went through periods of feast and famine. When the work was good, our stomachs were full. When we had to go deeper into hiding from the city enforcers, the garbage was our buffet.

I've built myself up from nothing more times than I'd like to count. I'll do it again now. I'll play Kaelis's game and keep his eyes on me and me alone. That way, they'll never turn to the people I love.

Speaking of people I love . . . I scan the tables again. I've looked over House Cups seven different times. Cups was the house Arina was going to bid for and was confident she'd quickly forged enough relationships to get into. It'd certainly suit her the best. Maybe she ended up somewhere else? I scan the other houses, searching for her. Nothing. I look again, as if something would've changed and she'd magically appear. Of course she doesn't.

My sister isn't here.

What. In. The. Twenty?

My fist shakes as I raise the goblet to my lips—from anger, and from the pain of the burns that still coat my hands. The skin is beginning to peel, gnarled and nasty. I try to wash away the taste of anger and bile with as much wine as I can tolerate without getting myself drunk. Which isn't much after a year of forced abstinence from the substance and a still mostly empty stomach. But a light wine-haze might be the only thing that keeps me from marching up to the faculty's table and grabbing Kaelis by the throat.

"You seemed tense to begin with, but the knowledge of the placements has taken it to a whole new level," Sorza says to me from across the table in that dry, even manner of hers. Her black eyes flick to Dristin as she tucks a lock of hair behind her ear. "Careful sitting next to her, Dristin, or I think she'll put that knife through your throat to reduce some of the competition."

"I won't hurt any of you." Not that they'd believe it from my tone, given how agitated I am. Kaelis asked for Arina's name in Halazar. *Why, if she's not here?* Unless he's already exacted his vengeance against her while I was kept unconscious. My blood is boiling.

"We'll make it into houses, or not, based on our skills, not our birth," Luren says optimistically. Her cheeks flush easily with the slightest bit of wine, overshadowing the thin spattering of freckles on her pale skin. "No need to be competitive beyond that. The academy is designed to reward the talented. We'll all do our best and it'll all work out."

Sorza snorts. Dristin blinks several times, as if he can't believe those words, in that order, just came out of Luren's mouth. I set my chin in my palm and stare at her as I take another sip of wine.

"What?" She picks up on our collective disbelief.

"Your naive optimism is refreshing." I set down the goblet. "But it's going to get you Marked at best and killed at worst if you're not careful."

"You don't really think—"

I grab her shoulder and pull her close, leaning in to whisper in her ear. "Do I think any of the people at this table would 'accidentally' kill you to further their own ambitions if the opportunity presented itself? In a heartbeat, Luren. *A heartbeat.* We've all killed our futures with our own bare hands just to get this far. What makes you think anyone would have any qualms about ending you?"

"Was that necessary?" Kel frowns as I lean away.

"It was if she wants to survive." I finish up the last few bites of my meal as Luren stares listlessly at her plate. She's going to find out what this place is like, sooner or later. It's kinder if I'm the one to tell her. I'm sure she doesn't see it that way . . . not yet, at least. But she will at the first opportunity that the deck is shuffled and none of the cards come up for her.

I pat her shoulder as I stand, giving her the same advice I was telling myself the entire time. "Eat up. You'll need your strength."

"Where are you going?" Sorza asks.

"To meet my fellow students."

"*Fellow* students," she mutters under her breath, with a snort at my hubris.

I'm the first to make my way from the center tables, so I can feel all the initiates' and students' eyes on me as I head toward House Cups. There are stares all around, none particularly warm, and more than a few whispers.

"Isn't she bold?"

"She's the one who killed her paramour, no?"

"A long-lost noble, a secret lover . . ."

"Is the prince truly engaged to *her*?"

"Couldn't be."

"He said it himself. Are you calling the prince a liar?"

"Clan Star . . . Liam . . ."

I fight to keep my head from jerking in the direction of the sound of his name. They could've just heard it from the future I sacrificed, but I doubt it. It was said with such familiarity. Of course someone here would know him. Most students are nobles, after all. I keep my head higher and my pace even—my focus solely on the man who spoke for House Cups.

There's a good shot he'd know what happened to Arina. If he is King this year, it's likely he was Knight or Page last year. My sister wouldn't mention too many people by name whenever she'd speak of her time in the academy—at least from what little I was able to hear about the school from her before I was taken to Halazar. So I can't be sure. But I know she was forging relationships with those in Cups to try and secure a spot, so he's a safe bet.

As I draw closer, I can make out a glassy, circular pin with a crown and an embellished Minor Arcana cup upon it, just like Arina described. Three others wear similar pins, each crown slightly different in shape to denote their position.

The four royals of the house.

They're not *actually* royals; they have no relation to the Oricalis family. But Arina explained them as "royals of the academy." They represent the nobility of each Minor suit—Page, Knight, Queen, and King. The Page and Knight are second years. The King and Queen are third years. All are the top of their class and exemplars of the cards they are said to represent.

"Hello, Clara Redwin of Clan Hermit." The man uses the same friendly tone as before. As though nothing has ever bothered him in his life. The go-with-the-flow nonchalance suits a King of Cups. "To what do we owe the pleasure of being the first house you would seek out?"

"I was wondering if perhaps I might impose upon you to take a turn about the room with me?" The music is picking up once more. The student performers have finished their meals. Dancing around the bonfires will surely follow soon, as is customary during the night of the Fire Festival. I'm sure just about everyone else will want to dance with the third-year King, especially the men and women of his house currently side-eyeing me. "There are many plants here that I have never encountered before, as I've spent most of my days among the cobblestone and iron of Eclipse City."

"If it is plants you seek to learn of, then perhaps a Coin would be a better escort?" Coins are associated with the element of earth.

"Perhaps I wish for *your* company," I say directly, adding a flirtatious note.

"As forthwith as a Sword and as bold as a Wand." There's a subtext to the remark: *not one of us Cups*. But I'm not bothered.

If I were forced to pick a house—which I suppose I will be—it would not be Cups. Arina was a Cup at heart. She could take one look at someone and know exactly what was wrong, and exactly what they needed to hear. Or how to break them from the inside out. The woman could talk her way out of Halazar if she needed to.

"I have been told such boldness can be appealing to a Cup," I say.

"By whom?"

"A good authority. Though, you are welcome to prove me wrong."

There's a glint of amusement in his warm brown eyes. He stands.

"Myrion, you can't be serious," the Queen at his left whispers.

"She is a guest in our home, Orielle. Let's not be rude." A *guest*. Not yet one of them. Something I doubt they will let me forget over the next year.

Orielle forces a smile. "Yes, of course."

Myrion rounds the table toward the opening that splits it from House Swords; I mirror his movement on the opposite side, meeting him in the gap, positioning the unburnt side of my face to him. If he notices the injuries, he says nothing of them. Myrion holds out his elbow. I can feel everyone still watching me as I take it.

The moment I do, it's like the rest of them have been given permission to make their moves. The other initiates stand and head to each of the house tables to strike up conversations. The music picks up in earnest, and Myrion guides me to a nearby pyre.

I've no doubt that he'll give me just a singular turn of the room, so I waste no time. "I am curious, are there any reasons a student could be Marked and cast out?"

"What an interesting question to lead with." He studies me through his thick black lashes. "Initiates, of course, can be Marked should they fail at any point in their first year." My sister wouldn't have failed, of that I'm certain. "But initiates aren't carelessly cast out. And, once an initiate is accepted and becomes a student, the only way they would be cast out is if they were removed by the headmaster himself. Arcanists within the academy are solely under the purview of Prince Kaelis."

I had already suspected that to be the case, but hearing it is somehow worse. My eyes burn from the effort of not shooting Kaelis glares. "And is such a thing common?"

"No. It's only happened once, I believe. Just before my time here." The answer is an odd relief. "Though, last year there were three initiates who ran."

If anyone would have had the means and possible reason to leave the academy and take others with her, it'd be Arina. She pushed hard from the moment she entered the academy—harder than I would've liked, and I let her know as much. *You're going to attract the wrong sort of attention,* I warned her, though it did little good. Within her first few weeks, she had discovered secret passageways through the long bridge that connects the cliffs of the academy and Eclipse City, spanning the opening of the Farlum River, and was using them to sneak out resources right under Kaelis's nose.

"They *ran?*" I feign shock. "Why would anyone willingly leave this honorable institution?"

"Perhaps they weren't the sort who were keen on serving a clan." Myrion inspects me and, for a moment, I wonder if he sees the similarities between Arina and me. But he doesn't seem to. Arina inherited our father's eyes—the color of golden leaves in fall—along with more of his cheek and jaw structure. Me, I'm all our mother. Though, we both inherited her brown hair.

"I couldn't imagine why," I say, distancing myself in ideology from Arina in the hopes of further avoiding any connection between us. "Disloyal traitors."

Myrion hums. I'd expect it to sound like agreement, him being a noble, but it doesn't. I can't make sense of this man. "More than anything, it was heartbreaking for me to see one who was such a prospect for House Cups leave."

Arina. It must've been her. I try to think of a way I can ask for the name without sounding suspicious, but I can't come up with anything. I don't want people making the association between her and me, to protect us both. Especially since she came into the academy using the Daygar alias Mother told us to go by instead of our true name, Chevalyer. Whereas I came in using Redwin. Bringing up Arina by name—when I have no reason to know it—would be an immediate signal that something is off with me.

"I must imagine, though, that it would be heartwarming for the prince to hear you speak so fiercely of loyalty. Especially following the scandal you caused immediately following his announcement of you as his betrothed."

I scoff, almost laugh, at the statement, flash Myrion a dazzling smile, and readily seize on the opportunity to move the subject away from Arina. Leaning closer to him as we cross in front of the faculty table is intentional. I don't think Kaelis would be jealous of Myrion, but I do hope that he takes it as a slight that I'd position myself so closely, so quickly, to another man. Especially after what happened with the Chalice.

"Would you suggest the prince is a man whose pride is so easily wounded? A man who's so easily threatened?"

"Certainly not. Though the prince is a man who gets—*takes* what he wants." Myrion's tone is unreadable, though I try anyway. Does he know Kaelis well? And, if so . . . do they get along? My gut is telling me no, but I don't have enough reason to trust it. Yet.

"If anything, I'd think the prince would be pleased with me," I say loud enough that Kaelis might hear as we pass. "After all, I removed a would-be competitor for my affections." Not that it was my intention . . . but I'll spin this to my benefit. No matter what that Two of Cups came up as, I was going to find a way to have it help me.

"All too true," Myrion says, somewhat sadly. I notice his cuff link. Two hands clasped with a ribbon. The symbol of Clan Lovers. Nobleborn, and someone who'd presumably idealize love. "With so many vying for your attention, I should perhaps consider myself lucky that you decided to seek me out first. I do relish in having a lovely someone on my arm."

It's been so long since anyone has taken that kind of interest in me, or since I've been willing to put myself out there, that I've almost forgotten what the chase feels like. The sensation of someone looking at me with something more than animosity. I've missed the rush of heat. The thrill of possibilities unknown. Of the push and pull of flirtation. I'm not looking for love here. But a bit of fun wouldn't be entirely unwelcome . . .

"Perhaps you should." I release him as we come to a stop at the edge of the Cups tables. "I imagine I will be quite the commodity among all the students, soon enough."

"Wands and Swords, indeed." He's referring to my confidence, or perhaps my bold spirit. Though I must also wonder if this is his way of subtly emphasizing that I shouldn't attempt to join Cups. They have five slots, but perhaps they're all already spoken for.

But would he be that kind to give me such a tip?

I can overthink everything in this place. Doing so might drive me mad. But it will also be my best chance to get out of here as quickly as possible.

"Take care, Clara." Myrion leaves, and I return to the center tables. I barely resist stopping him to ask about Arina by name. But I don't want to risk people knowing anything more than they already do about me. And Myrion already told me what I needed to know.

Kaelis removed her, Arina fled, or she was killed.

The music picks up, and most of the students leave their seats to mingle. None approach me, and I don't make the effort to approach any others. I've made my move for the night.

When Kaelis finally stands, I do as well. I make my way to the edge of the room, trying to avoid moving too quickly and drawing unwanted attention. Drifting with the ebb and flow of the music and conversations, I end up behind a group of individuals along the back wall.

As the prince strides through the center of the room, the students and initiates part and bow their heads reverently. The conversations momentarily fall to a hush. The large doors open for him without him lifting a finger. Once more, his eyes find mine among the masses. That cold, unyielding gaze is possibly the most unwelcoming thing one could imagine.

Yet all I see is an invitation.

Kaelis slips out the doors, and I am not far behind.

CHAPTER 12

Either no one notices or no one cares that I leave, because I'm not stopped. The shadows are already enveloping Kaelis as he strides down the opposite hallway. He doesn't even so much as glance back, though I know he must hear my hasty footsteps.

Yet no matter how quick I am, I still fall behind. Nothing about my body moves like it should. The rich food is making me heavy and sluggish. Kaelis turns, dipping down a curved staircase and disappearing out of view.

The stairs end in an unfamiliar stretch of hallway. I head left, initially drawn by the sound of footsteps, only to slow my pace when a conversation carries across the cold stones of the hall.

"You may leave, *now*." Kaelis's tone is curt and cutting.

"We have Prince Ravin's orders to search—" The voice is familiar. *It couldn't be.*

"Prince Ravin has no say here," Kaelis interrupts the other man. "The grounds of the academy are solely under my control."

I creep toward the entrance of a nearby room, keeping myself low and pressed to the wall. The open door casts a warm glow that reflects off a dark window opposite, the night beyond turning the glass into a mirror. Kaelis stands among five individuals dressed in simple canvas uniforms.

There are the Stellis, known for their shining armor adorned with raven and dove feathers. There are the city enforcers in their practical garb of green. Then there are the men and women who wear the drab gray-brown color that's nearly the same shade as the walls they patrol.

My blood freezes, and my heart works three times as hard to keep it flowing, the panicked pulsing drowning out the conversation for a moment. *The Halazar guards I saw during the procession are still here.* And I recognize the man Kaelis is talking to as Glavstone's current right hand. Savan is his name. I heard it enough times as Glavstone barked orders at him.

"... Given that this matter involves an Arcanist who escaped Halazar, the very same convict you came to execute, Warden Glavstone assumed you would want to pursue the escapee at all costs."

Kaelis's stance gives him the air of being completely unbothered, except for a twitch at the corner of his mouth that turns into a frown. "Thoughtful of him."

"Your highness, we respect that this is quite irregular. Please allow us to conduct our search of students and initiates quickly, then we shall be off," Savan says.

The prince doesn't move, and neither do I. *Send them away*, I beg silently. The academy is his domain. If he wanted, he could. But Kaelis is not known for his kindness. Especially not toward me.

"Yes, of course. I hope that we are able to find this escapee. Though I do not expect her to be here in the academy." Kaelis's expression relaxes into a smile. "Still, I shall allow you into the main hall so we might be done with this and I can return to my obligations for the night of the Fire Festival."

They turn, starting for the door. As I begin to back away, my eyes catch Savan's in the reflection of the mirror. The ice in my veins melts in the wake of searing horror as recognition dawns on him.

"What the—" he starts to say.

I run.

Back down the hall where I came from. Footsteps hurry behind me. Kaelis says something, but I lose the words.

I can't go back to Halazar. I won't. I'd rather die.

These frantic declarations propel my every step. I'm practically leaping down a staircase, darting through rooms that are now illuminated by lanterns—the whole academy lit up from the ritual of the Chalice, like a beast that's come to life once more, fueled by sacrificed futures. Those lanterns, though sparse, are far too bright. They feel like spotlights. Like the same spotlights that landed on me the night I was caught.

Side burning and chest heaving, I skid to a stop as I find myself in a room without any other exits. My gaze sweeps across the shelves, searching for a place to hide, but snags on the large metallic object that consumes the center of the space. The thing is so strange that, for a moment, I forget who and what I'm running from.

Before me is a machine unlike anything I've ever beheld. A metallic wheel is turned by an unseen force, with the heavy chain that spins it disappearing into the ceiling. A large block of steel rises and falls over a mortar. Worn down in the pit of the center of the machine are crystalline shards that fight against every hit of the grindstone, bursting with stardust at each impact and bathing everything in cold, hazy light.

Shelves line the walls, crammed with crates whose contents wink at me with a glow identical to the shards in the mortar. It's a unique cerulean hue, easily identifiable. It's this light that allows divers to find the crystals they harvest from the inky blackness of the darkest caves of the Drowned Mines. This room is a small treasure trove of the raw inking material for Cups cards. But the machine . . .

It's a powder mill, I realize. But, according to the crown, mills must be operated by hand. The process is too delicate and requires too much magic to be automated. So they claim . . . Is it a lie? Or are there Marked hidden in the walls of the academy working this small mill? Neither would be a surprise.

I approach it with the same care I might a feral animal, as though the machine is a sentient thing that might get spooked and run away. It's old but not ancient . . . The gears and pins are well worn but still in good condition. Some kind of rune has been engraved upon its hammer—what I think looks like a V with a P? E? attached on its tall side. But the details are hard to make out when it's in constant motion.

A blur is at my side, drawing my attention. I swing on instinct. Kaelis catches my fist with ease and our eyes lock. My arm quivers against his grip.

"What's that supposed to do?" His voice is low and ominous.

My breath hitches. His stare threatens to swallow me whole. He was holding back his agitation in the main hall, but he's not holding back now. The fingers of his other hand lock around my biceps, and he steers me until my back meets the cool stone of a nearby wall. My fist falls at the impact, my muscles beginning to struggle with the effort to merely hold myself upright.

The prince has nestled us between two shelves. His body is searingly hot against the cool air of the castle, his face ominous and outlined by the hazy glow of the crystals stored throughout the room.

"Are you going to give me to the guards?" I manage to make the question sound defiant even though the mere idea nearly sets my teeth to chattering.

A wicked glint sparks in his eyes. "Now, why would I allow my *future wife* to be sent to Halazar?"

My stomach churns at the words. "It should be obvious I've no interest in being your wife—in having anything to do with you at all."

"Ah, yes . . . I presume that's why you chose the Two of Cups." The shadows darken upon his face as he dips his chin, his expression turning sinister. "You wished to make a mockery of me." The words are barbed, and they sting with the venom of accusation.

"And here I thought you'd be smart enough to realize I'd helped you with that card." My voice is honed to a sharp edge to match his snarl.

"Helped me?" Kaelis's brow furrows further. He leans closer, looming over me, hair tickling my brow. Our chests nearly touch with every breath. The idea of bringing my knee into his groin to get him away crosses my mind. But I refrain.

Halazar guards are here; he could send me back with a word... Now isn't the time to antagonize the prince further. Even when it's oh so satisfying.

"What could make me look more like a long-lost noble than a secret, scorned lover from another clan? What could make our 'love' seem more legitimate than my devotion to you leading me to destroy any chance of a future with someone else?" I hate how well this worked out for him. The only solace I get is to try to use it to ensure I'm not sent back to that cell to rot.

"Who was he?" the prince demands to know.

"Why do you care?" I'm not telling him any more than he already knows about Liam from watching me fight my future, which is already far too much. "He clearly won't be anything anymore—can't be." The words are harder to say than I want to admit.

Kaelis's eyes widen slightly, then narrow once more. A low, amused growl rumbles in his chest. "You still love him."

"Silence," I hiss.

"Even after you've killed your prospects with him with your own hands... you *mourn* for him." The words are so full of hate, as if the idea of caring for someone—of loving someone so much that you yearn for them even when your better sense has screamed for you not to—is not only foreign to him but disgusting as well.

"What would you and your withered, cruel heart know about love?"

"A withered and cruel heart can't be broken, Clara. I've nothing to lose, and you'd do well to remember that."

"Or what?"

"Or I'll show you why you should reconsider being so eager for a good fuck that you'd open your legs for nothing more than an illusion before the whole academy."

I shove him away with a noise of disgust, guards be damned, unable to bear him being near me for a second longer. Kaelis catches my fingers. A hiss of pain escapes me. Confusion, rather than anger, overtakes his expression. He looks from my hands to my face. Slowly, almost gently, he brushes my hair from my cheek. It's the intensity of his focus that stills me enough that I'm not batting his hand away in an instant. His touch is almost . . . *kind*. And after a year in Halazar, I find myself completely confused by how to react when someone is reaching for me without intent to harm.

"You're injured." The statement carries as much emotion as if he were commenting on the weather.

Yanking my fingers from him and ignoring the pain, I retreat a step back. The wall affords me no more space to get away from him. I glower through my choppy bangs.

"I can help—" He's reaching for the deck inside his coat.

"I'd rather peel my skin off with my nails than accept your help."

Kaelis pauses, mid-motion. His gaze softens for a breath.

"You truly hate me." The words are little more than a whisper.

"You sound . . . surprised?" All I can do is laugh. "You have orchestrated—or supported—everything that has ever led to hurt or pain in my life. You put me in Halazar."

"It is *not* my fault that you were there." His mouth contorts into a scowl. I assume he means it was my fault for breaking the law. Laws *he'd* helped make and uphold.

"You have some kind of machination"—I motion to the machine—"that could process powder for inks, and yet you still Mark and send people to the mills?"

"The machine is an artifact from the previous kingdom. Its secrets are lost and can't be trusted." He speaks with authority he shouldn't have about "lost" sciences. It makes me trust him even less.

"And you'd prefer not to find them." If it were me, I'd be ripping the thing apart at the seams to figure out how it works. Something like that could change the lives of Arcanists everywhere. "You'd rather kill Marked Arcanists as if it's sport."

He grabs my face, fingers around my jaw, pressing into my cheeks. The pain of the burns is as sharp as the fire that caused them. How quickly his façade of caring vanishes. I wonder how many women would be taken in by it.

"Don't speak as if you know me," Kaelis almost snarls.

"Tell me I'm wrong," I challenge, unflinching. The memory of the first applicant taking on the Chalice is as fresh in my mind as Kaelis walking away from his corpse.

"Do you think letting that applicant live as a Marked would've been any better? You know as well as I that most *beg* for a quick death from the moment they arrive at the mills."

"Should I think you were being kind by murdering a man whose only crime was failing your test?"

"You should think of me as a man who would do whatever it takes to get what I want." There is no room for doubt at the end of his statement.

"Like taking a woman who *doesn't want you* as your bride so you can use her for who knows what—"

"You are going to help me get the World," he says, repeating his earlier sentiment.

"A lot of effort to hunt down a fable."

"The World is not a fable." His words drop to a whisper, grip relaxing, as if he doesn't dare say the name of the legendary Major too loudly. Kaelis's fingers fall from my face, gliding over my skin and leaving cold in their wake. "It is real, of that I assure you."

The World is real, Mother's voice echoes from my childhood, *and it can do* anything. *Which is why it must never be found. Do not trust anyone who would seek it.* There were times I believed her warnings, and times I didn't. Times when I felt like she wanted me to remain unsure of what was true in her stories and what were lies. But, much like her order to keep our Chevalyer name hidden, there were some things I knew better than to question her too deeply about.

"Of course it is," I say with sarcasm, showing the uneasy feeling that the mere mention of the World fills me with. "And if you want any help from me to get it, you're going to tell me what happened to Arina."

"Didn't I tell you? You're not in any position to bargain." Smugness wars with malice and the former wins. For now.

"Where is she?" I hadn't planned on daring to bring her up again with Kaelis and risking him finally seeing something in me that would bring the familial resemblance to the fore. But I hadn't formulated any kind of plan when I followed him from the main hall. I'm so tired. Everything hurts. All I want is to have something to channel all this pain and anger into, and Kaelis is an exceptional target for that.

"I don't even know who she is." Kaelis shrugs and steps away, as if he genuinely doesn't know. I don't believe it for a second. Not when he views all of the academy as his precious domain. It takes my mood from sour to outright venomous.

"*Arina.*" I repeat my sister's name and take a step toward him. "The one who you *forced me* to confess was helping me steal supplies from the academy." *Who, I know now, ran.* But I don't say so.

"Ah, yes." Such condescension in so few sounds. "*You* were stealing from *me*, and you're going to try to make it sound like I'm the one in the wrong?"

I don't take his bait, staying focused on my sister. Fortunately, it seems Kaelis didn't know her well enough to see the familial similarities in the shape of our eyes or the color and texture of our hair. "She should be a second year, and she's not here." I wonder if he's dodging the answer because it'd amount to admitting people can escape the academy.

"Perhaps the people you thought you could depend on are not as loyal as you imagined. You were in Halazar a long time; they might have thought you abandoned them and they moved on." The way he says it . . . it's as though leaving them behind was my choice. My heart hammers, and soon my ears are ringing from the rushing blood.

It's taking all my might not to throw another fist at his face. Usually I'd prefer more elegant means of retaliation against someone threatening or insulting me and my loved ones. But, seeing as I'm not armed with cards at present . . . I'll resort to what I must. My self-control is hanging by a thread.

"I. Don't. Abandon. People." I barely get the words out through gritted teeth.

A glint in his eyes makes me step back and relax, my walls quickly coming up. Exhaustion made me hasty. Clumsy. But it's too late. He's too clever not to realize the root of my anger—my hurt.

"But *they* abandon *you*." The words are searing hot needles pressing between my ribs and into the most delicate parts of my heart. The deepest fear I never want anyone to see . . . least of all him. Kaelis continues before I can think of any retort. "Now, we must return to the main hall." He offers his elbow.

"I'd rather eat glass."

"It's not glass you'll have to eat, but whatever they serve you in Halazar." His lips twitch into a smirk. I dip my chin and glower up at him. "Let's drop the pretense; you don't have a choice, Clara. Enough resisting."

He pauses for emphasis. For the first time, I contain my anger and don't rise to his goading. Approval shines in his eyes, as if I am a pet he's taught a new trick.

"Now, take my elbow." Every word is emphasized.

Reluctantly, I do.

"Good girl."

I refrain from demanding more information about Arina as he escorts me out. He's not going to tell me, and pressing further would only show more weakness and give him more carrots to dangle in front of me that he'd never actually let me have. I'll have to find out what happened to her on my own. Hopefully, she made it out and is giving Ravin and his enforcers headaches back in Eclipse City.

Kaelis pauses at the door and makes a show of locking it behind us. There's a flash of magic, but I don't recognize the card. The man already correctly assumed that I'd want to return to gather whatever information I could about the machine, regardless of his warnings. He glances in my direction, looking for a reaction. I give him nothing.

We're just about back to the main hall when the three Halazar guards enter the passage we're on from a side door. I freeze in my tracks.

"Keep walking," Kaelis commands under his breath.

I try, but my feet won't move. My head is spinning. Kaelis's biceps and forearm tense around my hand as if trying to anchor me, like he can sense my immediate need to bolt again.

"I have you." It's almost reassuring, even from him.

I'm just about to ask if we can take any other route when the guards turn in our direction. Savan's eyes lock with mine once more. But this time I can't run. Kaelis takes a step forward, and I have no choice but to follow him to my own demise.

"*You.*" That's all the Halazar guard says before charging toward me.

CHAPTER 13

Kaelis's arm tenses further, and he shifts with his next step. It's subtle, but I feel the change like a protective shadow gliding over my shoulders. He stands slightly ahead of me, wedging himself between me and Savan. But his demeanor is calm. From every purple-black hair on his head to the mirror finish of his booted toes, Kaelis oozes a nearly terrifying aura of control.

"Have you finished your search?"

"I'd say we have." Savan halts when he's close enough for me to see the yellow rings in his hazel eyes—they're nearly catlike in the low light. "Apprehend the convict," he commands to the other two guards at his flanks, men whom I don't recognize.

"Convict?" Kaelis glances back at me, and I see a flash of amusement dancing in his eyes. It's replaced with confusion when he turns his attention back to Savan. The prince's words are steeped in offense. "This, sir, is the last remaining member of Clan Hermit and my blushing bride-to-be."

"Your bride?" Savan nearly stammers.

"Yes. You would do well to remember this before levying such baseless accusations against her, thus deeply offending me." Kaelis's tone is more bitter than winter.

Savan's eyes dart between us. Confusion rakes deep lines into his brow that soon fold into anger and frustration. "This creature—"

Before he can finish, a card seems to materialize from nowhere, hovering right before Savan's nose, engulfed in an ominous ombré of magic. The card slowly spins, and I instantly recognize the Knight of Swords.

"This is my future *wife,* the woman who will become your princess. Choose your next words carefully. I assure you that having your throat cut out is not a pleasant experience." Kaelis acts so convincingly that it steals my breath when he drops my hand from the crook of his elbow and wraps his arm around me, pulling me close. Off-balance, I stabilize myself with a hand on his chest. I make the split-second decision to lean even closer to look like I'm leeching security and protection from him. The movement hides the tiny tremors at his proximity. For a dizzying second, I commit to the act; I am who he says I am and Kaelis—the void-born Prince of Oricalis—is really my star-crossed lover.

"Your highness . . ." Savan struggles to find words. Anger toward me wars with the instinct of self-preservation. "I do not know what lies she has spun, or how she has bewitched you, but—"

"You dare to claim that I, a Prince of Oricalis, could be 'bewitched' or otherwise led on? You dare to insult my intelligence and capability?"

"Of course not. However—"

Kaelis isn't about to let Savan get a word in, and I find I'm loving it. But I keep my expression as one of shock and confusion. "Then what are you trying to claim, Savan? That she is some escaped convict from Halazar even though I have told you otherwise? You forget yourself. The halls of Arcana Academy are my domain; she is an initiate—under my control. And my future bride." Kaelis looks toward me and his brow smooths with adoration, an expression I work to mirror. His face hardens once more as he looks back to Savan. "Unless you have undeniable proof otherwise, I would suggest you drop this claim and leave. I grow weary of your attempts to circumvent my authority."

Savan deflates. The two other guards remain frozen at his sides, clearly unsure of how to proceed. The Knight of Swords continues to hover ominously before him. "I only mean to serve the crown."

Kaelis leans forward ever so slightly and whispers, "I am the crown."

Savan opens his mouth to object. It's written on his face. We can all feel it. The unspoken words, *No, you're not,* hover in the air. Kaelis is the second-born prince. His father, King Naethor Oricalis, is the crown. Next in line is the firstborn prince, Ravin. But here, now . . . there is only Kaelis and the immense amount of power he wields. Standing in the stony corridors that are solely his domain.

Savan has the sense not to object further. He eases a step back, getting distance from Kaelis and me, and from the Knight of Swords that still spins threateningly before him.

"Forgive me, your highness. It seems that in my zeal to pursue the escapee, I was mistaken." Every word from him is begrudging, and I can't stop the satisfied smirk they draw upon my lips. Savan's eyes lock with mine at the sight of my smugness. I quickly tilt my head toward Kaelis, trying to hide it. "However, should I uncover proof, you will be the first I take it to, in order to defend the crown's honor."

"See that I am. Now, get out of my academy before my hospitality is entirely exhausted."

Savan dares to give me one last scathing look from the corners of his eyes. The guard turns on his heel and leaves, motioning for the others to follow him.

The Knight of Swords floats back into the pocket of Kaelis's coat, slotting into an unseen deck.

"Do you see?" the prince asks, drawing my attention to him. He looms over me once more, arm still tightly around my waist. Somehow stronger than any shackle of Halazar. "I am the only one who can defend you."

I shift, pulling myself from his person. I glare up at him but say nothing. Prince Kaelis is defending me. What an impossible thing. I can't deny it after that display, but I know better than to think it has anything at all to do with any compassion for me. This man was the one who let me rot in Halazar for a year . . . only to pull me from the depths of that abyss when he had a use for me.

He truly is so loathsome.

His fingers wrap around my chin and force my face toward his. I ignore the pain from the burns. Kaelis tilts his head slightly to the side. Strands of hair fall across his face.

"Yes, I like this expression."

I glower further, and his eyes shine even brighter in delight.

"Your tenacity will suit our ends." *"Our,"* as if we have a mutual goal . . . "Keep that fire, Clara." He releases me and steps away, gesturing casually to the right. "This way back to the main hall. I'll go and ensure Glavstone's minions see themselves out of here, or I'll flay their skin from their bones, whichever suits me more."

Kaelis's boots click down the hall with his departure. I head in the opposite direction—back toward the main hall. The feeling of his hand on me has the heavy dinner threatening to come back up. I walk faster, as if I could escape the sensation of him. But the prince is alive in this fortress. It lives and breathes him. There's nowhere I can flee that doesn't remind me of my current predicament.

Still, my haste serves me. I return not a moment too soon. Mere minutes after I slip back through the door and rejoin the students and initiates, Professor Thornbrow moves to the front of the room, in the center of the faculty table.

"If the initiates will please follow me, I will show you to the dormitories and explain your first-year arrangements."

Thornbrow leads us out through the doors and into a new passageway. Once more, I am stunned by the sheer scale of the place. Especially as the narrow passage quickly opens to a large inner conservatory—one I recognize from when Kaelis brought me from his tower. Except this time, I'm two floors up.

Not that I have much time to assess it. Luren materializes beside me.

"You missed the excitement," Luren says.

"*Why* did you miss the excitement?" Kel is at her side, as has been the case the whole night. She peers at me through narrowed eyes.

"Didn't you see? She slipped out with Headmaster Kaelis. Her betrothed, if what the students are saying is to be believed," Dristin says as he comes up on my left flank.

"It's true, then?" Luren is far too eager about this. "You really are engaged to be married to Prince Kaelis?"

"They said the prince announced it himself," Kel says.

"I am—we are." I force a smile, thinking of the Halazar guards. Of Kaelis standing between me and them. Until I can find my own way out, they all have to think I love him. "What was the 'excitement'?"

"Halazar guards were here." Dristin removes his spectacles, wiping them on his shirt. "Apparently, someone escaped the prison."

"I don't believe it." Kel shakes her head. "*No one* escapes Halazar."

"That's what would make it so fabulously scandalous if it's true," Sorza chimes in from behind us. We all glance over our shoulders and then make space as we're walking. Sorza tucks a strand of black silken hair behind her ear. "Think of how powerful someone would have to be to escape." I can't shake the sensation that Sorza is looking right at *me*.

"Or well connected," Dristin adds.

"I hope the person is found quickly. They must be dangerous if they were in Halazar, definitely not someone we'd want roaming free." I try to sound like all the nobles I've hated. Ignoring how many harmless Arcanists are sent to Halazar to rot alongside true criminals.

"At least we don't have anything to worry about in here. Prince Kaelis would never allow anything to happen on academy grounds." Dristin seems reassured by this. Meanwhile, the notion has my insides squirming and my waist hot where Kaelis's hand was.

As we walk, I hear chatter among the other initiates about the escapee and the Halazar guards. *There's no way any of them could know*, I work to reassure myself, even though I feel as if a broad target is painted on my back. I worry my every step might give away that I'm not who I say I am. *I must convince them all I am Kaelis's betrothed.*

We're led to a spacious lounge. There are bookshelves and gaming tables. Sitting areas cluster before four hearths to the right and left. In every corner is a stairway, the arch above bearing the circular signet of one of the four houses, identical to what the students wear around their necks. Directly across from the entry, in the center of the wall rather than a corner, is a fifth stairwell that's unmarked.

"This is the common area for all the houses. Each house has their own dormitory, as is marked." Thornbrow motions with an open palm at each of the four archways. The professor's movements are rigid and precise enough that I wonder if he was perhaps once a Stellis, or at least a city enforcer. The closely cropped hair on the sides with the tidy length on top gives me a similar impression. "You are not permitted into a house's dormitory without being a member of that house. Your current dormitories as initiates are opposite us. There are two to a room while you are initiates, as is marked. You'll find your things have already been brought up."

Things . . . I don't have those. But I do wonder who's carrying the luggage. It'd make sense for Arcana Academy to have attendants and other staff, and there were a few bustling around the hall. Grimly, I wonder if the staff has chosen to be here or if they were forced. My mind returns to Marked Arcanists.

"There, you will also find supplies for your classes that begin tomorrow. They have been furnished by the grace of the crown, so be sure to show your gratitude to the headmaster when next you see him.

"You will receive further information about the year's curriculum and what will be expected of you tomorrow at your first class. Please make your way when the bells toll. Tardiness will reflect poorly upon you." Thornbrow is already sounding impatient. I suspect most of the faculty, and students, see little point in investing too much in us emotionally when they know that roughly a third of us will be gone within the next two seasons. "Are there any other questions at this time?"

"Sir." A woman with pale blond hair that's more silver than gold speaks. She has honey-brown eyes and white skin, though not overly fair. As Thornbrow's attention swings to her, she places both fists at the small of her back, standing taller in salute. The pin over her left breast shines in the ambient light of the crystal chandeliers above. A streak of light glints down a lightning bolt striking a crumbling tower. *Clan Tower.* The generals of the Oricalis militia, leaders of the Stellis.

"Speak." Thornbrow shifts slightly; his hands twitch as though he is fighting giving a similar salute back to her. That, combined with his tone . . . He's of Clan Strength, or Tower. I'm nearly sure of it.

"What are the rules regarding the rest of the academy, beyond the dormitories? Are there any other areas we are or are not permitted to visit?"

Thornbrow smirks, as if he gets some kind of personal enjoyment or amusement from this question. "You are all of age, capable of conducting yourselves appropriately. If there is a room in which you are not supposed to be, it will be marked, locked, or barred. Use of cards is also permitted within the halls of the academy, but know that you will be held appropriately responsible for any damage or risks posed to others. Arcanists are valuable to the crown, and we cannot have any injury coming to royal property without proper cause."

Even Unmarked, we are tools. Just slightly better kept tools. I do, however, take note of how he specifies "proper cause." It sounds . . . intentionally vague.

"With that, I recommend you all seek out a good night's sleep. Your real work will begin tomorrow." The professor leaves.

I waste no time starting for the dorms. Others follow my lead. A few remain in the common room, no doubt continuing to court early favor with the different houses by waiting for the students to return to their dorms from the main hall.

Up the stairs is another, smaller common area, clearly intended just for initiates. A long hall stretches back from it with fifteen doors. Almost every door has two names on it. Which means they can only ever take thirty initiates at a time. Unless they remake this hall as needed during the dinner. It wouldn't be impossible with the right combination of cards . . .

I find the door with my name on it. It's underneath another: Alor.

I darkly hope that she's removed from the academy sooner, rather than later; I'm not exactly keen on sharing my space.

But, for now, I'm alone. And I'm going to make the most of it.

Kaelis does not seem to know the meaning of "restraint" when it comes to decor. One room's worth of finishings could likely support a family in Eclipse City for a year. The dormitories are no exception.

The stone walls are more polished here than in the rest of the academy, and the mortar is paper-thin, giving the entire wall an almost glossy appearance. The walls have been washed to an ivory color, and quartz has been embedded at the meeting of every four corners of stone. The tiny crystals catch the ambient light and reflect it throughout the room.

Two grandiose beds are separated by a plush, velvety rug the color of the midnight sky, embroidered with hundreds of golden stars. The bed frames are crafted from a dark mahogany, with tall headboards decorated with a lattice of gleaming gold-leafed vines. Linens and silks envelop the mattresses in the same deep jewel tones as the rug beneath them. The duvet is pillow-soft.

Between the two beds, along the back wall and underneath the large window, are two desks of equally luxurious craftsmanship. The motif of gilded ivy is carried across their surfaces, and around the arches of the two colossal wardrobes at the foot of the beds. Curiosity has me drifting toward the one with my name emblazoned on the front.

My breath hitches as I swing the doors open. Inside is a dream of fashion—perfect ensembles for a recently ascended noble. There are dark silks, light and airy in contrast to the heavy leathers. There are linens and velvets. Trousers and skirts and dresses. Every piece of fabric slips through my fingers like coins from my palms. *If I were to just sell this wardrobe, I could prep a handful of Arcanists fleeing from the Marking for the desert beyond the mountains . . .*

I snap the doors shut and hang my head. I fight a wicked urge to grab fabric by the fistful and run down to the common room and throw it into the fire.

Rage is worth little if it's not channeled. I told Arina that many times, just as Mother said it to me. I must listen to her advice now more than ever. I've already ignored more than a few of her warnings. Halazar has tampered with my self-control and my common sense. Two things I need to recover sooner rather than later.

The clothes can't help anyone if they're destroyed. But if I keep them, I might be able to fit in better here until I can sneak them out.

Lie. Survive. Resist.

I sound my resignation with a sigh. I quickly strip down and change into a pair of drawstring silken pants and matching shirt. Even with my stomach distended from all the food and grumbling at the richness of it following such a long period of hunger, my trousers must be tied tighter than I would like.

I'm pulled toward the other wardrobe. ALOR written in silver winks at me in the low light. With a glance over my shoulder to the main door, I pull open the wardrobe and take a quick peek.

The clothes are all in shades of gray. Embroidered swords dance down sleeves and frame cuffs. There are small lightning bolts in place of buttons. All my suspicions are confirmed when I see the symbol of the Tower.

Of fucking course Kaelis would make sure the person I'm sharing a room with is from the clan that supplies his family their dogs. I shut the doors in disgust and move to the desks.

I assume the desk on the right is mine, same with the bed, as that's the side my wardrobe is on. The top drawer glides open effortlessly, and I let out a noise that is somewhere between a gasp and a squeal of delight.

An array of arcane implements is inside, from shimmering powders and crystal inkpots to quills fashioned from eagle feathers and pens carved from precious stones. They glint in the lamplight cast from the lanterns hung over the desks, like little suitors winking at me.

"My only loves," I assure them.

The next drawer has more powders and pens and quills. I pull out the chair and the slim center drawer at my waist and find the paper I had been looking for—precut to card size. True luxury. Not the stolen scraps I usually have to fight for and trim to size myself. Or that I just squeeze and twist the inking on to make it work.

However, what catches my eye is an envelope on the top of the stacks of paper in the drawer, right in the center, so black it seems to absorb the light. I know who it's from without opening it, and I think, briefly, of ignoring it, or throwing it away. But curiosity gets the better of me.

I open the envelope with the aid of a silver letter opener and slip out the thin paper within. In a tightly spun, elegant script that is certain to belong to Kaelis are the words:

> **I hope it is all to your liking. Now show me what my bride can do.**

I can't ink an Ace of Wands fast enough to incinerate the note. I'll show him what I can do. Here, in the privacy of my room . . . no one will know I can already ink and wield *all* the Minor Arcana with ease. I will build my own deck. My weapons of choice. I will not be caught off guard and unarmed again.

I don't trust any of the other initiates for even a breath. These aren't my people.

My people are beyond these towering walls and windswept cliffs. They're back in Eclipse City. Arina found a way out of the academy, and once I regain my strength, I'm going to find it, too.

CHAPTER 14

The next morning is like waking into a dream. The soft mattress envelops me. The downy duvet smothers me. I've created a warm nest using every pillow, and, for a good minute, I curse the gray light of dawn.

Behind my eyelids, I'm in a different time and place. Mother gently smooths the hair from my face, planting a kiss on my forehead before she goes to the Descent. All non-Arcanists in Oricalis must work for five years at one of the harvesting sites to collect resources for the mills. Unless they pay a regill—a sum of money most never see in their lifetime, save for nobles. Failure to report is punishable by death. She'd already paid her time to the crown . . . but when the money dried up, she agreed to another stint. Every subsequent stretch of time earns a regill, *if* you complete it. Few things pay better than jobs that put one in mortal peril.

Look after Arina, she whispers, *I'll be home after the sun sets. You both have all my love.*

I force open stinging eyes and blink at the bone-pale wall. The mattress in my old room smelled of the damp hay inside it. The blankets were woolly. The room was half subterranean and so never got enough light, and the walls wept heavy beads of condensation for much the same reason. But I felt just as cozy in my family's home as I do now. More, even. What I wouldn't give to go back.

You think you appreciate what you have and then it's taken from you . . . and you wonder if you ever treasured it enough.

Emerging from the warm cocoon of the bed and my memories requires a significant amount of effort. It's been ages since I last slept comfortably, and I could probably spend an entire day just in bed. But I'm not going to have a late start to my first day. Swinging my feet off, I pause as I lay eyes on my roommate.

Alor is a soft silhouette beneath the rolls of the duvet. Her platinum hair, silver in the gray morning light, is a halo around her tranquil expression. Even in slumber, she possesses an almost unnatural grace.

I'd heard her come in last night. It was at some ungodly hour, but I couldn't fall into any kind of deep sleep until I knew she was in the room and wasn't about to stab me in my sleep. Perhaps she shares that sentiment and the slumber is nothing more than a façade she's putting on for me. As I stand, I catch a glint of silver—the hilt of a dagger peeking out from the top of the duvet, her fist curled around it.

A bitter smirk crosses my lips. My worries were founded.

Walking barefoot across the plush carpet and then cool stone, I open my wardrobe. Using the massive door like a changing screen, I tuck myself inside and quickly dress for the day. The sense of vulnerability that comes with being naked is overwhelming. Halazar might have been squalid, but at least the cell offered generally somewhat private squalor.

I select a pair of stiff, high-waisted cotton trousers in midnight, and a silvery silken shirt with billowing sleeves. A holster affixes to the wide leather belt that I fasten around my waist and is held in place with a strap that circles my thigh. Slinging a satchel across my body, I return to the desk, where I collect an array of basic supplies and the short stack of cards I inked last night. The former are in the satchel, the latter in the holster. I'm not supposed to have half the cards I inked, but that's a tactical risk as I'm not taking another step in this place unarmed.

Before leaving, I cast one more glance at Alor. She has yet to move. Her breathing is like clockwork. I don't think for a second she's sleeping. But I say nothing.

The common area for the houses is bustling when I descend. There is no official uniform among the students. They are dressed in as much of an array of finery as the night previous. The only consistent element of their garb is a medallion bearing their house symbol.

Each house's medallion has been cast in a different metal. Swords are in a dark, matte metal a shade lighter than iron—reminiscent of the alloy Kaelis's Oricalis family crest is cast in. Wands have a rusty hue that swirls with charcoal. Coins are made of gold. And Cups are almost translucent, done in a glassy crystalline material.

The only outliers are the house royals, who also bear a pin that signifies their status.

The students move in packs, keeping mostly to the other members of the same house. Initiates are peppered throughout. There wasn't an overly clear instruction on what we were expected to do this morning—beyond heading to class when the bells toll. So I assume all the other initiates are, like me, following the lead of the students.

We cast wary glances at one another. Every chest that's vacant of a medallion might as well be a target.

The grand hall is already bustling as I arrive. The tables practically groan under the weight of the food spread across them. Once more, I am in awe of the assortment of offerings and waste no time filling my plate with slabs of honeyed ham and towering biscuits that let out a mouthwatering billow of steam when pried apart. My stomach is already objecting to the rich food. But the sooner it gets accustomed to solid and not maggot-infested sustenance, the better.

"Good morning, Clara," Luren says cheerfully as she sits next to me, oblivious to the dark thoughts I'd been having of my time in Halazar. Consistent as ever, Kel is at her side. Sorza and Dristin are nowhere to be seen, so far.

"Good morning," I oblige her. Though her tone is somewhat confusing. *We're not friends,* I want to say. Judging from the look in Kel's eyes, she feels similarly. But Luren's sunshine smile stays both our tongues.

"Did you sleep well?" Luren asks.

"Well enough." I take a sip of my tea.

"How could you not sleep well in beds like this?" she says dreamily.

"She's probably accustomed to it, being a noble and all." Kel's nails run along the rim of her mug, as if she's trying to resist balling her hands into fists in frustration.

"Oh, right. I forget how many nobles there are." Luren's gaze quickly becomes a touch sad.

"I only uncovered the truth of my lineage recently." I'm not sure why I'm so drawn to reassure them. "I suspect our upbringings weren't so different for most of our lives." Despite my intent, their nerves don't abate. I decide to shift the topic slightly, hopefully in a direction that will emphasize our sameness. "Where are you two from?"

It's not Eclipse City, I get that impression based on some of her remarks.

"Grifton," Luren answers readily, confirming my suspicions.

"You don't have to answer every question she asks," Kel murmurs, stirring two sugars into her tea.

"It's not going to kill us to be friendly." Luren rolls her eyes.

"It might." Kel still won't look my way.

Grifton is a small community within the borders of Clan Lovers situated between the pulping houses that make paper for cards and the main road. It's just to the north of Eclipse City, beyond the mountains and hills that encircle the city. Grifton is off the main road by about a day and isn't frequented by anyone but merchants and Stellis going to collect paper.

I know it only because I once sent an Arcanist up that way who claimed to have family there. Usually, I'm adamant that Arcanists make for the border on the far western edge of the desert. But, they insisted. Grifton is under the oversight of Clan Lovers, the most lax of the clans, keeping it well out of the reach of the enforcers found in cities controlled by the crown. A place where an Arcanist, if they're lucky, can slip the Chalice and the Mark and make something resembling a life in peace . . . so long as they keep their talents hidden forever.

Despite knowing so much about the town, I ask, "Is Grifton far from here?"

"About a day, maybe two, to Eclipse City." Luren rolls a sausage around her plate. "Close enough that it seemed like no time at all to come here. Far enough that it might as well be a different world."

"I know that feeling." The Barren Mountains make a nearly impenetrable wall. Few people go in and out of Eclipse City as a result. Moreover, each region of Oricalis has its own unique quirks. Each noble clan has their land that they oversee on behalf of the crown and a purpose that corresponds to their house, making the High Lords' and Ladies' realms almost like tiny kingdoms. They just can't think of themselves as such . . . or they risk the fate of Clan Hermit. Only Eclipse City and the capital, Fate Hearth, are under direct control of the crown, rather than a noble clan.

"Where are you from?" Luren looks up at me through her long lashes, mid-bite.

"Eclipse City."

"Lucky you didn't have to leave your home to get here. Must make it easier to acclimate to these forsake— I mean, *prestigious* halls," Kel corrects herself with a murmur. I'm beginning to bet her dislike isn't personal. Her sour mood is toward this place in general. Which . . . makes me like her more.

"This is *not* my home," I insist. That brings her attention to me outright, for the first time without any kind of skepticism or contempt. "Eclipse City isn't Arcana Academy. I'm forced to be *here* as much as you are."

"Forced?" Luren pauses and nibbles at her breakfast, and I wait for her to get out whatever it is she clearly wants to ask me. Kel gives her friend the same space. "Wouldn't you be happy to be close to your beloved prince?"

Shit, that's right, I can't have too much resentment for Kaelis and his domain . . . "Oh, of course, that's wonderful. I'm exceedingly lucky for that." I take a large bite of food and chew slowly to give myself time to collect my thoughts. "It's only that, I wish I could skip being an initiate and student and go right to our future life together." I force myself to beam brightly.

"I can only imagine." Luren seems to believe me.

Kel does not. The latter continues to peer at me through her cherry-red hair, swooped to one side and shadowing half her face. Her skepticism is dangerous. I can't risk anyone believing I'm not exactly what Kaelis claims. Otherwise the Halazar guards might not leave so readily next time.

"Accepted into the Fire Festival last minute because you were busy finding out your long-lost lineage of Clan Hermit—revealed to you by the prince who destroyed that clan but whom you fell in love with anyway." Luren sighs wistfully. "It's quite the epic romance."

"You've heard all these rumors in the span of an evening?" I arch my brows.

"The people here . . . most of them, at least . . . they don't pay attention to people like us." She gestures between herself and Kel. *Common-born, not noble,* is what she means to say. I barely refrain from vocalizing my understanding of it.

"We can linger, and their attention will gloss right over us as though we're invisible," Kel adds. They're absolutely right, and it would've been my approach . . . if Kaelis hadn't ruined that chance for me by introducing me in the splashiest way possible.

"I think we could help each other out," I muse. I might not be able to blend in, but they can.

"How so?" Luren sounds curious.

"I don't know if we want your help." Kel nudges her friend and gives a pointed look.

What? Luren mouths in reply.

Kel rolls her eyes.

Just as I'm about to make my proposition to them, a woman approaches. I recognize her instantly from her pin. But also from her eyes, face shape, and silvery shade of hair, even if hers is cut short, midway down her neck.

All twenty Majors be damned... my roommate is related to the King of Swords. Arina mentioned that House Swords was not to be trifled with. And here I am with the King herself setting her eyes on me.

"Clara." She draws out my name. "I hear you've come into the academy as quite the inker."

I take a bite of biscuit, chewing thoroughly to keep her waiting before I respond, holding her gaze steadily the entire time. "And who might've told you that?" I know who. Only one initiate or student so far has had any indication that I've inked anything before, but I want to hear her say it.

She shrugs nonchalantly and pulls out the chair across from me, dropping into it with graceful ease. All the other initiates at breakfast lean away and focus on other conversations, intimidated by her mere presence. "Word gets around."

"Word from your ... sister?" I venture a guess.

The flash in her eyes, a brief and protective glare that's as deadly as a dagger, tells me all I need to know. "The half-full holster at your thigh speaks louder than any whispered rumor."

The table's chatter has now been silenced.

"What of it?" I shrug.

"A lot of inking in one night for a new initiate."

"How do you know they're inked?" I lean forward and rest my chin in my palm. "They could all be blanks, ready to absorb the knowledge of our great teachers here in the school."

"Don't insult my intelligence." She scoffs and leans back. "Anyone who wields the cards with that much confidence during the Fire Festival has used them before."

"As I'm sure you're well aware as a King of the academy, using cards and inking them are two different skills entirely."

She purses her lips. "How else would someone like you have access to cards if you didn't ink them yourself?"

"You know as well as I that inking cards is regulated by the crown, as is the sale of materials and finished cards. It's monitored by each of the noble clans, kept to those among their ranks." I put on my best innocent voice, as if I'm confused by what she's implying. "How would someone like *me* have any access to practice? I might be the heiress of Clan Hermit, but it's not as if we have any court Arcanists or deep coffers these days. I only found out about my lineage recently." I get my tone as close to mocking hers as I can without being overt.

She has no reaction. "Or, the prince has been supplying all the usual resources for a clan to you directly, given your attachment to him."

"Jealous?" I'm genuinely curious what her reaction will be. Kaelis did say there are those who would kill to be his bride, and she seems perfectly capable of murder.

"Hardly," she scoffs, and I believe it. She's clearly not someone who has any desire to be at Prince Kaelis's side. Smart woman. "I merely want to ensure all initiates have equal opportunities."

"That isn't how this academy works, and we both know it."

Her face remains passive. "Perhaps you are noble, after all."

Before I can respond, a chime resonates through the academy, loud and clear, cutting through the growing tension. Students begin moving, the King of Swords included.

"Stay out of my sister's way," she says with quiet malice as she stands. *That's what this is about.* She doesn't care about "equal opportunities." She cares about Alor. "If you so much as look at Alor wrong, you'll have the wrath of House Swords so far down your throat that you'll be shitting daggers, never mind what Clan Tower would do to you."

With that, she's among the first to stride from the hall.

"She's . . . cheerful," Kel says under her breath.

"I couldn't be luckier to have her sister as my roommate," I say dryly and stand with the rest of them.

Luren follows, leaving her half-finished plate behind. Mine's so clean it's like I licked it. I know I'll need every scrap of food I can get and then some if I want to return to my usual strength and get out of here. Kel isn't far behind.

"Alor is related to the academy's current King of Swords, Emilia Ventall. They're both daughters of High Lord Moreus Ventall," Luren says matter-of-factly. *Fantastic.* The heir of Clan Tower now has her eyes on me. "They spent their early years in the military rank and file of Tower before the academy."

"How do you know that?" I side-eye her.

"We know who all the initiates are related to," Luren says confidently. "We figured that out yesterday. There's not many nepotism house slots this year."

"Don't give her all our information." Kel hooks Luren's arm.

"I'll figure it out soon enough anyway," I interject before Kel can tug Luren away. "Perhaps we can help each other while we're here." I return to my earlier notion.

"How so?" Kel asks skeptically.

The walk to our first class is just long enough for me to roughly detail my idea: They will be eyes and ears for me; in exchange, I'll help ensure that they have all the skills they'll need for All Coins Day and the Three of Swords Trials. We provide one another with information and help one another with tarot—fill in any gaps in knowledge all around. Of course, I will censor myself as needed, but they don't need to know that.

We arrive at a large workshop just as our discussion wraps up. Light streams through tall, arched windows and dances on the polished surfaces of every desk—each initiate has their own place. Hanging from the walls are a variety of charts painted across long scrolls that nearly touch the floor. Each one contains diagrams of symbols inside carefully inked frames with rigid lines, all rendered with painstaking precision.

"We'd love—" Luren starts to say.

"We'll think about it." Kel cuts off her friend's excitement and begins to tug her away.

"Make sure you do," I say to their backs as they turn. "We're stronger when we look out for each other." And the true value of my offer will become apparent as my skills have an opportunity to shine in classes.

Kel casts one more skeptical glance my way and leads Luren to two desks a few rows back and one away from where I stand. Never have I felt so . . . othered. The nobles part around me and cast withering looks. The commoners regard me warily.

I bite back a sigh.

"This seat taken?" Dristin motions to the desk next to me.

"No." I hadn't even heard him come up.

"Excellent." He sits.

Movement at my left has my head swiveling in that direction. Sorza has occupied the other desk at my side. Her eyes dart my way, and a little smile crosses her lips, but she says nothing.

They're not your friends, a voice cautions. But they could be. I set my satchel down on the desk before me and waste no time filling the drawers with the supplies I brought. Excitement laces up my spine. For all the questions I still have, for all I must do, I can't deny the thrill at the opportunity to learn the academy's approach to inking, and with seemingly unlimited access to all the best tools.

The professor strides to the front of the room, positioning herself in front of a long table. Her rich brown skin is barely wrinkled, despite the age betrayed in her hazel eyes. Her jet-black hair is intricately braided and cascades down her shoulders, decorated with tiny silver charms whose symbols I can't make out from where I sit. She wears a flowing dress of sapphire silk, accented by a waist cincher of supple leather.

"Greetings, initiates." She has a kinder voice than I expected. Firm, yet warm. A Coin during her time in the academy, if I had to guess. "I am Lady Raethana Duskflame, head professor for inking. You may call me Lady or Professor Duskflame.

"Your first year here at the academy shall be divided evenly among the three aspects of tarot magic: inking, wielding, and reading. Each corresponds with a different test during the Three of Swords Trials in the winter. For four hours each morning, you will have guided instruction on one of these topics.

"Following lunch, you will have an opportunity for independent study to practice what you have learned in advance of your winter tests. The professors teaching you each of these subjects will make ourselves available in our respective offices, attached to our classrooms, should you require additional instruction during this time. Our assistant professors will also be available.

"Are there any questions?" she finishes, leaning against the table and folding her arms. No one says anything. "Excellent. Then the only other matter of housekeeping is to inform you that the desks you select in each classroom will remain your own for the first year. You may place your name in the slot at their front and lock them using the key in the top drawer. Do not forget to take the key. Just do not leave anything you might need for wielding tomorrow or reading the day after, as those will be in different classrooms.

"Now, let's begin with the basics." Details out of the way, she launches into her lecture.

I'd been expecting to have a slight advantage when it came to my inking and wielding. Hopeful I might learn something, but not holding my breath for it. Inking is second nature to me—even if it's been technically illegal for me to engage in. But this instruction might as well be in an entirely different language.

Attempting to take notes only brews frustration. Everything is so fastidious. Meticulous. There's no *soul* to the way she teaches. Card designs are treated like a formula. One blindfolded person, two swords, out at sea—all the requirements to make a Two of Swords are listed down to the tiny details. And then there's these intricate borders unique to each suit used to "contain the power" of the card that Raethana drones on and on about.

"Every line upon your card must serve a purpose. They are the channels by which the magic both is contained and flows," Raethana instructs, passing through the room as we work. She pauses at my desk. I don't bother looking up until her pointer lightly taps on my knuckles. "Clean up your lines, Miss Redwin, lest your wielding be as *chaotic* as those messy sketches. Look here . . ."

She goes over to one of the posters that line the walls, her pointer showing the precise swirls.

The frames don't matter. The words are heavy on my tongue, but I keep them to myself. My head is clearer today, and I'm not going to let emotions get the better of me. I didn't realize just how hard my skull had been pounding until I managed to get two meals and three carafes of water in me.

"Now we will—" Raethana pauses mid-instruction. Everyone turns to see what has caught her attention. "Headmaster." Raethana bows her head.

But Kaelis's eyes are on me, turning my stomach into a lead ball. His attention flicks to the professor, and his expression shifts to a pleasant mask.

"Forgive me for the interruption, Head Professor." He dips his chin slightly, the most deference anyone could expect from the prince. "I require Lady Clara Redwin."

All eyes pivot to me. A cheeky smile overtakes my expression as I try to exude the impression that I knew this was coming all along. I grab my satchel, lock my desk drawer, and rise to make my way to him.

"Lady Redwin," Raethana interrupts pleasantly enough. I pause briefly. "Since you will be missing the last hour of class, I would ask that you make it up this afternoon."

"She will be with me for the rest of the day," Kaelis interjects. I barely refrain from gagging.

Raethana's smile widens slightly, and the annoyance that lights her eyes intensifies. "How *lucky* that a student gets so much time with the headmaster himself."

"My apologies, we have much to go over before the wedding." Kaelis holds out his arm, and it slips around my waist protectively.

Don't. Grimace, I tell myself, making sure my smile doesn't twist my face.

Students exchange glances that are so transparent I can almost read their thoughts. If the rumors about me and Kaelis were bad before, they'll be unbearable now. *It's for the best,* I tell myself. Let the rumors run rampant, convince everyone, and then let them tire of it so I no longer have to actively keep up this charade.

"Lady Redwin, please seek me out at your earliest convenience so we may schedule time for your instruction."

"Of course, Head Professor." I nod, and Kaelis escorts me out. I wait until we're far enough away that there's no risk of anyone hearing before I say, "What do you want with me now?" I'm expecting it to be some frivolous reason based on a princely whim. But I'm very, very wrong.

"The first Prince of Oricalis has decided—yet again—to show up unannounced. And this time he's asking for *you*."

CHAPTER 15

"**M**e? Why?"

"I was hoping you could tell me." Kaelis gives me a skeptical look.

"Clearly, your brother and I are the best of friends because I am, in fact, a long-lost noble. He makes social calls all the time. Visited me often in Halazar," I say, deadpan.

Kaelis huffs and tilts his head in the opposite direction, as if he's not accustomed to someone calling him out when he's being utterly nonsensical. "Well, I don't know either why he's here, asking for you, specifically."

"Reassuring." My stomach is in knots, threatening to upturn my breakfast.

Kaelis's jaw tenses in reply. For a stretch there's silence, except for the echoes of our footsteps. And then he says, "Just . . . be careful. The goal is to get Ravin out of my academy as quickly as possible."

Everything here is Kaelis's domain—including me. He's made that much clear. I'm even wearing him on me . . . all over me. The reminder makes my clothes feel tight, as if the top button of my shirt is nearly choking me. Every time the fabric brushes my skin, it might as well be Kaelis's hands. I fight a shiver.

"*Your* academy . . ." I say under my breath.

"Yes. Mine. Everything within these walls is entirely, wholly, and exclusively mine." Kaelis says it with a protective edge—or controlling, more like.

The discussion evaporates the moment we reach a heavy oak door. Two Stellis stand on either side. Kaelis wastes no time waiting for an introduction and strides in. I'm a step behind, the door too narrow for us to walk through side by side. But his hand lands on my hip again, pulling me close, as if the movement is already instinctive. That same protectiveness I just heard in his voice manifests anew. But this time it's directed toward me, like I'm another ancient fortress to lay claim to.

Ravin's dark eyes flick to his brother's hand and then to my face. His smile widens warmly, a stark contrast to the cold halls and the even colder demeanor of his brother. "Clara, a delight to see you again. A few warm meals and a good night's sleep have already transformed you into a vision."

He scoops my hand and punctuates his final statement with a kiss on my knuckles. It's such a change from our last interaction that I'm left reeling.

"You flatter me," I say with a bow of my head. Flattery—that's all his pretty words are. I know how I still look. The dark shadows that sink my eyes. How dull and listless my hair is from months of undernourishment. Even the nails on the hand he kisses are broken past the bed.

A smile doesn't reach his eyes, because they're filled with recognition that I see right through him.

"I must apologize for our previous encounter," he continues. "I was . . . taken aback by the sudden news of my brother's most unexpected engagement, and by the revelation of someone from Clan Hermit having actually survived the annihilation of their clan."

Kaelis's jaw tenses briefly at the mention of Clan Hermit and the destruction. I'm reminded of Rewina's warnings to avoid bringing up the massacre with the prince. Something that Ravin must know . . . but clearly does not care about.

"Completely understandable." I keep my expression polite, even though I don't believe him for a moment. "You've nothing to apologize for, your highness. I was just as shocked as you were when Kaelis first told me the truth of my family."

"Now that you have made your remorse be known, is there anything else before you are on your way?" Kaelis cuts through the paper-thin façade of our making nice.

"But I have only just arrived." Ravin continues to wear his placid, but smug, smile.

"And just how did you manage to do that, again, without my knowing?" Kaelis tries to hide the frustration behind his words and fails.

"Where is the fun in my telling you outright? I thought you liked puzzles, brother."

"I like puzzles when they don't involve trespassers." A vein in Kaelis's neck bulges. Every word is strained.

"Arcana Academy is part of Eclipse—"

"*No*, it is not," Kaelis interjects. "Father has given us each a domain."

"Which he wants us to oversee together." Ravin's remark is ignored.

"*I* give Oricalis the protection offered by the fortress and Arcanists by guarding the Farlum River from any who would punch through to the heart of our kingdom. The futures of *my* students protect our kingdom, its trade, its resources . . . and your little city." If Kaelis hadn't made his possessiveness about the academy so recently clear, I would think his manner . . . protective, in an almost endearing way, even.

"Yes, the Arcanists make their sacrifices on behalf of all Oricalis, not solely for you. Just as the clans give their own protections in their lands, labors, and resources. Or the Stellis devote their lives to defending the crown." Ravin dismisses his brother with ease. "You do not own the sole responsibility for the well-being of Oricalis."

"Were it not for me—"

"Must we always spar?" Ravin's gaze lands on his brother and stays there. There's a tightness to his laugh that betrays it's not as light as he'd want others to think. "I came here for a reason, and it wasn't to discuss your security flaws."

"Then what was the reason?" Kaelis grinds out the words from between clenched teeth. I suspect he'd rather be asking about the details of those "security flaws," if he thought he'd get a direct answer.

All the while, I remain still and silent, as if Ravin might forget about me if I don't move for long enough. But the crown prince's eyes return to me anyway.

"Clara, it is my esteemed pleasure to invite you to a soiree at my residence in Eclipse City. I am a patron of the arts, and during the creative Season of Wands I invite my dearest friends to experience the fruit of the labors of Oricalis's most talented. Since you have recently reclaimed your title, I must insist, as it'd be a lovely opportunity for you to get to know your noble peers."

Surprise grips me at the invitation, followed by one immediate thought: *I'd be out of the academy.* And if he's hosting this gathering in the Season of Wands, then it's soon. Ravin's manor is right in the center of the city; I could quickly and easily get to the Starcrossed Club. So if I can sneak away during this soiree . . .

"You're absolutely right; it would be my honor to attend." I seize the opportunity before Kaelis can react.

The moment the words leave me, Kaelis goes as rigid as a statue. I can almost feel the agitation coiled in his gut. Frustration rolls off him and onto me like waves crashing against the cliffs beyond the fortress.

"*We* will be happy to attend," he corrects. I simply keep giving Ravin an easy smile. "You cannot expect my betrothed to go alone to an event. I am not a monster that would leave her unescorted."

"Of course not, I thought it was assumed." The way Ravin says it, though, makes me doubt he would've extended the invitation to Kaelis if not prompted. Or . . . perhaps "assumed" referred to Kaelis being a monster. I fight a smirk. "I am looking forward to this immensely. I'll send necessary details as I have them." He claps Kaelis's shoulder with an almost too-large, too-gleeful smile. Kaelis hardly moves as his brother attempts to shake him. "Now, before you lose all your composure, I'll see myself out. Do take care, brother."

Seeming very satisfied with himself, Ravin makes his exit. The sounds of the two Stellis follow him, eventually muffled by Kaelis clicking the door shut.

We square off. I'm beginning to think we don't know how to look at each other without an open challenge or contempt.

"What possessed you to accept his invitation?" He takes two steps toward me and then lets out a noise of disgust, shaking his head and turning away.

"Did you not tell me to play my part?" I turn his expectations back on him, saying nothing of my hopes to see my friends again. "Attending a social event hosted by the crown prince seems like exactly what the recently engaged second prince and his betrothed would do. And he is right. If I'm to be a noble, then I must act like one."

"It's not that simple," he mutters.

"Of course it's not." The moment I acknowledge it, Kaelis looks back at me with a hint of surprise. I fold my arms, mildly offended he thinks I wouldn't have realized the obvious implications of the dangerous game we're navigating. "I cannot begin to fathom your brother's motivations or what he intends for the night, but I know better than to think this invitation is as benign as he's letting on." I take a step toward Kaelis, my turn to close the gap while I feel like I have the upper hand. "But I will tell you this, Kaelis Oricalis, I am *not* going back to Halazar. And if that means that I must convince every High Lord and Lady of every clan and all the lower nobles beneath them that I am madly in love with you and am, indeed, a long-lost heiress, then I will do *whatever* it takes."

Kaelis's eyes widen slightly. He shifts, facing me outright once more. Somehow, that tiny motion tightens a thread between us. For a breath, neither of us says anything.

"My family is dangerous." The words are whispered. As if even Kaelis is afraid of the treason within them. As if . . . he's afraid of his family, too.

"I, out of all people, am the last one you need to warn about that," I say, both reassuring him and reminding him of my past. "I still have the scars."

Kaelis opens his mouth, but whatever he is about to say is cut off by the tolling of the academy bells. I wait, even as the halls begin to fill with the noise of students. Though I'm not entirely sure what I'm waiting for. Something in his eyes made me think . . .

I could laugh at myself for hoping for an apology from Prince Kaelis of all people.

"I'm going to lunch," I announce.

He doesn't stop me as I leave the room. Not that I had been expecting him to.

The halls fill with second- and third-year students pouring from the classrooms. After more than a few sidelong glances from the students, I step off to the side and try to find a route away from the crowd, debating my next move. I should go and eat lunch. But, while everyone else is busy, I could also work on finding Arina's secret passage. The only other person she mentioned being a fast friend with was "the man in the depths." But I've no idea who that could be . . .

I don't make it very far in my thoughts, or down the hallway, before a whistle draws my attention to another room.

As soon as I glance inside, my gaze meets a piercing yellow one. The man stands among empty desks. He smirks and tilts his head, his silver-white mess of hair, nearly the same shade as his skin, flopping to the other side with the movement.

It's him: the one from last night . . . The noble initiate who wouldn't stop staring at me from the corner right after the ritual of the Arcanum Chalice.

"Clara." He says my name as an invitation. Soft and sweet.

"Do I know you?" I pause.

"Not yet." The moon phases are stitched up his right sleeve—the symbol of Clan Moon. "Though you should."

"Should I?" Something about the way he looks at me has my hand twitching by the deck in its holster at my thigh.

"Oh, absolutely. Especially since I know so much about you."

"Do you, now?" I arch my brows.

"Two hundred and five."

Those words send an icy shiver up my spine. *Two hundred and five* . . . my cell number in Halazar. It's one thing for Ravin to have known that number. But this random initiate? And for him to direct it pointedly at me, something not even the crown prince did.

"Should that mean something to me?" My tone is casual even though every muscle in my body is now drawn taut.

"I think it does. You want to know what happened to your little co-conspirators while you were rotting away, don't you?"

I practically lunge into the room. The moment I do, the door snaps shut behind me. It's not just me and him. There are two others. My palm flies out, magic crackling, but strong hands close around my wrists. Thrashing against my captors does little. I'm still far too weak. Without being able to move to summon them, my cards are still in my deck.

"We've got a live one," the man at my right mocks.

"Do it, Eza. Let's see what Kaelis's new toy is made of."

My attention swings back to Eza—the man who drew me into the room, who knows far too much about me. A card is upright in his palm, tucked against his thumb, which curls around it. I don't have a chance to catch the image on its front. The world tilts sickeningly. Everything flips upside down. The floor is now the ceiling, and Eza hangs by his toes.

I blink, trying to force away the magic that's overtaking my mind. But every flutter of my eyes lasts longer than the last.

When I open my eyes anew, they're met with the near-perfect darkness of my cell in Halazar Prison.

CHAPTER 16

My body aches from sleeping on the hard floor, and my joints crack as I sit. Familiar patterns of mold and grime trellis up the corners of the room. The bars that keep me trapped here are locked tight.

My clothes are the same worn and tattered rags that I've been in for months. Heavy with filth, they cling to my skin. I run the fabric between my fingers, the rough texture both familiar and foreign. A far cry from the silks and leathers Kaelis had gifted me—finery I'd already been growing accustomed to. Or, at least, *thought* I'd been growing accustomed to. I put a palm on my aching forehead.

Kaelis . . . Why would I be thinking of the second-born prince?

As if summoned by the thought of him, a flicker of light flares into existence. My heart races, and I rise to my feet, staggering as my head swirls. The hunger pangs and dizziness that follow are nothing new, and yet they feel foreign. My palm presses into the concave arc of my abdomen and my bony ribs.

Did this place finally break me? I stare at the growing light dancing on the wall opposite my cell in wide-eyed horror. My mind feels torn in two, trapped both in the present—the cell before me—and in the academy that seemed so real moments ago. I can feel the weight of Kaelis's palm on my hip, tugging me ever so slightly closer. The powerful and defensive aura that perpetually surrounds him envelops me.

But this, too, is undeniably real. I can hear the guard's footsteps echoing through the hall. I feel the damp chill in the air. Was my time in the academy just a premonition? A dream of the future? The guard comes into view.

"Come," the guard commands gruffly as he unlocks the door to my cell. I stand, wide-eyed. "Now."

That spurs me to motion. I fall into step as they lead me down the dim corridor. The echo of every step seems to scream, *This has happened before.* But it hasn't . . . has it?

The shadows close around me and threaten to choke me. Had I been so desperate for freedom that I'd invented it for myself in my dreams?

The journey is short but familiar. I'm not taken up a stairwell where I can catch a rare glimpse of the outside world before ending in a new section of the prison where Prince Kaelis is waiting for me. Instead, I'm escorted into Glavstone's office and left alone with the man.

"What are you waiting for, girl?" Warden Glavstone snaps at me without so much as looking up from his desk. Pillars of curtains behind him block off what I've always assumed to be a window. He would never give me the satisfaction of catching even a glimpse of the sky.

I pull a hidden lever on one of his bookshelves and head into an adjoining chamber. This room—closet, really—is sparser than his office. A bare floor, stone walls, a chair, and a table covered with the minimum supplies necessary to ink tarot. I take my seat.

"I need ten copies of the Two of Cups." Glavstone moves so whisper-silent I didn't even hear him coming up behind me. With a look of disapproval that borders on disgust, he slowly closes the bookshelf door. I hear the mechanism lock in place.

It smells better here than down in my cell. And sometimes, I get small nibbles of food I wouldn't otherwise. At the least, it keeps my mind sharp. The constant scratch of the pen against paper fills the air.

Glavstone returns periodically, and each time, he seems more agitated than the last. "Faster," he barks when he sees I've done only five of the ten cards.

I'd like to see him ink faster than this. I've done half the cards in an hour. Anyone else would be gushing over my speed.

The next time he comes back, I am just putting the finishing touches on my eighth card. He hovers over me, inspecting my work. Without warning, he grabs my hair by the roots and pulls my face up toward him. I barely suppress a yelp that is part surprise and part pain.

"This is sloppy work. Do better." He releases me, slams a bottle of ink on my desk, and leaves.

With each visit, he grows more erratic . . . and more violent. My thanks for finishing ten cards is a demand for five more, of the Two of Swords this time. He comes back only thirty minutes after that, brandishing a hot poker, threatening to Mark me with an A himself and throw me to the mills if I'm not faster and my work doesn't improve . . . even though the inks he's giving me are barely usable.

Twenty minutes later, he makes good on his threats.

I swallow screams as the burning iron meets my flesh. Glavstone pulls the metal away and then immediately presses it to my other biceps.

"You are *nothing*," he snarls. "Trash. Not even worth the cell I've given you. I should throw you into the lowest level of the dungeons and show you what the real horrors of this place look like. You thought the first level was bad? There are two deeper."

I bite my tongue and fight my trembling to keep my pen steady even as the pain shoots between my eyes. My knees knock together. But my lines are as sharp as a dagger's edge.

It's relentless. The hours drag on, and I grow more exhausted with each card I finish. A body wasn't made to pour out this much magic, or to focus this hard for this long, on nothing more than sheer willpower.

But I will not let him win. I have endured everything he's thrown at me. Always. I will not stop enduring it now.

Don't let the bastard win.

"Sloppy," he growls. "Sloppy. Sloppy. Sloppy!" With a roar, Glavstone scoops up one of my silver-tipped pens and stabs it through my hand, pinning it to the table.

I stare at my hand, wide-eyed. My hands are my skill. My opportunity. My magic. While this wound would not be the end of me—I've taught myself how to ink with both hands, and some can ink with their mouths or with prosthetics—it is the end of my patience.

My uninjured hand grabs the first thing it can—a bottle of powder—and smashes it against his temple. With a dark chuckle that sounds almost like he's been waiting for this moment, Glavstone brings his fist to my jaw. I take the punch, focused more on how much pain I can inflict on him rather than worrying about my own. Besides, I suspect I have a much, *much* higher pain tolerance than the carefully coiffed Glavstone, and life in Halazar has only honed it.

He lunges for me, ripping my impaled hand off the table. My back slams against the wall. I bring a knee to his groin and duck out of his grasp. He's on me faster than I would expect, and I barely have time to swipe for his neck with a shard of glass from the smashed bottle.

I miss, and Glavstone has me pinned to the table, both hands around my throat. Squeezing. Tighter and tighter.

I wheeze. The shadows have come alive once more. Alive like Kaelis is near . . . *Kaelis? What does the void-born prince have to do with any of this?*

My thoughts scattered, I frantically reach for anything, and my fingers close around the one thing that has ever been my lifeline: a pen.

With a closed fist, I swing. The pen meets little resistance and plunges through the flesh of his neck effortlessly. Glavstone's hands relax. There's a little gap to his lips as if he's sighing. He's unable to form a word, his eyes wide and dulling. I kick him off me. He slumps against the wall and slides into a heap.

My throat is swollen. Rubbing it nearly pricks tears into the corners of my eyes. Glavstone's shape softens and blurs more and more every time I blink. I don't think I could scream even if I wanted.

Everything begins to tremble. *I killed him; the bastard is finally dead, and I was the one to do it. But . . . what does this mean for me?*

I scramble off the table. The cards I was inking were common, run-of-the-mill cards everyone would ask for from an Arcanist—the ones the average person would need in their day-to-day that could be easily sold. They don't need combat cards—the only battle they're fighting is for basic survival. I'd have to ink another, or several, if I wanted to use them for an escape. Did the guards stationed outside of his office hear our scuffle? I scramble for supplies. For my pen, now slick with blood.

My lines aren't straight. *Why won't they draw straight?* I scream within my own mind. The magic won't come. The shapes are blurring together.

Every shadow has come alive with nightmarish undulations. The evil that has seeped into the bedrock of this place will swallow me whole. I must leave or I'll finally be claimed by these walls.

Heart thundering louder than the banging on the door, I shove a handful of inking supplies into the waistband of my pants. There's no time, and if I can't get the inking done now, I'll do it later.

The door looks as if it's about to be ripped off its hinges. So I'm not going that way. I shut the bookcase and race to the curtains behind Glavstone's desk, pulling them open.

There's no sunlight. No sky. Only bars . . . looking into a familiar cell. *My* cell.

What . . . what's happening? This can't be real.

The door bursts open, revealing guards.

No! I launch myself toward a door in the back corner of the office and throw myself inside. There's a trapdoor hidden in the back corner. One that leads to the dungeons. It's the last place I want to be, but Glavstone tells few guards about the basements of Halazar. Glavstone is the only one to hold the key, but, lucky for me, the trapdoor is unlocked. It opens to a decrepit staircase.

Every step I take down the stairs and hall is overshadowed by the thundering of feet behind me. They're still on my tail. Down and down I spiral to the depths of the dungeons of Halazar. Every passage turns, funneling me in that direction. It's the last place I want to go, but it's the only place I have left. It looms large, yawning, swallowing me whole.

"Clara!" A familiar voice screams from the depths, one that pricks tears into my eyes. He screams my name from a world away, as if he's done it a thousand times. "I will find you!"

"You can't have me!" I scream back. *Give me a way out, please, someone, anyone,* I beg the unseen cards shuffling through my deck of fate.

I turn.

I'm back in Eclipse City.

"How are you doing this?" another voice asks, sinister. Annoyed. *It almost sounds like Eza?* "You should have no control here!"

The world seems to vibrate, and the familiar, safe streets I'd just been running to dead-end into the last place I ever want to be again. Spotlights click on, momentarily blinding me. I'm in the trap sprung by city enforcers—the one that landed me in Halazar. Tarot cards and inking supplies fall from my person, scattering. I'm caught redhanded.

Arina had cautioned me not to take the job. "Hold off, Clara. My readings about this one aren't good . . . Just wait. I can get you something beyond your imagining, next time I come. Something special. Inking supplies that will change *everything,*" she'd promised me with excitement.

But I'd told her that the inking supplies the man, Griv, had promised were only part of the deal. The other part I shared with her in secret—not even the rest of the club knew. Griv had claimed to know an enforcer who was working the Descent on the day Mother died. It was a chance at firsthand information from higher up than whispers among other workers.

The moment I told Arina, she stopped fighting. *We will find who killed you, Mother. We will avenge your death.* That vow my sister and I made years ago is marked on our souls, more gnarled and raised than a brand on an Arcanist's flesh at the mills.

I start running again in search of a freedom I put blind faith in finding. "Luck is on my side, *luck is on my side,*" I pant with every breath as Eclipse City blurs around me.

"Clara!"

"*Clara!*"

They're calling for me. Demanding me. I've killed their warden. I've fled their prison. Broken their laws. They're going to kill me this time.

"I won't go to the dungeons!" I scream in response.

"Where?" the first voice replies. It's disembodied and reverberating from every lightless corner. "Come back to me."

I stumble. Pain shoots up my arm from the wound in my hand. My throat opens once more despite the bruising, and I let out an involuntary scream. When I stand, I'm back in Halazar.

Knees bloodied and bruised. My whole body threatening to tremble apart so violently that Halazar will be brought down with it. I keep running through cell and city blocks that oscillate with every step. I run for my life—for the lives of everyone I've ever loved. For a future that might for once have some scrap of justice.

Please, my heart implores. *Please, luck is on my side. It must be. I* need it *to be. Give me somewhere safe.* For a moment, the city wins out. I'm almost back to the Starcrossed Club. Home and safety.

There's a grumble of frustration that rattles the foundations of the world. It evolves into a cry of rage. "How are you doing this?" Eza shouts from a distant place.

You can't have me!

I turn the corner that should lead to the Starcrossed Club, but instead I'm faced with a lone door in Halazar. Out of options, I throw it open and a warm, clean gust of air buffets my face. I'm on the precipice of a mountain right at dawn.

"Mother," I choke out, staring at the woman before me. Rope far too worn and thin is wrapped around her waist, tying her to a rock. She takes a breath as the wind whips up the cliffs of the Descent—the angry ravine that plunges through the heart of the Barren Mountains. It's the only place where the black falcons whose feathers can be crushed into the powder used to ink Swords cards roost.

She takes the rope in one hand as she turns to me. Her deep brown hair is wild, and her eyes, red like mine, glisten in the sunlight. She smiles as if she can see me . . . as if she knows I'm there.

"Mother!" I scream as she tips backward over the ledge. My luck gave me one last chance to see her face . . . only to make me witness the worst day of our lives.

It all happens in a second. The rope is pulled taut. There's the flutter of dark wings. A distant scream and a falling star. A strike of lightning and figures that move faster than I can see. In a breath, the rope snaps.

I launch myself forward, a primal sound ripping from me. A noise that is part the loneliness I feel every night since she left us, part disbelief that it could have happened to our strong and industrious mother at all—and part a rage so brutal it could unravel the world.

"Clara!" Two arms wrap around me, preventing me from throwing myself over the edge—preventing me from even seeing her face one final time.

I thrash. "No!"

"Clara, enough!" the voice snaps roughly. I'm shaken, and the world around me trembles. Fractures and shatters. "It's not real! I have you."

I blink, and the man who's gripping me comes into focus. The remnants of the mental prison I'd been held in fade from view. Instead, I see Kaelis as a dark outline against the late afternoon light. I'm back in the academy. My clothing is no longer rough, but supple and fine. I smell of perfume and the faint incense of powders that steeps in the air, not of waste and rot.

But . . . that place still lives within me. It will *always* live within me.

"Kaelis," I choke out. Never have I resented anyone more for being there for me.

Never have I been more grateful.

I throw my arms around his shoulders and sob.

CHAPTER 17

His whole body stiffens, and it's that reaction that snaps me back to my senses. I release him, absolutely mortified that I've just held him and cried as if he were a dear friend. His expression is utterly unreadable. He's doing a good job at concealing what I can only assume is equal horror.

The silence of the room is broken only by the sound of my pounding heart and my thin, shallow breaths. My panicked thoughts are so loud that I'm shocked he can't hear them. Yet his eyes search mine for an explanation I'll never give him.

What did you see? is the unspoken question. The one to which, I feel in my marrow, he already knows the answers.

Kaelis was the one to pull me from the endless tortures of Halazar both in that dream world and in this one. In his way, he was the one to offer me salvation and comfort. But he was also the one who put me there in the first place. Who turned my life into some kind of game to get me into the academy. Who's been the orchestrator of everything that has ever brought me suffering.

I hate him, I remind myself. *I hate him and all his ilk.* Every noble who treats us like tools rather than people. Who turns a blind eye to our suffering. All of them. And Kaelis is the head of that serpent. His father might make the laws about Arcanists, but it is Kaelis who is charged with their enforcement. Kaelis who manages the flow of all arcana throughout the kingdom. Which is why I've never doubted that the trap sprung to capture me was orchestrated by him all along.

"I . . ." I try to find words, but none come. Kaelis finds them for me.

"It was a card." He releases me hastily and stands, turning his back to me. He walks to the windows as if to give me space to pull myself together.

"Obviously," I mutter, rubbing my eyes. In the stars that bloom behind my lids I can catch glimpses of the visions that tormented me. "But, it was so real . . ." I murmur. I hadn't intended to let the errant thought escape, much less for Kaelis to hear.

"A prison of the mind, conjured by the Hanged Man." The twelfth tarot of the Major Arcana: a man suspended upside down by a single foot; one arm covers his face and conceals his expression. Kaelis's tone of voice is unreadable and somewhat detached.

"The Hanged Man . . . it isn't a card that can be inked, or used." I straighten and try to get my sluggish mind working again. I can still feel the hands of the two men as they manhandled me with ease. I must regain my strength quickly if I'm to survive here.

"I assure you, it can be inked. That was what was used against you."

"The Major Arcana cards are too powerful for any Arcanist to use." The only one said to have ever harnessed them was the Fool, which was what made him so legendary.

"Too powerful for *most*. Not all."

"Eza . . ." I heard his voice in that place. Could it really have been him controlling what I saw? Is that how he knew about me and my time in Halazar in the first place? A Major Arcana card? "He knows how to use the cards of the Major Arcana?" I try to focus on the facts at hand—on what Kaelis is saying and implying . . . Literally *anything* is better than thinking for too long on what I just experienced.

"He *is* a Major Arcana." Kaelis turns to face me.

"What?" That gives me pause.

"I assume you are familiar with the mythos of the Fool and the origin of the arcana?"

"I am." Just the mention of it fills my mind with stories Mother told me every night about the journey of the Fool. Stories similar to the ones other children knew, yet different enough that Mother told me they were never to be repeated. I might not have had a formal education, but I didn't go without intellectual pursuits, thanks to her.

"Tell me."

"You want me to tell you children's stories?" I fold my arms.

"I want you to tell me what you think of as history, so I can then tell you how wrong you are."

"And what if I'm not wrong?"

"You will be." He's goading me into speaking, I know it, but I can't stop myself.

"The Fool was the first to feel the whisper of the arcane," I start in as dull and dry a tone as I can manage, trying my best to accurately capture just how frustrating I find Kaelis's antics. "No one knows where the magic originated from, though some suspect the world was young and the primordial essence of creation still lingered, manifesting in some individuals.

"The Fool—because his name was lost to the ages, and we only know him through the accounts of those who at the time thought him 'foolish' for pursuing these 'magical currents'—set out on an odyssey to understand the truth of this power he felt. To comprehend and harness it."

I pause, allowing Kaelis an opportunity to say I'm wrong. He remains silent. As still as a perfectly carved statue. *Well, I guess I know more than he thought . . .*

"Along the way, he encountered trials that changed him. He first learned of the four elemental powers that would become the suits, working to harness them through objects first—Swords, Cups, Wands, and Coins—later as cards. Doing this transformed him into the Magician. He studied the sacred mysteries of the world and, in so doing, gained insight as a High Priestess would. He ascended to leadership and ruled as both Emperor and Empress. He—"

"You never thought it odd," Kaelis interrupts, "that the Fool ruled as both Emperor and Empress? That he embodied the High Priestess?"

"The tarot lives in us all. It is both feminine and masculine; it is also neither. It is the essence of life and nature in all its forms." I fight against my voice going soft and somewhat wistful. These words are an echo of Mother's own, and her face is so sharp in my memory right now that I ache. "You keep this tradition, even now, in the academy. Those who are the truest embodiment of a card's essence become King or Queen of a house. It does not matter what clothes they wear or if they prefer people to call them he, or she, or they."

"This is true," Kaelis admits. I think I've won, but with him? Of course not. "However, it is not true of the Fool's story. The story you know is centered solely on the Fool. His journey is far too long for one man's life, his roles and deeds too great."

"He was the first to master the arcana. Some say he became immortal after gaining all that power."

"And where is this immortal being now?" Kaelis holds out his hands and motions to the room, as if the Fool could stroll in at any second. "Clearly, not all the stories can be trusted."

"And what do you propose is the truth behind the legend?" The notion that he's right and I'm wrong—that I'm more ignorant than I think when it comes to tarot—is unwelcome and uncomfortable. But I work to shove this aside to hear what he has to say.

"The Fool was real. He *did* go on his odyssey. But what we know as the legendary Major Arcana do not stem from the Fool himself—from his own deeds or evolution. No." Kaelis *tsks,* but I don't rise to the goading. I stay silent, genuinely curious what he's about to say next. "The Fool met others along the way, others who embodied the aspects of the Major Arcana—who had mastered those powers—and these individuals shared their wisdom with him. What the Fool gave them in return was his knowledge of how to contain their powers within cards."

It's not utterly implausible. I can see how this truth could evolve over time and simplify to become the story of a single hero rather than a band of twenty-one individuals. There were times when I was a child that I even imagined it to be so. But in the end, Mother had always stressed it was only ever the Fool. Him, and his greed—a force I always imagined to be the ancient origin of keeping arcana from the masses. The way she told his story, the Fool was an entity of evil.

"And so . . . Eza is one of these original followers of the Fool?" I try to reason what he's implying and am met with a howl of laughter from Kaelis.

"No." He's barely composed himself. "And here I thought you were smarter than that."

"We were just talking about immortality," I say flatly.

"Eza is a magical descendant of the original Hanged Man—the one who first captured the essence of that Major Arcana."

"Magical descendant?" I've never heard that phrasing before.

"It's an honor passed along not by bloodlines or titles, but by destiny itself. Random chances of fate. The magic of each figure of the Major Arcana is always alive, transferring from one individual to someone new upon their death." Kaelis takes a step forward, and then another. The gap between us closes, and with it, my heart quickens once more. "And you, too, Clara, are one of the Twenty."

"What?" I breathe, barely audible. I'm not sure he heard me this time at all, even though he's just about upon me.

Would you have inked a Major Arcana, if you knew how? His words from Halazar echo back to me. I'd told him no one knew how to ink the Majors. Not even Mother could teach me how to harness that power. She discouraged me from ever even trying. But, she also discouraged me from ever entering the fortress, and here I am . . .

A smirk arcs across his lips, and Kaelis tilts his head slightly. "Shall we go and formally introduce you to your other Major brethren, Fortune?"

CHAPTER 18

Laughter is my response. "You're ridiculous. You had me there for a second with this 'unknown truth' about the Fool."

Kaelis takes a step forward, compressing the gap between us. My amusement is smothered by the cold voids of his all-consuming eyes. "It isn't a joke, and you know it."

"No. I *don't* know what you're talking about."

"You do, you've just refused to believe it. Closed yourself to it." A frown tugs on his lips. "You . . . are incredible, Clara."

It's as if he's disgusted with himself for even giving me that compliment. If it weren't for the deepening of his frown, I would've thought he meant it as some kind of jape. But hating himself for praising me? The jealousy that simmers in his gaze? That I expect. Which means . . . *The compliment was genuine?*

"*But* . . ." I can feel that "but" hanging in the air. He's not about to be that kind to me.

"No." His arm twitches. For a second, I think he is about to reach for me. The notion reminds me once more of the feeling of clinging to him. I forcefully remove it from my thoughts. "No 'but.' You *are* incredible." It's clear he's still forcing himself to admit as much. But he does seem to mean it, and I'm left in shock. He steps around me. "Your inking skills are only rivaled by your frustrating tenacity. So it is all the more astounding whenever you doubt yourself, or hold yourself back."

"I do not doubt myself, nor do I hold myself back." I whirl to face him.

"Prove it, then, and follow me." Kaelis leaves with a flap of his coattails before I can get another word in. I entertain the idea of ignoring him entirely. The afternoon is mine for study . . . once I've put in my extra hour of awful inking with Professor Duskflame. I've the library of Arcana Academy and all the inking tools I could dream of at my disposal, with ample time to plan an escape from Ravin's soiree once I'm in Eclipse City. I could be hunting for Arina's escape route. Or continuing to fill my belly and strengthen my body.

Any of that is what I should be doing. But . . . instead . . .

I race to catch up with the prince, and as I round the doorframe, I nearly run face-first into his chest.

Kaelis laughs deep and low as he leans forward, our noses nearly touching. "Took you long enough." With that, he's off again, and I'm left to assume he wants me to follow.

"If you intended to show me these other 'Majors' all along, then why have you not mentioned it already?" I keep my voice low as we walk side by side.

"We've been a bit busy." He has the look of a man who knows he's made a good point.

"You could've mentioned it earlier, before I walked off." Even I know I'm being a bit ridiculous. I haven't even been in the academy for two days. But I hate giving Kaelis, of all people, any slack.

"Forgive me for thinking it more important for you to get a proper meal for lunch and planning to find you later." It's oddly considerate of him.

"And then you changed your mind?" Now I'm trying to figure out how he knew to come find me.

"You weren't at lunch, and, given your condition, I couldn't imagine anything that would keep you from a hot meal would be good." The words harden slightly at the end. All I can imagine is him promptly leaving the main hall and coming in search of me.

Why do I matter so much to you? The question bubbles up, unbidden, unexpected. I keep it unasked, assuming that he'll give me the same vague explanation about obtaining the World for him.

Down a series of stone stairs so worn that they sag in the middle is an empty room that serves as nothing more than an antechamber for the structure that lies beyond. The entire back wall is glass, glowing with the light of the late afternoon sun. Kaelis wastes no time opening the iron-framed doors.

I've caught glimpses of this place from the outside, the fogged glass of the conservatory flush against the ornate arcades of the circling halls, but the moment I'm standing within its embrace . . . all movement stills. For a second, the entire world seems to stop to savor the sunlight with me.

"What is it?" Kaelis has stopped about fifteen paces ahead. A look somewhere between confusion and frustration occupies his features.

"It's been a long time since I saw sunlight. Unfiltered. Sunlight." My words are soft and wistful. The day I escaped Halazar it had been overcast.

"Eza put you in Halazar, didn't he?"

My attention drifts back to him. "Is that a touch of anger I hear in your voice, Kaelis?" His glower deepens at my tone—it's light, almost amused. As if to say, *Do* you, *of all people, have any right to be angry?* "Are you feeling protective of me?" I cock my head to the side. Though I phrase it as a question, my body language suggests it's a challenge. "Don't forget, you could've liberated me at any time from Halazar."

"And do what with you?" His hand balls into a fist, the supple leather of his glove squeaking softly as it tightens. "You saw the guards. A prisoner escaping from Halazar is already raising questions."

"If you took me out by decree of the crown, I wouldn't have 'escaped.'"

Kaelis *tsks*. "I do that, and then I have my brother and father wondering why I commuted a random prisoner's sentence."

"You clearly have power over Glavstone, don't you? Couldn't you command him not to tell them?"

"I am not the only one he answers to, or even the one he fears most." Though Kaelis's tone tells me he's tried to be.

"No, it's not only that . . ." I say softly; a new image is forming in my mind. I suspect what he's said is true, but it's also more than that. Kaelis would've known that if he'd just taken me on the night I was captured, I would've never agreed to help him with whatever his plot is. "You wanted me to escape not just to test me and my powers . . . but also because it's going to tie everything up neatly for you."

The flash of comprehension in his eyes tells me I'm right.

"You're going to let the leads run cold, wait for the search to come up empty-handed, and then 'kill' off the Clara Graysword that was imprisoned," I continue, taking a step toward him. "And, by allowing me to escape, you've put me in a spot where you know I've no other choice but to help you. Because at any minute you could expose the truth and put me back there."

"And?" he asks after a long, *long* stretch of silence.

I open my mouth and close it.

Kaelis laughs, as low and ominous as thunder rolling over the mountaintops. My blood runs cold at the sound. "Don't act like you're not getting anything out of this. You're engaged to a prince, after all."

"I'd rather die." I ball my hands into fists.

"That could be arranged." He shrugs. "Or something worse."

"Is that a threat?"

Kaelis tilts his head to the side, narrowing his eyes slightly. "A reminder. Play nicely, and you'll get your freedom at the end of this. As long as you're in the academy, I can protect you." Yet another reason he didn't take me out of Halazar sooner. I couldn't be admitted into Arcana Academy until the Fire Festival. *Is he really protecting me?* No sooner does the thought cross my mind than he reminds me who I'm dealing with. "Cross me, or give anyone a reason to think you're not my long-lost-noble bride, and you're sent back there."

I don't believe for a second that he'll give me my freedom. Whatever he's going to use me for, he'll want no one else to know of it, I'm sure. Which means, as soon as I complete his tasks, I'm dead.

"Now, do you have any other clever revelations about my machinations?" Kaelis keeps adjusting his coat. It must be sweltering for him in here, and I briefly consider letting him sweat a little longer, but I resist.

"No."

"Good." He takes a few steps and, with that, abandons the conversation.

I have a harder time letting go, even as we weave through plants both familiar and foreign. Lush vines with tiny, iridescent bellflowers drape over me. Trees with luminescent fruit glow in shady nooks. But none of it distracts me.

Kaelis plotted and schemed for at least two years to put me in a position where he is my sole protector, making me both indebted to him and at risk should I cross him. He's taking his own chances by maneuvering around his father, the king—I doubt King Oricalis would be keen to find out the truth of who his son declared himself engaged to.

What could he possibly need me for that badly?

A vine-trellised iron fence and locked gate finally jolt me from my thoughts. My curiosity is piqued when Kaelis shows me how to undo the locking mechanism built into it. It's a piece of work as marvelous as the mechanical mill from last night—though much smaller.

Inside, we come to a stop before a large mausoleum of weathered stone. Its walls are etched with a series of intricate carvings of mountains split by rivers, vast deserts, and low plains. An etching of a man mid-step on his journey adorns the timeworn doors. On the roof are a series of scrolled carvings, each winding toward a single, solitary number, framed by roses carved of marble: zero.

The Fool.

Kaelis guides us inside. A chill slithers down my spine—the cool air within is such a contrast to the warmth of the greenhouse. In the center of a surprisingly unadorned room stands a sarcophagus with the visage of a woman—not a man, as I might have expected given the Fool symbology—carved onto it. Stone cards have been scattered across her peaceful form, and her eyes are closed in an eternal sleep. Across her brow is a solid band with five unadorned points—a crown I recognize, though I've only ever seen it in portraits of King Naethor Oricalis.

"What is this place?" I whisper.

"All that remains of the last Revisan Queen." Kaelis places his palm gently on the edge of the sarcophagus.

The Revisan Kingdom is from a historical period only moderately more recent than the myth of the Fool. It's a kingdom that fell ages ago, giving way to the feudal clans and ultimately Oricalis. But every story about it reads more like legend than fact. I always knew the fortress was the remnants of the former kingdom. But . . .

"I never knew her tomb was here."

"Why would the current kingdom honor its predecessor in any fashion?" Kaelis's hand slides across the surface of the stone, coming to a stop at the woman's hand. "Don't worry, I'm not here to bore you with inconsequential histories or show you bones of forgotten queens—only powerful secrets."

He pushes on the shining sapphire inlaid into the queen's ring finger, the only feature on the sarcophagus not made of gray stone. A low click sounds somewhere deep within it. The sarcophagus slides on unseen tracks to reveal an opening in the floor leading to a staircase.

We descend, looping and looping, deeper and deeper into the heart of the academy.

The darkness of the spiral stairs lifts to reveal a cavernous room. Thick beams support a ceiling that soars so high above my head, it's impossible to make out the carvings and colors that dance upon them. The floor is covered in plush carpets that cushion our footfalls. Yet, even without any sound heralding our arrival, most of the occupants of the room all turn to face us in near unison.

There are seven in total, illuminated by a wall of tall, narrow windows that punch through the cliffs the academy sits upon, and within. I've never seen the waters of the ocean this close before. But my focus isn't on the churning waves, rather, the three men who lounge on one side in luxurious chairs and couches gathered around a blazing hearth. I instantly recognize Eza and the other two as my assailants, but I don't let any panic show on my face. I allow my gaze to move along, rather than lingering on them.

In the center of the room is an assortment of tables and chairs. Each sitting area has a different purpose, from reading tarot to gaming to inking cards. A woman I don't recognize stands with two others at an inking table.

"Myrion? Sorza?" I blurt.

"Oh, you're here, too?" Sorza looks up from what she was working on, startled.

"It's good to see you've joined us, Clara." Myrion smiles warmly. "I had a sense about you."

"What is this place?" I finish my inspection of the room, ending with the dueling floor to the left, where one last individual relaxes out of their stance.

"This is the Sanctum of the Majors," Kaelis answers. "A secret space where you all may work and hone your skills without having to hide the fact that your abilities exceed those of normal students." *So I'm not the only one who's been hiding my power . . .* Rather than excitement, unease courses through me. I thought I'd had an advantage. "Clara, meet your fellow Major Arcana."

"We're about twelve shy of the complete Major Arcana," I point out the obvious, still having a hard time believing any of this.

"Like all the Major Arcana would happen to have come into their powers within three years of each other so we could all attend the academy together," Eza says sarcastically, intentionally loud enough for me to hear.

I willfully ignore him.

"The other twelve went through the academy in their time, or not, if it was before the days of the academy proper. Either way, upon completion of their studies and their fealty to the crown, they were assigned a post just as any other graduated Arcanist would be," Kaelis explains and then starts back for the stairs. "And now I'll leave you to it."

"You're just going to leave me here?" I blurt.

"Yes, cling to your lover's coattails," one of the men by the fire jeers, his voice dripping with disdain, striking a nerve in me . . . and in the prince.

Kaelis's attention shifts off me and back to them, his stare turning colder. I step into his line of sight and harden my gaze. They're right. I can't depend on Kaelis of all people. And I won't. Not after all he and his family have done to me. It doesn't matter if he's protecting me now. He doesn't care about me; I'm safe only as long as I'm useful to him. The only people I can truly depend on are my family at the Starcrossed Club.

"I do hope she clings to me," Kaelis says, eyes still on them even though he takes a step closer to me. His attention drops to my face with a look that threatens to devour me whole. "After all, she is my bride."

Kaelis's fingers run down my shoulder to my hand and lace with mine. Then he brings my hand to his lips. Our conversation in the conservatory reminded me more than ever of the importance of our ruse if I'm to stay safe.

"I will see you again soon." I add a flirtatious note to my voice, trying to keep up the guise. My hand shifts as he releases it, and I caress his cheek and lightly touch his lip. *His skin is softer than I expected.* Kaelis's eyes widen slightly. My smile goes from somewhat forced to actually coy.

Two can play this game, I want to say.

"I look forward to it." His voice is deep with an implication that would send a rush across any woman's flesh. The air is colder as he turns and leaves, my hand hovering in the air for a breath where he just was.

Kaelis isn't gone for more than a second before I hear footsteps racing toward my back.

CHAPTER 19

I whirl. The deck on my hip responds to a flick of my fingers, three cards lifting from the pack and fanning out, hovering at my side. Each one ready to serve.

"Oh, there is some bite after all." Eza lifts his hands in a mockery of a motion of surrender. He clearly isn't threatened by me in the slightest. "I think our little welcome party upset her."

"Seems like it," the man at his right side says with a low snigger. A mop of brown hair shadows his dusky eyes. "Though look at how she must *move* to summon cards. Can't even do it with thoughts alone. I expected more from Kaelis's chosen bride."

"Really? I didn't. Seems about on par for our *illustrious leader.*" The third man, at Eza's left, shrugs. Hoops and bars line his ears, exposed by the shaved sides of his head. His only hair is a single strip of black, loosely spiked. A tattoo pokes above his collar, the dark lines intricate on his tawny skin. From his septum piercing to the severity in his shockingly violet eyes, it's clear he's honed his appearance to be as imposing as possible. Unfortunately for him, it takes a lot more than a sharp needle and little bits of metal to intimidate me.

"Leave it, Eza," Myrion warns, stepping between us. But it's clear his words do little to deter the angry man.

"Always a Lover, aren't you?" Eza sneers.

"You should try making love instead of war, for once," Myrion counters. "Goodness knows it might help you unwind a bit. I could help you with that, one way or another, if you wanted."

Eza scoffs at the implication and brushes past Myrion, their shoulders crashing together. I've yet to move. Every part of me is locked on to Eza's movements. Ready to react. I won't let him put me back in that mental prison . . . I'll kill him first.

"Know your place before I put you there." Eza tilts his head back, looking down his nose at me.

"I know mine." I flash him a coy little smile. "But if you want, I'll gladly show you yours."

"If you're going to duel, do it in the ring. Those're the rules," someone else says. I don't look to see who. Nothing in Eza's actions makes me think he cares at all for the "rules."

"Duel?" He scrunches his nose in disgust, but the expression quickly melts, his eyes lighting with amusement. "Perhaps I will. But on my time. Maybe I'll put you in the ground when the wielding test of the Three of Swords Trials comes around. That way everyone can witness how pathetic Kaelis's 'bride' is." Eza leaves, the other two in tow. As soon as they're gone, the air seems lighter.

"You didn't have to do that," I say to Myrion, easing out of my stance. The cards return to the deck.

"I get my own pleasure out of telling him he's an ass. It wasn't *only* for you." The man gives me a kind smile.

"I don't want it for me at all." They'll never respect me if they think they can walk all over me. Fantasies of revenge are already fluttering through my mind. But those things will have to wait until I'm stronger. As much as I hate to admit it, it's probably for the best that, right now, Eza and I didn't end up throwing cards.

"Noted." Myrion steps away, rejoining the remaining three.

"I'm Thal." The individual recently in the dueling arena steps over and perches themself on one of the tables, sending the little pieces of a forgotten game scattering without care. They have light skin and honey-colored hair that highlights the warm tones of their hazel eyes, so their Major seems apt when they say, "Nineteen, the Sun."

"Elorin." A woman of House Wands bows her head. She has waves of hair that are black at the roots but quickly fade into a rainbow ombré over her shoulders. Her rosy cheeks, bright blue eyes, and full red lips stand out against her ghostly pale skin, giving her an almost doll-like appearance. "Two, the High Priestess."

"Sorza, as you well know . . . I'm Justice, apparently." Her tone and expression betray that she's as unsure about all of this as I am, reassuring me the Majors weren't a secret she'd been keeping from me. She's still someone I think I can trust. Somewhat. At least for now.

"Of course, we've met as initiate and student. As Majors, I'm the Lovers." Myrion folds his arms, leaning against one of the tables. "And I see you had the pleasure of meeting the terrible trio."

"Eza is the Hanged Man," I start, hoping someone will fill in the other two blanks.

Myrion does. "Cael is his right hand, the Emperor. And the brown-haired one is Nidus, the Tower. Cael and Nidus are second years, and you'll have the delight of dealing with Eza as a fellow first year."

"He's already so close with second years?" It's half question, half musing.

"The delights of nobility. They all come in knowing each other. Nidus is also Clan Moon and even though Cael is common born, he's Nidus's best friend," Thal says dryly. "Though, I suppose as Miss I-recently-found-out-I'm-a-long-lost-heiress, you'll join that club soon."

"You're all second or third years?" I shift the topic off me and my fake nobility. Thal, Myrion, and Elorin all nod. "When you graduate, will you go to the clan of your namesake?"

The noble clans were said to have been founded by individuals who embodied and believed the ethos of their Major the most. Now that I think about it . . . such a claim lines up best with Kaelis's story of the Fool. If each of the Majors were people, long ago, then of course they would be powerful and respected enough to be leaders.

"Not necessarily," Elorin answers. "As Kaelis said, Majors are assigned to clans like other Arcanists, depending on need or, occasionally, personal relation to the clan. I'd bet that you will be 'assigned' to Clan Hermit, since you don't have your own Arcanist."

"Don't have much of anything thanks to your fiancé's work years back," Thal mutters.

"Most don't know of the Majors' existence," Myrion continues. I wonder if it's purely by chance he shifted the topic so quickly, or if he knows something about Clan Hermit. "Only King Oricalis himself, his inner circle, Head Lords and Ladies of clans, and those who are related to a Major know about us. Though we're technically supposed to keep what we are a secret, even from our families, should they not already have uncovered the truth."

"A few Majors are kept at the castle court, under the close watch of the king himself," Elorin adds.

"In *service to* the king," Myrion corrects.

"In service to," Elorin repeats. Her tone shifted when she began speaking about the castle court, but not in a way I can read.

"What noble clans do you all belong to, if any?" I hazard a guess that her opinions of the court would be shaped by her belonging to, or not belonging to, a noble clan.

"No nobility here," Elorin says. That surprises me, as those rainbow robes dotted with golden stars look quite expensive. "My parents work on the riverboats that ship powders."

"Myrion Leva, at your service." Myrion bows his head respectfully.

"Leva? I know that name." I knew he was of Clan Lovers from our turn about the room. But I didn't suspect he was the heir.

"I'm honored. Yes, my father is High Lord Ixil Leva of Clan Lovers." He looks embarrassed by the admission. *Why?* It should be a source of pride for him.

"I didn't know I took a walk with a man one step from royalty on night one."

"Hardly." Myrion rubs the back of his neck and glances at Elorin, who pointedly fixates on the corner of the room.

"Clan Magician, but not a family name you'd recognize," Thal says. "I'm pretty low, as far as us nobles go."

"Sorza Sprigspark." *Ah,* she's from northwest of Eclipse City, where the Blood Forests are. Sprigspark is the name given to the orphans there, much like Graysword here in the south.

"Clara Redwin," I say, careful not to mess up my newest fake name. I doubt many people can say they've been known by four names in their life: I was born to the name Chevalyer, though I never went by it in my life—my mother swore Arina and me to secrecy over our birth name from the first moment we learned of its existence. Then there was Daygar, the name Mother told us to tell people. That name lasted the longest. Graysword when I was captured and sent to Halazar. Now Redwin. Kaelis is lucky I'm so well versed in learning and responding to fake names. "Though I suppose you all know that by now."

"I'm fairly certain *all* the students know your name." The way Myrion says it, I don't think he believes that to be a good thing. "Are you the Wheel of Fortune, or the Star?"

"What?" It takes a good moment for the question to sink in. "Oh . . ." *Fortune,* that's what Kaelis called me. "Wheel of Fortune, I suppose."

"*Hah,* I was right. Star's last." Thal holds out their hand to Myrion with a catlike grin. The latter places a large silver coin in their hand—a doln—with a roll of his eyes.

These two were betting a whole doln on who would be the next Major? So much for thinking Thal was a "lower" noble. That kind of money is rarely seen changing hands so flippantly.

"Well . . . now that we all know each other and our Majors, what next?" I ask.

"Afternoon classes on the Major Arcana," Elorin announces with a swish of her hand, sending the flowing multicolored fabric of her clothes dancing around her arms. "And we're your teachers."

We all coalesce around the back table that she, Myrion, and Sorza had previously been hunched over. It's laden with exquisite papers of varying finishes, ink canisters filled with powders, empty containers, and crystal palettes. I hadn't thought it possible, but the brushes and pens are even nicer than what was in my room. I can't help but wonder what the prince himself uses.

"Let's begin." Myrion slides up to the table.

The instruction is familiar in concept: the Arcanist draws out their power and funnels it into the ink, staining it and locking it into a card for future use. But it is what follows that completely loses me. For the Minor Arcana, the materials are clear.

Swords are inked with an iridescent black powder made from the crushed feathers of falcons that roost in the Descent.

Wands require the pale ash of burned yew trees, which grow only in the monster-infested Blood Forests.

Cups' prismatic light blue powder is made from crushing crystals collected by divers in the Drowned Mines.

Coins' ink comes from green berries that fruit on delicate, thorny plants native to the flatlands that border the distant Desert Reaches.

Any Sword, Wand, Cup, or Coin can be inked with the necessary powder mixed with a bonder like oil or water. Each ingredient is hard to attain and harder to process. But straightforward . . . unlike inking a Major Arcana.

"So, then, as Majors, we can ink Minors with any powders we want, but our Major cards require something special?"

The three second and third years share a confused look.

"We cannot ink Minor Arcana with anything but the ink required." Elorin speaks for all of them.

I look to Sorza.

"Can't say I've tried . . . But I am new to all of this." She seems skeptical.

"Can you, Clara?" Myrion asks.

"Yes." Now I'm wishing I'd kept my mouth shut.

"Fascinating." He strokes his chin. "Every Major's magic is different but powerful enough that it gives each individual unique additional benefits. Our Major Arcana is our primary power—and the card is the way we actively access our power. When successfully inked, the card turns silver. Every Major also possesses the ability to use other Major Arcana cards—which regular Arcanists cannot use."

"A regular Arcanist can use a Major card if they're blessed by the Hierophant card," Thal chimes in.

"Well, yes. But generally speaking, using the Major Arcana is something only Majors can do." Myrion continues, "Finally, there are other powers that come with being the embodiment of a Major—those 'additional benefits' I mentioned. These are unique to each Major, and they're usually smaller, innate abilities that require no card.

"As for me, my primary power is the Lovers. If I or another Major cast that card, it can make two people whose names I know fall in love. My innate ability is that I can often tell at a glance if two people are in love."

"Can you?" I try to not sound panicked, thinking of Kaelis's and my display earlier.

"More or less." His smile is impossible to read. "It's not like using a card—not a surefire thing. But a pretty good instinct."

"And you two?" I ask, trying to move along from the notion of Myrion being able to tell Kaelis and I are very obviously not in love. If he hasn't said anything yet, then maybe he won't say anything at all. Or . . . he couldn't tell.

"People seem inclined to say things around me; they tell me things they might not otherwise admit, especially if I probe," Elorin says.

"My pain tolerance is ridiculous," Thal says.

"So yours, then, is you can ink any Minor with any powder." Sorza appraises me, then hums. "I wonder what mine is . . ."

"You'll find out in time," Elorin says. "But, for now, let's focus on the main way you access your power—inking your Major card."

"You'll have to find what your Major Arcana card costs for *you*," Thal emphasizes. "For example, mine's crushed poppies picked on a sunny day."

"How does that make any sense?" I shift my weight from foot to foot, working to not let my insecurity show. I've always been quick to grasp any lesson or concept thrown at me. But in this room, among these peers, I can't help but feel, for the first time ever when it's come to the arcana, that I'm starting from behind.

"The Sun . . ." Thal reaches into their loose vest and pulls out a vial filled with a crimson powder. It's unlike anything I've ever seen. Nearly the color of blood. Yet, when they hold it up to the windows, still bright with the afternoon sun, it splits the light into a dozen rainbows that scatter across the table we're gathered around. "It removes any pain from an individual. Pain of the body and of the mind. An enhanced and perfect version of what poppy medicine can do, and a hundred times more addictive."

"There's logic to that, I suppose." But then what inking material is "logical" for a Wheel of Fortune?

"Don't worry, we've all made it through this." Thal nudges my shoulder, reassuring me. "Remember, the card reflects you and your latent power. The cost is within you. You'll know it when you find it."

I merely nod.

"And, like a Minor card, you must have this inking material for every card?" Sorza asks.

"It's not *always* a material." Elorin lightly runs her fingers over the various inking tools, staring straight through them.

"What is it for you?" Her expression and movements make my question delicate.

Elorin's eyes flick to me. Despite their bright blue hue, they're even more void of emotion or feeling than Kaelis's eyes. "Much like your ability with Minor Arcana, I can use any inking medium—even plain pen ink. But to imbue it with power so that it can be made into a card, I must give up a memory."

Sorza lets out a soft gasp, her jaw slackening. "Do you get to choose which one?"

"I do. And, thankfully, it can be small." Elorin sounds exhausted, as if she's given this explanation a thousand times, even though it couldn't be more than a couple dozen, given the secret nature of our identities. "But that is why I must continually ensure I make new memories and be careful in which ones I give up."

"Even if you can make new ones . . . the cost is horrifying," Sorza says.

"It is a sacrifice, but we all must pay our costs in service to the Oricalis crown." Those are hollow words that Elorin doesn't believe, I'd bet my life on it.

"And the cost binds us all together," Myrion adds. "It's a sacrifice that only we can give, and only we can understand."

They all share a look that suggests there's something more. Though I wouldn't know how to ask. So, instead, I focus on the practical implications of what she's saying. "How do you ink a memory?"

"Much like how the raw materials for the powders must be properly processed to turn them into ink that can be used for tarot, it's the act of sacrificing the memory that charges whatever pigment I have to use, making it magical." Elorin plucks an oversized sheet of paper from the pile, handing it to Sorza.

Charges the pigment... I stare down at my hand briefly, thinking of how many times I've pricked my finger with a pen tip to ink a Minor with whatever powder I wanted. Maybe Thal is right, the cost is somewhere within me and I'll simply *know*, much like instinct led me to believing and discovering I could ink any card by mixing my blood with the ink.

I'm pulled from my thoughts when a slip of paper is placed into my hand. My eyes meet Elorin's.

"To begin," she continues, "start by meditating on the essence of your card—what it means. Draw what comes to mind. Don't force anything, and let the symbols and feelings flow. Follow them. Let them guide you to their inner workings."

She almost sounds like Mother. A fact I ignore.

"How does Eza already know how to ink his card?" I assume it's not a secret that he does. And, if it is, I'm more than happy to ruin Eza's secrets.

"Being good friends with other Major Arcana gave him a bit of a leg up before entering the academy," Myrion explains.

"Ah, so just like everything else, the nobles start ahead of the rest of us," Sorza murmurs. I wish I could commiserate more with her, but I fight to keep my face passive, or a bit guilty even, as I'm supposed to be one of those "nobles."

"You should focus on your own cards, for now." Elorin taps on the table, her long nails as multicolored as her hair.

Sorza and I each sit at our own inking tables, and the hours slip away, interrupted only when Myrion is kind enough to bring us some light refreshments in place of missing lunch. For the first time ever, my pen is still. I can't seem to think of a single mark. I replay my memories—of Mother and Arina, of surviving on the streets in Eclipse City, of the Starcrossed Club, of street fights, and of cold winter nights where the only thing that could do battle with the shivers was a warm body next to mine. I search for a sign or some kind of through line. Something that would make it all make sense when looked at through the lens of what I know the Wheel of Fortune to mean. Every possibility dances before me, taunting me, always just out of reach.

Luck is on my side. It's the only thing I can think of. Another sign of this supposed Major, I realize. Yet, now, when I need it more than ever, this luck doesn't materialize. If that is an innate power of my Major, I certainly can't call upon it at will.

The Wheel of Fortune can signify a change in one's luck, but also a major shift in their circumstances. Being acted upon by a force beyond their control. Apt, for never have I felt so out of control.

Mother . . . I wish I could ask her.

You don't need to worry about the Major Arcana, she'd said firmly. *They're not something that Arcanists can ink, or use. It's best not to concern yourself too much with them. In fact, much like the fortress across the bridge, avoid them at all costs.*

Had she known my hidden identity, then? She'd always turned down any discussion of the Majors outside of passing mentions in fables. Perhaps, though, with a bit too much conviction . . . She'd had to have suspected something was different about me when I discovered that I could ink any Minor with any ink.

Did you know? A question I'll never get to ask. Answers lost forever, taken by her murderer. I rub my neck in thought. If only I could see her one more time . . . Everything began to unravel the moment she died.

"You're trying too hard." Thal's warm breath has me jumping. I didn't even hear them get that close.

"Better than not trying at all." I set my pen down and rub my eyes, just now noticing how dark the room has become.

"It's all right to struggle, but don't worry, you'll find it. We all do. Sometimes, it's the things we can't see in ourselves that have the most power. You'll figure it out soon, I'm sure." They pat my back and lean away. "We're going to head to dinner. You should come, too."

The other three stand at the base of the stairs.

"I'll join soon, I've a bit more I want to do." I am *not* letting this get the better of me, even if I have to be here all night. "Go ahead without me."

"Are you sure?" Sorza asks. She can no doubt see how gaunt my face is.

I nod. "I feel like I might be close to a breakthrough." It's a lie, but it has them leaving me alone with my thoughts, and my work.

The pen tip hovers over the parchment, blots of ink dripping off its tip. Draw something, *anything*. My fingers tremble, aching with the weight of the blank sheet before me.

Draw. *Something.*

I take a shaky breath, trying to push down the rising frustration that threatens to swallow me whole as the shadows stretch longer and longer. The glaringly blank paper mocks me. I put the pen down and shake my head. *Why am I struggling so much? For who? Kaelis?* The thought is ghastly.

These Majors might be real. I *might* be one of them. So what? I can figure out the truth and what it means for me beyond the walls of the academy—beyond the reach of Kaelis, because he's the last person I'd want to have this power.

My gaze sweeps across the room, confirming what I already know: I'm completely alone. I might still be exhausted and malnourished. My body hardly feels like my own. But I have a deck of freshly inked cards at my hip and the knowledge that my sister found a way out of this place. And if Arina could find it, then so can I.

I'm leaving Arcana Academy.

CHAPTER 20

Arina didn't tell me much about the secret passage she'd found through the bridge. I also never asked. Part of it was my trust and faith in her—and probably an excess of it, given how reckless I knew my sister could be. But another reason I didn't ask was that I didn't *want* to know. The more details I had, the more of a weapon I could be against her. Even what little I did know probably put her in danger.

If she's not on the outside . . . if Kaelis did something to her . . . The thoughts have my blood hotter than the warm air of the greenhouse as I emerge from the Sanctum of the Majors. Kaelis might feign that her name is unfamiliar to him, but I know better. I know his nature and have seen firsthand how closely he keeps watch over his precious academy. He's toying with me, and I'm not going to allow it a second longer.

Yet, as the dark halls of the academy unfurl before me, my thoughts linger on him longer than I'd like. The feeling of his arms wound tight around me, pulling me out of that nightmare world. The worry in his voice, and the reassurance his presence unexpectedly brought—the same feeling as when his hand rested on my hip with Ravin and with the Halazar guards.

Protected. Safe. No doubt that's how he wants me to feel. Kaelis is a master manipulator. An expert at control. The longer I stay here, the more at risk I am of falling prey to his ploys. The invisible threads of his influence are already wrapping around me, as unyielding as his grip.

Students, initiates, faculty, and staff alike are all busy with dinner in the main hall, making now the perfect moment for me to slip away. Briefly, I consider going back to my room to collect supplies, but I don't risk it. I don't want to risk drawing attention to myself.

The one thing I wish I had done was scavenge some food. The snacks Myrion brought helped, but weren't a sufficient replacement for a meal. My stomach is screaming at me. Three proper meals and it's been reminded of how good it feels to be full again. The world tilts slightly as I descend a winding staircase.

There will be time to eat once I'm out of here. I'll savor Jura's cooking with Twino over a pot of piping hot tea. The ingredients will cost half as much as what they serve here and taste twice as good.

Knowing little about Arina's passage beyond its existence and a few vague mentions, I'm left to reason where it might be on my own. Using the windows as guidance, I navigate in the direction of Eclipse City and the mighty bridge that extends between it and the academy. The bridge is low compared to the rest of the academy, so I head down in search of the base of the fortress.

One passageway spills into the next. I use the Two of Wands to guide me. The card burns away, leaving trails of glittering orange light to point in the direction of my intent whenever I'm at a crossroads. But I'd inked only three of the card, and soon I'm left traversing on instinct alone.

The rooms become progressively darker as the magic sconces and lanterns that illuminate the academy become fewer in these unused and forgotten spaces. It's hard to keep my focus when slightly ajar doors beckon with the mystery of whatever secrets lie within. My thoughts wander to the machine Kaelis made it a point to bar me from. How many more secrets are locked away in the depths of the academy? What skeletons does the void-born prince keep entombed?

The farther I go, the higher the hairs on the back of my neck raise. The sense that someone is watching me won't abate. I keep glancing over my shoulders and stopping behind doors, back pressed against the wall, ears straining. Once I even think I hear footsteps. But they're gone so quickly that I can't be certain whether the sound was the soles of boots against threadbare rugs or the beating of my heart.

Move faster.

Every step is propelled by those two words. The shadows become thicker. My breath quicker. Rooms blur in my haste. Fading away.

You will never leave this place.

The thought is so vivid it's as if someone whispered it in my ear. I can almost feel cool breath on the nape of my sweat-slicked neck. *Faster. Faster still.* The walls are closing in, trying to squeeze me out—crush me.

Luck is on my side. Luck is on my side. Luck is on my side.

Shadows come alive in the same way as when Kaelis is near. My head is on a swivel. The sensation of being watched has yet to leave. Is someone chasing me? Or is it just the echoes of my footsteps? These mind games are exactly what Kaelis would play.

"Enough!" I snap, whirling in place. But nothing is there. I can hardly even see the hallway I've just been down. "No more games, Kaelis!"

As if in response, all light vanishes.

I run.

My teeth begin to chatter from cold and fear. Invisible hands push against my shoulders. They try to pull me back. I want to scream, but I won't give him—wherever he is—the satisfaction. My knees knock and lock. I stumble, nearly tumbling down a decrepit staircase and breaking my neck.

But sheer will and my hatred of Kaelis and this whole fortress are enough to hold my bones together. My lungs burn from the cold. My heart pounds from the sensation of hands upon me. Pushing. Pulling. Grabbing like the guards of Halazar would manhandle.

All at once, I stumble into a vast space. I can see nothing, but the claustrophobia yields. I gasp, chest heaving, side aching. The air here is so cold it stings my eyes.

I put my hands out, fumbling in the now complete darkness, and my palms meet the stone of one of the walls. I follow it along, still waiting for Kaelis to reveal himself with a roar of laughter and taunts. Halazar has made me no stranger to the absence of light. But there's something about this that's unnatural. Magic hangs in the stale air, sizzling across my skin. It cracks to the surface as my palm glides across ornate carvings.

Cold silver flames spring to life in iron braziers that flank a massive doorway. The flames give off no scent or smoke. Light dances off the imposing door, its carved surface adorned with an odd amalgamation of card symbolism.

I spin in place, expecting to use the light to scan the room. But its glow extends hardly more than a few steps beyond me. Everything else remains shrouded in obscurity. My unease has abated but not vanished. I wait to see if Kaelis will emerge, but he never comes. Perhaps I lost him . . . I turn back to the door.

It certainly has the appearance of a grand entrance. I've seen the students and faculty parade across the bridge every year for the Fire Festival, so I know the modern academy entrance connects to the top of the bridge. But, given how old the academy is, this might have once been the standard entry and exit.

I push on the doors, but they don't budge. Putting my weight into them yields nothing. None of the sculpted edges have any give. There are no hidden levers. No secret buttons nestled among the various carvings of cups and swords.

Stepping back, I assess the sculpted façade. There's magic at work here. Squinting, I tilt my head and push away all other thoughts and worries, trying to reason what the method to opening this passage might be. I've come this far; I'm not going to be thwarted by a lock.

A pattern emerges the longer I stare. Slowly, but it's clear. What I thought was pure chaos at first is anything but. I can make out a hand holding a sword aloft. Wands at a glance form a crown on a profile that could also be interpreted as a Queen of Cups. It's as if four cards have been layered on top of one another. Artwork blending, mixing in a chaotic but suddenly clear way.

The Four of Wands, Queen of Cups, Ace of Swords, and Six of Coins lift from my deck. As soon as they do, they are drawn into the doors by a force of magic not my own. They explode into silver light that illuminates the hidden patterns.

The doors silently swing inward, opening to yet more darkness.

Taking a deep breath, I step through the wall of living shadow, emerging into a dimly lit room with a floor of smooth sand. The only sources of light are ten beams. They're razor-thin, vertical, and set at even intervals like columns. I squint, trying to ascertain the source, but it's obscured from my vision. The rays of light seem to appear from nothing, punching between grooves in the ceiling.

On the distant side of the room is an arched opening. Inviting. I can already imagine the way out is on the opposite side.

It's too easy, instinct tells me. Especially given how difficult the doors were to get through. But, then again, perhaps the doors were the primary defense? *No, something is off here.* The beams of light with no source. The stillness that is so present it feels like another person . . . Though, Kaelis has yet to emerge, which causes me to doubt my senses.

Skimming through the cards in my deck, I search for something that might help. Once more, I'm left wishing I'd planned my escape better. But it wasn't as if I knew an opportunity would present itself so soon.

Three of Wands—safety in travel—it's the best I have. The *only* thing that might be mildly useful. I return the deck to its holster and drop the card, stepping on it. Magic rushes over my feet, trailing up my body as flaming vines that vanish before they pose any danger.

Gathering my courage, I step forward, easing my weight onto the sand. I'm not immediately sucked down. In fact, nothing changes.

Focus steady on the opposite doorway, I take another step, and another. A flicker catches the corner of my eye. As soon as it registers that one of the beams of light has vanished, the magic I cast with the Three of Wands surges. My boots move, feet carried along by virtue of being inside them. The magic takes me on what would be the "safe" path by taking two steps back. The beam of light reappears where I was standing.

Avoid the light? The realization has barely had time to register when another beam disappears, reappearing next to me. I pivot, this time using the magic protecting me to my advantage, moving faster than I should. But another beam has moved—or I was closer than I thought to begin with.

My arm clips the light, barely.

A stab of pain rushes straight to my head. It's bad enough that I'm left gasping. Stunned. The sleeve of my jacket has been cut through, perfectly clean. Blood pours from my forearm onto the sandy ground. A pale stone catches my eye, distracting me. I move my foot, shifting the sand around it. *That's not a stone . . .* What is undeniably a bone shard serves as a stark warning.

The Queen of Cups raises from my deck, flashing. Skin mends, but the pain remains. Another flicker. The light shifts. I dodge.

The beams wink in and out. I dance around them. One step forward, one back. Two forward. Three back. Side to side.

I can't make any progress, and the magic of the Three of Wands is quickly wearing off. My muscles are burning, and the fire escapes as a scream as I fail to dodge another beam of light. This one slices clean through my foot, blood exploding across the sand, the appendage rendered nearly useless instantly. Fingers twitching, I hunt for another Queen of Cups that isn't there. I used the other one I'd inked on the door.

The sheared tendons in my foot put my balance on a tilt. I try to compensate, and my foot twists in the sand. I tumble. A beam of light blinks out of existence, reappearing at my back. *Fuck.* There's not even time for my life to flash before my eyes when my shoulder clips the razor-sharp beam mid-fall. I contort enough that it barely misses the life-sustaining vein in my neck, but it cleaves deep through me. Deep enough that this time there's no sound for the pain to escape on, only a bloody gurgle.

As I blink up at the gray ceiling, the lights flicker. Closer each time, like they're chasing me—mocking me. The edges of my vision blur and darken. Every blink is harder than the last. I can't even move my right arm. My whole body shudders, going cold.

I want to think of the club, my mother, my sister. But I can't even muster the strength for a final thought that would bring me some comfort. All I can think is:

I'm going to die here.

CHAPTER 21

No sooner does the thought cross my mind than footsteps clamor over the stone. Sand scatters as a man lands with a heavy thud near me.

Ah, there he finally is . . . It seems Kaelis feels he's toyed with me long enough.

There's a flash of magic as two strong hands reach underneath my arms. A Queen of Cups knits the muscle and tendon of my shoulder, leaving a dull ache behind. The Queen of Cups might mend the wound, but the phantom aches are always left behind. Luckily, if there's one thing I'm good at, it's pushing through pain.

I'm dragged back through the veil of shadow, past the threshold of the door, and onto the cold stone floor beyond, where I am unceremoniously dumped. My consciousness fades in and out as the hands release me. A pause. Then footsteps fading away.

Honestly? He's going to leave me here?

"Kaelis, you bastard," I rasp. "If you want me dead, then fucking get on with it already."

Another stretch of silence after the last footsteps echo. But I can sense he's still there. I pant softly, the pain subsiding.

"You just wanted me to think I had a chance, didn't you?"

"I'm not Kaelis," an unfamiliar voice speaks. It's softer than Kaelis's, slightly higher, almost like a whispered song. Shock stills me.

Not Kaelis ... but someone who knew this place well enough to be nearby and hear my cries. Or maybe this was the person I sensed following me. I stare up at the ceiling, weighing my options with this stranger. At the very least, he saved my life. That counts for something.

"Do you work for Kaelis?" I ask.

"Don't we all?" The reluctance in the statement gives me hope. Not exactly a resounding endorsement of the prince—there's definitely no love in the emptiness of those three words.

I struggle to sit and twist to face him. The man stands at the border between the light and the darkness, mostly obscured. From what I can tell, he doesn't *look* like a student. He strikes me as being in his mid-twenties, a touch older than Kaelis. He wears simple clothes—a loose-fitting, long-sleeved cotton shirt and plain trousers of the type that went out of fashion four years ago.

An outsider? Twenty, I hope so. Maybe our paths crossed because he, too, was making his way to the secret passage. I hope he's a thieving little rat like me, scurrying right under Kaelis's nose and driving him mad.

"Don't go this deep into the academy again," he warns. "There are dangers in the depths, and you might not be so lucky to have me around next time to save you."

"I saw the danger firsthand . . ." I rub my neck. "That's the way out, right?" Arina is going to gloat until the end of time for managing to get through something that nearly killed me on my first attempt.

"I don't know. If you're looking for a way out, follow the rules and use the top of the bridge like all the other students. Don't go hunting through the ruins in the foundations." He begins to retreat.

"Wait." I scramble to my feet, stumbling once. "*Please,* wait." The man pauses. "You know about the academy, clearly. Are you a student?"

No response. It's hard to make out his face in the dim light of the flames.

"Were you a student? Staff? Faculty?"

Still nothing. He turns again.

"You're going to leave me here?" I take a step, still swaying as the world tilts. "I need your hel—" My feet slide out from under me. Dizziness caused by blood loss overtakes my balance. But I don't hit the floor. Instead, I'm met with the warm and sturdy side of this man. His arm locks with mine and half hoists me upright. I meet his eyes, about to thank him, but instead I blurt a question. "Do I know you?"

"I have that kind of face." He glances away. "I'm no one you need to concern yourself with. Better off forgotten. Think of this as nothing more than a dream." He starts walking, leading us away from the mysterious doors. I glance over my shoulder in time to see them shutting with a flash of light over the carvings like a seal. The flames extinguish as magically as they sparked to life, leaving nothing but darkness. When I blink, I can just see the blue outline of where they once were.

"What was that place?" I muse softly, mostly to myself. The night has come alive once more. Overwhelming. Threatening. I feel an irrational sensation that if I were to speak too loudly, I'd draw the attention of some dangerous, slumbering monstrosity.

"Nowhere you should ever return." He seems steadier than me, as if he's used to the unwelcoming oppression of this place.

"That only makes me want to go even more." My boast is a bit hollow, even to my ears.

He pauses, sighs, and continues walking. We soon travel up a winding stairwell and emerge into a hallway lit by moonlight. I blink, eyes adjusting; even the stars seem bright after being . . . wherever that was. The darkness behind us seems as normal as anything else, giving credence to his words, *Nothing more than a dream.*

"Where are you taking me?" I ask as we continue walking down a corridor I'm not familiar with—which still describes most of the academy.

"My room." That should raise my hackles a lot more than it does.

"Do you make it a habit of taking strangers back to your room?"

"Hardly."

"Then I should consider myself lucky?"

A brief and bitter chuckle before he repeats, "Hardly."

My better sense tells me to feel worried at that. But my gut objects. *This man isn't a danger,* it says. I put faith in my instincts. They're usually right . . . if I ignore the day I was caught.

As we walk, I glance at him from the corner of my eye. It's still hard to make out the finer details of his appearance, but the brief moments of lamplight give me the broad strokes. Dark hair, fair skin, and shoulders wider than most. He looks like a laborer, not one of the prim-and-proper regular occupants of the academy.

It isn't until he opens a door, warm light streaming out from the room, that I'm able to see him clearly. Black hair an utter mess, shorter on the sides and longer on top, falling just above heavy brows and sunken eyes of a green so pale they're nearly silver. The color is emphasized by the dark circles beneath them that almost mirror mine. The man has seen his share of horrors, I'd bet my life on it.

"I know you." This time, it's not phrased as a question. *But from where . . .*

"I assure you, you don't."

All at once, it clicks. "You knew Arina."

He halts. Wide eyes return to me as if he's seeing me in the echoes of Arina's descriptions like I'm seeing him in hers. She'd spoken of a friend on the inside—a man she was confident she could trust despite my understandable skepticism. The warmth in her voice, combined with the fact that my sister is usually as harsh as I am toward the ruling class and all those who abide them, led me to ultimately believe that she could trust him.

"Silas," I say confidently. His expression is all the affirmation I need that I've found the right person.

"Clara." Silas dips his chin.

"You knew it was me," I realize. "That's why you followed me—why you saved me."

"You're just like Arina, venturing deeper than you should." He shakes his head. I don't miss the fondness underneath the exasperation in his tone. "You even look like her, too. You have the same hair." He notices the one link others could not.

I shift, grabbing his arm, and I'm still so unsteady I nearly pull us both off-balance. My heart races. My fingers press wells into his thick biceps as I jerk him toward me. Our noses nearly touch.

"You're the first person I've found in this entire place who will acknowledge her existence." Relief wars with panic. "What happened to her?"

A frown furrows his brow.

"Tell me," I demand as the silence drags on. My voice thins as I struggle to not scream. "I know she ran." *At least, I'm pretty sure* . . . But Silas confirms it.

"Yes, the official story is she 'ran away' from the academy, was apprehended, branded, and sent to a mill."

"*Official* story?" I cling to the hope that word choice gives after the mention of a mill being her fate.

"All I know for sure is she went missing. Everything else is what they announced to the academy last year before the Three of Swords Trials." His mouth presses into a hard line.

I'm going to be sick. I sway, my grip going slack. He doesn't know. But Arina wouldn't have told a stranger, even one she trusted, of all her plans. Silas isn't one of our crew. Arina would've kept him at least a little ignorant. She still could've escaped, and Kaelis absolutely would've covered up a student slipping from his grasp.

"Come and sit." Silas leads me farther into what can only be described as a tiny one-room apartment.

The room has polished wood furniture crafted in a similar style to what's in my dormitory. However, the carvings are different. Rather than ivy, feathers line the edges of wingbacks and low tables. Plush carpets are works of art across the floor, their vibrant colors outlining a map of Oricalis Kingdom. Pieces of art are pinned to the walls, all handmade by Silas, I suspect, given their similarities in medium, format, and style.

It's like walking into a person's diary. Every worn track in the carpet and scuff on the furniture can be read as a clue to who he is. Those paths in the rug are in straight lines from what must be endless pacing. The finish on the handles of the chairs is worn down, gripped a little too tightly for a little too long. The bindings of the books on a lone bookshelf look like they'd fall apart with one more read. So well loved that they've come undone.

I can't stop myself from asking, "Do you live here?"

"Yes." There's more wrapped up in that word than I can comprehend.

"The man in the depths," I whisper. I didn't need further proof of who he was, but it seems I have it. Even though I've never met Silas before, he feels like a friendly face. There were few people Arina had mentioned more often than him.

"What?"

"That's what my sister called you." I ease into the wingback thanks to Silas's help.

He chuckles as he crosses the room, retrieving a thin, crusty loaf of bread and salted meat. I can tell it's of the same quality that's served in the main hall, but its far simpler presentation puts me more at ease than I've been in days. "She would have called me that."

"She said you knew the deeper passages of the academy." And those passages were allegedly leading her to something big—bigger than the passage through the bridge. *But what?* I never had a chance to find out before my arrest. "Were you the one to show her the way out?"

"No." Silas sighs. "She found that on her own. And, somewhat the opposite, I cautioned her against going too deep."

"But *do* you know of the way out?" I ask as I devour the food. I needed sustenance desperately.

"Not her way out." He catches himself, raising his hands and trying to verbally backtrack. "No, I don't know of *any* ways out."

I narrow my eyes at him. Silas makes it a point to avoid my probing stare.

"Please," I say.

"I can't."

"If you knew Arina, then you already know who I am and what I fought for. What's happened to me." There's no point in attempting the fake noble ruse on him.

Silas averts his eyes, as if the truth of what I've endured is too much for him to bear. Yet I force him to anyway.

"No more than five days ago, I was in Halazar." I'm not sure how long I was unconscious for after Kaelis dragged me out of the water, so I make a guess. "I was there for almost a year. *A year*, Silas. I've had no contact with the people I care about most in the world. Arina—" My throat closes, and, for a moment, I choke on emotions I've been working so hard to keep in check. "She is my sister, the only blood family I have left, and I don't know what happened to her. Last I knew, she'd lied about her age, made it into the academy and through the Fire Festival, and was eying Cups as her house."

"Arina lied about her age?" He seems genuinely surprised. I was right, she didn't tell him everything.

"Only a little. She was nineteen." Not that you could tell by looking at her. And her magic had fully matured. "She was supposed to be here in her second year, but I can't find her, and I've yet to get solid answers I can believe. The people I love—people I swore to protect—might be in danger. I don't know anything about any of them, either. Every second I spend here, ignorant and at the whim of my enemies, rots me from the inside."

I wrap my arms around my sides and dip my head for a second, drawing a shuddering breath. I'd been doing so well keeping myself together. But now I'm a ribbon, spinning endlessly. Waving on the wind. Forcing myself to linger in these feelings, I turn my eyes back to him. I want him to feel the weight of these emotions threatening to crush me as though they were his own.

"Don't you want to know what happened to Arina?"

"Of course I do."

"Then help me get out of here. Do that, and I will do *anything* you want to repay you." I continue to keep my eyes locked with his. My voice quiets with severity. "You've no idea how rarely I give out an offer like that."

Silas opens and closes his mouth. He nearly breaks. But ultimately he shakes his head. "I *can't*."

"Are you some kind of prisoner?" Kaelis clearly has a thing for keeping people locked up.

"No more than any of us are." *Isn't that the truth?*

I pick up on more. He's hiding something. "But you can't leave."

"It's because of my card."

The ambiguity. Kaelis keeping this man close and hidden . . . "You're a Major." I piece it together.

"The Chariot."

"And what does the Chariot do?" I get the sense that the moment I stop asking questions, he's going to force me to leave.

"Much like you'd expect . . . Transportation instantly between two known locations."

I'm on my feet. "So you can get out."

He continues avoiding my stare. "You're new. You don't know all the rules of the Majors yet."

"Fuck their rules," I blurt.

Silas's eyes widen with shock. "The use of the Major cards is only for High Lords and Ladies, or the king himself. We can't—"

"I don't care what people who have never spent a day of their lives worrying about me think," I interrupt him. Anger laces my words, but I keep my composure so it's clear the rage isn't directed at him.

"They will punish you."

"I don't care," I repeat.

"You don't know what they can do to you."

I bark laughter. "I know *exactly* what they can do to me." Silas is silenced. "Eza doesn't play by the rules. He uses his Majors as he pleases. Don't be the only one heeding the crown's limitations on us."

"Eza's cost to ink is less than others'. Those of us with rarer requirements are far more scrutinized. We can't get away with as much."

"What is your requirement?" I ask, in part to keep him talking. Though, Silas doesn't seem to be the type of man to respond well to brute force. *Soften yourself, Clara.* As if I know how to make any part of me "soft" anymore . . .

"I can only ink my cards in a location I've never been before. One new location, one new card. So I'm kept here. The Chariot is too useful to risk me going somewhere new and not getting a card out of it."

My stomach churns with the poison of his solitude. "Kaelis keeps you locked up because of your card?"

"I'm free to wander most of the academy so long as I stay out of sight; that way, no suspicions are roused, or questions asked, about why I don't look like a student." He speaks as if that should be enough.

"How long has it been like this?"

"Since I entered the academy four years ago. As soon as my Major and the cost of inking it was known, I was put here." A man of roughly twenty-four years . . . I was right that he's a little older than Kaelis.

"One year in Halazar and I nearly broke."

"This is far more comfortable than Halazar, I assure you."

"A prison is a prison."

He pauses, eyes drifting to a shadowed corner, where they linger. I know all too well the look of a man consumed by his ghosts. It prompts me to close the gap. The touch of my fingertips on his elbow brings him back to the present.

"If you can go anywhere, Silas, then leave," I say gently.

"I must first know a place to go to it with the Chariot."

"Your floor is a map."

He pauses, and the soft lighting casts shadows over the chiseled planes of his face. "It's not a matter of what I do or don't want . . . It's what must be done for the good of the kingdom."

"You don't believe that." It's a far nicer thing for me to say than the first several thoughts that crossed my mind in response to the phrase "good of the kingdom."

"You don't know me," he reminds me. My hand drops from his person. He's right.

"I don't. But no one should be forced to give up the world."

"The World is precisely what we're all fighting for." He gives me a reassuring smile, but it doesn't reach his eyes, which only makes my heart ache more. "Once we have unlocked the twenty-first Major, Oricalis will prosper, more than it ever has before. We will usher in a new age." The words sound recited. Hollow.

"You believe all that nonsense?"

"I assure you, it's not 'nonsense.'" The solemn severity of his words . . . his grave expression. It strikes me more than any of Kaelis's claims have to date: Silas truly believes it's real.

The World, the ultimate wish card. If it does exist, then I could use it for myself . . . The frantic hope that flared in me when Kaelis first mentioned it returns. It could change my life—put everything back to the way it was before Mother died, the way it should have been.

"Leave this place with me, tonight."

He sighs, realizing we're back at the start. "I can't. You can't."

I bite back a groan of frustration. "If not for me, then for my sister and any fondness you had for her."

"It's not—"

"Two cards, Silas. We go and come back. No one will be any wiser that we even left." The words are ash in my mouth, and I still don't know if I mean them. But I'll say anything to get out of here. Silas's skeptical expression is well placed. I shift tactics slightly. "What constitutes a 'new place' for you?"

"Standing in a location where nothing I see is something I've seen before."

"Excellent. Then you'll be in lots of new places as we go to find my family; you can ink two new cards—more than two, probably." I take his hand in both of mine, staring up at him, pleading with my expression and words. "Please."

He sighs and withdraws his hand, crossing to his desk. I think I've lost until he plucks two tarot cards from among the clutter and inking supplies scattered across the surface of his desk. He places the first into a nearby satchel along with the inking supplies before rolling up the sleeves of his shirt, exposing the ropey muscles of his forearms.

He takes a moment to admire the second card before turning to me. I notice that the ink shines with a silver sheen.

"I've never seen ink that color before."

"When a Major inks their Major card successfully, the ink turns silver. It's how you know you've done it true," he explains.

"No matter what ink is used?" Myrion had said as much earlier, but I want to verify everything I'm told. If two people tell me the same thing, it's more likely to be true, I think.

He nods.

"Fascinating..." At least I have a marker for success should I make another serious attempt at inking a Major Arcana.

"Are you ready?" His voice is steady. But his eyes are shining with what could just as easily be excitement as fear. "We go, and we come back."

"Give me the card and I can—"

"No." Even though he's firmly shot me down, he wears a slight grin. "I know how Arina was when it came to being sneaky and getting her way; I assume you're even worse. I'm not letting you touch this card and disappear. I'm coming with you and I'm bringing you back. It's too risky for me if you go missing."

"Fine." I nod. "I'm not going to put you at risk. Not when you're the one who's being kind enough to help me."

He must believe me, because he holds out the Chariot. The opportunity to see a Major in action—when it isn't being used to hurt me—*and* get out of this place? My dizziness is from a lot more than blood loss now. Hope is a potent draught.

With practiced ease, he exhales softly. The card rises, balancing on its corner at the tip of his finger. It shines, and I hear the distant whinny of a horse. The paper unravels into thousands of shimmering strands of white light. The ribbons of glowing silver fall into a circle around us. Silas's expression turns almost nefarious as the haze casts eerie shadows across his face.

But I don't doubt him. Not for a second. Arina trusted him, and so shall I.

As the circle engulfs us, the world shifts, and Silas's haven fades from view, replaced by somewhere far beyond the academy's walls.

CHAPTER 22

The brilliant light of the circle that surrounds us fades, revealing a dilapidated bedroom. Vaulted ceilings support a chandelier that has recently seen more spiders than flame. A grand four-poster bed is covered in as much dust as it is threadbare blankets.

"What is this place?"

"An abandoned manor house at the edge of Starburst Row. It was once used for the education of Arcanists in the city, and as a secret point of rest for nobles making the pilgrimage to the Chalice . . . before all arcane education fell under academy control and Kaelis's command."

Before the academy's founding, every clan educated their own, raising their own Arcanists born into their families and onto their lands. Mother told me of how the clans would endlessly war over Arcanists just as they had once warred as kingdoms over the resources used to make cards. Tensions arose from some clans simply being luckier and having more Arcanists born on their land, which led to jockeying for power and then, ultimately, to the Clan Culling—a legendary war that wiped out half the clans. From that war, Oricalis rose, and the laws governing Arcanists were put in place.

This history almost makes the academy seem . . . fair. It created an equal education for all Arcanists and gave clans—and theoretically the people high and low who belonged to them—equal access to magic. It allowed all Arcanists to go before the Chalice and unlock their full potential regardless of innate ability. But, just like the old ways, the academy is merely a different system for treating people like cattle and herding their services and powers into the hands of those above them.

"How do you know of it?" I remember him saying he had to know of the place to teleport to it, and that he had entered the academy under Kaelis. He shouldn't have been here.

"After I was discovered as a Major, I was taken here—to this room. The academy was very new, and my powers manifested earlier than most." His expression is hard, closed off. Voice as hollow as the abandoned rooms that surround us. "My family . . ."

"What happened to them?" I recognize that blank stare, the emptiness. "What did *they* do to them?" Silas's eyes drift to mine, coming back into focus. I offer him a bitter smile. It's not necessary to say who "they" are, we both know. It's Kaelis, the crown, the clans, the whole bloody system. "I know what they do to people like us—to the families and loved ones of people like us. Especially if those families would have the audacity to hide you."

"As your family did for you?" The question is a gentle probe. But I fold anyway. I can't help it; I see myself in him—a kindred spirit.

"You're not the only one who showed aptitude early. My mother . . . she knew what I was well before I did. Did everything she could to hide me . . . and herself."

"She was an unrecorded Arcanist," he whispers, as if there are enforcers here with us. "Unmarked, even?"

I nod. "They killed her for it." Perhaps for even more . . . if my growing suspicions have merit. Kaelis has clearly known what I am for some time. While he was founding the academy, Arina and I were living on the streets just across the bridge. "My sister and I swore to do whatever it took to find her killer and avenge her."

"She mentioned."

"Did she?" I'd assumed she'd been more sparing when it came to the information she gave him, but . . . perhaps not.

He nods. "Did you manage to get your revenge before you were sent to Halazar?"

I shake my head. "My search started with nothing but disbelief and a hunch. Then, I found people my mother had worked with who had conflicting stories compared to what the enforcers had told me of what happened that day. I found a man who said he saw her rope at the Descent and it looked cut. I managed to sneak my way into an enforcer's record hall once. But there was nothing."

"Do they keep records of accidents at the Descent?" he asks delicately. I hear the real question: *Do they care enough about lowborns like us to even keep track of our deaths?*

"Not detailed, but there's usually at least a note in a ledger. Especially since she'd already done her mandatory stint at the Descent and this was a second stint for payment. I found out that Stellis were called to the Descent the day before. But the page for the day my mother died had been torn out of the book entirely." I frown. After Bristara had taken Arina and me into the Starcrossed Club, she told me to give up the search. When she learned I hadn't, she warned me that I was hunting down ghosts that shouldn't be found. That if it was something the enforcers hid . . . then powerful people were likely involved. That only cemented my need to search even more. Mother was engaged in illegal activities, that much I knew. She did everything and more that the crown hated, and they had the means to kill her. But why they murdered her covertly when they could've put her on trial and condemned her to death still eludes me. "Every lead went dry for a while . . . until I had one lucky break. Or so I thought. It didn't work out."

I cross to one of the windows, as if I could physically remove myself from this conversation—and from the memory of the failure that got me caught. I should never have trusted Griv. In the brief time I knew him, he always seemed to know just what I needed to hear—what to say to get me to blindly trust him. But it's not like I made it hard for him, being as transparent as I was and am when it comes to Mother's death and the nobles.

The curtains are pockmarked with holes left behind by hungry moths. I'm surprised the fabric doesn't disintegrate between my fingers as I peel it back, unveiling the view of Eclipse City.

The districts are stitched against one another as in a patchwork quilt. Neighborhoods that gleam with lanterns and spotlights stand seamlessly flush with neighborhoods where the windows are so thickly coated in grime that not even candlelight could penetrate them. A dark swath is lit more by starlight than by magic or practical illumination. The slums sprawl to the east, toward the foot of the mountains that arc around the city, a pit of despair . . . and a nest of resistance.

Silas comes up at my side. "I'd stare out this window for hours."

I hum and shift my weight, leaning against the windowsill. I'm surprised it holds my weight given the condition of everything else in this room. I say nothing, waiting.

"I'd imagine that, maybe, I'd see my family walking in the streets below," Silas says finally.

"What happened to them?"

"I . . . don't know." Silas rubs the back of his neck as if he's unsure. As if he's never told this to anyone else before. "I think, sometimes, if I follow the crown's rules and do everything right, then I'll be able to find out."

There's the reason he was so hesitant to leave. My vague notions of ditching him begin to vanish. I can't do that to someone else . . . not after what I've been through, and if there's still a possibility his family could be alive.

"Use them, Silas," I advise. "But never trust them."

"Do you trust Kaelis?"

"No."

"Even though you're engaged to him?"

"It's a temporarily beneficial arrangement," I tell both myself and him. "As soon as its use has dried up, there will be nothing between us, and we'll be enemies once more."

"Do you think he can help you find your mother's killer?"

"Perhaps." I sigh. Stale air that clings to the upholstery fills my lungs. That singular mission is all I've known for years. The one thing that gave Arina and me purpose when all else seemed lost.

Nothing was the same after Mother died. We lost our guide and guardian. Our home. We threw ourselves into finding the truth. Into pushing every boundary if it meant acting against the crown and its laws. Vengeance won't bring her back, but it might bring some amount of peace.

"But first things first, I just want to make sure my family is safe, and be with them again, that's all," I say.

Silas's chin dips slightly, eyes drifting to the floor. "I'd give anything to see my family again . . ."

"Maybe the club can find a lead on them. We've helped people out before in similar ways; it's what we do." I push away from the window. "I know where we are. We'll get to them quickly." I can't see the Starcrossed Club from this vantage, but I know certain landmarks like the back of my hand.

"With necessary stops for me to ink." He shrugs the shoulder his bag of inking supplies is thrown over.

"Of course." I'm curious to see a Major card being successfully inked. Perhaps it'll give me some clarity on my own card.

He leads us out the bedroom door and through the decrepit rooms of this remnant of a bygone era. Down a staircase, we turn away from the main entry and into the kitchens. In the back is a small receiving door—an alleyway is a much better place to slip out. Who knows how busy the main road this manor sits on is. Though I suspect not very, given its condition.

Silas hesitates at the threshold of the door, eyes shining in the low light. He seems to shrink in on himself, shoulders arcing inward. For such an imposing figure of a man, and even with all his muscles, he's quite good at making himself seem small and demure.

They have his family. He didn't say so outright. But given the circumstances . . . we can both assume it to be true. A physical cage wouldn't work on a man whose magic can go anywhere.

"Silas . . ." I hesitate, unbelieving of what I'm about to say. I'm honestly going to abandon the idea of leaving him and truly reclaiming my freedom. But when he looks my way, curious, all doubt is forgotten. "If you want to stay here, you can, and I'll come back. Or, give me the other Chariot card and I'll return to your room when I'm done."

"I'm not letting you out of my sight."

I shift to face him. "You're right, the idea of running crossed my mind. But now that I know they have your family, I won't. I can't. After what they did to me and mine, I'm not going to put someone else through that pain."

He shifts uncomfortably, an internal war tugging on the tiny muscles of his face. "I can't trust you."

"I understand." I nod. "We've only just met, and I hardly trust you."

"But I saved your life." He seems genuinely surprised.

"So did Kaelis." That silences him. "Whenever you're ready, then."

In his own time, Silas crosses the threshold. He stops and tilts his head to the sky, inhaling deeply. It reminds me of what I did the first moment I stepped into the greenhouse. That first taste of freedom on the wind. Even if the "freedom" is little more than an illusion.

Slowly, we take another step, together. And another. I match his pace. Every pause. Every step.

Before I know it, we're running.

We sprint down the alleyway and onto the street. I take the lead, guiding us toward the Starcrossed Club. Weaving around people in their capes and dresses like two street urchins running from the law. Shouts chase us, but no other feet follow. We're too much of a blur.

Running from the darkness. From the grime. From the tiny boxes we were squeezed into.

When my side feels as though it's about to rip open, I pull us off into an alcove. We're on the fringe of the Gilded District. The gold-dipped iron lampposts that give it its name are becoming less frequent. I can almost smell Rat Town from here. Which means it's only a short jaunt through the Stone Steps and then up Coin Hill to the Starcrossed Club.

It's so close I can almost taste the bubbly wine that we serve in the main salon, as sweet as each gulp of warm summer air.

"Mind if I take a second?" Silas asks. He isn't nearly as breathless as me. Another reminder of just how much my physical prowess has slipped.

I shake my head and wipe sweat from my brow. He sits and draws his knees up, propping his bag on them and pulling out some inking supplies. It's the same paper as I'd use, and ink as plain as any other. Yet I can feel an immense surge of power as he draws. I try to conceal how attentively I'm watching.

"Where are we headed?" he asks.

"The Starcrossed Club."

He makes a noise of comprehension; Arina must've mentioned it to him. I sink down next to him. We're on the stoop, so the few people out for a late-night stroll on the sidewalks don't pay us any mind. Still, Silas conceals his inking by resting his cards within a journal, so that it merely looks like he's scribbling notes about something. Carriages clatter past, their occupants oblivious to us.

"It's odd to be back here."

"I can imagine, after Halazar." He doesn't look at me as he speaks, focusing on his inking.

"Not just that . . . My sister and I were born not too far from here, if you can believe it."

"Really?" His pen pauses. "She said you grew up in Rot Hollow before living on the streets."

"We weren't always there. But she was too young to remember anything different . . . Our mother fell on hard times, and we ended up in Rot Hollow when the collectors came knocking. That was how Mother ended up doing another five years at the Descent. She did her first five before I was born. The money from the second was helping us make ends meet." But even a whole regill over five years wasn't enough, fast enough. So Mother did other work helping Arcanists—for money, and for her beliefs. A labor of love I gladly carried on.

I continue, "After she died, the enforcers came around and nearly saw the inking supplies she'd left for us. They were already talking about starting my assignment at the Descent early, since I was now the head of the house . . . I wasn't going to let harvesting inking resources take me from Arina like it did Mother. So we left and lived on the streets, dodging the enforcers."

Mother's face is still sharp in my mind thanks to Eza. I can't decide if I hate him for it or am oddly grateful. Time had begun to blur the little crow's-feet and smile lines she'd hard-earned. I don't want to forget those.

"Would they have really forced a child to go to the Descent?" Silas seems skeptical. The assignment usually isn't mandatory until twenty, mirroring the academy.

"Maybe? Maybe not. I wasn't sticking around to find out if it was an empty threat." I shrug. "Plus, if they were behind Mother's death, I didn't want to be where they could find us."

Silas's expression tells me he can understand that much. "Where's your father in all this?"

"Never knew him." Vague, hazy memories of the man fill my mind from back when we lived in that stately home where everything gleamed. But I've no solid recollections. "Mother didn't talk about him. All I know is, it was after he left that we fell on hard times. He didn't care enough to ever come around again, and that meant I had no reason to seek him out. If we were dead to him, then he is dead to me."

"Was there no one in the extended Chevalyer family you could've gone to?"

A shiver tries to rip through me despite the balmy air of the summer night. *Arina told him our name? Our* real *name?* The name that Mother impressed upon us was to be shared only with those we would trust with our lives? *Our name is like our special card,* Mother would tell me. *It is our greatest treasure and deepest secret.*

"Arina mentioned," he says softly, as if reading my mind.

"No other way you could've known the name." I force a smile and try to dismiss my unease. "You should've addressed me by it from the start. I would've been much less skeptical of you."

"Oh?"

"We're private people." *That's one way to put it.* "If she told you our real name, then she trusted you." Silas must feel my stare, because he lifts his chin and meets my gaze. I hold his stare for several long seconds. "If she trusted you that deeply, then so will I."

He opens and shuts his mouth, clearly searching for the right words. His expression slips into a slight and sincere smile. "Well, I'll call you by whatever name pleases you." *He chose the right words.*

"Redwin, for now. Put the rest from your mind."

"Redwin it is." He finishes his work with a flourish. I'm in awe as the black ink dries to a shimmering silver. Silas slips the card along with his inking supplies back into his satchel and slides the strap across his body.

I take his unspoken cue and stand.

The remaining journey to the club is slower. We set a brisk pace, but that initial drunken rush of freedom going straight to our heads has left us. Every few blocks, we stop in some quiet spot—a park bench, an alleyway, a small table outside a closed cafe.

It's after the last one that my feet find momentum again. *We're so close . . .* Close enough that there won't be any more stops or detours. My friends—my family, the living and breathing heartbeat of my world. I will hold Arina so tightly her eyes pop. I will eat all of Jura's cookies and debate whatever stupid thing Twino wants to debate until we're blue in the face while Ren rolls his eyes at us both.

As the streets grow more familiar, I move faster again. So fast that I don't notice the little oddities. The signs that Coin Hill might not be quite the same as I left it. Signs like a boarded door, a shattered window left in its pane rather than being replaced, the quiet emptiness of streets that were once bustling. It's all lost on me.

Until . . . I round the last corner.

My steps falter. My toes drag across the ground and snag on a crack. Silas keeps me from falling to my knees. Though I wish he hadn't. I wish he'd let me crumple.

The Starcrossed Club . . . The place that took Arina and me in after years on the streets. The first place to feel like home after Mother died, and the last place I saw my sister's face . . .

In its spot is nothing but a gaping chasm of cold, singed rubble.

CHAPTER 23

Numbness threatens to overtake me. It's the same full-body tingling I felt when I was told of Mother's death. And the same numbness I felt as the enforcers held me down on the floor in front of the judge who sent me to Halazar.

"It's . . . gone." I wish I could scream so loud that it would fill the chasm before me. The rubble looks like it's been there for months. This brutality wasn't recent.

"The building is, but the people might not be." Silas's optimism is a balm.

He's right. Even as my heart is fragmenting, as despair pulls me down and questions spiral, I find my legs beneath me once more. I'm not helping anyone, myself included, if I crumble.

"Do you know where they might have gone in a time of crisis?" Silas is clearly trying to help guide me through this. I don't have the capacity to thank him in this moment, but I know I will have to when I can think clearly again.

Blinking through tears that I refuse to let fall, I cling to the last fragment of hope that got me through Halazar. "There is somewhere else."

"Where?"

"The start of a network—a passage out of the city." Close enough to the club for easy access. Not attached, to avoid discovery in case of a raid.

"Out of the city?" He sounds surprised. I nod. I'm glad Arina didn't tell him *everything*. Since Eclipse City borders the sea and river, it's heavily regulated, to maintain Oricalis's iron-fist control of trade.

Silas follows as I lead him away from the pit and narrow alleys that splinter off from the square the Starcrossed Club once stood in. I stop before an inconspicuous metal door, then glance around the alley and up at the windows. No signs of life anywhere. When my attention returns to the door, my chest tightens.

The lock has been smashed in.

I throw it open. It's empty. No supplies. No messages. The hatch in the back has been left sickeningly ajar.

"No . . ." I stagger into the room to get a view of the inside of the hatch. Where there used to be a ladder descending into the tunnels underneath the city is twisted and gnarled metal that ends in rubble. The passage collapsed. "No, no, *no*."

"Maybe they went somewhere else?"

"There is nowhere else." I bite out every word, fighting to keep my voice steady. "This path was our escape route. Our fail-safe. It led to where we had our storehouses of supplies. It would've never been left open like this. If it was compromised . . ." I run a hand through my hair, trying to think of whether Bristara ever said anything about an alternative. I'm sure she had other routes. But where they'd be is a mystery. "Fuck!" I slam my fist into the wall. But the word echoes louder in the small, empty space.

"Clara." Silas is at a loss. He's run out of hope to give.

"I don't know where else they'd go." The weight of the admission chokes me. "If the enforcers knew of this path, I must assume they knew every path." I round to face him. "Did Arina tell you anything else?" Perhaps after I was taken, they correctly assumed there might be a threat to them and left well before the club was destroyed and our passageways raided.

He shakes his head.

"Of course not..." I sigh heavily. The one thing she didn't tell him was the one thing I would've wanted her to say. Arina and the rest might be alive—I choose to believe they are until I know otherwise—but I've no idea how to find them.

"Let's keep looking around," he suggests.

"I promised you we'd get back."

"We will. But we have a bit of time still." Silas clasps my shoulder, and I shift to face him. He wears an encouraging smile. "You've come this far... you'll regret it if you don't try."

I nod, and we emerge back into the alleyway. Every route I can think of leads to a dead end. Every building that was once familiar is distorted. Dull outlines where there was once color and sharpness. Everything becomes a blur, building after building, street after street.

But then Silas's sudden inhale jars me. "Clara—"

He doesn't have time to get another word in. A rough hand clamps over my mouth. Panic and anger rush through my veins as I'm snatched off the street and dragged into an alley.

I grab the offender's thumb and use it as leverage to rip his hand away from my face. I might still be recovering from the torture and neglect of Halazar, but I'm still the same Clara who grew up on these streets. Years of survival in Eclipse City have honed my instincts to a deadly edge that can never be dulled.

Hand at my hip, cards fly from my deck. I spin, ready to strike.

Thank the Twenty I don't.

"Gregor?" I say with a breathless mixture of shock and relief.

"The one and only." He shifts his left hand away from the deck he always wears strapped to his right biceps and envelops me in his arms. "Sorry for manhandling you. I didn't want to make a scene where others might see."

Human touch still feels like an oddity after my time in Halazar. I don't mind it. I never have. But after months of beatings as my only contact... There's now a stiffness in my shoulders I must consciously relax out of them. I need to force my arms to return Gregor's friendly embrace. I don't want to let Halazar pull me from my friends. I won't. As if knowing all of this, Gregor squeezes me tighter. I try to exhale the last dredges of the prison from my body.

As I pull away, I take stock of him. He's in a familiar, worn-down leather jacket that highlights his broad shoulders and hefty midsection. Thick brown eyebrows shadow his dark bronze–colored eyes. Stubble coats his jaw, set against the pale of his skin, identical to the stubble that coats his head where his hair once was.

"You shaved your head?" I can't stop myself from running my palm over his prickly head.

"You haven't seen me in almost a year and that's what you say?" He gives a full-bellied laugh. "Fuck, Clara. I thought you were dead."

"Me? Never." I grin slightly.

"Half the hair fell out from stress and worry. Figured I'd just shave the rest." He touches the thin layer of fuzz as well. "Whatcha think?"

"Hair or no, you look like the same oaf you've always been." He's got the same goofy oversized smile, which nearly makes me weep with relief at the sight of it.

"But a lovable one at that?" He seeks reassurance he shouldn't need.

"No doubt."

"Damn straight." Gregor steps away, and his entire demeanor shifts when he turns to Silas. The warmth evaporates like gutter water on a summer's day. "You are?"

"A friend," I reassure Gregor. "It's because of him that I was able to get here." Would I have found a way out on my own? Eventually, yes. But Silas certainly helped expedite the process. And I didn't have to risk discovery by doing something rash at Ravin's soiree.

"A story I want to hear. The rest of us will, too."

"The rest of you?" My heart skips a beat.

"Yeah, this way, let's get off the streets first . . . it's best if I don't linger too long."

"Still making trouble?" I fall into step behind him. Silas takes up the rear, though I can sense his hesitation. I try to give him an encouraging look, but he doesn't seem convinced.

"Don't know any other way." Gregor wears a wry grin. "Now, keep your head down; last thing we want is someone else—less friendly—to recognize you. Even with your own hair chopped off." I duck my chin. It takes no small amount of effort to keep my questions silent.

We stay off the main road and keep to the side streets between brick-and-mortar homes. Not a word is exchanged out of an abundance of caution, even though the questions threaten to burst from me. Behind an iron gate is a garden path that leads to a narrow townhome. The front façade is simple, but the building is as stately as the rest in this affluent district. My muscles relax, my pace slows, and the tension seeps from me as I feel the same sense of safety I always had around the Starcrossed Club. I admire the building for a moment, a knot tightening in my chest. Already, it feels like I'm returning home.

We enter into a tight coatroom. As I shut the door, I notice that just above the curved door handle is a four-pointed star stylized in the shape of an X. On the left side of the X is a brass S, on the right a C. The same symbol is inside the silver bracelet I'd gifted Arina when she left for the academy.

"Starcrossed Club," I whisper, running my fingers over the almost insignificant detail that was once my entire world.

"Bristara says we have to keep the spirit alive, somehow," Gregor says warmly, though the words are twinged with sorrow. The club would still be alive and well if not for . . . whatever happened. "Let's go to the lounge. We'll be more comfortable there."

Through the second door and out of the coatroom, the hall splits in two. A narrow, straight staircase rises to the second floor on the left. The right pathway is perforated with doors, ending with one of framed glass that leads to an inner courtyard in the back. The first door to the right of the entry is shut, but the second one we pass is not.

I halt.

It's a galley kitchen. Jura is there, humming to herself the jaunty tunes she picked up from her days working on the riverboats. To think . . . I was once sick of those songs. Now I feel like I've never heard finer music. Her long raven-black hair cascades in waves down her back, the light brown of her skin complementing the richness of her brown eyes. Eyes that now turn to me.

She stops all movement. With a clatter and a crash, the pot she was holding drops to the stove—luckily it wasn't very high to begin with and it leaves only a small splash of red sauce on the tiles. Jura runs to me, throwing her arms around my shoulders. She goes limp as soon as mine wrap around her waist, her knees giving out. But I'm more than happy to support my somewhat dramatic friend.

"Clara! No. No. It couldn't—" She pulls away and grabs my face, eyes widening. "It is. It *is* you. I thought you were dead."

"Told you it was her that escaped." Gregor leans against the doorframe.

"You said you thought I was dead, too." I glance over my shoulder at Gregor.

"Well, I did, until I heard about the escapee." He shrugs. "Couldn't be anyone but you to escape Halazar."

"Word has already spread that widely?" I separate from Jura, my heart sinking.

"Someone escaped Halazar, how could anything else be the talk of the city?" Jura has a point.

"The boat crews down at the docks said they saw someone swimming in the water in the distance—coming from Halazar," Gregor adds. "By the time they called the enforcers, the person was gone. It was all rumors, but I guess the enforcers confirmed the talk. The city has been a mix of high alert and gossip ever since."

Damn it. I don't know why I'd been foolishly hoping that if I escaped the academy I'd somehow be safer in the city. But Ravin said that guards were searching Eclipse City, too . . . The best protection I have still might be my fake nobility and engagement to Kaelis. As nauseating as it is to even think about.

"Gregor has been going out every day looking for you around the old club since." Jura squeezes my hands.

My attention settles on that lovable mountain of muscle, my face easing into a grateful smile. *No wonder he found me . . .* He knew where I'd go. After a year of surviving on my own, I'd almost forgotten how incredible it is to have people look out for you.

But before I can say anything, the stairs sag with slow, uneven steps.

"What's the commotion?"

"Late again," I tut with a heavy layer of sarcasm even though my heart is about to burst. "What am I going to do with you, Twino?"

"No," he breathes. "It couldn't be . . ."

"It is," I assure him loudly. Twino rushes down the stairs as quickly as he can manage, and I move to meet him in the hall. Much like Jura, he stares at me with wide eyes and parted lips. Emerald silks offset the rich brown of his skin. *Good to see he hasn't lost his sense of style amidst the chaos of whatever's happened to them.* "You look like you've seen a ghost."

"I think I have." The tap of his cane accompanies the quick shuffling of his feet. Thin, twisted locs fall from the low bun at the back of his neck. I hold out my arms, embracing him tightly and offering him a moment to stabilize himself following such quick movement. When he's steady, he pulls away, and I get a good look at him. He's just the same as I remember. Probably keeps the same habits, given he was up at this abnormally late—or early—hour.

"I was right," Gregor says to Twino triumphantly. "Pay up."

"Please don't tell me you two placed a bet on me being the one to escape Halazar." I narrow my eyes, glancing between them. My focus sticks on Twino. "And please don't tell me you bet *against* me."

He rubs the back of his neck, looking guilty. I let out a gasp. But before I can playfully chide him, another person interrupts.

"The prodigal child returns at last," a soft voice says from midway up the stairs. I look up. I've always looked up at Bristara—the matron, owner, and original founder of the Starcrossed Club.

She's a towering figure of a woman. Imposing, even though her muscle has lost some definition over the years. Her salt-and-pepper hair is pulled into a tidy bun at the nape of her neck, and she peers down at me over horizontal spectacles with her sharp lilac eyes.

"Hello" is all I can manage to say. I'm left feeling like a child who's been out way past curfew.

"Welcome home, at long last, Clara." Bristara's eyes drift to Silas. He stands a bit taller. "And who is this?"

"He helped me get here." I instantly know she doesn't approve of Silas being in this sanctuary, and I can't keep the defensive edge from my voice. Disappointment from the woman who raised me since I was sixteen is heavy.

"I should . . . give you some space?" Silas shifts awkwardly.

"I think that'd be best." Bristara is a master at keeping her emotions from her voice. A feat I always admired . . . when that coolness wasn't directed at me. "The first door is a small study. You may make use of it." Her attention shifts toward the back of the house, motioning to the last room in the hall. "The rest of us will sojourn to the lounge."

"I'll put on the kettle." The normality of Jura saying so helps calm me. Even though this place isn't the Starcrossed Club that I remember, the people who were the closest to me—who were the soul of the establishment—are here. It already feels like I've been down this hall hundreds of times.

The decor of the lounge is reminiscent of every detail I've seen in my dreams for months. Velvet drapes in deep purple line the entire left wall. A black rug patterned with falling stars cushions my feet as we make our way between two wingback chairs, reminding me surreally of the rug in my room at the academy. The chairs form one side of a square that's completed by two parallel sofas and a large marble fireplace opposite that Twino sets about lighting. Cups dance with Coins, Swords duel with Wands, all around the frame of the fireplace. A globe chandelier of crystal etched with stars casts the room in a warm haze. I know instantly who's behind this design.

"Good to see you haven't lost your aesthetic sensibilities," I voice my earlier thought to Twino.

He straightens and preens, running a hand down his long emerald robe. "Did you ever have any doubt?"

"I've had doubts about many things this past year, and many more after seeing what's left of Starcrossed," I say gravely as I sit.

"I'll get Ren." Gregor moves for the stairs as Bristara enters the lounge. "Ren!" Nothing. "Ren!" Still nothing. "*Ren,* get up! Clara's back."

There's a thundering from above that rumbles down the stairs and appears as a blur of fire-red hair, skidding to a stop in the hallway. I breathe a small sigh of relief as I meet eyes as green as Twino's shirt, framed by freckles. His clothes are loose on his wiry frame and he rubs sleep from his eyes, blinking, staring at me, rubbing, and blinking again.

"Clara?" He bounces over and pulls me into a tight embrace. Ren was the most recent addition to the group. But the moment I knew Twino's relationship with him was serious, he had nothing but my support in joining.

"In the flesh."

"What? But I thought— How?" Ren's questions are punctuated with yawns. He always was the first to bed and first to rouse, sleeping like the dead between sundown and sunup. He sits with Twino opposite me.

"Literally what I was going to ask." Gregor joins them.

"Close the doors, if you please, Jura." Bristara settles herself in a leather wingback at the end of the table in the center of the sitting area as Jura enters from a pocket door that connects the kitchen.

She has a silver platter laden with tea accoutrements and a small plate of her famous lavender cookies—no doubt sourced in part from the courtyard garden I saw earlier. Ren has quite the green thumb. As soon as she sets them on the low table between the sofas, I help myself. Jura does as Bristara instructs and then sits next to me.

Feeling more myself than I have in almost a year after a sip of tea and a bite of cookie and with all my friends around me, I return to the most urgent matter on my mind. Someone is missing. "Arina?"

The five of them share a look that has the cookie falling from between my fingers, clattering across the plate, instantly forgotten.

"The night you were taken . . . enforcers stormed the Starcrossed

Club within an hour of you leaving." Bristara is the one to speak. "We tried to fight, but there were too many and they came prepared."

A sinking feeling pulls me deeper into the cushions. It is all my fault. I know it is . . . *If only I hadn't gone, if only I hadn't played into their trap* runs through my mind, echoed by Bristara's disapproving look.

"They didn't even bother taking the club guests alive." Gregor's hand balls into a fist.

"Arina?" I repeat, softer, weaker, yet more frantic. I want to hear what happened to them, but my sister . . . I must know what happened to my sister.

"It was all we could do to escape. We tried to get as many out as we could, but it was chaos." Jura ducks her chin. "Arina . . . We haven't seen her since right before that night. We thought she was lying low for the first bit after, maybe couldn't risk leaving the academy, but she never came back with the haul she was getting from the academy. Never said anything else."

"I heard she ran. Silas told me she was sent to a mill; that was the 'official story.'" I can hear the desperation in my own voice as it quivers up slightly at the end of the statement, nearly making it a question. Though everything I want to ask is left unsaid. They already know.

"We heard as much, too." Twino's tone gives away nothing, and that causes my panic to rise further. "So we looked into it."

"And?"

Twino looks to Bristara. The rest of them follow, pained expressions that tell me everything. The silence that fills the air is as grim as death.

"*And?*" I repeat.

"According to rumors that reached our ears, and what records we could find, she died." Bristara remains expressionless as she delivers the news.

The color drains from my face. Despair strikes me like a thousand panes of glass shattering. Blood rushes through my ears, deafening me. My fingers grow numb again. And yet, my heart doesn't seem to beat at all. It was halted by the one scrap of hope I have left.

"Did you find a body?"

"No." Twino shakes his head.

"Then there's a chance," I insist.

"Clara . . . You know Arina," Gregor says softly, pain lacing tightly between his words. Even though it's been a year, his eyes shine with pain. "She was precocious, bold, arrogant, and had a streak of doing whatever in the four suits she wanted. If she was alive, we'd know—either because we'd hear of it, or she'd come back."

"Maybe not, if she thought coming would be dangerous."

"Not for this long," Bristara says grimly.

"They could have her captive."

"You know Oricalis, they don't take people alive." Every word Bristara says is a separate blow.

"They kept me alive."

"Curious, that." Her eyes narrow slightly. I can't deal with Bristara's skepticism. Not now.

"*There is a chance.*" My words are like a dagger point at the throat of any who'd dare say otherwise. Bristara and I lock glares. But, finally, she says nothing. "Arina is just as strong as I am, and you all know it. Until I see her bones, until her ashes pass through my fingers, there is a chance she lives."

"We *have* looked for her," Jura offers. "And we still keep an eye out, of course."

"Good. I have a lead of my own to follow." I stand. "And it's back in Arcana Academy."

CHAPTER 24

"What?" Gregor balks. "You were in the academy?"

"Infiltrating it?" Jura clarifies.

"Sort of . . . as a student," I correct.

Ren scrunches his face in disgust. "I thought you'd be lying low since escaping. Not going straight into the enemy's lair."

"Why would you join as a student?" Gregor asks.

"It was safer, at the time." I don't know how much I can bear to explain, even though I know I owe them the truth. Unexpectedly, Twino saves me from elaborating.

"*Why* would you go back?" Twino focuses on what's ahead, rather than what's already happened.

"The last place anyone knows for sure Arina was is the academy. Which means that's going to be the place I'll find the start of any trail." *There's one person who would know the truth, and this time I'm going to* make *him talk.*

"Do not go back there, Clara. You know what your mother said about entering the fortress. Don't make her memory endure a second daughter ignoring her warnings." Bristara says it flatly, but I can hear the hint of scolding in her voice. She knew Mother. Not overly well. But was close enough to her that Bristara knew of the tunnels in the mountains—where she ultimately found Arina and me one day and offered us a place in the club.

"My mother is dead." I don't shout or whine. I'm stating a simple fact. Yet, for some reason, it scatters their gazes—all except Bristara. She continues to stare at me calmly. "Whatever she did or did not want for Arina and me died with her."

"Honor her wishes and heed her warnings," Bristara says, like she was the one my mother told those wishes and warnings to.

"Arina is all I have left. I'm not ignoring any chance I have to find her."

"What about *this* family?" Bristara motions to everyone seated. None of them looks my way.

My stomach knots. "You all know . . . I . . ."

"You must find her," Twino finishes for me. "We don't abandon family, by blood or by bond."

The rest of them nod. But Bristara seems unconvinced. She continues to pierce me with that unyielding expression of hers. I don't flinch, and I don't back down. I might have a lot of shortcomings. I can be brash and bold. I can rush in, and I can say too much when emotions run high.

But no one, *no one*, can ever claim that I am not loyal to those I love.

"I'll come back," I say, even though I'm not sure when I'll be able to keep that promise . . . But Arina found a way out of the school, one I'll eventually find, too, with or without Silas's help. I start for the door.

"Wait." Jura stands, rushes into the kitchen, and returns with a bundle of cloth-wrapped cookies. "Be safe, please. We understand you need to find her. But don't forget we thought we lost both of you. You already came back from the dead. Don't die on us again."

"Never." I kiss both her cheeks and pocket the small bundle of confections. "Don't weep for an empty coffin," I remind them all with a final pointed look and depart.

But before the door can close, Bristara slides out behind me. I'd hardly heard her stand, much less move. Now we're alone in the hallway.

"You think you can trust this Silas?"

"I do." I keep my voice low so he doesn't overhear. I assume he's still in the front study.

"And you trust your own judgment after what happened with your last job?" The words sting, and I look away, balling my hands into fists and relaxing them. She lets me stew. Then, far gentler, "Clara, I worry for you is all. I worried for you then, and I do now, too. I worry for this home we've managed to rebuild. If we trust the wrong people again . . . there might not be a second chance for any of us."

"I know." I hang my head. "But I had to get out, somehow. I had to find you all and know if—if . . ." *If I truly lost everyone.* I can't finish it.

"Keep a close eye on him." It's half command, half advice.

"Already planned on it."

Her long, slender fingers settle on my shoulders. It's the closest thing to an embrace she's ever given. I always wondered if she knew that I didn't need her to mother me and respected that. I had a mother. I needed a boss.

"For now, keep lying low. Learn what you can. As much as I hate to admit it, you might be right in that the truth of what happened to Arina is in the academy."

"It is." I'm sure of it. "Once I know, I'll return for good."

"See that you do." A brief pause. "And, if you continue ignoring your mother's will and going to the fortress, at least keep your true name a secret." Bristara knowing my true name at all was a sign of her closeness with Mother. Even if they didn't know each other well, Mother clearly had trusted her. So I did as well.

"I always do." With a final nod, I head to the study. Part of me doesn't want to leave them, but I *will* find a way back.

And, for now, I have a prince to interrogate.

I find Silas hunched over a desk that overlooks the front walkway. He closes his journal. He must've already finished his card. "Time to go."

A frown briefly passes over his lips as he stares out the front window and up at the sky. It's still dark, but slivers of dawn are bleeding at the sky's edges. "I suppose it is."

"You said you know the back passages of the academy, right?" I slide up beside him.

"As well as anyone can be expected to, given the nature of the place." He eyes me skeptically.

"Exceptional. I want you to take me as close to Kaelis's apartments as you're able."

He hesitates. "Why?"

"I have some questions for the prince."

"Kaelis doesn't take kindly to people showing up unannounced." Silas slowly puts his inking tools back into his satchel. It's so obvious he's stalling.

"So I've noticed. But that'll be between Kaelis and me. Get me as close as you can without him suspecting you were involved." I amend my earlier statement. Silas has been good to me. The last thing I want is to bring the misfortune of Kaelis's wrath upon him. Silas is worth more to me as an unknown ally. I grab his wrist gently, reassuring him. "Kaelis won't know you helped me. I already have some idea of how to get to his apartments, so he won't suspect a thing. I appreciate what you've done for me tonight; I won't repay your kindness by putting you in danger."

Silas sighs softly and then turns his hand palm up and pulls his arm so my fingers slide up his wrist and into his palm. He holds my hand with a warm and steady presence. "Very well."

Without another word, he grabs the card he placed into his pocket earlier in the academy. The world distorts and folds into the magic circle that appears around our feet. In an instant, the cozy townhome is replaced by the ever-oppressive gloom of the academy. I don't recognize the office we've appeared into, but judging from the thick curtains of cobwebs that serve as the only window coverings and the layer of dust that blurs the details of two rose motifs at the window's corners, I'd say that it's been abandoned for some time.

"I should get back," Silas says but doesn't move.

"You should." Now that I'm here, the simmering rage in my veins at Arina's disappearance has sparked into a fire threatening to consume me if I don't unleash it on Kaelis.

Silas moves toward one of two doors in the office, stops, and points at the other. "We're in the professors' wing; his apartments are not far. Through there, straight, up the stairs, right, down the hall, and then out to the bridge."

"Thank you." I mean it.

He nods, hovering in the frame of the door he's opened. For a breath, he holds me with an unreadable stare. "If you need me, Clara, you know how to find me."

The offer startles me. But not so much that I can't say, "I appreciate that. And much the same to you."

We both depart in our opposite directions.

My footsteps echo through these familiar yet unwelcoming halls with an agitated and purposeful rhythm. Just as Silas instructed, I make my way to the bridge that connects the heart of the academy with Kaelis's tower. Two Stellis remain positioned at the opposite doorway, and they eye me warily, armor gleaming under the two sconces whose firelight rages against the mountain winds.

I ready excuses, barters, bribes, and even my magic to fight . . . if that's what it takes to get me inside. But neither guard tries to stop me. They want to. I can feel it in their stares. The way they hover. Their hands at the ready by swords. But neither even flinches.

The mere idea that Kaelis has told them that I am welcome here—that I may come and go to his chambers as I please—makes me inexplicably angry. This is something I can use to my advantage, eventually . . . when I have a clearer head.

For now I waste no time retracing the path in reverse that Kaelis led me on the last time I was here. The doors to his bedroom tower before me, massive and imposing. I don't even bother knocking and push them open, surprised to find them unlocked after Ravin blew them down.

Kaelis lounges on one of the sofas before the fire he'd pinned me next to, facing the doors. The poker is once more taken from its place. He passes it from hand to hand, swinging it to point in my direction.

"I knew you would come." An air of power clings to him. He is probably trying to seem mysterious. But all I see is arrogance.

"Fuck you." Not my most eloquent moment. But barely contained, shaking-in-my-boots-because-I'm-one-more-smart-ass-remark-from-murderous rage is rarely eloquent.

"You know, at first, I thought that'd be a punishment worse than Halazar. But I've begun to wonder what you're like in bed. Do you bring that same tenacity to your endeavors as a lover? Are you one to break? Or do you enjoy an opportunity to submit when you strive so hard to control everything around you?" He looks at me through the shadows cast by his hair falling into his face.

"I'd rather die."

"Your foreplay could use some work."

I am struggling to keep my voice steady. He's just doing this to get a rise out of me.

"Arina." Her name is the only thing I can confidently manage.

"Who?" His brow furrows, and I honestly can't tell if he's doing this intentionally. I'd hardly be surprised if he hasn't paid her any mind and has completely forgotten her since our last encounter. I'd also hardly be surprised if he was just toying with me.

I stalk over to his sitting area, falling into the sofa opposite. I spread my knees wide and lean back, trying to take up as much space as possible, and claim what's his as mine.

"My friend. The one who was helping steal academy supplies. Who would ferry them out through a secret passage, who I'm so, *so* sure you knew of because she disappeared not long after I was captured." If Kaelis orchestrated locking me up, then why not capture Arina in the chaos of the same night he brought down the Starcrossed Club? Then he would've also known to use her to further motivate me to escape Halazar and continue playing into his grand schemes. It all makes so much sense. "The woman whose name you ripped from me by force in Halazar for no other reason than to torment me—*because you could*. I know you know who I'm talking about because you control this whole place like it's your own little kingdom; you *know* there were runners last year and she was one of them." My words grow rougher. Colder. They're like a saw through ice. I'm done being fucked with. "Where. Is. She?"

"Ah, *right,* after our last encounter I did look into this, as you clearly won't let it lie." Kaelis stands, returns the poker to its place, and starts toward a door in the back corner by the windows. "Come."

"To where?" I don't move.

"To show you the records. I assume you will not take my word for what happened. So . . ." He motions to the door, and I reluctantly stand, following.

Kaelis leads me into an adjoining study. Books upon books line the three walls that are not a massive window overlooking city and sea. They pile around a lonely settee where an all-black cat lifts its fluffy head, blinking dully at us.

"You have a cat?" For some reason, that's all I can focus on. Finding another sign of life in these dreary, cold apartments is startling.

"Why does it surprise you?" He goes to the center of the room, where a large desk dominates. His every movement is calculated and purposeful as he shifts through papers in a drawer.

"Because you . . . you're . . ."

Kaelis pauses, hand splayed on the desk. "The second, void-born prince who's incapable of human affection?"

"Yes." If it's obvious to him, I'm not going to deny it.

He snorts. I can't tell if it's bitter amusement or an appreciation for my directness. "Her name is Priss."

"Priss," I repeat, still in shock.

"It's a perfectly acceptable name for a cat."

"I never said it wasn't."

"Your face said it for you." He puts his back to me and goes to one of the shelves behind the desk. Long, elegant fingers trail along the spines of books. He selects one, flips through it.

I'm taken aback by the surreal nature of being in Prince Kaelis's personal study . . . now scratching *his cat's* chin. Priss is a ball of long, silken fur. Friendly with a purr-box that takes no time to activate. She might have Kaelis's severe all-black look with resting sassy eyes. But unlike him, she's nothing but sweetness inside.

"Here." Kaelis points to one of the pages. "Once you brought her up again, asking where she was, it did jolt a memory of three initiates going missing last year. Your Arina was recorded alongside them as unauthorized departures from the academy. Runners. An investigation was launched, of course. We found her and sent her to a mill. She was declared dead before winter was over."

It's similar to what Myrion, Silas, and the club all said, giving credence to Kaelis's claims.

My fingers pause. Priss lets out an indignant meow. "What happened to her body?" The question quivers slightly.

"Would you like the official answer? Or the truth?"

I straighten and lock eyes with Kaelis. What an odd, uncharacteristic thing to offer . . . "The truth. Always the truth, Kaelis."

"Officially, parts of her body—enough to 'identify' her—were pulled from the wreckage of the explosion. They were put in the mass grave by the mill." Explosions are not uncommon at mills, given how reactive the magic in the powders can be during processing. "Unofficially, no body was ever found."

The mantra of the club echoes in my mind: *Don't weep for an empty coffin.* "What about the other two who escaped with her?"

"One left earlier in the year. They were also apprehended and are accounted for at the mill." Kaelis clearly expects what I'd ask next and is ready. "The other initiate was never found."

Arina might have been caught getting someone else out . . . "What was their name? The other initiate?"

"Selina Guellith."

I don't recognize the name. Whoever this person was, Arina never mentioned them to me. *Could be a lead in the future, perhaps. I'll mention it to the club when I see them next...* "Was another search launched to try to find Arina after she escaped the mill?"

"Secretly, yes." They wouldn't advertise that someone escaped from the mill. "And, before you ask, that search ended a few months ago. She wasn't found."

Then there's a chance. I hide my swelling hope and excitement with a dull tone and expression. "I'm shocked they're not continuing to hunt to the ends of the world. Your enforcers would lead one to think a single missing Arcanist could be the undoing of Oricalis."

"They are not *my* enforcers." It is his voice now that is as cold as winter.

The harshness in his tone stuns me to a brief silence. I resume scratching Priss as a thousand thoughts fly through my mind. In so doing, I lose track of Kaelis for a moment. He's looming over me when my awareness next returns. I narrow my eyes at him. "What?"

"Who was she?" Kaelis still doesn't seem to recognize any similarities between Arina and me. I'm grateful that he seems to pay more attention to names on paper than actual faces.

"Is," I correct him, still not ready to admit to the possibility of anything else.

"*Is* she?" he relents.

"I told you, a friend. Nothing more."

"I can help you find her," he claims. But I don't believe it for a second. If he could find Arina, he would've by now. Arina has always been slippery. If anyone could flee a mill and keep herself hidden for months, it would be her. *But where would she go, if not back to Eclipse City and the club?* The question is as intriguing as it is maddening... and frightening.

"Oh, like you've 'helped' me already?" I challenge, to shift the topic from Arina. I wish I were a little bit taller so I could look him evenly in the eyes. I hate feeling like my stature keeps me from being on equal footing with him.

"I took you out of Halazar, didn't I?"

"You don't get to make a problem and then take credit for fixing it!" I prod him in the chest. He doesn't so much as flinch.

"*Make* a problem?" Without warning, his fingers close around mine, holding my hand tightly. "Didn't you 'make' that problem yourself when you decided to illegally ink and sell cards?"

"Perhaps if you and your family didn't feel the need to control every last Arcanist to ever breathe in the Oricalis Kingdom, then—"

He has yet to release my hand, but with his other he reaches up and grabs my face, fingers curling around the back of my neck. I had already been looking directly at him, but now I lack any choice. Our noses nearly touch.

"I had no choice. I had to find *you*."

"Me?" I blink.

"Yes, you, and all the other nineteen Majors." It sounds a bit like he's backtracking. *Find you* was said with such purpose. As if I'm different, somehow.

"Once more, back to this children's story about the World." I narrow my eyes at him. Silas believed in this story. *Prove it*, I challenge Kaelis without saying the words.

"If only it were," he says softly. His gaze drifts beyond the entry of his study. "Perhaps I should show you."

"Show me what?"

Kaelis releases me and steps away. "Come, and I'll take you to the place where everything you know met its beginning, and will soon meet its end."

CHAPTER 25

I consider saying no. The last thing I want to do right now is follow Kaelis anywhere. But saying no is a luxury I don't have . . . not if I'm being sensible about my predicament and what is most likely to yield information I need. And my better sense has left me too often in dealing with this prince. Bristara is right—*I need to pull myself together.* She didn't say it in as few words, but I know her well enough to hear it without her saying it.

"Fine," I say begrudgingly.

We cross through the main bedroom to the exact opposite corner. He opens a side door neatly tucked into the stately molding. I'm met with a perfectly normal—by a prince's standards, at least—dressing room. Decadence drips from floor to ceiling, with tailored fabrics on the walls and plush velvet chairs. A long table stretches down the center, its polished surface gleaming under the light of a chandelier.

"Does dressing exhaust you so much that you have to sit down in the midst of doing it?" I nod at the chairs.

"It's exhausting being this good-looking."

A snort of amusement escapes me. I quickly scowl at the look of triumph that Kaelis wears.

"'Good-looking' for someone who seems to only dress in the dark. Is everything black and gray because you don't have to think about it matching?" I run my fingers along the garments hanging on the racks. If my grubby hands touching his clothes bothers him, he doesn't let it show.

"I have a look, and it suits me."

I pause, getting a glimpse of an equally lavish bathroom through a cracked door. The door stands between rows of shelves holding everything from perfume bottles to jewels of state. But the bathroom isn't what distracts me, nor is it the other locked door that Kaelis is moving toward. I can't help myself; I lift one of the dark gray crowns off its place, shift over to a mirror, and settle it upon my brow.

The circlet, inlaid with obsidian stones, looks utterly out of place on me, and not just because it's a little too big. My cheeks are still slightly sunken, and my eyes and hair lack their luster. I *look* like a pauper wearing a prince's crown.

"Are you that excited to wed me and claim your crown as princess?" Kaelis's movements are soundless. Without warning, he's at my side again. His fingers curl around my shoulders, and, for a shared breath, we both occupy the mirror. Him behind me, so close that I can smell the scent that must've come out of one of these crystal perfume bottles.

"Hardly." I remove the crown and settle it back on its shelf.

The prince leans in, tilting his face toward me, as if he were about to kiss me on the cheek. I inhale slowly, about to tell him off yet again, but he whispers, "A crown suits you, you know."

"You're a wretched liar." My words are even and dry. They don't betray the treacherous quickening of my heart.

Kaelis releases me with a low laugh that I feel almost as if it were in my own chest. "That usually works on most women."

I turn, glaring up at him. "I've no interest in your crowns or titles . . . or previous escapades with women or men or whomever else."

"I know, and it's quite refreshing." He steps away. "It did suit you, though, as queen of the rats."

I make a noise of disgust.

Kaelis produces an intricate silver key from his coat pocket and unlocks another tucked-away door that I hadn't noticed on entry with a soft click. The dimly lit passage beyond beckons, and Kaelis takes the lead. Once more, I follow him into the unknown.

The passage is straightforward. A downward slope, a turn, another, straight on again. I can taste the warm summer air before I see the narrow, arched windows that line the left and right sides. They offer glimpses of the mist below the academy that consumes its base, and of the main structure ahead of us.

"We're inside the bridge to your apartments," I realize as I get my bearings. Kaelis nods. "Why not just walk across the top?"

"You think I want everyone to know all of my comings and goings?" He glances back with a sly smile. "I'd lose most of my air of mystery if I can't be seen popping up at random places throughout the academy, with everyone unable to figure out how I got there."

He seems rather proud of this and says it like it's all a game. But all I hear is: *I can be anywhere, and everywhere.* As if I weren't already always looking over my shoulder.

Back into the bowels of the academy, downward, and downward still, we continue. The walls become rougher and the air cooler, to the point that my breath curls into frosty puffs despite it being summer. We're deep in the cliffs, and I can feel the weight of the stone—of history and magic—all around me.

Finally, the passageway opens to a vast, cavernous room. The only competition for its magnitude is its beauty. Both steal my breath away.

A monumental sculpture of an androgynous figure stands proudly in the center. It's carved from a marble-like stone, primarily alabaster in color, but instead of gray veins roping through it there are streaks of glowing magic, as if the stone is nothing more than a façade for pure power within. The glow of the sculpture, though bright enough to see by, doesn't even touch the highest point of the ceiling.

Their face is one of serenity and ageless wisdom, eyes closed and smile coy. They extend their arms, cradling a globe in their hands on which is rendered in intricate detail all the oceans and continents of our world. Lands I recognize . . . and ones that I have never even imagined.

I'm drawn to the base of the statue. A ring of what appears to be glowing water separates the figure from an outer wall with twenty numbered slots, each clearly crafted to house a card. The meaning is clear.

"Twenty slots, twenty Majors," I murmur, resting my hand in the center one labeled with a 10—the Wheel of Fortune . . . my slot.

"The journey of the Fool. Each encounter exposed the true, magic nature of the world. All must be accounted for before the World might be summoned once more and used." Kaelis speaks quietly, but his voice carries on echoes in the empty space.

I look between him and the statue. "It's real, then." This would truly be an intricate lie if it weren't. Everything he's said, the Majors, how the others acted, what Silas said . . . It's too much evidence stacking up to believe the World is a ruse any longer.

"You stand before the nexus of all power. The one card that matters more than any other. Where everything has ended, begun, and will end, and will begin again. Where kingdoms have risen and fallen. Over and over for time eternal." He looks up at the statue with awe and reverence.

I lean against the base of the sculpture, studying him. "What do you want with the World?"

"What anyone would." He drags his eyes to me, and with them a chill runs down my spine. "To change everything."

Folding my arms, I ask, "Change it to *what*? Does this world not suit you enough as it is?"

A rumble of bitter amusement rises in his chest. The noise coils tension within me. I can't tell if it's arousal . . . or fear. The way he looks at me is as something to be claimed. Possessed. Owned. I tighten my arms slightly around myself, as though I could protect my person from the man who already has me in his palm. *Maybe,* something in me whispers, *he was right about you. Maybe, for once in your life, it'd feel good to submit.* I push the thought violently away and keep my focus.

"No. Not in the slightest." His answer is so simple, raw, and direct, it almost catches me off guard.

"Oh?" I shake my head, and disgust creeps into my words. "The prince with his own castle, who has a direct hand in controlling all the magic of the kingdom, who personally ensures the futures are stolen from every Arcanist, who—"

"Had his own future stolen," Kaelis snaps. I'm startled to silence, and he uses it as an opportunity to speak over whatever thoughts I had that are now lost. "Oh, Clara, you didn't think that highborn and lowborn Arcanists were the only ones who were made to sacrifice futures to the Arcanum Chalice, did you?"

"But you . . ." I honestly thought it'd be the case.

"I am an Arcanist, above and before all else. That puts me in service to the crown and under the laws of the land just as any other." Kaelis closes the gap between us with purposeful steps. For once, I don't feel as if he is pursuing me as a predator . . . but instead as someone trying to meet me as an equal. The idea is so foreign that my mind instantly rejects it. "I was brought to the fortress and, before none but my father, made to give up my future. I surrendered all three cards to the Chalice."

"He forced you to do that, even as a prince? As his own son?"

"I am the spare. I exist as a tool to my father and my brother. To manage their magics, fortify their borders, maintain their trade, and keep them safe." Kaelis comes to a stop before me.

He's telling the truth. That, or he's an even better liar than I ever gave him credit for. But everything in my marrow tells me he's being honest.

"Forgive me if I don't feel sorry for you." I unfold my arms and grip the edge of the pedestal. My gaze is sharp, I know it is, but I do nothing to dull it. He's trying to claim that we have something in common when we don't. "You might be struggling, but it is not the way the rest of us are. You still have spent your days in gilded halls with tables and cups full. You might be seeking freedom, but you aren't just using the cards. You are using *people* to obtain it. You're no better than anyone else in your twisted family."

Kaelis takes a step forward, closing on my personal space once more. His chest swells to the point that I think I am about to see the usually in-control prince lose his temper. But, when he speaks, his words are soft. "And how much worse do you think it was when my father had unfettered access to the world's Arcanists before I was at the helm of this institution? If he made his own son give up his future, do you think he used strangers more gently?"

Realization strikes. "You're not looking for the World for him, are you?" Kaelis simply holds my stare as a response. I'd always assumed the entire royal family to be at the behest of King Naethor Oricalis—operating as one. When he doesn't speak, I fill the silence, waiting for him to tell me I'm wrong. "Maybe your father did task you with finding the World . . . but it's not for him. You're doing it entirely for yourself."

"Precisely. And you are essential to my plans."

"Why *me*?" The way he says it further emphasizes that my role in this is more than just my being one of the last, formerly missing Majors.

Kaelis leans forward, forcing me to lean back. His arms frame me. The glow of the statue softens the usually harsh lines of his face.

"You are the Wheel of Fortune, the least understood Major because your power is luck itself—changing fate. That luck has given you the ability to craft any Minor Arcana with any ink."

My escape from Halazar, the inks available to me then . . . even Glavstone giving me fewer and lower quality supplies across the months. My suspicions were right: *It was all a test.*

"Every Major Arcana will ink from these waters a *single* golden card."

"Not silver?" I'd understood silver was the sign of a successful Major card.

"Silver signifies Major cards that can be used. Normal cards. The one inked here is special—*gold*. It is a card that captures the Major's entire essence, and only this card can be used to summon the World itself. These cards can only be inked once, cannot be cast, and there is only ever one in existence. The Arcanist who can place all the Major cards in their slots and offer a vessel for the World to take shape within will be the one to claim its powers." His fingers slide across the grooves of the divot at my side, the one for my card, the Wheel of Fortune. "I have thirteen of these golden cards—soon to be fifteen, when you and Sorza perform your task. I've gathered them either from seeing the individuals through the academy myself or by bringing them here to ink from the waters of the World."

"And the other five?"

"No one has the Star yet. My father has the other four."

"He didn't make you give up your gold cards?" My words are steeped in skepticism.

"They were inked before me, not him, so they fell into my hands. And he thinks them safe with me." Kaelis shrugs in a manner that betrays he finds his father foolish for that thought. "And neither of us can summon the World without all the cards."

"So it's a stalemate," I murmur under my breath. His father demanding the cards could potentially put him at odds with his son who controls all magic. A risk that, unless he was about to use the cards, would not be worth it.

"Which is where you come in. I cannot get these cards for myself, and my father would never give them up. But . . ." He dips his chin slightly. "Never before has there been an inker like you. Never have I met someone so lucky that the only way for even a prince to capture them was with an elaborate trap."

"But only a Major can ink their own card." I remember what the others told me earlier.

"A card that *works*, yes."

"You believe that with my skills, I can make convincing counterfeits of all the four Major Arcana your father has." I'm finally seeing the design of the web I find myself in. "You plan to steal them."

"Very good." The praise rumbles up the back of his throat. My body tries to shiver in response, but I refuse to let it.

"My father will visit on All Coins Day. We'll find an opportunity to get you close to him; he's never without the cards on his person. He'd die before he let someone else hold on to them." Kaelis rolls his eyes. I bite back a remark that killing the king could be a compelling option. "Once you see the cards, I trust you'll be able to make the fakes. I'll give you the rest of the year to perfect your work. Then, at the ball for the Feast of Cups, we'll make the switch. He'll be none the wiser, and I'll have everything I need to call upon the power of the World."

"What about the Star?" The last missing Major.

"I know where the Star is." Kaelis shrugs nonchalantly. "Not something you need to worry about."

"And the 'vessel' for the World?"

"Leave that to me as well."

"If you want me to work with you, you can't leave me in the dark about everything." I frown.

"I'm hardly 'leaving you in the dark' given everything I'm telling you—showing you." He motions to the statue behind me, but I don't turn, keeping my eyes locked with his. "You have a hard enough task ahead of you, I think. Stay focused on that, and when you are successful, we will move on to the next part of the plan."

We. I haven't lost sight of who still holds the power in this arrangement. But . . . something is different about this interaction. Something has shifted between us. He is telling me more. And, if all he says is true, he's letting me know of a treasonous plot.

"Fine," I say, for now. I can research this "vessel" on my own time anyway. I've a lot of information-hunting on the World ahead of me.

"All I need from you are your skills as an inker. Show me what made you so in demand in Eclipse City's underworld." He levels his eyes with mine once more. Even though he's not touching me, I feel him along my entire body. An errant desire to touch him flits through me, and I quickly banish it.

"Did you destroy the Starcrossed Club?" I whisper. It's so easy to blame him for everything, yet every time I try . . . my accusations unravel.

"I never touched it."

Somehow, I continue to believe him. "What's in it for me? If I help you, what do I get out of it?"

"Beyond being engaged to a prince and all the comforts that come with it?"

"You're remaking the world; you can do better than that. I don't even have a guarantee our engagement will stick after you get what you're looking for from me." Every steadying breath nearly has my chest brushing into his. I blame Halazar for how hyperaware I am of his proximity.

"I can give you what you know you always wanted." His eyes are alight with amusement. "A new world, a better one. One where Arcanists are free to do as they please."

I consider it, but only briefly. "Empty promises."

He's not surprised in the slightest by my skepticism. Eyes lazily trail down my face and land on my lips. "What must I do to prove to you that I need not be your enemy?"

I can't stop myself from licking my lips, the attention making me realize how dry they are. "Change your name—your destiny. Give up the Oricalis Kingdom entirely when you remake the world. Shatter it."

"Give me the World, and I will. *Gladly*." His eyes bore a hole straight through me, as if he can see everything I am and have ever been. All my thoughts.

"Arina." I keep my focus. "While I'm helping you, help me find her."

"Done." Given that he offered as much earlier, it's good to see he's consistent.

I search his face. Instinct is screaming not to give in to him. But what other choice do I have? This might be my best path forward in so many ways. "You didn't have anything to do with her disappearance?"

"No, I swear it."

I still don't know if I can trust him. Why would he admit to possibly harming someone who I've made clear is important to me? After all, he needs me, and that truth—if it were true—would result in him losing my compliance. Which also means it'd be pointless to ask outright about my mother.

But I can leverage my proximity to him to continue my own investigations into her disappearance. Like I told Silas, *Use them.* The crown sees us as tools. It's only fair.

If Kaelis is speaking the truth, then he will use the World to rebuild things and make them better. That's the bare minimum outcome. Hopefully my inquiries have led him to believe I have faith in that.

Meanwhile . . . at the very least, I will find out the truth of my mother's death. Uncover what happened to Arina. And find a way to steal the World for myself. That'd be the best outcome.

"So, will you help me?" Kaelis arches a single brow. "No more sparring or resisting, and we work as a team?"

"Very well," I say reluctantly, reminding myself over and over that this is a means to an end. Nothing more.

"Good." Kaelis pushes off the pedestal and his arms glide away, no longer framing me. I'd forgotten how cold this cavern was, and it highlights how warm his body is. He looks me up and down one more time, but there's a shift in his expression. Something more thoughtful. Almost sincere. "Now let's find you something to eat."

"What?" The change in his demeanor has me startled.

"You still look like a breeze might blow you over." He must really believe everything I said and see us as a partnership. "I prefer my women with more substance."

"I don't care how you prefer your women."

"The way you looked at me just now said otherwise." He smirks, and I scowl. Kaelis waits until I open my mouth to tell him off before he speaks again. "Besides, you're not going to prove to all of them just how talented you are if you pass out in your first week, and I know you missed dinner." He must have been looking for me in the main hall. "So come, eat an early breakfast, then rest some before your morning class. We have work to do, you and I. But I will not have you suffering further through it."

"Have I suffered enough already for his highness?" My usual bitterness returns readily.

Kaelis's expression falls and turns serious once more. His hands twitch, as though he wants to ball them into fists. There's rage simmering in his eyes, but not for me . . . *Who?* I wonder.

"I thought we were past this," he mutters.

"You can't sweep a year of Halazar away with a few words."

"*I* never wanted you to suffer there. Were I able to remove you sooner, I would have. But I couldn't risk it before the Fire Festival. The engagement alone wouldn't have been enough. You needed the protections of the academy as an initiate, then student."

Once more, I nearly believe him. If we're to work together, then maybe I *want* to think that I'm not making a deal with my mortal enemy. But I can't let him get the better of me. He's already wormed his way too far under my skin for one interaction.

"Clara—"

"I'd like to leave," I say firmly. I might be his reluctant partner, for now, but I'm not his lapdog. "Show me the way back to the dormitories."

To my surprise, Kaelis does. He guides me through the passageways up to a point at which he ventures no farther. The prince tells me how to find my way from there and leaves me with a respectful tilt of his head. My ears are ringing from the deafening silence and the sense that there is still much left unsaid behind his eyes.

As soon as I get my bearings, I head toward the library instead of the dormitories. It's empty in the small hours of the morning, but the lamps still glow. I hunt for any mention of the World. Mother's stories are alive in my head as I nibble on Jura's cookies in place of the dinner I missed hours ago.

The World . . . It could do anything. Fix everything.

Everything spiraled out of control when Mother died. We lived on the streets. Arina and I fought and stole, breaking almost every law. We became reckless, obsessed with Mother's murderer. But, with this, *I could bring Mother back.* And if she were here again, somehow, I know it'd all make sense. That one thought has me up past the sunrise and dragging my feet to classes.

CHAPTER 26

Vaduin Thornbrow, head professor of wielding, strolls down the center of his classroom. His hands are gathered at the small of his back. His mere presence commands silence. And his eyes, sharper than a rapier's edge, slice across the room.

He knows exactly what he's doing. We sit around him in a ring, no desks; I'm more relaxed in my chair than the rest. I allow him his survey and remain unflinching in the wake of his assessment. In a way, he reminds me of Bristara. I overheard the other students talking about how this is only his second year at the academy. So I wonder if this imposing display is compensating for people thinking he hasn't yet earned—or isn't worthy of—his position.

This is my fourth class with him, and today is the first day he seems ready for us to move on from the mere theory of wielding. It's surreal to think two weeks have slipped by already. There's a monotony to the flow of classes that I've found myself drawn into. Acting like a normal initiate to keep my cover has resulted in me feeling very much like nothing more than that.

"Wielding is not just about skill, but about your connection to the cards," he begins, voice resonant and deep. "You summon the cards you need from your deck with nothing but your senses—by your power calling to that which has been imbued in the paper.

"To ink cards is to channel the primal forces of nature on ink and paper.

"To read cards is to surrender to the fates that guide your hand.

"To wield cards is to make the true power of the undercurrents of this world unquestioningly your own."

It seems Kaelis isn't the only one who has a taste for the dramatic in this academy.

"I saw each of you attempt wielding at the Fire Festival, and I must say, you are all lacking." He turns about the room, leaving no one out of the assessment. Myself included—which I take mild offense to. "All Coins Day will be here before you know it. It's possible you will manage to earn a coin or two from a house without skill in wielding, depending on how you approach the day. You can present a good showing with inking or reading alone. But there is no escaping the Three of Swords Trials. One of those trials will be a duel. Initiates will be paired against each other, so it is only possible for half of all initiates to pass the wielding portion of the trials."

Eza's eyes dart to me at the mention of duels. I don't shy away from his stare, and I run my fingers over the short stack of cards in my lap, which had been waiting on each of our chairs when we entered—the Ace, Two, and Three of each Minor Arcana. I knew what the cards were instantly by touching the small deck.

"We shall begin by practicing summoning from the deck," Vaduin continues. Eza is the first to look back at him, and I do as well only when Eza's eyes are off me. "Hold the cards before you."

Obediently, all the initiates balance the short stack on their open palm, myself included.

"Ace of Cups," Vaduin declares.

As students begin concentrating, they murmur and furrow their brows. Many look as though their stomachs are in knots. Some have their mouths twisted in what one could misinterpret as pain.

I lift my right hand, and with a little wave of my fingers, the Ace rises from the deck, hovering in midair.

"Redwin." Vaduin's eyes rest solely on me. "Without movement."

"Pardon?" I relax my focus and allow the Ace to settle back on the deck.

Vaduin approaches slowly, looking down at me. "Summon the card *without* movement. Two of Swords."

"What does it matter if I use movement or not?" I ask as the rest of the students are already focusing on their decks. Or pretending to. My question has them looking at me through bangs and lashes.

"Excuse me?" A frown quirks Vaduin's lips.

"What does it matter if I summon the cards with movement or not, as long as they're summoned?"

He straightens slightly, looking down his nose at me. "Two of Swords," he repeats coldly. Pursing my lips, I raise my right hand again, determined not to let him get the better of me. His hand moves faster than a viper. Cold fingers wrap around my wrist as he leans over and pierces me with his emerald eyes. "Two of Swords."

Fighting a frown of my own, I stare at the deck, willing the card to move. It quivers, nearly sliding out. The cards part and—

Tumble to the floor, scattering. Paper sliding against stone has never been so loud, or so mortifying. Never have the cards been rebellious toward me.

"*That* is why." Vaduin releases me. "Wielding is about connecting your raw essence with your deck. If you rely on movement, then you're not fully allowing yourself to find that connection. Moreover, you'll give your enemies an easy way to incapacitate you."

Like Eza, Cael, and Nidus . . . Damn it. I hate that he's right. Cael and Nidus must have taken notes on how I was wielding during the Fire Festival and reported back to Eza as they hatched their plan. I try to stop my eyes from darting back to Eza and fail. He's grinning like a fool.

The sick, sinking feeling overtaking me is made worse when Vaduin adds, "Besides, movements like that make you look like an illegal Arcanist running from enforcers on the street. Those with *proper train-*

ing, as someone of your status should have, would never." The way he holds my gaze. The sharpness in the words leaves nothing but silence in their wake.

It's broken when another initiate, Marlon, mutters something to a man at his side about how "The prince's whore is probably as messy in the bedroom as she is with her tarot."

My fist closes around the half of the deck still in my palm to the point that it shakes. I bite back a retort. A *lady* wouldn't *lower herself* to acknowledging the jab. But, by the Twenty, I wish I could just let out that illegal Arcanist in me that Vaduin is so ready to insult.

"Again, Redwin. But this time without your embellishments." Vaduin acts like he didn't hear Marlon, even though there's no way he didn't. "Three of Wands," he calls to the class.

I quickly collect the cards that scattered across the floor. The deck is heavy in my hand now. The ease, the thrill, and any joy I might have felt at wielding is gone. I wedge the fingertips of my hand not holding the deck under my thigh and give the cards all my focus. The Three of Wands trembles. Hesitates. Sweat beads on my forehead. *Rise, damn you.*

Shuddering, slowly, almost begrudgingly, it does. Never has a victory felt so small or empty.

It's like I walk through the academy with one arm tied behind my back and every day is more frustrating than the last because of it. I can't ink or wield any cards higher than the fifth—as it isn't something first years should be able to do. It's outright banned for first years to even attempt to try more advanced cards, to lower the risk of a card reversing from someone reaching for magic more powerful than they can handle. My level of skills would raise too many questions.

The cards I do have access to are like strangers to me. The lines I'm required to draw on them look nothing like the shapes Mother helped me master. The way Vaduin teaches wielding has my mind, magic, and body moving—or not moving—in ways they never have before.

And reading? Four suits, that was always more Arina's thing than mine...

Everything about this place is foreign and uncomfortable. When the second and third years can spare us initiates even a glance, their eyes dissect us with a scrutiny that picks us clean. There's little relief to be found among my peers. Cliques have begun to form, but I don't quite belong to any faction. I'm not "noble enough" to sit among those from the clans, despite Kaelis's lie and my attempts to present myself as a long-lost heiress. However, that same lie also keeps me from the common-born groups. They don't see me as one of them, either.

Haunting me throughout it all are the occasional whispers that I can't ignore, no matter how hard I try. "Have you heard about the escapee from Halazar?" "Didn't the person die in the river?" "The enforcers said no body was retrieved." "How frightening." On and on they go... I refrain from saying a word about the rumors. Even when, one night in the common area, I hear Eza mention it in passing: "It happened right before the Fire Festival. You don't think one of us initiates could be the escapee, do you?" No one seems to pay it any heed, but I swear the gossip gets worse after.

My only reprieve is the unexpected camaraderie with Sorza, Dristin, Luren, and even Kel that I find at mealtimes and in the afternoons. But, come nightfall, I always split apart from them to slip into the quieter halls of the academy—into those unlit and shadowed passages I once found oppressive but that now feel like sanctuary.

Away from everyone's prying eyes, I work on strengthening my body.

I run laps, up three flights of stairs, down three, past four rooms—more and more—until I am dizzy, stumbling, throwing up. I push a desk underneath a window and use a well-wrought curtain rod to hang from and then try to pull my chin over its top edge. I lift and lower fallen statues, returning them to their place, then back to the floor, and then back to their place once more. I move my body until my legs and arms quiver and the rooms spin. But the second I manage to catch my breath, I do it all again.

It hurts. Everything hurts. But the ache is sweeter than the honeyed breakfast that follows every morning. It's as if I can expunge those cursed passages of Halazar as sweat through my pores. As if I can ensure none of the rumors are cast my way if I physically change myself enough from the woman I was when I left the prison.

I intentionally avoid the Sanctum of the Majors, instead making my own areas for study and practice. Facing Eza, Nidus, or Cael again before I've recovered more of my strength isn't worth it. But that doesn't mean I don't run into the other Majors.

Like Silas . . . who I nearly literally run into one night.

I'm mid-run through a corridor that rings the outer edge of the fortress—one of my favorite places to lap—when I hear, "Out for a stroll?"

I come nearly stumbling to a halt.

Silas looks as guilty as a kid filching cookies from the corner of a street cart. "It's just me, no one to worry about."

"You might be a lot to worry about," I say

He relaxes with a slight smile. "I was taking a walk myself."

A walk? This is a lot more than that. Sweat is pouring from me.

"Trying to not feel so . . . pathetic," I admit to myself and him.

"You're anything but."

"You're sweet. And a liar." I grin.

He gives me a look that suggests he's *barely* refraining from rolling his eyes. "Someone 'pathetic' doesn't escape Halazar. Nor hike through Eclipse City when they're skin and bones."

"I do what I must." The compliments are sincere, which makes them mildly uncomfortable.

"What has made you feel pathetic?"

We start walking side by side while I catch my breath and tell him of my struggles with the academy's style of magic. How it's the first time I've ever felt inadequate when it comes to tarot. He has some good pointers for me to try to incorporate both in and out of the classroom.

Silas is surprisingly easy to talk to, so I find I don't mind when he shows up the next night. Or the one after.

I can see what made Arina speak so fondly of him.

The routine becomes a rhythm. One day and then the next, my sole focus is on getting stronger. I can't do anything if I remain as weak as Halazar left me. Finding the truth of Arina and Mother. Escaping the academy. Helping the club. Stealing the World from under Kaelis's nose. None of it will happen until I'm back to my old self.

My focus is so singular, so intense, that I don't realize it's been nearly six weeks since I last heard Kaelis's voice or saw his shadow-clung form slinking through the halls around me. Morning classes; afternoon study in the library with some combination of Luren, Kel, Sorza, and Dristin, or them all; evenings to myself, or training with Silas's help.

But the monotony of my routine is unexpectedly shattered one afternoon—by a box that materializes in my wardrobe. It's so unassuming, a simple slate-gray package with a black silk ribbon tied in a bow.

And a card, with a date, time, and address that I recognize as the regent's manor in Eclipse City, but with no signature.

When I open the box, my stomach sinks. I hook a single finger through a cord of leather strung with a lace so fine it might have been spun from spider-silk.

"Oh, Twenty Majors, no."

CHAPTER 27

I stride across the bridge to Kaelis's apartments. My breasts strain scandalously against the almost-too-small bodice of sculpted black leather covered with a layer of intricate lace and beadwork. Pauldrons of dove and raven feathers cover my shoulders, and from them strips of chiffon cascade down to my ankles, turning me into a living shadow. The skirt is made of silk, two shockingly high slits expose both legs while I walk.

My efforts to regain my strength have been working. I suspect this was made to my first measurements on arrival; everything is a little too tight. My skin swells against its leather-and-lace prison with every breath.

But . . . that's obviously part of the appeal of it. I look delicious, and I know it. So I hold my head high as the Stellis that flank Kaelis's apartments let me pass. Their eyes linger on me, and it's another reminder of how long it's been since anyone last paid that kind of attention to me. A reminder that it feels . . . *good*.

I cross to Kaelis's doors and, briefly, debate knocking. But the high of feeling so exceptional in my skin gets the better of me, and I ultimately decide against it, letting myself in with a bit of a dramatic flair.

I chose wrong.

Kaelis stands by his bed. The dim light of the apartment reflects off his skin, giving it a near-ghostly pallor. He tilts his head at me and pauses, not even troubling himself with the appearance of modesty even though he lacks a shirt and his trousers are dangerously unlaced. The thin, dark line of hair down the center of his stomach draws my attention right to the cords that hang lazily in his unhurried hands.

"If you wanted to see me with my clothes off so badly, you could've asked," he drawls.

"At least you have clothes." I gesture to my cleavage and the exposed midsection between my bodice and skirt, keeping my composure even when my cheeks warm slightly. "Rather than whatever the tailor could throw together from their rubbish bin."

Kaelis tilts his head, dark eyes trailing slowly over my body. One look brings the sensation of unseen hands on my exposed skin. Tiny bumps rise along my flesh, and I am glad for the dim light of the room so he can't see what he can do to me with just a look. Perhaps it's the clothing, but for a moment it doesn't seem like either of us is ourselves. For the first time, I really believe we can slip into these pretend roles.

"The 'rubbish bin' suits you," he says.

I fold my arms and lean against the doorframe, keeping my distance as I compose myself. "I bet you say that to all the women you keep imprisoned for a year and then decide to marry."

"Every last one." He finishes lacing his trousers then pulls his shirt over his head. I get one final glimpse of the muscles in his back shifting as he tugs the fabric down.

Kaelis is a ropy, lean creature. A man of hard contrasts, with a body that looks . . . *aching*. It's the only word that comes to mind to describe him. It's as if he aches for a nourishment food can't give him. He aches for a comfort deeper than the velvets and furs he surrounds himself with. Aches for the touch of something kind . . . or at least of a pleasure deep enough to forget himself for a while. His body is full of valleys and hollows for the shadows that love him. He's so full of voids that I can only imagine he's struggled to fill for years. That, I unexpectedly can relate to.

"We're going to be late if you don't hurry," I point out as he's leisurely affixing his cuff links. I ignore the unexpected sense of camaraderie I feel with him. I know I'm seeing things where they're not.

"A prince is never late. Everyone else is early." Now I know he's moving with deliberate slowness.

"Is that another thing you tell your partners?" I jape. "That you're the last to come?"

"Don't you hope it is?" A satisfied smirk slips as slowly across his lips as the crisp black jacket that slides over his shoulders.

I roll my eyes and force my gaze away, feeling the heat that threatens to rise back to my cheeks unbidden. *Get yourself together, Clara.* The prince might be, objectively, if I had to be completely honest . . . physically appealing. In a sort of strange, unnerving, and yet you can't look away kind of way. He's like some gangly yet stunning, lithe and lethal, bird of prey.

If Kaelis notices that I'm avoiding looking at him, he does me the rare decency of not pointing it out. Instead, he slips into his boots, and with one more adjustment of his jacket, he crosses and offers me his elbow. "Shall we get this over with?"

"Lead on." My fingers slide into the crook of his arm. The warmth of his body envelops me as we walk side by side through the academy.

I ensure I'm half a step closer to him as we stroll by the Stellis, like I'm all too happy to be at his side. We separate some as we navigate rooms and passages to a darkened hall where a carriage and driver wait. I allow him to help me into the carriage, his hands lingering on the small of my back, my hips . . . my thighs. Though the moment the door closes and we're out of sight of the driver, Kaelis sinks back into his seat as if he can't get far enough away from me.

"We're going to need to be convincing," he murmurs. "The other nobles will be watching us. Clan High Lords and Ladies might be there. Word will get back to my father and—"

"Kaelis," I stop him. "Clearly, I know."

It dawns on him that I was already doing what he was in the process of trying to tell me to do. I give him a curl of my crimson-painted lips. He chuckles, low.

"Let's give them a show, then." Kaelis folds his arms, expression turning serious once more. "Here's what you need to know if you're to mingle with the nobility and have any chance of them believing you deserve to be among them . . ."

I bristle at the word "deserve" but keep my mouth shut and stay focused on what Kaelis tells me next. The truth is, I don't know the nuances of clan life or politics. I've spent so much of my life resenting the nobility that I never bothered to learn anything beyond what I thought could be useful to tear them apart.

Now this knowledge is the only thing that's keeping me from being thrown back into Halazar.

The carriage crosses the long bridge that spans where the Farlum River meets the sea and ambles into the city proper. I lean back, watching the glamour of the wealthiest parts of the city glide by. I can feel Kaelis's eyes on me, studying me as he speaks. Perhaps . . . a little more closely than even he intended.

Well, he is the one who picked out the dress. If he's distracted, he has only himself to blame. I sit a little taller and slowly cross and uncross my legs, allowing the hip-height slits to fall open. I think I see him lick his lips, but I can't be sure.

"Are you listening?" His voice is slightly husky.

"I can look out the window and listen at the same time," I assure him.

"Just have better manners when you're around nobility."

"Whenever I see someone worthy of actual nobility, I'll be the portrait of politeness."

He huffs with amusement, rather than offense.

The regent's manor built for Prince Ravin is a grand building, brightly illuminated by spotlight and sconce to put his wealth on display. The carriage slips between sturdy gates and proceeds up a driveway that lazily slopes between gardens. Kaelis is the first to step out of the carriage when it comes to a stop, shooing the driver away so he can help me out himself.

Music and laughter spill from the many open doors that line the wraparound veranda. Paintings are propped on easels, against walls, and on furniture. Sculptures stand among them. Bards roam, and contortionists slowly move their bodies, to the awe and delight of the nobles who mill about. Women and men hang from the ceiling on nothing but strands of silk.

My fingers brush Kaelis's as we ascend the steps. The movement, though unintentional, draws his eyes to mine.

"I have you," he whispers, fingers slipping between my own. There's something in his eyes that makes me feel . . . safe. "Just follow my lead, and I'll make sure no harm comes to you tonight."

"I won't let either of us down." My grip tightens on him. I don't think I imagine a soft sigh and a slowing of his breath. But neither of us lingers long in the moment.

We're swept into the currents of the soiree. Kaelis moves us from one room to the next. His hand is always on my person. Hot on my thigh. Caressing up my side, dangerously high on my ribs, as he introduces me casually to people we pass. I don't miss the occasional chatter about someone escaping Halazar, though it seems none of the nobility is too concerned about it. After two months of no leads on the escapee, the enthusiasm for the mystery is dying down.

I'm about to say that I think it's going well . . . when Ravin appears.

"Clara, Kaelis! *So glad* you both could make it." His dark eyes are nearly black in the dim light of the veranda.

"Wouldn't miss it." I smile, shifting a bit closer to Kaelis for emphasis. "*We* wouldn't miss it."

"Indeed," Kaelis agrees, pulling me tighter. "Where's Leigh?"

Leigh Strongborn Oricalis. *The Wind's Bane,* they call her. She's a warrior rumored to be so fierce that she can go toe to toe with even the most skilled Arcanist despite possessing no magic herself.

"Oh, you know how she is." Ravin shrugs and laughs. "These parties aren't much her thing. She's back in the stables with her stallion, I think." A pause. His eyes dart to me. "No hidden meaning in that. She loves her horse more than most people."

"And loves her falcon at least double as much as her horse," Kaelis adds. "Perhaps more than even you, brother."

Ravin brings a hand to his chest, feigning injury. "You wound me. Though I doubt you're wrong. Not all of us can be as deeply, madly in love as the two of you. Or as well matched. A love story for the ages, they're calling it. One of the few things that the nobles seem to be more eager to gossip about than the Halazar escapee." Ravin's eyes dart to mine, gleaming.

I do nothing but smile politely. Kaelis attempts the same. I think, at least . . . It looks more like a sneer.

"Oh, Clara. I've a special guest I'd like you to meet." Ravin's words are said lightly enough . . . but there's still that look in the firstborn prince's eyes that's putting me further on edge. He shifts back, waving someone over.

That's when I see him.

Liam.

The past I thought I'd long buried and the future I killed suddenly stands before me. His bright blue eyes are as vibrant as I remember—as they were in the iteration of him in the Arcanum Chalice. Those blue eyes lock on to mine, and I feel my hand go limp at Kaelis's hip. It'd fall away if the prince didn't pull me closer, jolting me to the present.

"Clara?" Liam exhales. The sound of my name is a surprise. It somehow encapsulates the raw, aching truth of everything—*so damn much*—left unsaid between us.

A woman stands beside him, her golden eyes darting between her betrothed and me. I remember her. Her fiery hair spun into tight curls. The way she pins little gemstones through her tresses like the stars of her clan's namesake. I remember everything down to the shining ring on her finger.

"Liam?" she probes gently.

"Yes." Liam clears his throat and finally tears his attention from me to look at her. "Elara, my love, this is Clara Ch—"

"Redwin," I interject hastily. The past has finally loosened its grip on my throat enough for me to speak. I see Liam's brows briefly furrow. But it's hardly noticeable, since I keep the focus on me. "It's Redwin now that I've uncovered my lineage, thanks to the prince—Clara Redwin."

"*Lady* Clara Redwin," Kaelis adds firmly.

"An old acquaintance," I continue. "Liam knew me before my family history was discovered," I try to quickly explain, shoving my true name as far as possible from the conversation. I'd forgotten I'd told Liam the Chevalyer name—something I should've never trusted him with. I did stupid things when I thought I'd met the love of my life at seventeen.

"Yes, I knew her back from my days on Silver Street." Liam's tone is neutral, which is a relief, because it betrays nothing of our deeper history. I silently hope that if he held any love or fondness for me at all, he picks up on the need for discretion when it comes to everything about me. Did he even know I was in Halazar? The only safe thing for me to do is assume he has more than enough information to damn me.

"Ah, yes." Elara gives me a practiced smile and politely extends her hand. "Liam mentioned you."

What does that mean?

"Oh, did he now?" Ravin seems utterly delighted as I take Elara's hand. "Clara is quite unforgettable. How else could she ensnare my brother? Though, I suppose her delicious, story-worthy history helps her allure."

"'Ensnare' . . ." Liam breathes. "The woman engaged to the prince . . . is you?"

I nod. My throat is gummy.

"Oh, please accept my warmest congratulations." Elara beams. I can't tell if her obliviousness is intentional.

"Thank you," I say.

"Yes, congratulations," Liam clearly forces himself to say.

You were the one who left me, I want to scream. But I can only smile because of this game of pretend I'm stuck in.

Kaelis remains silent. But his hand on my hip might as well be burning a hole through my flesh. His energy shifted at the mere sight of Liam.

"Please excuse me, I'm quite parched." I step away, freeing myself from Kaelis and the whole circumstance.

One room. Then the next. Another. A stairway to the second floor and past some minstrels and a couple who sneaked away into a coat closet they forgot to close.

I can't breathe. Every strap of leather is constricting me. *All this time I thought of you. It was you I wanted. Only you.* I can hear Liam's voice from the Arcanum Chalice still inside me. As if he's still there. Still a part of what could be . . .

Footsteps have me slowly unwrapping my arms from around myself. I'd wound them so tightly, as if I could ward away all my racing thoughts and find some comfort. I turn, part of me hoping to see Liam there.

Though I know it's not him by the pace and gait. How have I already learned what the prince's footsteps sound like?

"I don't think this is where you'll find drinks," Kaelis says slowly, motioning to the canvases that surround me. The spotlights on the ceiling cast his face in dramatic shadow.

"I got lost."

"You ran."

Frustration and embarrassment tighten my chest. "I made a strategic retreat. I didn't want him saying something he shouldn't."

The gap between us closes to almost nothing. Kaelis looks down at me. Every light and shadow frames his sharp features more elegantly than any statue on display.

"He knows too much." It sounds like a threat.

"He won't say anything," I assure Kaelis.

"Even if Liam won't"—Kaelis's voice dips low at Liam's name—"Ravin will see this as a victory. He suspects you, for good reason, and if he gets any proof you're not a noble as we say—"

"Liam will say nothing," I insist. "And I'm not going to give him proof." I can hear the accusation in Kaelis's voice.

"Your actions say otherwise." There's fire in those dark eyes. "You still love that man, don't you?"

"Hardly," I say bitterly. Defiant to the pull of my own emotions. "He's nothing but an old wound."

"One that won't close or mend." Kaelis is so confident, and I hate how right he is. I glance away, but my attention is drawn back as his knuckles graze up my arm, brushing against my cheek. "How many wounds do you have that you just let bleed, Clara?"

His words are little more than a whisper. The pad of his thumb grazes against my lower lip. I fight a quiver and lose.

"How many wounds do *you* have?" Turning the question back to him is a weak retort and I know it. As weak as my knees feel.

"Enough that I'll remake the whole world to fix them." His voice is deep. I didn't expect him to answer.

From the corner of my eye, I see a figure appear in the doorframe. An all-too-familiar visage I'd know anywhere—from my sweetest dreams, my worst nightmares. Liam's eyes are searching. He came alone, no doubt with endless questions that mirror my own. This could be our moment to air it all.

But what could he say that would make it better? There are no excuses.

Panic and anger race through me. Part of me doesn't want to be seen like this with Kaelis. Another part wants Liam to know that I don't care about him any longer. The nasty urge to hurt him like he hurt me wins. I reach for Kaelis. My hand slips around his neck, and I pull him to me. My lips find his in a sudden and fierce kiss.

Kaelis stiffens, and I grab his hair. *Don't you dare pull away,* I try to convey with the grip I have on his waist that wanders toward his ass. But the prince surprises me by melting into the kiss. His hand falls from my face, and he envelops me in his arms. Pulls me closer.

I feel every inch of that hard body I caught a glimpse of earlier. The ache the sight of it filled me with is palpable now. It's alive in me. I'm yearning for something to make me *real* after a year of cold captivity. The touch I was so sensitive to weeks ago now overwhelms me. Without my permission, the world falls away—and Liam with it.

There's a clatter as one of the paintings falls. The easel topples over with it. My back hits the wall.

Kaelis's tongue is in my mouth. He kisses me like he's been waiting years for this. My leg rises to wrap around his upper thigh, my skirt hiking up dangerously high. The prince bites my lower lip with a low growl.

I can hardly breathe. He rolls his hips into me and I shudder. *Fuck.* I hate this. I hate how good it feels. How badly I want to be touched, and how I had no idea. But what I hate most of all is that it's *Kaelis* sparking these sensations.

Kaelis finally pulls away, and I open my eyes to see him staring attentively down at me. We're both breathless.

"He . . . Liam . . ." I desperately try to justify my actions to him, and to myself.

"I know. I saw him, too." Kaelis tilts his head toward a mirror. It's positioned perfectly to give a view of the entry. I wonder if Kaelis had one eye open the whole kiss, waiting to see when Liam left. The prince's eyes drag over me one last time, fingers following down my cheek, my neck, to my clavicle. They pause, trailing on the wrapping just above my breasts. My heavy breaths press into his fingertips—as if tempting him to go farther. Tempting both of us. "Well played . . . I always knew you were dangerous."

"More than you realize," I whisper.

His eyes hold me for one last, long moment, and then Kaelis pulls away. "Let's make a hasty departure. Keep your hair a mess, your lipstick smeared." He runs his thumb over my mouth for emphasis. "Our clothing stays askew. Let them all gossip about us to the point that there's not even a mention of your lineage being suspect or anyone who escaped Halazar."

When I nod, Kaelis escorts me out. He doesn't touch me again after we enter the carriage. Not even when we say a somewhat awkward, muted goodbye back at the academy. But I feel the ghost of his touch and the heat of his mouth on mine long into the night.

CHAPTER 28

The next morning, Kaelis is at breakfast. For once. Of course he makes it a point to be here today.

And I make it a point not to look at him.

Running again, Clara? I can almost hear him purr into my ear as I finish eating as quickly as I can and make my way to wielding. My feet pick up the pace despite myself. As if my body is trying to sabotage me by proving even the phantom of him right.

"Are you okay?" Sorza asks.

"I hear she had a busy night." Dristin's tone is harmless, but I'm fighting a scarlet flush anyway. If Dristin of all people heard . . .

I look to Luren. "Word got around already?"

"It always does." She offers me an apologetic smile.

"I thought students couldn't leave the academy," I mumble.

"*You* left." Dristin adjusts his spectacles, sounding mildly offended that he didn't get to as well.

"Well, yes, but . . ." I fumble in search of the right words.

"But you're a long-lost noble who's engaged to a prince; clearly, exceptions can be made," Luren finishes and hooks her arm with mine, patting me as if to say, *It's all right.*

"Exceptions can be made to lock lips with Kaelis in a secluded gallery, I hear," Kel adds with a tiny, self-satisfied smirk.

I can't tell if I'm relieved that part of the story has made it around... or if I'm so mortified at the idea of people knowing I kissed Kaelis that I want the floor to open and swallow me whole.

"The same exceptions that are made for almost all highborn nobles," Dristin murmurs.

Luren ignores the rest of them. "Was the soiree fun, at least?"

"It was fine."

"So Kaelis isn't good in bed?" Kel remarks dryly.

"I never said anything of the sort," I object hastily.

"Then you have slept with him." Kel regards me from the corners of her eyes, looking rather pleased with herself for forcing the omission from me.

"A lady doesn't tell." I huff and look ahead, knowing it's probably for the best I'm fueling the gossipmongers with tidbits beneficial to the story Kaelis and I need to sell... But I still can't stand it.

As we walk to class, I don't miss the glances and whispers. Kaelis's and my showing has run rampant. I would've hoped that having new fodder to gossip over would've turned mentions of a Halazar escapee into old news. Ideally forgotten. Though that doesn't seem to be the case, as new whispers circulate about even that. The soiree did nothing but add fuel to the rumor fires.

Class can't come fast enough.

Vaduin wears a long coat today, patched at the elbows as if worn through from years of leaning against his desk. He ushers us all into our seats and launches into his lecture on the nuances of wielding the Aces—how each one can cast a small elemental feat, and the variety of ways in which these elemental magics can be applied.

"Lady Clara Redwin"—he motions to the center of the room—"would you care to demonstrate?"

The room suddenly grows colder as all eyes swing to me. I stand. "Which Ace would you like me to use?"

"The Three of Swords Trials aren't that far off."

"One hundred twenty nights away," Sorza murmurs.

If Thornbrow heard, he ignores it. "Why not choose the card of the house you will be seeking to join?"

If I hadn't done so many back-alley deals and honed my face into giving nothing away, I would've narrowed my eyes at the professor. Declaring my intention for a house, this early, is a dangerous thing. It could close doors prematurely to potentially necessary opportunities.

"Very well." I fold my arms, making it a point to show that I summon the card without a single flick of my fingers. In my past life, Wands had always been my preference, but, here, I think Swords will be what I can depend on to carry me through.

The card glows, lengthening into a crescent of light and shadow. It rushes forward, toward Vaduin. The dark hair on the left side of his head barely moves, followed promptly by a gust battering the training dummies in the back of the room.

Eza snorts. He leans toward Alor—I've noticed over the past weeks that the two are closer than I'd like. "Is that it?"

She turns to him, and I can't see what look they give each other or hear what they might be saying.

But not a second later, the center training dummy's head silently slides off its neck. It falls to the floor with a dull *foop*. Straw stuffing scatters. The room is utterly silenced.

"Very good." Though Thornbrow doesn't sound impressed in the slightest. Not that I needed him to be. Not that I need any of them to be.

I sit, and Thornbrow resumes his instruction.

When the bell tolls a few hours later and everyone begins to gather their things, Alor wastes no time in approaching me. I acknowledge her with a glance. Since we arrived at the academy, we've yet to speak more than a few words to each other. My nighttime training has ensured our paths very rarely cross. And her still sleeping with her dagger tells me all I need to know. She's not here to make friends, either.

"There are only two spots in House Swords," she says matter-of-factly. "One of them is mine, and the other will be Eza's." I say nothing and continue packing my things. But what I want to ask is why in the Twenty she's sticking her neck out for Eza, of all people. Probably as simple as nobles looking out for nobles, and that explanation makes my blood boil. "So there is little point in making an attempt for one."

My eyes flick in her direction again, and I pause briefly to give her an incredulous look. It has the effect I wanted. She stands a little taller, as if bracing herself against an oncoming attack, even though I've hardly moved. I smile faintly, and this seems to only annoy her more.

"I'm trying to be helpful." Her voice lowers as she leans in. "You might be a noble, maybe even a High Lady once you've graduated . . . *if* the king carves out Hermit's old lands from the lords and ladies he parceled it to on their demise." Her tone betrays skepticism that such a thing will happen and, if it does, that it'd probably be a bad idea. Even I can reason that the High Lords and Ladies wouldn't be too keen on giving up land. "But let's not lie to ourselves . . . Even then, you'll be the High Lady of a giant hole in the ground."

I almost falter at that, the Starcrossed Club flashing before my eyes. Did Kaelis have something to do with it despite claiming otherwise? If he already annihilated a clan by reducing it to nothing . . . what's to say he didn't do it to the club?

"Those in House Swords are cunning; they're not going to pick someone who doesn't offer a tactical benefit to them," Alor continues, oblivious to the sudden turmoil swirling in me. "Since you're new to the world of the nobility, let me emphasize that there are ways things are done and times that we step aside and out of each other's way."

I hum, making a show of contemplating her advice, as if she really has imparted to me some profound secret. "To make sure I have this right . . . you're telling me that you're the sort of person—that your *sister* is the sort of person—who is fine with being accepted into a house through nepotism rather than on your own merits?"

"Keep my sister out of this." Her voice sharpens, and the remaining initiates who have yet to filter out to lunch halt in their tracks.

"I'm merely trying to understand, since you are so kindly educating me." I smile thinly. "As you are the sister to the King of House Swords, and a high-ranking member of the prestigious, noble Clan Tower, I would've assumed that you would want to prove yourself to your peers and to your family. That your noble sister would want that as well. That you'd accept nothing less than the best. And, to that end, neither of you would be afraid of a challenge."

Alor leans forward. I don't move back at all. If Kaelis can't intimidate me, she won't. "You should watch your tongue."

"Threats aren't very befitting of a lady." I *tsk*.

"How—"

"Let me teach *you* something, *Lady* Alor." I slowly stand. "I might be a recent noble. I might deeply appreciate your kind assistance in trying to guide me." I let my tone do the work of conveying everything I'm not saying overtly. "But don't forget that because I am 'new,' I didn't grow up with the same privileges as you. I grew up in a world where if you threaten someone, it has consequences. So be *really sure* you want to make me your enemy before you say another word. I know where you sleep, after all."

"I am *not* trying to be your enemy," she whispers.

"Well, you're not doing a good job of it." I notice the shifting expressions on the other initiates' faces. I seem to have gained some respect with the common-born . . . and lost some with the nobles. But I'm too far in now to back down. Not that I would, anyway, not when Eza is approaching.

"Need help convincing this one to show some respect?" Eza runs a hand through his perpetually wild, nearly white tresses.

"No." Alor eases away. "It's not worth our time."

I can't help but snort.

"What?" Eza narrows his eyes.

"Leave it, Eza." Alor's encouragement is ignored.

"I think it's adorable how close you two are," I lie. She spoke to him like a dog. All right, perhaps Alor isn't all bad. "I had no idea."

"There are a lot of things we don't know about each other, I think." Eza gives me a slightly wild smile, reminding me just how much about my past he knows. It's more of a threat than anything Alor has said.

For her part, Alor is silent. Though I do catch a sidelong glance from her in Eza's direction. They suddenly don't feel as close as I once thought . . . interesting. "It'd be a shame if too much came to light, don't you think? Especially with such wild rumors flying about that escapee still at large. People might draw dangerous parallels."

My hand balls into a fist.

He notices. "Movements, still? Such a bad habit. Maybe I'll break you of that one day by showing you how a real Arcanist wields."

"Name the time and place," I say before I can think better of it.

"Enough." Thornbrow cuts through the tension. "Lady Redwin, my desk. The rest of you, out."

I'm not sure how I'm the only one marching to Professor Thornbrow's desk while the rest of them leave. But Eza's smug smile follows me the entire time I cross the room. The fist at my side is shaking.

"I must caution you," Vaduin begins, folding his fingers.

"I fear Alor and Eza already beat you to cautioning me," I interject.

The corners of his lips twitch toward a frown. But he doesn't, outright. "Displays like that are unwise."

"Alor and Eza were the ones who came up to me," I mutter.

"I'm not talking about them. I'm talking about what you did in class; it's only going to put more of a target on your back if you show too much, too soon."

I didn't expect to get seemingly genuine advice from him of all people. "*More* of a target?"

"Kaelis might not be well loved, but there are many who would desire the power proximity to him brings." He leans back in his large leather chair and splays his hands across the desk.

I think of how Vaduin is always at the prince's side and wonder if he's one of those people. But instead I say, "I'm not afraid of them."

"A rumor can be more deadly than a poison." Is he honestly trying to help me? I can't make sense of it.

"If they're already talking, I might as well be a part of the conversation." I shrug.

"Having people's eyes on you is not always a good thing here, Clara."

"It's never been a good thing for me." I shift my bag on my shoulder. I never asked to be wanted, hunted, or thrust into the spotlight. "But here I am."

"Yet, here you are," he repeats, voice low and ominous but tinged with a hint of amusement. "Aren't you a lucky one for it?" His eyes narrow slightly. "A young woman pulled from obscurity thanks to a fortuitous history and a prince's love."

"A lucky break, I guess."

"Lucky, indeed," he says thoughtfully.

I purse my lips, not liking his not-so-subtle implications. I'm also on edge because of the rumors. "Is that all, Professor?"

"It is. For now." He dismisses me with a wave of his hand, and I'm ready to be rid of him. Still, I can feel his eyes following my every movement as I leave, and I fight to prevent myself from taking double steps.

The days fall into a monotonous pace. Morning classes—a rotation of inking, wielding, and reading—followed by afternoons spent in the library or practicing. Luren, Kel, Sorza, Dristin, and I keep one another company at meals as well. Their companionship makes the days a little more bearable. I learn that my suspicions about Dristin were correct; he's a lowborn noble, specifically of Clan Chariot.

I finally feel confident enough to go back to the sanctum now. While not all my strength has returned, I no longer feel like I'm made of glass. Sorza is a friendly presence and the sense of safety in numbers she offers helps, too. And—as much as I hate to admit Thornbrow was right about something—being able to summon cards without movement is reassuring, given how Eza, Cael, and Nidus got the better of me last time by holding my arms.

The days continue in their steady pace.

"Have any of you given any thought to what you're going to do for

All Coins Day?" Luren asks as the five of us head back to the common area. She's been, politely, in my ear about helping her ink for the past week. I finally decided to give in and assist rather than running off to the sanctum to work on my Major card. She has more than kept up her end of the bargain by keeping me appraised of all the rumors of the academy.

I've cautioned Luren that my approach to inking still isn't quite what Professor Duskflame would want—a point the professor made painfully clear when I made up time with her not long ago—but the cards I ink *work*. Which is more than Luren can say about most of her cards.

"Probably inking." I shrug. "It's what I'm best at."

"And it's a good strategy. You'll get to know other nobles, as many come to All Coins Day to stock up on additional cards beyond what their clan's Arcanists can make," Dristin says approvingly.

"Exactly my thought," I lie. They say that All Coins Day is designed to give back to the community. But given that only noble clans are permitted to possess cards and they hoard them, the only "community" it helps is the wealthiest.

"You could also do some wielding." Sorza adjusts the stack of books she's carrying. She's made it a point to regularly raid the library, an endeavor I've gladly assisted with on more than one occasion.

I'm still on the hunt for information about the World card, as often and as subtly as I can. But there's precious little to be found. I wouldn't be shocked if Kaelis had expunged it all from the library.

"It's amazing how you can use so many cards in a row without getting exhausted. I use three cards and I'm spent for the day," Dristin laments to me as we enter the common room.

"Lucky like that, I suppose," I say as we all sit around one of the side tables. Students come and go but pay us little mind.

"Seriously, though, you use cards like a third year would, perhaps even better." Dristin leans in, lowering his voice.

"Oh, stop," I say, brushing it off.

"Perhaps she has some secret power she's not telling us about,"

Sorza jokes. I shoot her the fastest of glares. She purses her lips, clearly resisting giving more of a reaction.

"Just think of how much you'll be able to do after your next offering to the Arcanum Chalice." Luren opens one of her journals. It's filled with sketches of symbols and notes for inking. Dristin follows suit. It seems Luren isn't getting a private lesson today.

"Funny, that . . ." Dristin adjusts his glasses and lowers his voice. "Any of you ever think that maybe there are ways to use more advanced arcana without sacrificing to the Chalice?"

Sorza and I share another look. Both of our minds no doubt instantly go to being Majors. But there is some truth to what he's saying, and Kel is the one to confirm it.

"I've heard that it's possible for some Arcanists to innately be able to use more advanced cards," Kel says. "That, with the right practice or training, they can even unlock these abilities on their own without the Chalice."

"Kel!" Luren gasps her name, scandalized. "Saying so is against the law. The only way to progress in tarot is through sacrifice to the Chalice."

"I'm not saying I'm going to do it, just that people have said it's true. Gossip isn't going to get me taken by city enforcers." Kel grins mischievously.

Luren shoves her shoulder. "Better just be gossip. I couldn't handle it if you were hiding power from me."

"I doubt any of us are hiding power from each other if we're all trying to help each other pass." Dristin rubs the back of his neck.

Sorza snorts.

"What?" Dristin looks at her.

"Oh, nothing."

"Really, what is it?" Dristin perks up.

"Nothing." Sorza laughs.

The conversation fades away as I flip through my books and pull out my inking supplies. I hadn't even considered my next offering to the Arcanum Chalice . . . *That's next year's problem.* First, I have to get at least one coin from a student on All Coins Day. Then pass the Three of Swords Trials. Make a declaration for a house that gave me a coin and then have them accept me. All while keeping up the illusion of being an heiress who's madly in love with Kaelis, while somehow simultaneously figuring out a way to forge copies of the Major Arcana cards he wants. And staying out of association with any rumors of the escapee from Halazar.

That's more than enough to keep me busy for now. Whatever I'm forced to sacrifice in my second year is too far away for me to worry about. But being able to finally use *all* the cards I can wield and ink will be a relief. Hiding my power isn't something I particularly enjoy.

Reading is possibly the worst class ever. I've known the principles of it for years, but Arina was always the one who took to it like a falcon on an updraft of the Descent. My general disinterest in the subject is only made worse by Professor Rothou's demeanor.

Las Rothou is a rather eccentric-looking woman with fair skin and black eyes. She's always weighted by all manner of quirky jewelry that contrasts with the perpetual breeziness of her usually silken clothes. Her long, black, wavy hair is often free with a streak of white.

But her manner of teaching is in stark contrast to her artsy fashions. Las teaches reading like Professor Duskflame teaches inking. Her method is rigid and relies entirely on the traditional symbology of the cards. There's no room in her approach for nuance. Something Luren has the misfortune of finding out firsthand.

"Professor, in your example, would it not be better to read the Seven of Cups more positively?" She brushes hair from her eyes with her usual demure manner. But she speaks her question with confidence. If there's one class Luren shines in, it's reading.

"The Seven of Cups represents the illusion of positive choice," Las repeats what she just said as she laid out her example for the class. As she does so, she adjusts an ornate headband on her brow. Today's is a row of tiny obsidian starbursts. "An abundance of options that, upon deeper inspection, is not as ideal as it appears on the surface."

"But with the Ten of Coins also present in the spread—signifying wealth and long-term success—would it not suggest that all the options in the Seven of Cups are good?"

"The Ten of Coins is in the future position that has no bearing on the Seven of Cups in the present conflict position." Professor Rothou takes reading *so seriously*. There's no room for the cards' meaning to shift depending on the other cards in the spread, the querent, the situation . . . or merely reader's intuition.

"Right . . ." Even if she doesn't say it, I can see Luren's objection in her eyes. Her reading style reminds me so much of Arina it hurts.

Whenever Arina would read, her eyes would flutter closed, and she'd sway slightly as her hands moved over the cards. As though she were conducting a symphony of whispers from the universe itself. Singling out the voices she needed to hear. She read from her gut and said every word during her reading with nothing but confidence, and as a result her readings were always shockingly accurate.

"What if our cards come up reversed—upside down, Professor?" Kel asks. The question is met with murmuring among the class.

My ears perk up. Reversed cards are one thing I've yet to truly probe Kaelis on, although the lore about him demands answers—especially if I'm to truly know the man I'm aligning myself with. But I also suspect he'll tell me little, so I pay close attention now to Las's answer.

Las clasps her fingers together over her stomach, all the rings she wears clanking softly. She does the motion whenever she's frustrated, as if trying to remind herself not to yell right from her belly. An odd image for the usually soft-spoken professor. "In reading, if the cards come up reversed, you turn them the right way."

"Are reversed cards not an ill omen in a reading?" Sorza asks.

"Reversed cards are nothing more than stories told to frighten children," Las insists. "There is only one way to *properly* read and use the tarot."

"Technically, reversed cards do exist," Alor dares to point out. "In wielding, if the Arcanist isn't skilled enough to use the card, or it wasn't inked properly, then the card can reverse and become volatile. The magic twists. Backfires, even."

"Exactly." Las smiles with a slight twinkle in her eye, as if Alor has just proved her point. "Reversed cards only 'exist' briefly because of poor execution in wielding. Arcanists cannot *intentionally* wield a reversed card any more than they can read one. Fortunately, in reading you can at least correct the card painlessly. The cards have one power, one meaning. Nothing more or less."

Eyes dart my way as she speaks. I represent the clan that was rumored to be destroyed by a reversed card. But the rumors deviate from one another: Was the card intentionally wielded as a reversed card? Or did Kaelis lose control of it? The former is a legendary level of terrifying. And suggesting the latter would be treason.

So I keep my mouth shut.

"Now, if we can get back to the task at hand, today's reading—one for the upcoming change of season as we welcome in the fall, the Season of Coins. Remember, All Coins Day is just over thirty days away. Now is the time to focus on perfecting your reading skills, as they might serve you well in impressing a student enough that they award you a coin."

All students are supplied with a full deck for reading class, though we're not allowed to take it out of the room, to avoid the temptation of trying to use cards that are supposedly beyond our abilities. I give the deck a good shuffle and then fan out the cards.

I start by drawing the card that goes at the top of the spread—my present position. Beneath that is the central challenge that lies ahead of me for the next season. To the left and right of the center card are what is known and what is unknown about that problem, respectively. Beneath it is the likely outcome.

Each card is placed face down so they're read in order, and then holistically at the end. My hand hovers over the top one. But I don't move to flip it. There's an uncomfortable energy radiating off it, as if the card is trying to push my fingers away.

I force myself to flip the cards, one by one.

Top—Present Position: Seven of Swords

Center—Problem: Ten of Coins

Center Left—What Is Known: Prince of Swords

Center Right—What Is Unknown: King of Swords

Bottom—Likely Outcome: Ten of Swords

After staring at the spread for a second, I rotate the only card that appeared upside down, the Prince of Swords. My fingers linger on it. *A prince of Swords.* I see Kaelis instantly in the man on the card—he has a severe jaw and deep-set eyes that stare at the world with barely contained ferocity.

What is unknown . . . the King of Swords.

My thoughts are so loud that I don't hear Professor Las until she's at my side, letting out a low noise that sounds almost like disapproval but is something even worse: pity. "You'll have a harsh fall ahead of your winter, Clara."

"The cards only show what might be," I counter.

"Is *most likely* to be," she tries to gently correct.

"But still not what *will* be."

"Perhaps, for a better reader, they might." Her comment makes me think of Arina. Her readings were never wrong. If she were here, she'd know exactly what was to come. Las taps my desk. "Study hard, Clara. The Three of Swords Trials are about more than fighting and fancy card work. The right reader can also gain an advantage by knowing what's to come."

I stare at the cards as she leaves, willing them to be something different, to tell me something I don't already know. But there is only the

Prince and the King of Swords, flanking the card that represents All Coins Day—the Ten of Coins. There aren't a lot of ways for me to read this spread. Kaelis and King Naethor are going to consume my All Coins Day. And the final outcome?

The Ten of Swords, a card depicting a man skewered by ten fiery blades, predicting nothing but agony.

CHAPTER 29

"Easy, easy!" Myrion lifts both his hands before placing them on his knees and panting. "I yield."

I straighten, relax my magic, and wipe my brow. On occasion, I still train on my own. But coming to the Sanctum of the Majors in the evenings has given me the opportunity to practice wielding against others on the small dueling strip. After the rocky start to my year, I'm determined to learn tarot the way the academy wants me to. The mere idea of failing at something I *know* I can do well is downright unpalatable. Plus, this is the only place I'm able to really flex my skills against people who are also capable of wielding a full deck.

"Unlike you to be beaten so thoroughly," Elorin says to Myrion in her melodic, almost dreamy way. Her eyes then drift to me. "Now, if you could only channel that same competence into inking the Wheel."

"Rude." My tone is as dry as my throat, and I make my way toward the large pitcher of water that Thal set out for us.

"You must figure it out eventually." Elorin continues to hover.

"You think I don't want to?" I drink and give her a side-eye.

"Avoiding inking practice isn't going to get you any closer to mastery." Every word is said with detached beauty, fitting her usual demeanor. Elorin's features rarely betray happiness or sorrow or any emotion at all. She's like a colorful porcelain doll: Everything about her is perfect—her aura peaceful and calm, her appearance flawless—and though she's always clad in a rainbow of cheerful hues, she sometimes feels utterly soulless.

"She'll get it in her own time." Myrion comes up beside me and pours a drink from the pitcher. As he raises his glass, he gives me a warm and encouraging smile. Myrion is one of the few people I've ever met who has never put me on guard.

"I'm going to wash up for dinner," he announces after draining his glass. "Nothing can be done on an empty stomach."

"I'll be on my way in a bit. I should work on my inking." I make my way toward a desk, giving Elorin a pointed look. She merely smiles, somewhat coy in her triumph.

Myrion heads off, and Thal isn't far behind him. Elorin perches herself before the fire, leafing through a book that she plucked off one of the shelves that line one wall of the sanctum. There are better, rarer books here than even in the library. But unfortunately, I've found no material in them about the World. I keep glancing at Elorin from the corner of my eye as I set to inking. If she notices, she doesn't react.

Sorza finally departs with a loud stretch and a declaration of "That's enough for today." She's been hunched over for hours working on her own card. She's been as unsuccessful as I have been, but she seems much closer to a breakthrough. "Coming, Clara?"

I shake my head. "Go on without me."

"I'll stash some food in your room." It's not the first night she's offered to help, and she's always come through.

"You're too good to me."

"Isn't that the truth?" She waves and leaves.

Now it's just Elorin and me. I am not going to let her leave before me after the remarks she made—I am not going to have Elorin claim again that I'm not putting in the effort. I keep my head down and persist in scribbling on the page. My drawings mean nothing. I don't feel any particular connection to them—they're as soulless as the lines Raethana Duskflame teaches. But I *look* productive.

The moon is up and we've both surely missed dinner when Elorin finally yawns and shuts her book with a dramatic flair. She tucks the dusty tome under her arm. I feel her eyes on me before I bring mine to hers again. Wordlessly, she holds my stare, and time seems to stretch on even longer than our little game did over the past few hours.

"It's not going to work, you know."

My pen stops moving. "What isn't?"

"Trying to stall your learning to avoid getting an assignment. It's not going to work." Her listless eyes take on new meaning. Their blue has clouded, becoming almost stormy with a tumult that she clearly fights to hide. I wonder just how much agony brews beneath the placid surface she presents.

"I wasn't trying to stall."

"Sure you weren't." She's skeptical.

"I wasn't," I insist. Then my mouth runs away from me. "If anything, I'm frustrated I can't ink the card. This is the first time tarot hasn't come naturally to me and it's completely and utterly maddening." I stop myself promptly before I say more. Elorin tucks a strand of hair behind her ear, looking guilty.

People seem inclined to say things around me; they tell me things they might not otherwise admit, especially if I probe, Elorin said on my first day in the sanctum. I didn't understand what she meant until now. That outburst was completely true, but not what I'd been intending to say.

"You should want to stall," she murmurs, looking away.

"Why?"

"Once you can, they will have you and all the powers they can wring from you."

"*They?*" I set my pen down. I can surmise what she means, but I want to be sure.

"The nobility you'll be assigned to . . . the king himself." Her gaze drifts out the window, and she stares with longing at nothing, as if the only times she's ever been truly free are when she's looked at the horizon. "We exist for them."

"We exist for ourselves." I refuse to accept anything less. She looks back to me, but, rather than arguing, she just smiles in a way that makes her disagreement palpable. I ask, "Do you know what clan you'll be going to?"

"Not a clan, to the court at Fate Hearth. My power as High Priestess is too valuable to be anywhere else but at the king's side."

"What is your power?" I realize just how little I know about each of the Majors' unique magic. Myrion told me earlier that with the Lovers card he can make two people fall in love. Eza showed me his card's skill when he attacked me. Thal told me their power to remove someone's pain with the Sun on my first day. Sorza is still figuring out her magic, just as I am. And I know Silas's . . . But Cael, the Emperor; Nidus, the Tower; and Elorin, the High Priestess, I don't know what their cards do.

"I can look into someone's mind and learn their innermost thoughts—their truth that they hide from the world." I lean back in my seat. She laughs at my reaction. "Don't worry, I haven't used it on you, nor would I without being asked . . . or ordered to by the crown. I don't delight in giving up my memories. I'd rather keep them for myself than exchange them for others'."

"I can only imagine."

"I hope, for your sake, the inking requirements for Fortune are much more forgiving."

She leaves me to my thoughts. I stare at my page of half-hearted scribbles. My inability to ink isn't just from not knowing the right symbol for Fortune. A sinking feeling pools in my gut. I don't know what I must sacrifice. Until I do, I doubt the magic will ever coalesce into shape. What if inking the Wheel of Fortune takes more than I can bear to give?

When I hear footsteps, I think it's Silas come to find me, as he does from time to time when most are tucked into their dormitories. But the moment I turn my attention to the sound of his footsteps, I realize they're not his.

A man whose hair looks white in the moonlight smirks back at me, his hand already hanging by the deck on his hip.

"Eza." All warmth has left my voice. Our paths have crossed only briefly these past few weeks, and when they have, others have been present—all by my design. Now we're alone. As if he sought me out.

"*Graysword.*" He sneers the name I went by in Halazar. Goading me from the first moment. I pretend to look down at my paper again, picking up my pen. But he isn't one to be ignored. Every tiny hair on my body is on end. "I've heard you've been making use of the training grounds here."

"My name is Redwin," I correct. How does he know so much about me? When he first attacked me . . . and now.

"We both know it's not," he scoffs. He's right, of course. But my real name isn't Graysword, either.

"It is. And what I do here is not exactly a secret." I make a few annoyed marks with my pen.

"I want to see what a Halazar inmate can do."

"I'm not sure what you think you know about me, but I assure you that your information is wrong." I drag my eyes back to him, hate welling in my stomach. But I keep my cool. "Moreover, I'm not interested in showing you anything."

"You seemed willing to earlier in the year."

I'm not going to let you get the better of me this time. "I changed my mind."

"And if I don't give you that option?" He wears a wild smile as he crosses the room to me. "Why don't I tell everyone that you are the person from all the stories—the escapee from Halazar—and put you back into the cage where vermin like you belong? Can't imagine the king would take too kindly to a harlot lying her way into his son's bed."

His question, as rhetorical as it was, sticks . . . *Why hasn't he had me sent back to Halazar?* He's clearly certain about my identity, and he's right. So why hasn't he done anything more other than goad and attack me personally? Why not tell a professor to call the enforcers?

"Because you *can't* put me back." I keep the realization from seeping into the words. No matter what he might know, or threaten. He can't put me back there. "Otherwise you would've by now."

Eza's gaze hardens.

"You think you're so strong, don't you? But you're just as afraid of Kaelis as anyone else." I want to laugh. *Damn it, Kaelis was right . . . being engaged to him does come with its own protections.*

"You don't know anything," he growls.

"Don't I, though?"

"Halazar was too kind for someone like you." A card lifts from his deck, spinning around him. With every twirl, the visage of the Hanged Man flashes at me. Whatever he needs to ink that damned card isn't enough of a cost. "Maybe we can find somewhere else in your history that's more fitting. Somewhere darker still. Or I could invent a little mental prison of my own design for you. See whose mind is stronger."

I release the pen, heart racing.

"After all, it took only a few strikes and a pen through the hand to make you snap. Hardly anything at all."

How does he know what happened in the vision down to such a specific detail? An icy rush coats me, freezing hard, stopping my movements. Could he somehow see my vision? Did he design it, as he said?

No matter how hard I've trained myself, around Eza I am once more left raw, exposed, and vulnerable. The notion that he was watching what played out in my mind while I was under the influence of his Hanged Man is sickening.

"Resorting to a single Major Arcana card to always win is hardly impressive." I stand, wanting to be ready for anything. The tension in the air is about to snap. "It makes me wonder just how strong you are if you're always forced to rely on one trick."

His nostrils flare. Men like him are so predictable. "I could beat you without my Major."

"If you say so." I almost sing the words, partly mocking. I'm goading him into a fight and I know it. But I'd rather see the attack coming than have him launch into one when my back is turned. "Not that you'd try without Nidus and Cael. Or Alor, I suppose. Incredible how unwilling you are to fight when you're not outnumbering your opponent."

I expected that to be his breaking point. I didn't expect him to lunge over the table and forget his card entirely. The Hanged Man falls like a silvery star, abandoned. He grabs for me, hands at my throat.

The world tilts. We hit the ground.

Eza and I roll across the floor. Every bit of my training with Gregor over the years, every street fight, every close call with enforcers, it's all called into action along with all the strength I've regained. My fist connects with his jaw, eliciting a sharp grunt. It feels *so bloody good* to destroy that too-pretty face of his. He loses his grip on my throat and rolls off.

Retaliation comes in the form of a crackle of ice across the floor, created by an Ace of Cups. I scramble out of the way, my hand swinging over my own deck. Old habits die hard in an actual fight. A card rises magically at my summons. Fire explodes around me as the Ace of Wands burns, holding back his ice with a hiss.

Breathing heavily, we both regain our footing and circle each other. Moonlight dances along with the flickering candlelight of the sconces. Ice and fire illuminate our faces.

"You have quite the punch." He moves his jaw around, blood dripping from his lips.

"You have quite the weak jaw."

Face twisting into a scowl, he grunts, two cards rising from his deck. I'm ready for him. I dodge another blast of ice, but my feet stumble as one of his cards releases a pale purple haze that fills the air around me. My eyelids feel heavy.

Four of Cups. Sleep. Sluggishness. I call the Four of Swords from my own deck—healing—before I collapse into a dreamless sleep.

The haze clears with just enough time for me to see Eza moving toward the Hanged Man card he dropped earlier. The card quivers to life in response. Before he can reach it, I retaliate with a mental attack of my own—the Two of Swords. Eza staggers as the world no doubt spins before his eyes. Confusion causes his body to go limp instead of continuing its pursuit of his Major Arcana. I lunge.

The line between physical and magical combat blurs. Cards evaporate, unravel into threads of light, burst into multicolored stardust, disappear into a haze. The room is upended as we go for the throat—for the kill.

It's been ages since I fought like this. Since I really, truly stopped holding back. Breathless, bloody, every muscle screaming. Anger and desperation keep me moving. My pain tolerance is so much higher than his. I'm betting my life on it.

"Stop. Moving. You. Bitch," he snarls. I don't see the next card that hits me.

I'm thrown, tumbling over the far table, my body's momentum stopped only by the wall. Blinking stars away, I see Eza moving for his Hanged Man card. *No . . . I won't go back there.* But my body doesn't heed my commands. I can't move a finger.

"I won't go back there," I rasp. *Going back to Halazar, even if it's only in my mind . . .* "I'd rather die."

It's difficult to even stand when my hand keeps sliding down the wall, slick with blood. Eza is almost in close enough proximity to his card to cast it with a thought. I stagger to the table I was working at and fall into it. The papers from earlier are still scattered, coated by my scribbles, my nose dripping constellations of blood onto them.

If there was ever a time that I needed luck . . .

The Wheel of Fortune, a turn of fate. It's not complicated. Not even something that can be controlled. It encompasses everything and nothing at the same time. I draw a circle on one paper, then another circle, half finished, on the outside of it. Lines stretch from the outer ring to the center point of the inner circle. I slam my hand into the paper and pour out every bit of magic, of myself, every scrap of luck I've ever had and watch as it illuminates with a silvery haze and vanishes.

But whatever I did wasn't enough. Eza is finally at his card. It hovers. I brace myself. But the attack doesn't come.

Peeling my eyes open, I see what he's staring at in disbelief. His card has inexplicably shredded into a dozen pieces and been rendered useless. A twist of fate. Not what I'd imagined . . . but everything I needed.

Seizing my opportunity, I hurl myself at him. Not with magic. But with my whole body.

I'm atop him. Eza is helpless beneath me. He's no longer fighting back, and yet I can't stop myself. I punch and punch, our blood mixing. All the pent-up pain within me finally finds its outlet.

He's never going to make me feel small again. No one will. I'll kill anyone who ever threatens me or those I love. There will be no quarter for them. No peace. *I'll remake the whole fucking world if that's what it takes to have my family and keep them safe.*

I might actually kill him . . . until a force yanks me away.

Kaelis's grip on my wrist is ironclad as he hoists me off Eza. I stumble back, falling on my ass. Eza wastes no time spitting up blood and rolling onto his side.

"Monstrous wench! She attacked me in cold blood!" he sneers.

The prince's gaze is as unyielding as his grip as his eyes take in the chaos we've wreaked in the Majors' once-cozy haven. Then his gaze lands on me, and it softens before immediately hardening again. Danger pervades Kaelis's aura, and it's apparent enough that even Eza leans away from him.

"Call her a wench again and you'll answer to much worse than her fists." Kaelis's words are like cold fire. Bitter and biting. Little more than a deadly snarl.

"But, but—"

"I have your golden card, Eza. Even if you died, it could still be used to summon the World. I don't need you any longer." Kaelis doubles down on his threat.

"Your father would say different."

That hits a nerve. "Leave. *Now.* And learn some sense before I set eyes on you again, or we'll test that theory."

Eza somehow finds his footing, though it's shaky. He shoots me a withering glare. "Hide behind his coattails like the coward you are. We will finish this."

I don't have time to respond before he stumbles away. Kaelis turns to me. "He started it," I say, before the prince can get in a word.

"I know he did." There's no longer a tone of reprimand in his words, not toward me. "When I didn't see you at dinner, I went looking . . ." Kaelis's free hand shifts, as if to touch my face. I realize it's the first time we've been this close and this alone since the soiree weeks ago.

A shiver runs down my spine. Vulnerability sneaks into my veins, replacing the rush of the fight. Worry from Kaelis? For me? *Impossible.*

"I don't need you to save me." I object to the way he's looking at me now. To the notion that he'd fear for me.

"No, clearly you don't." Kaelis shakes his head. "But you do need me to ensure that my father doesn't inflict all manner of torture on you for slaying one of his Majors after you ink your golden card." The prince stands. I don't miss how "all manner of torture" is something different from Halazar . . . something that sounds worse. "Now, come with me."

"Where?"

"My apartments."

"I don't want to go." The objection lacks its usual bite.

"I wasn't asking." He smirks slightly, but it does little to subdue the worry in his eyes. "Consider it an order from your prince."

"How dare—"

"You're a mess, Clara. And I'll not have my future wife looking like she fell down several flights of stairs lined with daggers and I did nothing about it." I don't move. He arches a dark brow at me. "What now?" Kaelis sighs.

"I don't care how I look. I'm not your prize to be dressed up and paraded around as it suits you."

He kneels before me, eyes level with mine. The oddity of a prince on his knee in front of me has my head spinning from more than just Eza's blows. "Fine. I don't care how you *look*. Be a bloody mess. Be the rat queen of Eclipse City that you so want to be. But I will not ever have it be said I don't care for those closest to me."

The words settle on me like a poultice for my wounds. Words that sound like my own. Warm heat floods me. For the first time, I feel as though I can understand something about him.

"I am close to you?" The words have gone soft.

"You don't see me surrounded by copious amounts of company, do you?"

That elicits a weak laugh from me. Even Kaelis smiles, before the expression is abandoned.

"Unless you will reject my help again this time?" The question reminds me of my first night in the academy. Of the wounds I carried from the Fire Festival that I refused to even let him touch. I say nothing. Still a skeptical, wounded creature. "Please, let me help you."

It's the "please" that does it.

With a grimace and a concomitant grunt, I give in and take his hand so he can help me up. Kaelis fights a little smile and loses, as if my moodiness is somehow endearing to him. He tidies the room with some deft card wielding and then begins to escort me out. When it's clear my body can no longer support itself, he slips an arm behind my legs and hoists me.

"Excuse you," I protest, though it lacks any real force.

"What am I going to do with you?" he says with a sigh.

My arms are folded on my chest to prevent myself from wrapping them around his neck, even though it'd be more stable as we ascend the stairs. "Let me go."

"Trust me when I say, that's the one thing neither of us wants."

CHAPTER 30

We take the hidden way in through the interior of the bridge that connects to his apartments, up the winding passage and in through his closet. The entire time he holds me as though I weigh nothing, even though I know after all my weeks of training the very opposite is true. Kaelis brings me to one of the sofas before the fire.

He disappears through one of the many side doors. I hear him calling for Rewina. His words are muffled, and I don't bother straining my ears for something I can't hear anyway. Instead, I sink deeper into the soft cushions and allow them to gently cradle every wound and tender spot on my body.

It smells of the prince . . . ink, cedar, oiled leather . . .

"You look quite content ruining my sofa with all your blood." Kaelis is at my side, holding a bowl of water with a rag draped over the edge. At some point, I must've closed my eyes. Long enough that a purring Priss has taken up residence on my stomach. At least she doesn't mind my state.

"It's not just *my* blood."

"That makes it worse." He grimaces. "The only place I want Eza's bloodstains are on the floor. And maybe my knuckles."

"I didn't take you for one to resort to blows."

"I'm not, usually."

I glance his way. "Am I to believe you'd get yourself dirty for me?"

"Believe whatever you like," he says aloud. But his slight smile says simply, *Yes*.

"So you'd get your hands dirty, but not the sofa?" I try to keep levity in my voice even though that look he gave me caused my whole body to tingle.

"My hands are easier to wash."

I fight a laugh. I never thought I'd be *laughing* in such a state. "You're a prince. Buy another sofa. Buy several." I scratch the cat between her ears and under her chin, which she readily sticks out for me.

"I like *that* one. More important, it's Priss's favorite."

"And here I thought she was sitting on me because she likes me." I meet a pair of bright yellow feline eyes. "Was I just in your way?"

"She has a habit of getting what she wants, like someone else I know." He sets the bowl down on the table between the sofas and sits on the floor.

"Now I know you're not talking about me." My eyes flick to his.

"You have a prince personally attending you right now." He produces a card from his pocket, and I barely get a glimpse of the Queen of Cups before it vanishes. My flesh knits, wounds mend. It takes three cards to get most of the injuries healed, though I can still feel the ghosts of my wounds all over.

Kaelis takes my hand in his. Priss lets out a loud meow in protest that he dares to take away the fingers that had been so dutifully scratching her. Kaelis shoots her a mildly offended look before he begins to gently dab away the blood that is both mine from my split knuckles and Eza's.

"Only because he insisted." I'm fascinated by the oddity that is a prince—Kaelis, of all the princes—wiping away the blood and grime from my body. It's the only thing that keeps me from pulling my hand away. Well, that, and I don't want to disturb Priss.

Kaelis sighs heavily. When he next speaks, he sounds very tired. "Someone must; you clearly won't look after yourself. Was that scene with Eza really necessary?"

"I'm not going to be Eza's punching bag whenever he wants. And I'm certainly not going to let him use the Hanged Man to throw me into Halazar again . . . even if it's only in my mind." I make sure there's no room for question between my words.

"I've no issue with you defending yourself, but did you have to go so far?"

"You're really scolding me?" I blink at him.

"My father does like his Majors alive so he never will run out of their silver cards to use as he pleases," Kaelis begrudgingly admits, reminding me of one of Eza's last remarks. "He's nearly found the complete set of twenty and isn't a man who handles disappointment well."

"I don't give a damn about your father," I say bluntly.

Kaelis snorts, and his eyes shine with what looks almost like fondness at the remark. "Perhaps not. But I give a damn about keeping his attention away from that which is mine."

That which is mine . . . He's talking about me. A shiver courses through my body, the cool air highlighted in the wake of Kaelis's touch and the warm rag he runs over my skin.

"So, the next time, I recommend quitting while you're still ahead," he finishes.

"What happens if you kill a Major?"

"A Major's magic always exists in the world, so it lives on in another."

"A sort of reincarnation?" I ask.

"More of a transference. The magic moves to another individual instantly. It could be an old man, or a young baby. The person could be across the world, or right next to the Major who died," he explains. "But that person must be found, and then they must learn of their new abilities. As you can imagine, it's quite the process."

"Eza will be fine as long as he doesn't mess with me," I say defensively. Then, after a stretch of silence and a soft sigh, I add, "You don't know what it's like to, for your entire life, be told you're a *thing* that can be used, beaten, discarded."

That has Kaelis stilling. The rag sits in the bowl, ribbons of red unspooling from it into the water.

"Perhaps you do," I whisper. His attention still fails to return to me. His own family forced him to sacrifice his futures to the Chalice. I wonder, for the first time, what those futures were. "After all, you knew I'd fight back at the first opportunity I had. Which is why you gave me one when you tested my ability to use the cards to get out of Halazar."

Kaelis doesn't respond and instead reaches back for the rag. He continues up my arm, and I continue lying limply, staring at the ceiling. Saying as much to him leaves me more exhausted than the fight.

"Am I just a game to you?" I whisper.

"No."

The fact that I believe him makes tears of frustration prick at the edges of my eyes. They don't fall. I'm not that broken. But they threaten to. It'd be so much easier if he told me I was nothing, less than nothing. But he's both looking after me and using me. I'm trapped between, and it threatens to tear me in two.

Don't let him win, Clara, a voice that isn't quite my own cautions. I hear my mother's whisper laced through it. *Beware the void-born prince.*

"Eza is stupid," Kaelis says after a long stretch of silence. "No matter how badly you beat him, it'll only make him come for you again. And harder than the last time. Try to make peace, even if it's of a begrudging sort."

"I know. He'll probably bring friends again, too, now that he knows he can't take me one-on-one." I sigh and sink farther back into the cushions as Priss nudges my hand toward scratching her cheek. "He's not the sort of man to tolerate being beaten—literally or figuratively."

"Much like his father . . ." That remark has me turning to face Kaelis, but he stares through the fire instead of meeting my eyes. His hand holding the rag has stilled once more. "You have suffered much as a result of me." There's the thinnest thread of guilt lacing his words.

"*Nooo*, have I?" I suck in a deep gasp of air and let sarcasm flood my voice.

A bitter laugh escapes through a grimace. But his expression turns serious once more. "I am sorry."

"For what?" I want to hear him say it. There's a lot for him to be sorry about, and it will mean nothing until he acknowledges what it is he's apologizing for.

"Many things." When he says it, I almost laugh at how well it mirrored my thoughts. "Not least of which that it's my fault Eza hates you."

"What do you mean?" There's not a lot of love for the second-born prince in the kingdom, to be sure. But he sounds especially convinced.

"His father is Warden Glavstone."

I inhale sharply, and our eyes lock. "*What?* But they don't have the same last name." Something like that would've stuck out to me at some point in one of my classes.

"Bastard children are not uncommon for nobility. And his mother was of higher status in Clan Moon. Eza took her name and was accepted into her family. But the fact remains." Kaelis has ceased his ministrations, as if he's unsure he can still touch me.

"He got his mother's looks and his father's *charming* personality," I mutter, unsure of what to do with this information. It doesn't fundamentally change anything, but . . . "That's how Eza knows I was in Halazar."

"Yes, I can only assume his father told him. But Eza won't say anything. I made *that* clear to both him and his father." The defensive edge in Kaelis's tone has my eyes searching his face for deeper meaning in those words.

"It's a lot of faith to put into Eza . . ."

"It'd be my word against his, a battle he can't win and knows it." Kaelis sounds more confident than I feel. Perhaps his princely aura has made him ignorant. But, as the one to bear the risks, I've even more to be wary of.

"That's why he's attacking me in other ways, when he can. He can't go after me in the most obvious way," I murmur.

Kaelis nods. "And I suspect his resentment toward me for what I did to his father is being taken out on you as well. Given that it's not as if he can attack me—you're far more accessible."

What Kaelis doesn't say is, assuming that's true, it means Eza believes Kaelis cares for me. He thinks that hurting me is a way to hurt Kaelis. Our ruse seems to be working, if other people really believe we're madly in love.

"Priss, time to move," the prince says.

"She's fine."

He's already shooed her away and lifts my shirt without asking, baring my side from rib to hip. The fabric has been reduced to little more than tatters, yet I feel oddly exposed, and the cooling washcloth against my hot skin sends a shiver through me. The phantom pains from my ravaged body that were so recently there still tingle.

Priss resettles by my feet. I'm not imagining the huff that comes from the fur ball. I echo it with a sigh of my own. I'm not sure what I want to do with this information about Eza yet. But at least now I have it.

"And I am sorry that I did not find a better way to save you than keeping you in Halazar for the year." He's explained it before, but . . .

"Forgive me for not feeling overly grateful."

"I might be a prince, which gives me enough sway to help some, but I couldn't completely overrule a formal judgment. Especially not when it was my brother, regent of Eclipse City and head of the enforcers, who sealed the decree." He can barely finish his sentence, his jaw is clenched so hard. "I have no say about what happens on the other side of the bridge, not really."

"Your *brother*? Prince Ravin decided my fate?" I sit up now. The conversation has my full attention, and I don't want sleep to take hold of me. "He was involved?"

"It was his men that caught you, and their trap that ensnared you. I didn't know where you were until you were taken in. I happened to notice that some matters weren't adding up about the case. I began looking closer into it all. Had Glavstone run a few tests—though I did not find out his methodology until I came to collect you this year." Kaelis turns back to the bowl and uses my new position to access my left thigh. I'm vaguely aware of the feeling of his fingertips sliding over my skin as he pushes back the frayed scraps of my trousers to continue cleaning the blood.

"Ravin's men . . . caught me . . ." I repeat. Griv, the man who had come to me asking me to help him get out of the city . . . The trap that he led me into. Arina's cautions about the job, that something was starting to rub her the wrong way. Griv was a mole for *Ravin*, not Kaelis.

"Ravin is the head of the city enforcers, as regent. So of course he had a direct hand in it. Though, I cannot be sure if he knew you were a Major or not. Or if he even recognized you on the day of the Fire Festival. I suspect not, as that would've been his best chance to send you back to Halazar—before you became an initiate. I declared you my bride out of panic that he might have known who you were," Kaelis continues, oblivious to the fireworks of thoughts exploding across my mind. "I've been trying to figure it out. I expect Ravin, as my father's lapdog, to know everything, especially when it comes to another Major. He would no doubt want to find a Major before me so he could get their card to my father first. Sending you to Halazar just to toy with me . . ."

The words fade away as I bring a palm to my head, suddenly hot and cold at the same time. The room spins.

"Clara?" Kaelis's voice is distant. Concerned.

Arina knew the Arcanist who came to me was someone to worry about. She'd said she had a bad feeling about it. I'd assumed it was a reading she did. But could it have been something to do with Silas? If it was, does that make him Ravin's mole? Or did Silas know of a deeper plot and warn her out of kindness?

Griv's musculature was similar to Silas's. His hair was a shade lighter . . . Eyes a different color, weren't they? But he'd worn glasses.

Perhaps tinted. Dye could explain the hair. He was never able to meet Arina, never showing up to our meetings whenever I mentioned she might be there. My stomach churns. I might be looking for enemies in all the wrong places. But there's one thing I now know . . .

"It wasn't you." I slowly tilt my head to look at him. "You really weren't the one to imprison me." Nor orchestrate all of my other pains. Ravin controls the city enforcers, not Kaelis. Could *he* be behind Mother's death?

"I told you I wasn't," he murmurs, not meeting my eyes. He did, all the way back to my first night here. But I'd had no reason to believe him. Until now.

"Because you need me to steal from your father." In all the time that's passed, in all my classes, I haven't forgotten my real purpose here.

"Among other things." Our eyes lock, and my throat goes tight.

"What other things?" I manage to say.

"Your card."

"Right, absolutely . . ." Yet, why does it feel like there's so much more to this? The feeling is made all the worse by how the scent of him still lingers on me from when he carried me earlier. I try to focus on anything but him and myself. "Speaking of, I think I might have successfully used my Major?"

Kaelis sits straighter. "You do?"

"I *think* so." It's easier to speak about cards, and I hide behind the subject. "When I was fighting with Eza, I used my blood to ink a card . . ." I trail off as it dawns on me. "That's it. I've always been able to ink Minor Arcana with anything so long as I dropped a bit of my blood into the ink—added a piece of myself to the card, as Mother would say. I think my Major must be the same. Or it must be inked entirely in my blood."

"Let's hope not the latter," he says grimly. Though, given what other Majors sacrifice, it seems somewhat minor in comparison.

Before either of us can say anything more, the door that Kaelis had disappeared through earlier opens and Rewina appears with a silver platter.

Kaelis pulls his hands off me so quickly that I would question whether they were there at all, if not for the warmth they left behind. "Rewina, thank you." He goes to meet his maid, taking the platter from her.

"You are most welcome." Rewina respectfully ducks her head. Her eyes turn to me. "Goodness, sir, you did not tell me she would be in such dire need of fresh clothes."

"I'm fine," I start to object.

Kaelis speaks over me. "A grievous and shameful oversight on my part, without doubt. Do you mind remedying this?"

"With haste." Rewina excuses herself and departs the way she came.

"I said I was fine."

Kaelis sets down the platter on the table, far enough away from the bowl of bloody water that splashing isn't a risk. "I said I cannot have my betrothed looking in such a state."

"And *I said* that you should really let the whole 'we're engaged' thing go." I add, "At least when it's just the two of us, we can drop the pretense."

"It's safer for us both not to." He reaches down and plucks a grape off the platter, popping it into his mouth. "Last thing we want is to get so comfortable in private that we make a mistake publicly."

"I suppose you're right . . ." Especially when it comes to the "getting comfortable" part. I help myself to some food, preventing myself from saying anything else.

Rewina reappears even faster this time. Perhaps she'd already been expecting this oversight on Kaelis's part. "My lord, lady." She bows her head to each of us as she places the clothes on a nearby chair.

"Thank you," I say after her, just before she leaves. My focus sticks on the clothing. "Do you just keep outfits in my size lying around?"

"I don't question what Rewina thinks is best when it comes to managing the storerooms of my apartments. Which, speaking of . . ." He stands and starts for the entrance to his study. "I'll give you some privacy to change. Give a knock when you're finished."

He's gone before I can say anything more. Begrudgingly, I stand and engage in a staring contest with the door. Even though I'm alone, I feel as if the world's eyes are on me—*his* eyes are on me—as I reach for the hem of my shirt and pull it over my head. Everything in me aches, still.

Using the bowl and rag, I try to finish cleaning myself up as much as possible before dressing in the new clothes. They're simple loungewear. Buttery silk from head to toe with enough structure that I don't feel as though I'm comically underdressed. But, also . . . I'm still vulnerable.

"I would've preferred the leathers or stiff velvets you gave me in my wardrobe in my room," I announce as I open the door.

Kaelis turns away from what he was inspecting on the desk, quickly lowering his hand from his mouth. Was he biting his nails? The act seems so unlike the usually composed Kaelis.

"I would bet that Rewina suspected you'd be more comfortable, given your injuries."

"Injuries that are mended, thanks to you." I follow him back to the sitting area, choosing the clean sofa. Kaelis does as well. Which I don't blame him for. But there were chairs as an option to not sit next to me . . . farther from the food, though. *Why am I overthinking his proximity?* "Really, it would've been fine to leave me in the other clothes. Twenty know I've been in worse."

Kaelis reaches for another grape, but rather than putting it into his mouth, he gently presses it into mine. I'm too shocked to object. "Stop fighting, Clara, and accept my kindness. It'd be a shame to waste it; I give it to precious few." He turns back to the platter, and I can't properly read his expression in profile. "Besides, you will not have to 'be in worse' ever again. Not so long as I'm around."

"You don't have to do this."

"But I want to." Kaelis glances my way. "Consider yourself *lucky*."

I can't help a laugh. *I'll take this luck.*

"Who was the first to teach you about the cards? Your mother?" Kaelis casually asks as I reach for more food.

My hand freezes midair. All the suspicions I've ever had about the prince return. "How do you know about my mother?"

"You mentioned her earlier, that she was the one to first say to put 'a piece of yourself' into the cards. Clever, though I doubt she meant it literally." He doesn't seem to realize the panic that those words instill in me.

I grab one of the oversized sandwiches, stand, and announce, "I should get back to the dormitory. My roommate already suspects me of a great many things."

"Clara—"

"Thank you for everything, Kaelis," I mumble through a large bite of the sandwich.

"*Clara.*" He says my name like a command. Like a plea.

"I won't let anyone see me leave. I know the way." He doesn't stop me as I help myself through his closet. As I sprint for the back door and into the dark tunnels.

It isn't until I'm most of the way back to the dorm, sandwich long gone, that I realize I'm not looking over my shoulder to see if Kaelis is following . . . but for Eza, or any other threat. For the first time, I realize his apartments are the only place in the academy where I feel safe. That Prince Kaelis, of all the people in this world, for reasons I don't want to fathom, is a balm to my frayed nerves.

CHAPTER 31

I make it a point not to miss dinner the next night, and the entire time I can feel Kaelis's eyes on me. Eating at the center tables of the hall with the other initiates feels more and more like we're caged animals. Everyone is always watching everyone else, sizing one another up.

But I can ignore a thousand stares as though they are little more than passing glances—save for *his*. Kaelis's attention carries with it the weight of the world. That stare fills my mind with the memory of the sound of my name on his lips.

He says my name like a command. Like a plea . . .

Conversation offers minimal distraction, but I keep at it anyway. I hadn't expected to make friends here, but I've grown admittedly fond of Sorza's quips, Luren's fussing, Dristin's unexpectedly thoughtful insights, and even Kel's constant dry skepticism.

It takes two days before I'm ready to go back to the Majors' hideaway. Each afternoon I tell myself I'll go. But there's always an excuse. Luren asked for help . . . I had to re-ink the cards I used when fighting Eza . . . I want to run through the halls and train my body instead . . .

They are just excuses, though.

At night I can feel Eza at my throat as viscerally as I can feel Glavstone's pen skewering my hand. They alternate places in my nightmares, the familial resemblance in their hard jaws and sharp stares now undeniable. I hardly sleep, despite the comforts of my bed. Knowing that Alor is friendly with Eza and she's *right next to me* makes it even worse. It's like my first nights in Halazar all over again—staying awake, afraid of what the guards might do if the opportunity of me sleeping were presented to them.

The third day, I make it a point to go back to my room early enough that Alor won't be there. I can take my time undressing from my daytime outfit and then re-dressing into a sleek pair of leather trousers and a simple silken shirt. Leisurely, I go through all my cards—even the ones I'm not supposed to have—tucking them into my deck, which I strap to my thigh. I pack my satchel with inking supplies and sling it across my body, then crawl into bed and pull the covers to my chin, putting my back to Alor's side of the room.

A light slumber overtakes me, but I wake instantly when Alor returns. I don't move, though. It's agony listening as she goes through the movements of her evening routine. The sheets slide. I wait until her breathing is even before I slowly roll over.

Her back is to me, and she doesn't move as I shift. The swell of her chest is consistent as I push my covers aside. My boots meet the carpet without a sound, and I pad to the door. The hinges and latch ease open and shut with hardly a whisper.

The initiates' common area is empty at this hour. But the main common room for the four houses isn't. As soon as I emerge, Kel calls to me.

"I thought you went to bed early?" The moment she says it, I feel like all eyes are on me.

"Trouble sleeping." I cross over to where she sits with Sorza. "Looking to see if I can't find a certain prince to comfort me."

"Disgusting," she says with a pleasant smile.

"Now, now," Sorza scolds lightly. "If Clara wants to make heinous life choices, then that's her business."

"You two are the absolute best," I say dryly.

"Don't forget it." Sorza gives me a wink.

"Pleased to see you finally acknowledge my greatness." Kel preens, sinking back into her chair. She adds, loudly, "Now, don't let us keep you from going to the prince's apartments suspiciously late at night."

Rolling my eyes, I head out. I only look exasperated. Anything to have people believing Kaelis and I are a real couple is worth it to me.

The academy and its endless passages are second nature to me now. It takes no time for me to get to Silas's tucked-away abode. I give a few solid raps.

"Silas, it's me, Clara." I brace myself.

"Clara." He lets out an audible sigh of relief at the sight of me. Without warning, I'm engulfed in his crushing embrace, and I stiffen instantly, thinking of my conversation with Kaelis. Of the suspicions that have been swirling within me over the past few days. "I was worried about you. After Eza . . ."

Silas slowly unravels his arms. There's a familiarity in the way he holds me. He's unhurried to let me go, so I'm the one to initiate it. I try not to be awkward, but it's hard when I'm searching his face and asking myself if *he* was the one who led to my being caught.

"You heard?"

"I was coming to see you. But then . . . I'm sorry I didn't help." He averts his eyes and releases me. "I wanted to, but—"

"You're supposed to stay secret." I initiate contact, fingertips landing on his forearm, hoping the motion alleviates any suspicions. This brings his stormy gaze back to mine, and I try to offer an encouraging smile. "It's all right. I'm not upset. And I can take care of myself."

His sigh sounds unconvinced. "I wish I could've done more than fetch Prince Kaelis."

"You went to Kaelis?" *But he told me . . .*

"I found him in the halls, conveniently headed in that direction, actually." Silas nods, unknowingly confirming Kaelis's claim that he was out looking for me.

"Is it Kaelis you answer to?"

He tilts his head slightly, and I instantly know my question was too direct. "I answer to the crown."

Not what I wanted to hear, Silas . . . Torn about what I've come to him for, I remind myself I made up my mind and say, "Well, you can make up for it by helping me tonight. Can you take me back to my friends' townhome?"

He tenses, and I wait. Through the conflict in his gaze, I know he's going to say yes. His guilt over Eza will—

"You shouldn't. It's not safe for you to leave the academy."

"There is nowhere safer for me than with my family," I assure him. Even though I'm not sure I can trust Silas, he already knows of the townhome, and I have no other way out of the academy. Until I have proof, it's better to keep my suspicions a secret: I could be wrong, and I won't ruin a key alliance and friendship by being hasty. "And it's precisely because it's not safe that I must go. I've thought through this, I swear."

He inhales slowly and exhales agreement. We move into his room and back to his desk. Just like the last time, he collects his inking supplies and two cards with the Chariot already emblazoned upon them.

Silas holds out his hand to me and, in a blink and with a whinny, we're standing in the entry of the townhome.

"Go ahead and ink in the lounge before we get there," I say. Silas wasn't allowed in the lounge last time, so he didn't see it. Which means, I think, it'd still be a "new" place by the rules of his card. His lack of objection affirms my suspicions. "I'm going to wake up the rest while you do."

Silas nods and heads toward the back.

Unlike last time, not a single candle or lantern is lit. I slowly make my way up the stairs in nearly complete darkness. The building is set so far off the main street that the lamplight can't reach its windows. The second floor is a repeat of the first—half stairwell, half hall with connecting doors. All shut. All silent.

Except one. In the far back, the faintest slit of light cuts across the floor. Not too late for all the night owls, I see. I make for it and knock softly.

"Enter," Twino says from within, suspecting nothing.

I ease open the door to find a cramped study—little more than a closet, really. In the back, spanning from wall to wall, is a little desk that faces a window. Above the window is what looks like a signet of Clan Tower. *Odd.* It likely belonged to the previous owner. The desk is flanked by floor-to-ceiling shelves on both sides that are crammed so full of books and scrolls and inking supplies that one wrong breath would be likely to trigger a costly avalanche.

"Still burning the midnight oil, I see."

Twino jolts upright, spinning in his chair. He tries to blink sleep from his eyes. "You're not making a good case for not being a ghost when you show up out of nowhere like that."

"Please, I've always shown up out of nowhere." I scoff. "Here, I have presents for you."

"Presents?" His brows lift. I step in so he doesn't have to stand, squeezing to his side. I hold out my satchel and Twino sets it on the desk, letting out a gasp that could rattle the foundations of the house. "For me?"

"All for you."

"You shouldn't have." It's somewhere between a jest and completely serious.

"They're keeping me well stocked at the academy—I have everything I could want and then some."

"Not even Arina could sneak out this much."

"My sister still had a lot to learn," I say. "Did she ever mention anyone else? A Selina Guellith, maybe?" I ask, suddenly remembering what Kaelis said about another student disappearing at the same time. "Or anyone who'd been sneaking out with her?"

"No . . ." His expression turns serious as he looks back to me, and I know it's not solely a result of bringing up my still-missing sister. "In all our searching, we didn't come up with any mention of another student going missing. What aren't you telling us?"

"I really wish you missed something, sometimes." I take the bag back from him. He made quick work of emptying its contents and is already sorting out all the powders, papers, brushes, and pens I could spare.

"I'd be a shit strategist if I missed things, Clara." He never has. It's why I've always trusted him. "Though, clearly, I've had quite the blind spot." I can tell how much it frustrates him from his tone. "So, are you going to tell me, or should I start guessing?" He doesn't look at me as he speaks, instead decanting the powders into larger, half-empty containers already at the corner of his desk.

"Prince Kaelis has taken a special interest in me and has fed me some information as a result. Oh, and we're engaged." No point in hiding it.

Twino blinks. "*Oh, and we're engaged,*" he repeats in a mockery of my phrasing. "You and Prince *Kaelis?*" He forces the name out as though it's in a foreign tongue. The clanking stops as he stiffens. "*You're the one the void-born is engaged to?*"

"Rumors do spread widely." Yet, as someone who generally doesn't care for gossip, I'm always amazed by it.

Twino is focused on one thing. "You're engaged to the same prince who put you into Halazar?"

"It wasn't him."

"And you believe that?" Twino gives me a look that suggests I'd be foolish for thinking so. I don't blame him.

"I do." I'm shocked at how much conviction I have.

Twino mirrors the emotion. He still oozes doubt. "Who, then?"

"I'll tell everyone at the same time. I've important information to share."

"I'll go get them." Twino slowly rises to his feet. "You might startle them a bit too much if they woke up and saw you over the side of their beds."

Twino makes his way to the other rooms, and I head downstairs. Silas is still in the lounge, finishing his inking. The black lines dry silver as I enter.

"You'll be using this room again, I assume?" he asks.

"Likely."

"No problem, I'm done." He begins collecting his inking supplies back into the small pouch he wears around his hips. "It must be nice . . ." The sentiment is little more than a whispered murmur.

"What must be?"

"Having people you're so close to." The words are full of longing I don't want to hear. *Don't make me feel for you.*

"They're pretty amazing." I sit across from him, meeting his gaze firmly but gently. "And I'll do anything to protect them."

He nods. "I can understand that."

Jura is the next one up; we hear her in the kitchen before she pops her head through the door. "Hello, Clara, Silas. This week is a cinnamon swirl shortbread cookie with a vanilla drizzle."

"Yes, please." It's one of her best recipes.

"May I have one, too?" Silas asks shyly.

"You may have several, because I only know how to cook in single serving, or for small armies, there is no between." Jura enters with a heaping platter, placing it on the table between us.

Silas seems shocked and delighted as he helps himself to three. Then he excuses himself for the study. I bite my tongue and keep from telling him not to go upstairs. I don't want him to suspect anything. I need to keep acting normal.

Within ten minutes, everyone else is up. Gregor has stoked a fire and leans against the mantel. Ren is half falling asleep on Twino's shoulder in the sofa opposite. Jura assumes her position next to me.

"What's the emergency?" Despite the hour, Bristara is still sharp in her usual seat.

"Prince Ravin was behind my imprisonment in Halazar, I'm nearly certain of it," I say solemnly and quietly, leaning forward to speak only for them—even if Silas's ear were pressed against the door. "And I'm not sure if this place is safe any longer."

A long stretch of silence, filled with wide eyes.

Jura reaches for the platter. "Well, this is cookie news if I ever heard it."

I tell them *everything* this time. About the Majors and myself.

About Kaelis's bid for the World and my intention to steal it when the time comes. To their credit, everyone takes the fantastical tales in stride. If anything, it seems to provide an explanation they were missing on why I can do half of what I'm able. "Now I feel less bad about not being able to learn how to ink with any powder," Twino murmurs at one point. The rest of them nod in agreement.

At the end, I explain why I now believe Prince Ravin was the one really behind my imprisoning, and how we all need to be more careful than ever because Silas—the man milling about right now—might have been, could still be, his mole.

I cannot stand the disapproving glint to Bristara's stare. Her silence throughout it all has been deafening. She was skeptical of Silas from the first moment. I want to defend myself and double down that I was only doing what I thought was best. What I had to. But I also know I've proved her instincts right.

"We could just kill him now." Gregor cracks his knuckles.

"No, Clara is right. It's best not to arouse suspicion without solid proof," Twino says begrudgingly.

"I was getting so comfortable here." Jura sighs heavily.

"Better to know what might be coming and act than to be caught off guard again." Ren seems to have deflated into the sofa, looking far more awake. "What do we do now?"

"With the additional supplies Clara can bring us, we can do enough jobs to find another place to buy—or rent." Twino stares at nothing and no one—his usual look when he's running the finances of the club in his mind. "We'll be able to find somewhere else within half a year, a little more."

"Nowhere as easy or as comfortable as this," Jura laments. She looks to Bristara. "You don't know of any other homes abandoned by noble clans we can take over, do you?"

"Unfortunately not. But let's not be hasty." As Bristara speaks, she presses her fingertips together. "We will make our own subtle preparations, certainly. But until we know for sure, we will not make any bold decisions." Her eyes swing to me, landing hard. "I expect you to come up with the truth of what happened and if it involved Silas or not. The rest of it, we will carry on as normal, for now."

All I can manage is another nod. I hate the weight of her disapproval. Of feeling like I failed them all once more. The fateful night that I was caught will forever haunt me. *But my mother's murderer . . . I thought it was a lead.*

"If Silas was behind you being caught and the club being destroyed . . ." Gregor's attention is affixed on the door. "He's mine when the time comes."

"Get in line," Ren adds. The rest of them murmur their agreement, and I have yet another task on my growing list of seemingly impossible tasks: find out the truth, once and for all, of what happened the night I was taken.

CHAPTER 32

"No." Kaelis looks up at me from behind his desk. I'm not sure what he's doing, but he's doing a very good job of making himself look important while doing it.

Meanwhile, I have taken up residence on the settee. I've put an upside-down tray on two stacks of books as a makeshift table where I work on sketching out my Major. The memory of the symbol I inked when I fought with Eza is in my blood now—literally and figuratively. But it's all so . . . rudimentary. There are no flourishes. Nothing that would truly suit a card of its nature. Hence why my ink has yet to dry silver. I can feel the card demanding more from me to fully master its magic, and I am determined to rise to the occasion.

Priss is curled up next to me, a bit offended that I keep crossing and uncrossing my legs to the point that my lap is not a viable sleeping option. I scratch her chin on occasion with my free hand to try to mitigate her fuzzy wrath.

"It makes the most sense, and you know it." The plan I've suggested is a good one. Kaelis sighs in a way that tells me he knows it, too. "You said your father *never* shows anyone the cards. But you're also certain he's never without them. The only way he might give us a clue as to where he keeps them on his person is if we give him a new card. With any luck, I'll get a glimpse of the rest of them when he stores it." If King Oricalis is that paranoid about the cards he has, then he'll want to store a new one right away. I hope.

"And what if you don't? He ends up with another golden card." Kaelis rests his temple on his fingertips and stares at me in a manner that could make paint peel. "That's the opposite of what we want."

"I'm stealing them at the Feast of Cups anyway, aren't I?" I shrug and lean back into the cushions. Priss wastes no time seizing the opening in my lap. "What's one more card to forge and take at that time?"

Kaelis points his quill at his four-legged companion as I give her a good scratching around her entire face. "Opportunist. Traitor."

"Don't be bitter just because she likes my chin scratches better. Don't you, Priss?" I give a few extra for emphasis. Then I turn back to Kaelis, briefly catching a smile directed at the feline, before the tone shifts to serious once more. "If there's one card I'll be able to make a convincing fake of, it's my own." I'd give him a fake to begin with, but I've been so focused on making my own card that I haven't even started trying to figure out how to make fakes of the other legendary Major tarot. "And if I fail to steal them for you at the Feast of Cups, it doesn't matter if your father has one card or five cards."

Kaelis rubs a palm over his face, suppressing a groan. His hair is even more of a mess than usual as he rakes his fingers through it. The same fingers that now twitch as he pulls them away from his mouth before he can bite on them—a habit I've just noticed over the past few weeks.

"It's the best opportunity for me to see the cards that doesn't involve us concocting a reason for me to be around your father again after All Coins Day."

"I know." He sighs and hits the desk lightly with the side of his fist. "I do . . . But my father will kill to keep those cards a secret." Kaelis's attention darts to me with a look that could cut diamonds. "You trust these people?" He's referring to the members of the club. I've mentioned bringing them in for the job. The last time I worked on my own, it got me caught. I'm not making the same mistake twice.

"With my life and then some. Besides, they managed to thwart your brother once by surviving and escaping his attack on the Starcrossed Club—something not even I managed." I had to tell Kaelis that I had found a way out of the school to more easily plan with the club. But he hasn't asked for too many details. The headmaster seems pleased to remain willfully ignorant when it comes to when and how I'm breaking his rules. Which is good, because if he did ask, I'd outright lie to protect Silas.

"And they have the skills to get these cards if my father doesn't show them to you?" Kaelis slowly stands.

"I think so. It's not the first dangerous thing they've done." I focus on Priss for a moment to avoid the overwhelming guilt that follows. I know the danger I want to put them in. And I still need to get Bristara to agree to it.

"This will be the *most* dangerous thing they've ever done." Kaelis crosses to me.

"I know," I say, softer.

He stops in front of the makeshift table. Wordlessly, he reaches for the paper I was sketching on. His eyes dart to mine, almost like he's asking for permission to look at it. I don't move, other than continuing to lavish affection on Priss. He lifts the paper and studies it.

"Beautiful." The feeling behind the word is deep.

Never have I seen anyone admire anything I've created the way Kaelis does. It is as if the secrets of the world are wrapped in my rough lines and hasty inking. As though he is entranced wholly and completely.

I wish someone would look at me that way. The rogue thought has me ducking my chin to look at Priss rather than Kaelis. It's been so long, too long, since anything like that has materialized for me. I've been busy focusing on keeping myself and Arina alive, then proving myself to Bristara. Liam was a fluke, an error that should have never happened. It's been too dangerous to entangle myself with anyone outside of the club, and I decided early I wouldn't sleep with the people I worked with. Which now includes Kaelis . . .

"All right." Kaelis sets the paper down with another heavy sigh. He turns to the window opposite his desk. "We'll go with your plan."

"You're sure?" If he's not fully on board, I don't want to move forward. That's a recipe for sabotage.

"No." His hands ball into fists at the small of his back as he stands a little taller, as if every muscle in his body is tensing. "I loathe the idea of my father having another card—*your* card." The way he says it—shifting his feet to half face me, his stare—suggests that the latter might be even more unpalatable to him than the former. "But you're right, it is the best approach. The best we have. And . . . I have faith in you. And because you trust them, I will have faith in your friends, too."

The last admission makes me completely still. The warmth from him is so strange that I'm instantly on guard. In the absence of any other response, arrogance becomes my defense. "I agree. My plans *usually* don't fail."

"Here's hoping we have your luck, rather than mine." The sun is setting behind him, outlining him in gold. For once, he looks touchable. Warm. Human. "The main hall is far, and our time is short. How about dinner here, with me? You can continue working. The dining table in my apartments would be a better space anyway; you'd have more room."

"Sure." The word slips from my lips before I can think about it too much.

This morning, instead of the wielding classroom, Professor Thornbrow has taken us to one of the academy's rooftops. It's one of the largest towers and so has ample space for us all to spread out and practice. Given how close we are now to All Coins Day, these rehearsals for the tests we're going to face feel so much more real.

Allegedly, this rooftop is where we will be dueling in the Three of Swords Trials, too, which seems to have put everyone a bit more on edge.

Luren stands opposite me. We square off. She shuffles her deck for the seventh time.

"You can't be afraid of your own cards," I say under my breath, glancing toward Vaduin. The professor is on the opposite side of the circular rooftop. "You *made* them, with your own magic."

"My inking isn't the best, what if—"

"What if it goes off perfectly and you're the best wielder to ever step foot in the academy?" I arch my brows and give her a pointed look.

"You know that's not the case." Luren sighs. "If anyone is, it's you."

"Four of Cups, Luren." I harden my tone and my stare. From the corner of my eye, I see Vaduin begin rounding back toward us. He's been relentless today, demanding that everyone practice with Threes and Fours only.

"I don't want to—"

"Now," I interrupt. Then add, gentler, "Please." *For your sake.* Vaduin pushing her will be a lot worse than me doing it.

With trembling fingers, she draws the Four of Cups from her deck. I refrain from scolding her for not summoning it with magic. Getting her to just draw the card is progress. She returns the deck to the oversized pocket of her knitted coat and holds out the card.

Luren closes her eyes, and the card quivers like a leaf in the autumn breeze that now cools the backs of our necks. I feel the moment her magic surges. But it's too much, too wild and uncontrolled. The ink on the card shifts, as if alive—sentient. Frost coats it and then hisses into the air. As the ice disappears from the card's surface, a new image appears.

It's similar to the old image but subtly changed: What was once right side up is now upside down.

The card has reversed.

"Luren!" Her name is nothing more than a gasp. I dash forward, casting an Ace of Swords. It's probably futile. An Ace couldn't stand up to this magic. But I try anyway, even though I already know it's too late.

The frost explodes off her card with a burst of magic. Like a winter geyser, it drenches half the class, ice-laden waterfalls pouring off the edges of the rooftop. The Ace of Swords that had been hovering under my palm disintegrates. I brace myself, twisting my body and shielding my deck. Other students aren't so lucky. The force knocks them back just like Luren. Groans and frustrated shouts rise with the shock of ruined decks.

As soon as the blast is over, I continue rushing to her side. Frost coats her chattering lips and tries to fuse her with the stone rooftop.

The Ace of Wands jumps from my deck and becomes a tongue of flame that hovers above her. It fights against the runaway frost magic trying to slow her heartbeat and end her life. Without warning, I'm shoved away.

"Move," Vaduin says gruffly. The Queen of Cups is hovering over his shoulder. I withdraw my flame and my person, giving him space. My magic seemed to steady Luren just long enough for Vaduin's skilled card work to mend her. The ice retreats, and Luren's eyes crack open.

"What . . ."

"Your incompetence nearly got you and half the class killed, that's what," Vaduin snarls.

"It wasn't her fault," I snap. "She wasn't ready for that card."

"Was it a Five or less?" His attention swings to me.

"She wasn't—"

"Was it a Five or less?" The professor's patience is gone today.

"Yes," Luren answers, sitting. Her head hangs in shame. "Four of Cups."

"A card any first year should be able to wield without losing control." Vaduin looms over her. "How did you manage to survive the Arcanum Chalice?" he asks, even though he was there. Even though he knows we all fought for our places.

Before Luren can answer, Sorza shouts, "Professor, *Professor!*"

Vaduin's head swivels, attention swinging to another dueling ring next to us, where Sorza and Kel were paired. The latter is on the ground, with Sorza hunched over her. Icicles skewer Kel's body. Blood pools around her, mixing with the puddles of water and seeping between the stones of the rooftop.

"Kel," Luren chokes. She practically lunges for her friend.

Vaduin throws Luren back, forcing her to the ground with a shove. Luren blinks up at him, still dazed. "You've done more than enough," he snaps and rushes over to Kel.

"Kel." The name quivers on Luren's lips.

I wrap an arm around her, unsure of what else to say or do.

"I . . . I . . ." Silent tears stream down Luren's face as she stares at the unmoving body of her friend. "It reversed. How could . . . How did . . ." The words fade away.

"Dristin," I call over to him. He rushes to our side. "Stay with her."

With a nod, Dristin does as I ask, and I cross to where Vaduin is hunched over Kel. Sorza has been pushed away. She doesn't move. Simply stares, wide-eyed. Horrified.

Magic flashes as Vaduin uses card after card. Nothing lands. The swirls and sparks of tarot releasing its powers cascade off Kel's cold flesh. Her body is horribly still.

"Let me help," I whisper, not knowing what I can do. Vaduin doesn't acknowledge me. I say, louder, "Let me help."

"I don't have time for your insolence, Clara Redwin." The professor has yet to look at me. But fewer cards fly from his deck. He pants softly.

"I can—"

Vaduin stands and somehow feels a thousand times taller. He stares down at me, and at Kel's lifeless form. "Unless you have some special card that might bring someone back from the dead, there's nothing you can do."

At the word "dead," Luren lets out a howl. She doubles over, clutching her stomach, retching.

"Class is over. Dristin, get Luren to the clinic. The rest of you get out of my sight." The initiates begin to move.

Luren shouts, clawing at the air to try to seek purchase on imaginary walls as Dristin pulls her away. "Kel. Kel! Let me see her! I killed her. I killed her. *I killed her!*" Her howls are worse than the cries of the dying in Halazar.

"Dristin, let her go," I say.

"Take her to the clinic," Vaduin snaps.

My whole body jerks to face the professor, shoulders squared. "She has a right to say goodbye to her friend."

"She will be where I tell her to be." He practically snarls. "Dristin, do it now. The rest of you. *Go*." The commands are barked, and everyone shuffles away. Sorza pulls herself off the ground, and I move to join her. Vaduin stops me. "Not you." I shoot him a glare, which only deepens his glower. "You're spending the afternoon with me. I will not tolerate disrespect."

Sorza gives me one sidelong, wary look, but she ends up following the rest, staying at Luren's right side. Dristin is at Luren's left. Knowing she has them to look after her is the only thing that keeps me somewhat calm in the face of Vaduin's command to stay.

It's just Vaduin and me left. He doesn't tell me what to do, so I simply stand there as he walks back to the rooftop entry and calls for three robed staff, who silently collect Kel's body. They carry her unceremoniously back into the academy.

I've seen my share of death. And while I'd come to know Kel better than most here, she wasn't a dear friend. Not like she was to Luren. Perhaps it is the pain that I know Luren is in that twists my insides into aching knots.

She lost the only person she truly trusted . . .

"Luren didn't even get to say goodbye," I whisper.

"Enough," Vaduin says briskly.

"Luren lost her only companion here and—"

"All because she couldn't control her magic."

"This was not Luren's fault." I narrow my eyes.

Something in the way Vaduin looks at me has me bracing for a strike. His green eyes are alight with rage. But he hardly moves. "Perhaps she will learn how to better control her magic now that she has witnessed the cost of not doing so."

"You are a monster." I don't even care what he might do to me. I've had worse.

"I am a teacher who lost a student!" Vaduin takes a step toward me so suddenly that I can't move backward fast enough. Hurt spills over into his voice. A pain I didn't expect from him. Like he . . . *cares*. "Since you know so much, Redwin, tell me what happens when an Arcanist wields a reversed card once?"

"They're more prone to doing it again."

"*They're more prone to doing it again,*" he repeats the second I've finished. "You're right, I wanted Luren to hurt because she needed to know this pain. Otherwise, she's going to harm others and likely kill herself when her magic reverses again."

It's heartless. Downright cruel. But also . . . fair, in its own way.

Perhaps Vaduin is more like Kaelis than I thought; they both seem to care a lot more than they let on.

"Now, scrub away the blood. You're dismissed when there's not a drop left."

I reach for my deck.

"Not like that." He motions back to the entry, where a bucket, rag, and brush have been left. "Without magic. So you have ample time to think about all the reasons why you should heed commands when they're given. That you might not have the full picture."

I hold his stare for a few more seconds. Vaduin is unyielding. So I'm the one to back away. Wordlessly, I do as he asks. I retrieve the bucket and set to scrubbing.

Hours pass. The stone is porous, and Vaduin is slow to bring me fresh buckets. For a while, I'm just moving around blood. But I don't complain. In a way, the act feels like a vigil. Vaduin leans against one of the columns that supports a pergola over the entry, watching me the entire time.

It isn't until the fourth bucket that a strange glint catches my eye. It's no mere reflection of the sunlight in the tinted water, nor is it a fleck of quartz trapped in the stone used to build the academy. It's a tiny shard of what almost looks like colored glass. Except, there's a brief sting of magic that pricks my fingertip like a needle plunged right to the bone.

Wincing and shaking it away, I glance in Vaduin's direction. He continues watching me. If he notices the movement, he says nothing. I return to scrubbing. There's a few other strange shards. All an identical shade of teal. All with stinging magic. Something with the card reversing, perhaps? It seems likely . . . I've never encountered a reversed card before, so I'm stuck with an educated guess. I doubt Vaduin will answer if I ask.

And the next person to emerge I know will not want to talk about reversed cards.

"What is the meaning of this?" Kaelis's voice slithers on the wind. As dangerous as a viper. Eyes flashing as they swing from me to Vaduin.

"I'm teaching her a bit of respect. She needs to learn the importance of cleaning up one's messes."

"My bride is not to be made to scrub on her hands and knees," Kaelis says, seething, and begins to cross to me.

"No." I lean back, sitting on my heels. "Your highness, respectfully, no." I want to go, desperately, more than anything. I want to follow Kaelis all the way back to his apartments and collapse on his couch in front of that massive fire. Ask kindly if Rewina would be up to bringing me a tall glass of something hot to get the chill of death from my bones. Maybe I'd even be bold enough to steal Kaelis's bathroom, which is far, far nicer than anything I have access to as a student, for a much-needed bath. But I can't.

"See, this is what I'm talking about." Vaduin motions to me. "The audacity of her to—"

"Professor Thornbrow gave me a task, Headmaster," I interrupt, still speaking to Kaelis. His focus hasn't left me. "I intend to see it through to the end."

Kaelis purses his lips and then his face relaxes into a neutral expression before Vaduin can see his momentary frustration. "Very well."

Vaduin narrows his eyes at me. He can't argue. I'm giving him exactly what he wants.

Even if it means we stay out here all night for me to do it.

Kaelis leaves.

The moon is rising when the last of the blood is expunged from the stone. Kel was gone in a breath, her body carried off like little more than luggage. But it took hours to clean the remnants of her. And, in the end, it was my honor to offer what meager service it was to her memory. It will likely take Luren much, much longer to wash her hands of what happened here today.

Vaduin and I have both missed dinner at this point. The second the last bit of water dries on the late breeze, I stand and stretch then make my way to him, looking down as I pass. He sat long ago.

There's no thank-you. But also no snide remark. He doesn't say a word as I stride into the academy.

CHAPTER 33

It's three days before Luren returns to classes. When she does, she doesn't say a word to anyone. She just appears at her desk for inking one morning. Silent and studious. I don't miss how the other students regard her warily, their too-loud whispers asking, "What's the point of inking if your cards reverse on you?" I silence them with a scathing stare. Luren doesn't even look up.

When I try to approach her after class ends, she quickly flees.

Later, at dinner, Sorza stares at the two empty chairs beside me and asks, "Did you see her at all this afternoon?"

"No." I don't have to ask who she's referring to.

"Me, neither." Dristin sighs and pinches the bridge of his nose. "Probably for the best that she's making herself scarce, though. I heard some people celebrating that not one but two initiates were out of the running, since Luren's now 'basically comatose.'"

"Bastards," Sorza murmurs under her breath.

I'm inclined to agree with Sorza. Whoever said that was lucky it was Dristin who overheard and not me. "We should find her." I stand.

The other two readily abandon their meals. Together we make our way to the dormitories. Luren's room is easy to find—all our names are plastered on the doors. But my heart sinks when I see the placards.

Kel's name is underneath hers.

I exchange a look with the other two, then knock, but there's no answer. So I open the door without an invitation. There are two trunks, one next to each of the beds. Luren sits on the edge of her bed, in the dark, staring out her window. She doesn't acknowledge us. Doesn't even move as I approach.

Her eyes are red and puffy, but her cheeks are dry. I imagine she's cried out every tear she had and then some. I know all too well how it feels.

Luren still doesn't move as I sit next to her. Sorza sits on her opposite side. Dristin closes the door and then leans against the wardrobe.

"I thought it'd be easier if our things were packed." Luren's voice is void of all emotion. "Though, the staff still hasn't come to take her things back to her family. I—" She chokes on her words. "I wrote a letter explaining what happened. They deserve to know."

Over the months, getting to know the two of them, I learned that my initial suspicions had been right: Luren and Kel grew up together. I saw them practically finishing each other's sentences. I can only imagine what the letter in Kel's trunk contains.

"Where are *you* going?" I ask softly.

"To the mills."

"Luren . . ." Sorza is at a loss for words.

A bitter smile crosses Luren's lips. One of resignation. Her eyes flutter closed. "My magic turned on me. I know what happens to Arcanists who have a card reverse . . . You can't be trusted to live, otherwise you might cause something like Clan Hermit."

"Clan Hermit was because of Prince—" Sorza stops herself, eyes darting to me, as if she's afraid of my opinion of the prince. Like I don't already know what's said about him. Still, now isn't the time to get into it, so I don't correct or interject, allowing her to say, "No one knows what happened to Clan Hermit. Not really."

"First it's one card, then many." Luren sighs. "Once your magic turns sour, it never goes back."

"That's not true," I insist.

"Clara's right. Arcanists are too valuable for the clans to lose them due to one mistake," Dristin says matter-of-factly. "They're not going to kill you for a single error; it has to be repeated. And there are many stories of an Arcanist only having one card turn on them."

Luren finally moves. Her head turns slowly, almost mechanically, as she looks back to Dristin. Never have I seen her expression so cold. "This was more than a 'mistake.' Kel is dead."

A heavy silence crosses through the room at the last word.

"Still, you can't give up." Sorza is the one with the bravery to speak first. "Don't just hand them your wrist and walk to the mill."

"What does it matter?" Luren turns to her. "No house will want me now. I'm heading to the mills no matter what: It will be either now, of my own volition, or later, when I don't get a coin on All Coins Day. I might as well take the Mark and be done with it."

"You have power that you can use. You passed the Arcanum Chalice," Sorza says optimistically.

Luren hangs her head. "Only because I cheated."

The three of us share a confused look. I'm the one to say what we're all thinking. "It's impossible to cheat for the Chalice; you had to conquer it by your own merits."

"Not true," Luren objects. "I managed to get my hands on a deck and gave myself a few readings before I came to the academy."

"Where'd you get the deck from? You shouldn't have had access," Dristin asks. The noble, ever the stickler for rules.

"I worked at a club in Eclipse City for part of the year. They did readings there for the nobility."

"Reading for yourself would've been illegal." Dristin frowns.

"What's done is done, and unless you intend to report her to the enforcers . . ." I let the statement hover, looking pointedly at Dristin.

"Of course not!" He seems aghast at even the suggestion, which I'm relieved to see. "I'd never do that to Luren. I only meant it's surprising . . ." He glances away, adjusting his glasses.

"What was the club's name?" I ask Luren out of curiosity.

"The Fatefinders Club," she answers. I should've guessed. "The nobility would talk as if I wasn't there about everything, including things not meant for my ears. Even the students who would come in on winter break. Especially if I kept their cups full and my tits out." There's a side to Luren I never imagined. I'd applaud the boldness but now isn't the time.

"You learned about the Fire Festival test from the students and nobles—so you did a reading for it," I surmise.

"I'm still not entirely following," Sorza says. "How did giving yourself some readings help you 'cheat' the Chalice? Readings are only what *can* be, not what *will* be. At best you had a rough idea, but that's a far cry from *cheating*."

"Think about the theory behind reading: A really good reading is what is *most likely* to be, should circumstances not fundamentally change." Luren's voice is monotone. But at least reciting fact is keeping her talking. "And there weren't many ways my circumstances would fundamentally change before the Arcanum Chalice. We're all shepherded in together in one identical procession and presented with the same script and the same choices. The cards I picked during the Fire Festival were as much up to fate as the reading I did beforehand—there's nothing that could happen that would cause the cards I drew to change. So I knew what cards would be presented before me at the Chalice well in advance and which one would probably be the easiest to face."

Her skirts. Realization hits me. That was why she undid them. Why she pretended like she didn't know what was going to happen and seemed uninterested in what I had to say. She didn't want to risk altering her fate by doing even one thing differently.

"Luren . . . You are *brilliant*," I breathe.

"If I was brilliant, I would've told Kel I foresaw her death." She hangs her head and draws a shuddering breath. Tears still refuse to fall. "I tried to change it. Even when I knew she wouldn't want to trust you all, I tried to force it. To do everything possible to deviate from what I saw in the cards. But . . . what I saw ultimately came to pass."

Luren is two for two. Two readings where what she foresaw became reality, identical to how the cards said. At that rate, she might be as good of a reader as Arina.

I reach for her hand, taking it in both of mine and squeezing tightly. This draws her eyes to mine. "Luren, listen to me, you are a rare talent. You cannot go to the mills."

"But—"

"We are going to make sure people see your gift at All Coins Day." My conviction is partly selfish. I need this ability. Desperately. Arina would always give readings before our operations. The one time I didn't heed her warnings was the time I got caught. With Arina missing, this is one key area that the club is lacking before our operation on All Coins Day. I might not be inducting Luren into the Starcrossed Club anytime soon. But that doesn't mean I can't make use of this ability . . . and it'd be good for Luren, too. She needs to keep moving forward. "You can make it through All Coins Day with reading alone, and then we'll all train for the Three of Swords Trials together—we'll do even more than we're doing now. There's plenty of time before winter. We will make sure you stay."

"Why should I have time here in the academy and a chance at a better life when Kel cannot?" she whispers.

"*Because* Kel cannot, you should have it." I hold her hand tighter still, as if I'm her sole lifeline. I look at her and see the outline of my sister. Of us clutching each other with viselike grips, vowing that we will not die until Mother's killer is brought to justice. Sometimes the living must breathe because the dead cannot. "Do it for her. Live for her."

Luren's eyes shine in the moonlight. I wonder if she sees me—the real me underneath all of Kaelis's expensive fabrics and makeup. The me that has been dirty and scrappy and hungry, surviving only on determination. The type of person that she needs to be now, too. "You really think I can do it?"

"Unequivocally." I nod, wrapping an arm around her shoulders.

Luren leans on me. "I owe you. All of you."

"We're all helping each other survive this place," I say, surprised at how sincere it is. "You owe us nothing, because you help to us, too. More so . . . you're a friend."

We all keep our promise. Little by little, Luren reintegrates with the rest of the initiates. But they're still skeptical toward her, and that serves only to insulate the four of us further.

Let the other initiates underestimate and dismiss her. I don't mind her being an Ace in my pocket. The students are the only ones whose opinions matter anyway.

We spend our time together in the library, discussing inking. In dedicated rooms, to practice wielding—something she must work herself up to doing again. And reading for one another.

Luren's state improves steadily over time, as well as can be expected. I still find her staring off at times, her silence weighty. But as the academy moves on, so does she. At least that's what she presents. I doubt her innermost thoughts are as peaceful as her tone of voice.

I wait weeks, until All Coins Day is five days away, to finally ask her for a reading on what's about to happen. I use my intimidating reading from Professor Rothou's class months ago as a pretense. "I want to see if anything has changed," I say.

The results are not what I expected in the slightest.

The second the evening quiets, I help myself into Kaelis's apartments through the usual passage inside the bridge and through his closet. He's not in the main room, but the door to his study is ajar, as if left open just for me.

Our eyes lock the moment I enter.

I waste no time. "Someone is going to try to kill your father."

Kaelis, very slowly, returns his pen to its stand and steeples his fingers, as though I have come to him with a business proposal and not news of his sire's impending demise.

"Clara," he starts slowly. "You cannot just barge in here and talk dirty to me."

"Excuse me?" I lean back, nearly bumping into the doorframe.

He lets out a brief laugh. For some reason, the sound almost makes a hot flush rise to my cheeks. "Pray tell, how did you come to find out about this regicide plot?"

"One of the other initiates is an incredibly talented reader . . ." Ignoring my usual settee, I perch myself on the corner of his desk. I'm too worked up to lounge—I need to be ready to pace at any moment. I tell him about Luren and the readings she did for me tonight. And about how, in every spread, there were ominous signs for the king. "Of course, Luren didn't *quite* read it as an assassination attempt—she doesn't know that I have plans to actually meet with the king—and took the presence of the King of Swords more figuratively. But it was all there. I could see it, and I'm not even the best reader. So if it's obvious to me . . ."

Kaelis hums deeply, sinking back in his chair. "Luren, that's the woman whose card reversed, is it not?"

"It is." I try to read him and fail.

"Are you certain you can trust her abilities?"

"Are you questioning my judgment?" I lean back, aghast.

"You associate with the void-born prince; how could I not?" Kaelis taps his desk with his long fingers.

Void-born . . . Well, since he brought it up . . . "What do you know about reversed cards?"

His eyes narrow slightly. "If you're going to ask questions you probably shouldn't, then you can do better than that."

"Fine." I straighten. "Is it true? Can you wield reversed cards?"

"No," he answers without hesitation. Though it's not as if I really would've expected him to admit it if it were true. He smirks. "You don't believe me."

"Given what you've done, I—"

"What I've done?" he repeats. A shadow crosses over his expression. His words grow harsh. "You mean Clan Hermit."

I remember what Rewina told me and take it to heart. "I was going to say founding the academy at such a young age. You did so at eighteen, when most are just beginning to show an inkling toward magic. Two years before your first crop of initiates. You command with both fear and fealty some of the best Arcanists in Oricalis as your faculty. Stories of your prowess are not hard to come by."

He leans back in his chair, tapping his desk once more, as if he can't decide whether I'm telling the truth. Either way, Kaelis lets drops the subject of reversed cards, and the air feels instantly lighter. "So you think—because of what your 'talented' friend said—that someone is going to try to kill my father on All Coins Day."

"Yes. Do you know anyone who wants your father dead?" I ask.

"Please tell me that *you*, of all people, didn't just ask that." Kaelis gives me a look that suggests how painfully obvious the answer is.

"Fair."

"There are many foreign adversaries—and people inside our own kingdom—that are always considering making a move against my father. We have secured control over all the means of production of arcane powders, and we have more Arcanists than anywhere else in the world. The clans, while they have been forced to submit to the crown, still have memories in their bloodlines of the days when they ruled their own lands as kings. There are many who would like to see a return to those days, especially now that they've seen the power an absolute monarchy can wield."

I stare out the window at the city I've spent my life in. In all that time, I thought little of the world beyond Eclipse City, never mind Oricalis and beyond. The only time I have, it was to help an Arcanist escape through the desert to the east—the best chance they'd have of making it out of the kingdom.

"Does it matter who attacks our king, should such a thing happen?" Kaelis asks, returning my thoughts to the present.

"I don't think so." I drum my fingers against the desk.

"The real question is how does this change our plans?"

"I'm going to consult with my friends, see who can position themselves where—what information we can find. If we move quickly and there's some kind of advance warning, I can save the king and look like a hero.

"If there's an opening, Jura can lift the cards in the chaos—if she's managed to see where he keeps them. Twino will wait back at the regent's manor and be flexible support. Should the king be injured, they'll probably take him there. Same with Ren. Gregor will act as support behind the scenes." I pause to repeat everything in my mind. It seems to be a solid plan on its face, but I know I'll need to work out a few kinks and refine a few things before All Coins Day arrives. And I can rely on Twino and Bristara to poke at my plan and find the little holes. "All this is assuming your father isn't killed."

"He won't be killed." There's not even a whisper of doubt around Kaelis.

"How can you be so sure?"

"He never goes anywhere without the Twentieth Major, Quaelar—Judgment—right at hand. The Judgment card can revive anyone within five minutes of dying." Kaelis curls and uncurls his fingers into fists, as if barely containing rage. "At no small cost to Quaelar. But the man will continue shaving off years of his life if it means keeping my father alive. And that's not to say anything of the other Majors, and trained Stellis, that constantly surround him. Unfortunately, my father has made it nearly impossible to assassinate him."

I study Kaelis. It's the prince's turn to stare intensely out the window. But he looks past the ocean-filled horizon and mountain-wrapped city.

"You really do hate him." His dismay that his father is so hard to kill is evident and potent.

"There's much to hate." Kaelis steps around his desk. I have the sense he's done with this conversation. "For now, we should focus on what must be done—inking your golden card."

"Tonight?"

"With only five days left until All Coins Day, there's no time like the present." Kaelis stretches out a hand.

And, taking mine, he escorts me back the way I came—through his closet, past the secret door, and down the alternate tunnel. Already waiting on the pedestal surrounding the statue are an assortment of inking supplies, or at least two-thirds of the materials I'd need: pens and paper. But the ink itself is notably absent.

"You were prepared."

"You are ready. We both knew it, even if neither of us has said it aloud." There's a note of pride in his voice. "Use the water that surrounds the statue as the base of your ink." He guides me toward the statue and then releases me.

I cross the rest of the way on my own. Hand still tingling from the sensation of his fingers around mine, I study the different writing implements he left out for me. Each is as fine as the last. Even the paper, arranged in a small, neat stack, is perfectly cut.

"You clearly don't have that much faith in me if you think I need this many attempts." I tap the blank cards.

"Most don't get it on their first try."

"I am not like most."

"No . . . no, you're not." There's something more than admiration for my skill behind those words. I hear it, despite not wanting to. The meaning catches on me, halting my movements.

"Kaelis, may I ask you one thing?" My fingertips settle on the cool stone instead of the supplies.

"Anything." He says it like he truly means it.

"Why have you been so . . . kind to me?" The moment I ask, I instantly regret it. I don't want the answer. Maybe because, in part, I don't want to acknowledge the hidden truth to begin with. Yet, ignoring it is somehow worse. There's a knot in my chest that is only tightening, and I will him to tell me he secretly hates me so I can move on.

"You're essential to my plans." The statement is void of all emotion. Almost carefully so.

"You could get what you needed from me without giving me access to your apartments—without looking after me the way you have." Despite my better judgment, I can't let this go.

His footsteps echo off the high ceiling as he comes to stand next to me. He hovers for a moment before leaning against the pedestal. "It's because Priss likes you."

I snort in reply.

"She does. And she's an exceptional judge of character, far better than me; she doesn't warm up to just anyone." He smiles. *Really* smiles. It's painfully apparent he doesn't do it often because Kaelis ducks his chin slightly, as if trying to hide it. The movement puts his face in even deeper shadow, giving a contradictory, sinister aura to the sincerity of his expression.

I stand for a moment in stunned silence. He mistakes my reaction, and his expression quickly falls. Before I can say anything, Kaelis folds his arms and shifts his gaze to stare at the wall. But I suspect the wall is not really what he's seeing.

"Clara, I know what I am. I know how the world sees me, and that they're not all wrong. To be honest, most of the time, I don't even care." He shrugs. "If to bring about a new world—a *better* world—I must be the villain, if I must do evil things for the greater good, then so be it. I'll play the part now and be reborn a hero in my next life." There's a long pause that seems to encapsulate a thousand thoughts, a thousand long nights of inner turmoil I suspect I'm the first person to ever catch a glimpse of. "But it's also true that, sometimes, even the worst among us want a moment of absolution. To feel our humanity isn't entirely rotted away, that we aren't just a cold and lonely husk."

My fingers twitch. They move on their own, lifting from the stone. Instead of reaching for supplies, I reach for him. My touch lands on his forearm, tense under the thin cotton of his shirt. My fingers trail down, landing on the side of his thumb, a breath away from interlacing with his.

"You're warm, Kaelis."

"What?" He startles but doesn't pull away.

My eyes drag up from our hands to meet his. "You're too warm to be a husk." My lips arc in a slight smile, slowly, as if to show him how it's done. "You're a man of flesh and blood, whether you want to be or not."

He opens his mouth and closes it, abandoning all words. I leave him to the silence and pull away, turning back to the cards.

Kaelis, you annoying creature. I didn't want to like you even a little bit.

I lift a pen and dip it into the glowing water. No . . . it's not water. It's something else. Its viscosity is more like a thin jelly than water. It clings to the metal tip of the pen as I lift it, and with my every gesture, it trails light through the air.

Placing one of the blank cards before me, I close my eyes, steady my breath, and center myself. *All the power you need is within you,* Mother reminds me from wherever her soul now rests. As I press the metal tip into my finger, crimson swirls into the liquid, racing through it. Never have I seen anything more fascinating . . .

Never have I felt more magical.

Power surging, I set the tip of the pen on the top left edge of the card. The border is first. Swirls and dots. Intricate but meaningless designs that are little more than a warm-up. I imagine that they are like the lines of fate—rather, of luck, one of the few things that can defy destiny itself.

Even before I lift my pen, the lines break free of their outer confines and swirl inward. They take the shape of circles. Spinning inward and inward. All looping around a central symbol of a wheel. The sun winks through clouds above, and the moon goes through its phases below. Hidden in the chaotic patterns are hands and eyes that all reach and watch for the same point in the middle of the wheel—a tiny star.

And then, all at once, it's finished. Drawing even one more stroke would be wrong. I lift my pen and admire the finished product as the faint glow of the liquid dries to a golden metallic sheen.

Kaelis leans over my shoulder and whispers, "It's perfect."

He stole the words from my lips, so all I can do is nod. Reverently, I lift the card and run my finger over the now-dry image. The lines are raised slightly and cool to the touch, as if they were actual gold. Even the paper feels different, thicker, as though it were cast in a superfine metal rather than pulped river reeds.

The magic within is also changed. Normal cards thrum and pulse with power, waiting to be unleashed. But this is different. I can feel what Kaelis told me the last time we were here—this card is not meant to be cast.

"Now . . ." He extends his palm expectantly.

I hesitate for half a breath. Something in me unexpectedly balks at the idea of handing the card over. Even though it's the first time I've ever held it, it feels like I'm giving him a part of myself when I place it in his waiting hand.

Dark eyes meet mine. I can see that his restless energy seeks release. A slight, almost ominous expression crosses his face, highlighted by the faint glow of the water, but the danger is not directed my way. His words send a shiver up my spine. "Now our work will truly begin."

CHAPTER 34

All at once, All Coins Day arrives. Despite our weeks of preparation and planning inside and out of the classroom, it seems to appear out of nowhere, just like the chill that's settled in the autumn air. Initiates and students alike buzz with excitement as we gather in the common area to head into the city for the All Coins Day festival—where we will offer our services as Arcanists to the community and be judged by the students of the academy.

It strikes me that this will be the first time since entering the school during the Fire Festival—now sixty days ago—that most of my peers have left the fortress. A few seemed to have had exceptions made for them for Prince Ravin's soiree . . . but only the highest born. Perhaps I'd be shuffling in my boots and restlessly readjusting my scarf and coat countless times, too, if I hadn't been able to find my own way out.

The three department heads—Las Rothou, Raethana Duskflame, and Vaduin Thornbrow—lead the procession, with the students in four lines behind them. The King, Queen, Knight, and Page lead the other students in their respective house. Then come the initiates, who fall naturally into four lines as well. Finally, a handful of other faculty walk behind us. I've seen some of these professors in the halls, but they seem to teach only second and third years.

We're led through the academy, around the central conservatory that houses the tomb of the last queen of the ancient kingdom of Revisan, and down into a grand entryway that I recognize from the night of the soiree. However, that night it was shrouded completely in darkness. Today, with the wide doors open to the morning light, I can see the thick layer of dust that has blanketed the stone carvings around the room and turned them silver.

The stone carvings are of all the Majors, I realize: There are twenty columns, each with a cloaked figure representing one of the Majors at its apex and stoic guardians—wielding a variety of weapons, dressed in armor both familiar and foreign. Sculpted lines swirl around them, weaving every statue together like a tapestry. Every carved ribbon connects at one point, right above the doors. But the statue they'd connect to is missing, as if it has been ripped from its place. Wind blusters through the open doors, and a shiver runs down my spine. Would that statue have been the World? Or the Fool?

"Look, it's the Wheel of Fortune," Sorza leans in and whispers to me, gesturing with a tilt of her head toward one of the statues opposite where the World would have been. "Maybe it'll grant you luck today."

"Hopefully." I could use it.

"I'll take all the luck I can get." Luren overheard us. Fortunately, Sorza hadn't said anything too suspicious.

I grab Luren's hand. "You'll be great. And, when the sun sets, you're going to come right back here with us."

"I'll try my best." She smiles, but it doesn't quite reach her eyes. When she pulls her hand from mine, staring out the main entry of the academy, I wonder if she's thinking about how the last time she walked through these doors was with Kel. I stand a little bit closer to Luren as the procession begins to walk.

There are no carriages this time. We march across the big bridge that spans the mouth of the Farlum River, connecting the cliffs between city and academy. Wind threatens to rip off scarves and hats. Luren sinks deeper into the thick wool of her coat, her eyes red from more than the cold, I suspect.

Midway across the bridge is a slightly wider section. I can't see it from here, but I know that it houses a massive, fortified portcullis that can be opened and closed to control vessels entering and leaving Oricalis.

At the other end of the bridge is another gate: The three department heads combine their powers to unlock it. From here, I know the way. As I pass through the gates, my head swivels, and I find my eyes drawn back to the stony archway that houses them—inset in the wall that curves around the cliffs. The black ironwork of the gates is somehow stronger than steel but more delicate than lace, and I remember . . .

> *I'm a little girl, no older than ten, standing before this same gate. I clutch the cold ironwork instead of my mother's hand as she waits patiently for me. She indulges me often by taking me here. Though, even as a child, I know it is begrudgingly so. It is before the days of the academy, before Kaelis . . . a time when the education of Arcanists is much more decentralized and the fortress is nothing more than a relic from a kingdom that fell centuries upon centuries ago. It is both a forbidden place; the crown does not take kindly to mentions of its predecessor's glory. And it is sought after by Arcanists braving the journey anyway to seek the blessing of the Chalice in secret.*
>
> *"Little one, we should go, it's getting late," my mother says.*
>
> *"It is not," I object, even though it's so cold I can see my breath.*
>
> *"The stars will be out soon." She kneels next to me, wrapping her arms around my little body and holding me snug. "And the moon, and the night birds, and all the things that will say, 'It's time to sleep.'"*

My focus on the building that will become the academy can't be shaken. It's almost as if I feel something there. Whispering softly, calling to me . . . "One day . . . can I go inside?"

"You want to go in there?" she repeats softly, even though she heard and knows my current obsession well. "That place doesn't hold your destiny, only danger. You and your sister must never go there, Clara."

"They say the Chalice—"

"You don't need the Chalice," she repeats for what must be the thousandth time. "The Arcanum Chalice is a cursed ritual. You are plenty powerful all on your own."

"But—"

"Swear to me you will do as I say and stay hidden. Keep your true name and your powers secret. Stay safe. Protect those like you."

"Like you protect other Arcanists?" I turn my eyes to her, finally.

She gives a slight nod and holds me closer. "One day, I will tell you of all the little passages through the mountains. Of those like us, and all the precious reasons why we must fight for them. But you will never learn those things if you go to the fortress. That is a place of foul magic and ill omens. So give me your word that you will never go there—and that you will keep learning all I have to teach."

"I swear."

"Good." She kisses my cheek and stands, holding out her hand. Our shopping basket is tucked into the elbow of her other arm.

> "Now, come along, we don't want to keep your sister waiting. And tonight we'll keep working on your special inking..."

I'm sorry, Mother. I almost whisper it as I turn my attention forward once more. The gate is now far enough behind that it strains my neck to keep looking at it. I shift my grip on my bag. She was right—that building that became the academy ended up holding only danger for me.

But maybe danger is my destiny. Maybe I felt drawn to this place because it was what I was meant for all along. A part of fate that couldn't be taken.

The festival for All Coins Day is held in the heart of the city, in the main square by the expansive greens of River Park. On other days, the square is filled with temporary stalls set up on blankets and under sunshades by farmers and craftsmen who have traveled to Eclipse City to sell their products. Local merchants also line the square, peddling everything from staple goods to luxury indulgences from the far reaches of the kingdom and beyond. The Eclipse City merchants have still set up shop today, but the enforcers have prevented the seasonal vendors who usually migrate into Eclipse City for the day from setting up, to make room for the students and initiates. I can only hope that they're able to set up their stalls in the other smaller squares found throughout the city. Or that one day without being able to sell their goods won't mean their produce spoils and their families go hungry.

In place of their humble establishments, a labyrinth of small but stately tents have been erected. There are five colors in total: dark gray for Swords, blue for Cups, gold for Coins, red for Wands, and a plain cream for initiates. Full-fledged students participate in All Coins Day by simply enjoying the spirit of abundance, and also by giving their magic and skills to the community at no cost. In addition, students get an opportunity to assess the initiates' skills to determine who they deem worthy of being potential future housemates, as this is the day they will bestow their house coins upon us.

"Shall we claim our spots?" Sorza asks.

"Might as well. Let's go this way." My tone is casual, but my strides are purposeful. I'm replaying what Jura told me as I walk—*third row down, midway* . . . I was able to make it back to the townhome twice more before this event to coordinate. I just wish I didn't have to do it with Silas's help while I still don't fully know if he can be trusted. Bristara has continually reminded me not to act before all information is in hand. Something that is still sometimes a struggle for me.

The tents for each house aren't clumped together but rather are intermingled: Swords alternate with Cups in some aisles, Coins with Wands in others . . . every row looks different. I look for the cream tent set up over a table with a chipped corner. "I'll take this one," I announce and set my bag on it, grateful that the club's plan to pick a tent a bit farther away worked—most of the students pour into the first two rows.

After we wish one another luck, Sorza, Luren, and Dristin all find their own spots, diagonal and down from me. I can't worry too much about them now. They've been making their own preparations, as have I. And theirs are much less risky. Now is the time that we must all focus on ourselves.

"Lovely day," Jura whispers through the back of the tent fabric.

"I think we can expect a sunny afternoon." I would have replied the same way no matter what the sky looked like. *Glad you made it*, I'm saying in code.

The citizenry of Eclipse City flows in. They flood the stands and survey the offerings of the students and initiates, eager for free arcana work. I pick up the gossip of the day. Most of it is benign, but I hear a few mentions of people seeking cards to protect them from the escapee from Halazar. I catch sight of a few professors milling about with the rest. Vaduin moves up and down the row I'm in several times, looking agitated, eyes whipping about. I wonder if he's annoyed that most initiates seem to be favoring inking and reading over wielding. When Las passes once, she seems much more at ease.

Some students follow dutifully behind their new patrons for the day, having agreed to lend their services until sunset, when the All

Coins Day festival ends. Many initiates, like Luren, are busy reading cards. Dristin consults with his clients with zeal, giving suggestions to highborn and lowborn alike on what cards might be best for their specific ailments, wandering off with one or two and then returning when services have been rendered.

It takes a few hours of selling my inked cards to graduated Arcanists who flash me their academy badges and the lords and ladies who wear the sigil of their clan before, eventually, Jura makes her way to me again. Rather than lurking between the densely packed tents and staying out of sight as she had been this morning, she's now on the other side of the stall. She's wearing a satin dress along with a fur coat that I've never seen before. Even though she doesn't bear any clan sigil, she exudes the ease of wealth. Her hair is a brilliant shade of red today, a long wig trailing down her back and over her shoulders. *Was Silas wearing a disguise as simple as that? A wig and tinted glasses . . . Is that why I didn't recognize him immediately? Or are he and Griv different people and I'm grasping at straws?* I push away the questions and stay focused in the moment.

Jura meanders over, studying the cards.

"He's starting on this row, he'll be here soon," she whispers as I look out for any others that might come up to my table.

"Are you ready?" I ask. Her makeup is incredible. The contours she's painted have almost completely transformed her face.

"Yes." No hesitation.

No sooner have I asked than the Stellis carve a path through the citizenry for the king. Jura steps off to the side of my table—the one missing its corner. The position gives her the ability to be out of the way yet right at hand.

It's the first time I've ever laid eyes on the king. He's a towering, hulking man—I can see where his sons get their height from. But his frame is bulkier than both combined. Muscles bulge from underneath his tailored silks, the kind that are more for function than form. At his right hand is his heir, Ravin. After what he did to me at the soiree with Liam . . . after finding out he might have been the one behind my time in Halazar . . . my body instinctively readies itself for an attack. But I keep my cool.

At Ravin's side is a woman of equal height and an even more imposing build than Ravin. Leigh Strongborn, the Wind's Bane, wedded to the first prince. The first daughter of Clan Strength lives up to her namesake. She rests her hand lightly on a heavy broadsword at her hip. Her stormy gray eyes constantly survey the surrounding area with a keenness like that of the falcon on her shoulder.

The queen and the youngest of the three Oricalis princes are absent. Kaelis had told me during our final preparations that'd likely be the case.

Behind the king, crown prince, and princess are three cloaked figures. Their oversized hoods conceal their faces. But, if what Kaelis said is to be believed, one of them is Judgment. The other two must be the Hierophant and Temperance—the other Majors Kaelis said live at the high court.

Will Elorin end up wearing one of those robes as well? She had said on graduation she'd be sent to the court, her power too valuable to give to a noble clan. My stomach churns for her. These Arcanists are little more than dogs on invisible leashes.

The king makes his way to me, acting as if it were on a whim. As if I'm not the one he's sought out. He's large enough to cast a shadow over my entire table. His eyes are as black as Kaelis's, short-cropped hair like raven's feathers. There's a flicker in the inky depths of his stare that suggests he might have once been attractive in his younger years, but now that spark has cooled and hardened with age. Only a dangerous shadow of it remains.

"It is good to finally meet you," he says, as if it has been years he's waited.

"My liege." I duck my chin respectfully.

"I hear you have something for me." His voice is a low rumble, like the earth itself is groaning—and about to cleave in two.

I'm taken aback at how quickly he cuts to the chase, even with Jura standing right there. Perhaps it's because she keeps her head bowed in deference to him. Or perhaps it's because the king knows that with a snap of his fingers he could have her ended, now or whenever he wanted in the future.

"Yes, your majesty." I dip into a curtsy. "I have prepared a special gift, just for you."

"Well? Do not keep your king waiting," he says before I can even straighten.

"Father, perhaps not here." Ravin's eyes dart to Jura, his brow furrowing. *Does he recognize her?* It's not possible. We planned for him potentially knowing the names and faces of everyone from the Starcrossed Club, hence Jura's disguise. Hopefully, he doesn't recognize her, and she looks like just another noble.

The king ignores his son and holds out his hand to me.

I reach into the pocket of my coat. The card has been wrapped in black silk. While cradling it in one hand, I slowly unwrap it.

His eyes light up with a flash of gold. With a hunger so keen it could make milk curdle. The moment I see it, I know, *This man should never be allowed to harness the power of the World.*

Just as he reaches for it, a gale sweeps up the row, rattling the tents. I grab the card on instinct, throwing the silk back over and protecting it. I'm only slightly faster than the king. His large hand closes around both of mine. Hunger has turned to murderous intent that I'd dare block his access to his prize.

"Sor—" My quivering apology is cut short.

Over the king's right shoulder, the head of one of the Stellis slides off his neck, falling to the ground with a clang and a crimson splatter.

CHAPTER 35

Just as Luren predicted. Damn, she's good.

"Majesty!"

"Father!"

The prince, princess, and Stellis all spring into action, lunging toward the attacker. The cloaked Majors huddle closer to the king. None of them reaches for their deck. Does he keep them unarmed? Disgust, but not surprise, courses through me.

Three assassins emerge from the crowd. Some students fumble for their decks with clumsy fingers. Most are frozen solid by panic and shock.

"Stay back!" Ravin shouts to the students and initiates, moving around the king and toward the first assassin. Ravin's attack comes so fast it has me sucking in a sharp inhale. The prince's movements are flawless and well trained.

Dagger. It's the one word that seems to encapsulate him: Elegant. Deadly. Hidden up the king's sleeve until the moment he's needed.

Leigh is also in motion, her falcon launching off her shoulder as she draws her sword to engage with the second assassin. Without the bird's interference, the assassin would've launched another card at her. But the bird shreds the card easily with his talons, and Leigh nearly gets a hit in with her heavy sword.

The final assassin engages with the Stellis who were at the rear. Even outnumbered three to one, the killer makes the Stellis look as helpless as the students. Whoever these people are, they're positively lethal.

No sooner have Ravin and Leigh joined the fight than movement to my left catches my eye. Time slows, and the chaos is muffled and a moment of lucidity overtakes me. With each breath I take, the scene expands before me and details sharpen. Fingers tightening around the silk-wrapped card, I rip my hands from the king's grasp and throw the card into the inner pocket of my coat.

A fourth and fifth assassin make their move.

The king makes some kind of gruff objection to me taking back the card, but I don't hear it. Action and instinct override my hesitation. I slam my hand on the table. The impact throws the cards on my table upward. A Four of Cups glows, bursting into a haze of fog that makes its targets sluggish and sleepy. One of the assassins staggers. The second resists and readies an attack.

I use the momentum to jump up onto the table, tucking my legs under me. The strength I've regained from my weeks of training propels me forward. A card lifts from the deck at my hip—but it vanishes midair.

My opponent cast a Ten of Swords—which has the power to instantly destroy another card.

Damn it, she's powerful, too.

My fingers twitch as though I'm flipping through an invisible deck. Pointer and middle finger come together, selecting a card. The Five of Swords barely has time to blink into existence before a sword materializes from a whisper of wind and I grip the summoned saber.

And my blade is hungry for blood.

Keeping clear of the king and the Majors, I slash through the air, aiming for the assassin closest to me. She's still swaying, eyes blinking heavily, trying to overcome the effect of the Four of Cups. The other woman—the one who resisted my fog—intercepts me with a dagger of her own, parrying my blade.

Muscles strain, weapons quiver, and stares link; there's something in her eyes that can only be described as recognition. But her clothing bears no markings, and her face is completely wrapped in unadorned fabrics, nose to chin, brow to the back of her head, so that I can't see anything but her eyes, and I can't recognize her from that alone.

"You . . ." she whispers.

I grit my teeth and say nothing, trying to twist her blade from her grasp.

"*You* would defend *the king*?" Her snarl underscores her shock.

I'm even more horrified by it than you, I wish I could say. I wish I could tell her their mission is futile. That even if they managed to kill the king, he'd be revived within minutes by one of the Majors at his side. That I'm defending him because the best chance we all have for a better future is keeping him alive and letting him think that I'm on his side so I can get the World, or, at worst, Kaelis can. But there's no time.

Perhaps, though, more than anything, I wish I could ask, *Do you know me?* She is looking at me with such familiarity . . . and an equal amount of disgust. But I can't risk being associated with the assassins in any way—even talking to them is too much.

Metal shrieks against metal as we disengage.

"Your majesty!" Jura's voice cuts through the chaos. I glance back as I spin. She pushes the king out of the line of attack of the other assassin, who has now shrugged off the Four of Cups haze.

"No you don't!" Yet another defender enters the fray. Alor. She immediately engages with the other man.

I need to end this quickly before the chaos becomes too unwieldy . . . and before anyone else can get too much credit for saving the king. The woman lunges for me again. I dodge, my muscle memory and training taking over. My deck swirls with power, but since I'm an initiate I limit myself to only the first five cards of each suit. There're too many eyes here to risk using anything more advanced.

Magic flies and sparks. I predict almost every move the assassin makes, and that ultimately gives me the upper hand. My blade eventually finds its mark, skewering her abdomen.

She grips both my hands, leaning over me, impaled on the sword that, its job complete, will vanish at any second. "Be careful, Clara Chevalyer . . . don't forget . . . who you are."

The words are the woman's dying gasp. No sooner do they register in my mind than her whisper is taken by the wind. The blade vanishes, and her hands go limp. She falls to the ground, eyes wide.

I want to rip the wrappings off her face. To figure out who she is and how she knows my true name. I didn't tell her. Given her age, I doubt Arina had . . . *Did Mother?* Did I just kill one of Mother's dearest friends? Because that's the only explanation I can think of for her knowing my true name. A thousand questions blur through my mind, but I push them all aside. The battle isn't over.

My eyes dart to Alor. She's fighting desperately but is outmatched by the other assassin. Since she's an initiate who's able to manage only a handful of cards in a day and can't wield anything greater than a five, the battle is wearing her down. The king, for his part, has stepped back and is allowing the scene to play out before him with little more than slight amusement illuminating his eyes. Jura hovers next to him, looking for an opportunity to capitalize on the chaos. The Stellis—well, they're down to one Stellis—Leigh, and Ravin have almost finished with their assassins. They're now two against one.

A spike of magic jolts my attention back to Alor. She's been backed into a corner. Her face is desperate and unfocused. She raises a card, and I can feel it before my eyes settle on the image—she's reaching for a level of power her body has not yet been trained for. Volatile magic crackles off her shoulders like bolts of lightning. If I hadn't seen a card reverse mere weeks ago, I might not be able to recognize what's happening.

"Alor!" Emilia shouts over the chaos. She runs up with a group from House Swords, pushing through the crowd. But it's too far, too late.

I race forward.

The card Alor holds is a court card—the Knight of Swords. The magic is reversing. Crackling miasma lifts from her shoulders and takes the shape of a phantom sentry looming over her. Its sword is lifted, but it wavers. A growing storm sweeps up the dirt around her feet.

Alor lets out a primal scream. It's the sound of her every muscle tearing from her bones. The color drains from her eyes until they are completely white.

This isn't like Luren taking one step beyond her comfort zone. This is several steps too far. It is going to tear Alor apart.

Damn it all. I skid to a stop opposite Alor, the assassin between us, king at my right. I reach to my right hip with my left hand and swing it across my body. The Ten of Swords flashes out of my deck. A thousand tiny slashes of light and wind wrap around the card clutched in Alor's trembling fingers. The card is shredded, along with some of her skin—a minor casualty.

My power rolls like thunder, like the crash of waves against the massive pillars of the academy's bridge and surrounding cliffs. I reach for another card with my right hand—the Eight of Swords. As soon as it evaporates into the air, eight spectral swords forged of light and shadow cleave through the assassin and pin him to the ground. He screams in agony, but there is no blood.

Even as reality rushes back in, the aftershocks of the explosion of power ripple through my body. The magic is so potent that it leaves my fingertips sizzling and courses through me like liquid fire—pain and pleasure. I'm exhausted, and yet I've never felt so alive.

Ravin has made it over to Alor, and he catches her before she falls. *Isn't he the very image of a knight in shining armor?* I sway. *At least Kaelis looks the part of the void-born. I'd rather a man who shows you who he is on the outside and isn't a tyrant in a hero's outfit.*

I'm about to stumble as my exhaustion overtakes me. An arm wraps around my middle; another pulls my arm around a pair of sturdy shoulders. I'd been half expecting it to be Sorza. Maybe Jura . . . But it's Emilia.

Her expression is cold and harsh. But she holds me steady while I regain my footing. Power still drains from me to the magic swords pinning the last assassin in place.

"Well done, using the Eight of Swords." But the king is praising Ravin, not me. Even though I know he must've seen *me* use the card. He can probably even sense that it's my magic fueling the swords keeping the killer in place. But the king protects me by not drawing attention to the fact that I'm skillfully using cards I shouldn't be able to wield as an initiate, giving credit to the prince. "Now, kill him."

The assassin says nothing. I can't even see his expression as Ravin passes Alor to Leigh and crosses over to the assassin. In a moment, it's over. I breathe easier as the drain on my magic vanishes.

King Oricalis rubs his temple with his right hand, looking like all of this has been some great trial on him even though this is the first time he's literally lifted a finger all battle. Then, he slowly turns to me. Emilia releases me and steps back to join a group of Clan Tower knights and additional Stellis quickly approaching, a minute too late. At its head is a man covered in plate. Perhaps she moves away because she can feel I'm steadier on my feet without the draw on my magic.

Or she wants to be nowhere near me for whatever judgment the king is about to render.

The king now looms over me. I know the look of someone trying to be intimidating. But there's something about the king that makes it almost, *almost* work. A tiny curl of fear unfurls in the back of my mind. He hardly moved the entire battle, and yet, somehow, it almost seems like that was for the best—that seeing the king attack would have been akin to watching a living nightmare.

His hand reaches out, and, for a second, I brace myself for a blow, though I'm not sure why.

That large palm meets my cheek, but not in a slap—instead, it's a gentle pat. It would be fatherly if not for his sinister smile. And that same hungry glint in his eyes.

"It is clear what my second son sees in you," he says softly, for only me to hear. Though I suspect Alor is close enough that, now that she's coming to, she'll pick up on his words as well. Leigh helps her to Emilia's side. "Come, Clara Redwin, claimed heiress of Clan Hermit, and allow me to show you my gratitude with my hospitality so that you might recover from these labors in comfort."

The king steps away, and I am left to drag my feet behind him. I swing wide to sweep the remaining cards from my table, barely exchanging a look with Jura. So far as I can tell with a glance, she's fine. Her hand raises to the center of her chest, and she bows her head. The movement is just odd enough that I know it is a signal of some sort. But what she's trying to communicate is lost on me.

CHAPTER 36

We go to Ravin's estate, not far from the main square. The atmosphere is vastly different from the night of his soiree. The building is instantly more somber and serious now that its veranda is devoid of revelers and all its doors are closed.

Still, I can't help but mutter under my breath, "You have any guests of honor this time, Prince?"

He lets out a barely audible chuckle, knowing exactly what I'm referring to. "Only you."

I think I can believe him, and it puts me a bit at ease. Not that things in there will be easy for me, even without Ravin playing his games . . . But the last thing I want is more surprises.

Heavy doors creak open, and we're greeted by staff dressed in silvers and dark grays.

King Oricalis strides ahead, purposeful but not hasty. He hands his cape to an attendant who whisks it away. Ravin and Leigh do the same. No one offers to take my coat. Which is fine. I think it's colder in here than it was outside.

"Please have the kitchen prepare some light refreshments, and some tea for the king as well," Leigh says to a servant in that restrained and steady way of hers. The man nods and steps away. "Your grace, my love—" The two words are said almost identically, out of duty and nothing more, making me wonder just how deeply she cares for the prince. Not that it's my place to question his relationship—my own with Kaelis is a charade. "I beg your leave so I may take Storm to his aviary."

"Granted," the king says. Ravin merely nods. With a respectful bow, Leigh strides toward the back of the house. King Oricalis then turns to the three cloaked figures that continue to follow us. "You both may take your leave as well."

Two of the three Majors break away, starting for the staircase I remember fleeing up weeks ago. Thoughts of Kaelis return unbidden, and I forcefully push them away. The third Major walks alongside the king as we enter a parlor—Judgment, if I had to guess. I wonder if that man sleeps in adjoining rooms to the king—in the same bed, even. I try to get a sense of him, his age, his demeanor, but it's impossible with the oversized cowl that covers half his face and shadows the rest.

A fireplace crackles warmly, warding off the autumn chill coming from the large windows overlooking the gardens. Plush armchairs with intricately carved wooden legs are arranged in a circle around a low tea table.

"Sit," King Oricalis commands more than invites, as he eases himself into the largest armchair. It's positioned in the center on the right-hand side of the room, offering a view of the street through the glass doors by the veranda. Both entries to the room are at his left, a wall at his back.

I hesitate for a moment, assessing my options in the seating arrangement, ultimately choosing the chair opposite the king. It offers me a view of both doors to the interior of the house as well, though my back is to the veranda. This leaves both seats next to the king open, and Prince Ravin, expectedly, takes the one at the king's right hand. The Major takes the one at the king's left, his movements little more than a silent breeze. *Protocol is a language all its own,* Twino told me once, and I can only hope that I'm able to speak it fluently enough. That my selection has shown I'm ready to be an equal player—to face the king head-on. But, simultaneously, to do so respectfully.

As we settle in, the second of the two doors opens and two servants enter. They keep their heads bowed, but I'd recognize one anywhere. Twino does a good job of hiding his limp. There's not a trace of magic on him, so as not to arouse suspicion. I wonder what pain-killing tea or tincture Jura and Ren drafted for him to perform this role.

They place two trays on the center table—one with two teapots and cups, the other is laden with snacks. The servant beside Twino carefully lays out the cups. I notice that the liquid in the king's glass seems to be a slightly different shade and is poured from a different teapot than the rest of us. It could be as simple as a rare or exotic tea he has a taste for . . . Or, there's more to it I don't know yet. Then the servants step back, positioning themselves, heads bowed, along the wall, becoming more furniture than living beings. I grip the arms of my chair—the room's atmosphere is tightening like a coiled spring.

I know Kaelis planned to make himself scarce. "My father will never take out the cards if I'm around," he'd said. Yet, a small part of me can't help but wish he were here.

"I doubt there will be further interruptions." The king motions with an open palm to the center of the table.

"Forgive me for earlier." I reach into the pocket of my jacket and pull out the silk-wrapped card. "I was afraid the card would be blown away, damaged, or destroyed. My instinct to protect it took over."

"These cards become much more than mere paper and ink when they are completed." He doesn't seem agitated, and I'm hopeful I've avoided his ire.

I set the card in the center of the table and unwrap it. The cream parchment, illuminated with gold, is a stunning contrast with the black marble of the table. The king must feel safe here indeed, because he doesn't immediately lunge for it. In fact, his silent stillness drags on for long enough that I'm afraid the card is somehow wrong. Yet eventually the same smile from earlier creeps across his face.

"So, Clara Redwin, you have worked hard on my behalf, fought commendably today, and have given me this most precious gift. I suppose it would be good and proper, as a benevolent ruler, to impart a boon upon you to show the depth of my gratitude for your service." King Oricalis holds out a hand, as though he already has the World itself in his palm. "Tell me, what is it you desire? Name it, and if it is within my power, it will be yours."

A chill sweeps through me, even though I'm still bundled in my coat and scarf. It sends a shiver that whispers across my skin. It's dizzying, like I've had one too many sips of mulled wine. *Within his power...* Quite literally *anything* is within his power. But I doubt he'd truly give me whatever whim I asked for. Nothing is ever that simple . . . or gifted that freely in Oricalis.

It takes all my energy and effort to keep my expression serene. I lean back as if I am giving the offer a great deal of thought.

"My king, what I have done with this card is my destiny. What I did today to protect you is what any of your loving subjects would do, especially as one who hopes to rebuild a clan someday." The words are as bitter as bile in my mouth and just as comfortable. But I say them with every scrap of grace I can muster and hope this pays off. "Serving you is its own reward."

"Such humility." His eyes gleam. "Though, surely, even the most pious and humble among us have basic needs. Have secret wants."

Do I dare? Is it too bold to ask to see the cards outright? My heart is racing so loudly that he must surely hear.

"Then, perhaps . . ." I lower my eyes respectfully. "If it is not too much trouble, could I perhaps see another card like this one? I had nothing to serve as an example while working on my own card and was worried it would not be up to your standards. But now that I know it is—now that I've seen its beauty—seeing others would be reward enough."

The seconds of silence that follow are excruciating. Then the king moves. I slowly draw my eyes up, bracing myself. The king lifts a hand and undoes the first five buttons of his shirt. There, underneath, is some kind of card-carrying apparatus connected by four chains around his torso. This was what Jura was trying to signal me about.

"Father—"

He lifts a hand to still Ravin's objection. The way the king unlocks it is almost like he's issuing a challenge. He's showing me the mechanisms out in the open. Showing me that there is a special way the various gears must be twisted to get the front latch to release.

The king is so confident that his cards won't be stolen—that they *can't* be, that he's letting me see everything.

One by one, he lays out the four cards in his possession at the four corners of mine: Death, the Hierophant, Judgment, and Temperance. Three robed Majors surrounded him today . . . I wonder if the fourth, Death, is back at court. I shudder to think of what that particular card is capable of.

But where the Death Major is isn't my concern. I slide to the edge of my seat, looming over the cards. From the corner of my eye I see Twino shift, ever so slightly.

"May I?" I ask, holding out my hand.

The king motions with his palm. One by one, I lift the cards, turning them to the light. Tilting them so Twino and his photographic memory can catch all the designs across their surface. He'll immediately make sketches while the drawings are fresh in his mind, and we'll compare notes later. Then, I will begin making my forgeries.

Setting them down, I lean away and say a simple but sincere "Thank you."

"No, Clara, thank you." King Oricalis collects his cards—mine included.

Within the hour, I'm back in the square and lined up with the other initiates. Students are gathered by house and surround us in a large half circle, general faculty behind them. At the front is the royal family. Behind them are the three department heads, interspersed with the king of every academy house.

King Oricalis steps forward and offers warm platitudes to the denizens of Arcana Academy and the collection of nobles and citizenry also in attendance. The cheerful tone of his voice contrasts with the clanking of metal directly behind the initiates: The cozy smell of woodsmoke fills the air like a false sense of security as the fires are stoked for branding irons.

When the king is finished, Kaelis steps forward. Seeing him is an unexpected flood of relief.

"Citizens of Eclipse City, it has been our honor serving you this day—showing you our great Arcanists at work. Now the final event of our All Coins Day celebration will begin. Each student of Arcana Academy can gift an initiate with a coin from their house. Whether they choose to or not is up to them. An initiate can receive more than one coin. But initiates who receive none do not have a place in the academy and will be Marked." Kaelis steps to the side and motions for the King of Coins.

The ceremony is simple enough. The King of Coins calls the name of one of the initiates, who steps forward. There might be some notes from the King about which student in the house the coin is from, or what merits the house sees in the initiate. A coin is bestowed upon the initiate, which symbolizes an opportunity to pledge for the house following the Three of Swords Trials. Then the initiate returns to the lineup and the next name is called. The cycle repeats. In total, House Coins gives out ten of the ceremonial tokens, four more than the six slots available for that house.

Next is Wands. I realize they're likely going from the houses with the most openings to the least. Wands also decides to give out ten coins, but five overlap with individuals who received coins in the first round.

Fifteen initiates now have the ability to pledge for a house. Five have their choice of two houses. Cups is up next.

Myrion speaks in his usual light and easy manner. I'm drawn to the present when he calls out, "Sorza Sprigspark."

The woman beams at me triumphantly, going to collect her coin.

"And lastly, a coin from me, for a heart unshakable in loyalty and duty, Clara Redwin."

I blink, staring at Myrion before I move forward.

"I thought you said not to try for House Cups?" I whisper under my breath as he places the coin in my hand.

"I like you enough that I thought I'd help you stick around." He smirks slightly, the expression falling as I step away and return to my place.

So four then, myself included. That means that there are now nineteen initiates who can pledge for eighteen total spots.

It's Emilia's turn. "House Swords has decided to give just three coins this year."

It's the stingiest of all the houses. Not that I'm surprised.

"The first, from our Queen, goes to Alor." There's a warm smile between the sisters as Alor collects her coin in her bandaged hand. I find a small knot of tension I felt toward the women loosening some. They're just . . . two sisters who want to be together above all else. Who'd do anything for each other. A younger sister who wants to follow in her elder's footsteps, and the older sister who wants nothing more than to protect her.

I can't fault them for that. Even if it makes me ache deeper than my marrow and beyond my years for my own sister . . . wherever she might be.

"The second, from our Knight, to Eza."

Shocking.

He flashes a smile to Alor on his way up, gathering his coin with pride. Two coins, for two slots . . . But Emilia said there was a third.

"The final coin is from me. To a woman who acted with the swiftness, bravery, and skill of a Sword." Out of everyone in the crowd, her eyes land on *me*.

Oh, Twenty—

"Clara Redwin."

Murmurs, louder than before, surround me as I make my way up to her. "You don't really want this," I whisper as she places the coin in my upturned palm.

"I want the best, nothing less." Emilia's eyes are cold but fair as she echoes what I said to Alor in the classroom months ago. Not for the first time, she proves why she is the King of her house.

Twenty-one initiates out of twenty-four have received coins. The field has narrowed some. I look around as I return to my place. The weight of the realization settles on those who didn't receive an invitation to pledge any of the houses.

Luren's expression is as stony as the night Kel died. The slightest hint of a smile tugs on her lips, as though she could laugh at the irony of it all. As if she's once again seeing a future she foretold, and feared.

No . . .

"Initiates who did not receive a coin, please report back for your Marking and mill appointment," Kaelis announces. No one moves. "With haste." His words are like the crack of a whip.

No.

Luren turns to leave.

I catch her hand. Already, pink eyes meet mine. "Have it." I thrust Myrion's coin into her palm.

"Clara?" She chokes out my name with confusion, her brow furrowed and upturned in the middle.

"This one is yours. You're not being Marked today."

"But—"

"You can't do that," Eza sneers. The way he looks at me is positively murderous, no doubt resentful that I got a coin at all, nevertheless two when he got only one. "Coins are invitations, and she did not get one. No student thinks she's worthy to stand among them."

"You can shove your coin so far up your ass you choke on it," I snap back. "If it's an invitation, then I extend it to her. People thought me worthy? Well, *I* think she's worthy."

"What did you say to me?" A growl rolls up the back of Eza's throat.

"What is all the commotion?" Kaelis's voice cuts through the rising altercation.

I look to him and, for a moment, I am fire incarnate. I burn brighter than the sun—unrelenting and undeniable. Kaelis could be the darkest night of winter, and it won't cool my rage at the injustice of one of the most talented initiates, a woman I need—a friend—about to be Marked.

"I give my coin of House Cups to Luren," I announce, thrusting her fist holding the coin into the air.

"That is not done," Kaelis says coolly.

But I look past him to Myrion. "King of Cups, you gave me this coin to pledge your house. But you know as well as I, as well as anyone who bears the crystal signet of Cups, that I am not one of you. I am too sharp and too fiery. But Luren is one of you—or, at least, she should be. If you saw anything in me, then take me at my word that you would be *honored* to have her among you. She is the epitome of your house. Give her a chance in the upcoming Three of Swords Trials, and she'll prove it to you."

"What are you doing?" Luren whispers, each word quivering through tears.

"What is right," I answer without taking my eyes off Myrion.

"If . . . his highness, Headmaster Oricalis, would allow it, House Cups would be willing to consider this most unorthodox adjustment," Myrion says cautiously.

Everyone's attention is back to Kaelis. But his focus is solely on me. His eyes narrow slightly, and I can swear I hear him shouting in his mind, *What the fuck do you think you're doing?* I stand the slightest bit taller, not backing down.

"This irregularity . . . will stand." The words sound like he forced every one of them through a jaw clenched so tight it could crush diamonds to dust. Murmurs ripple through the crowd. I feel the weight of hundreds of eyes on me. *The prince's favorite,* they're calling me. "Now, students and initiates, we return to the academy."

I lower Luren's hand, shock overtaking me as the students fall into place. *That worked . . .*

"Clara, thank you," Luren whispers. "You . . . you changed my fate."

Like a turn of the Wheel of Fortune. The thought stills me. But for only a second.

"You deserve it," I remind her. "Show them."

"I will. I swear it." And for the first time, I see a conviction in her that assures me she won't have trouble following through.

We begin to march back. I position myself on the outer edge of the group, brushing against the masses of citizenry that line the streets to watch the students and initiates of the academy depart. I meet Jura's eyes and work my way close to her. By the time I return to the academy, the coin is not the only thing that is burning a hole in my pocket. But I don't have time to inspect what Jura's nimble fingers left there.

Halfway back to the dormitories, I'm pulled to the side by a living shadow and slammed against the wall.

CHAPTER 37

Kaelis presses his palm firmly against my mouth. I give him the dullest *Are we really still doing this?* look that I can manage. He slowly pries his hand away, but rather than saying anything, he grabs me by the arm and takes us farther into the abandoned depths.

I can vaguely recognize the rooms on the path to his apartments now. But Kaelis loses his patience long before we get there.

He releases me, spins, glares, looks away, paces, spins, and then crosses the distance again in a blink. It's as if he can't be far enough from me, and yet at the same time anything more than a breath away is too much. His restlessness transfers to me, and I fight to keep my heart from quickening so I don't lose my better senses.

"What were you thinking?" he snarls.

"I was saving your father? Seeing the cards? Having the whole plan go off without a hitch?" I know what he's asking about, but I don't want all of the day's successes to be overshadowed by one bold, slightly out-of-line choice.

"Giving the coin to another initiate." Kaelis runs a hand through his hair. "A *Cups* coin at that."

"I'm *so sorry* I went against the precious decorum of your academy." I throw up my hands. "Without Luren, our plan wouldn't have gone off nearly as well. She's too good to be Marked and sent to a mill to die. This academy needs her—*I* need her."

"*And I need you!*" The words rip themselves from his throat, loud enough that they echo both through the empty halls and within my mind. My control snaps, heart races. "I . . ." Kaelis brings a hand to his mouth as he stumbles back, biting at his nail. With a shake of his head, he looks deep into the shadows that cling to the halls, as if he's about to run into their welcoming embrace. "Cups has more spaces than Swords. It would've been safer for you to have options."

"You're not mad because I broke tradition. You're mad because . . . you're worried about me not making it into a house?" I tilt my head. Kaelis looks away, and it's all the answer I need. Suddenly, I'm hot and cold all over. I don't want to be here, and yet, I don't want to be anywhere else. Panic rises in me, making my next words as hastily spoken as they are chosen. "Right, of course. You need me at the Feast of Cups to steal from your father. If I don't get into a house, I won't be there."

The look he gives me is akin to that of a wounded animal. It says pages upon pages. Yet what comes out of his mouth seems like only a fraction of what he's thinking. "If that were merely the sum of it . . ."

There's so much not being said out loud, and I want to ignore all of it.

"Well, don't worry, I'll earn one of the two spots in Swords," I say hastily. Emilia proved it was possible with her words and actions today.

"That's one of the most difficult houses to get into."

"Doubting me is unappealing," I say.

"I'm being realistic."

"Then be realistic about the fact that you don't really *need* me once I give you those forgeries, and I can do that well before the Feast of Cups, even the Three of Swords Trials."

"Who else will steal from my father, if not you?" he snaps.

"You're clever, I'm sure you'd figure it out."

A growl resonates from the depths of his chest. "Must you always be this frustrating?"

"Yes." I can't stop myself. "And you know what, Kaelis, I think you like it."

"*Like it?*" he repeats incredulously. "*Like it?* Why would someone like me like anything about someone like you?"

"You tell me." I shrug, knowing I'm getting under his skin. I'm trying to play it cool, but all the while my heart is beating so fast I'm getting dizzy. "You're the one keeping me around. The one looking after and worrying for me much more than you need to."

"You are insufferable. You are too talented for your own good. You are so—fuck—*so* arrogant at times and more stubborn than I have ever imagined a person capable of being. You are angry, fiery, passionate, often impulsive, and more determined than any creature I have ever met. And what's worse is that—for as annoying as you are—you're so gorgeous any sane man wouldn't be able to take his eyes off you." Kaelis approaches, but this time, every footstep has purpose. I hold firm and stand tall to meet him. I don't move. "You delight in being a criminal. Your whole existence is the antithesis to all I am. You would have killed me and my entire family several times over if you had the chance."

"You would've done the same to me and those I love," I counter.

Kaelis halts at that. The shadows on his face seem only to deepen. We're illuminated by nothing more than the fading sunset blazing through the dust-coated windows. "Must you always strive to get the last word?"

"Only if I'm right."

"You're problematic, disruptive, unsuitable, bothersome, ill-timed—"

"Ill-timed for what, exactly?" I counter with a shallow breath. He's so close now that if I were to take a deeper one my chest would brush against his. He'd be able not just to hear but to feel the frantic beating of my heart, what he's doing to my body without even touching it.

"For me. You are somehow better and worse than I could've ever imagined—everything I needed and the last fucking thing I wanted." Kaelis's hand rises, as if he's about to touch me. He touched my face at the soiree. But this . . . *this* is different, and we both know it.

So I cross the gap. I rest my hands on the sides of his waist, gathering fistfuls of his jacket. I pull him to me, our bodies flush against each other.

"To be honest, Kaelis, the only thing I ever thought I'd want from you is your heart, carved from your chest."

"Say the word." His head tilts slightly, long bangs teasing across my forehead. Our lips hover so achingly close. Every rational thought is gone as the warmth of his breath mingles with mine. I can still taste the chill of the autumn air on his lips. I can still taste *him* from the last time his tongue was in my mouth.

"And what word is that?" My voice is barely audible, almost lost to the storm that brews in the voids of his eyes.

Kaelis's hands finally find me. One skims along my waist. The other delicately trails the edge of my jaw. Each point of contact is like a tiny star landing on my skin. Bursts of light in the darkness.

"Surrender, or conquest?" The words are a velvety murmur.

"Aren't they the same thing?" The question hangs heavy in the air, as heavy as our lids. As our bodies sink into each other, the room around us blurs into inconsequence. Fading until it's gone.

"We can't." His breath escapes with a ragged sigh, as if his entire body is ready to snap. It quivers with the effort of holding himself back. Of not acting on whatever it is that "we can't" do. I know, deep in my core, what he's referring to. But his self-control refuses to release its hold on that bowstring. "They'll wonder where we are at the All Coins Day Feast."

"Let them wonder." I'm not ready to give up, or give in. Not when this ache is so deep and raw and could finally be satiated.

"We're both being stupid. Neither of us really wants this." Yet even as he says so, neither of us moves. Every word is hot across my lips, the gap so achingly small. "We're simply . . . overcome with carnal desires."

"So?" I say plainly.

He tilts his head back to get a better look at me.

"*Obviously.*" I draw out the word this time for emphasis, holding him tighter. "You think I'm not aware of how this is a terrible idea for us both? How this will impact our ability to work together? How much we mutually, generally, *hate* each other?"

"'Hate' might be a strong word," he murmurs.

"This doesn't have to be anything, mean anything." I run my hands down his chest. He's as sturdy as a wall. Breathing shallow. *Four suits, I want to break him.* "Let's be honest, I was in Halazar for nearly a year. Despite what you say, I'm pretty sure you're the least desirable bachelor in all of Oricalis." His eye twitches slightly at that. I smirk. "We both need a good fuck, Kaelis. This doesn't have to be hard."

He groans softly, both hands back on my hips, gliding over the curve of my ass. Hooking on the top of my pants. As he yanks me close to him, I can feel just how hard this situation has become for him. It excites me further.

"They will suspect us if we're late to the feast," he repeats.

"They've already called me your 'whore.' I might as well give them a reason." I smirk. "Besides, wouldn't it give more credence to us being *so* in love?"

He moans. "We really shouldn't—can't." I open my mouth to object but don't get a word in. "'They' are my father and brother."

My eyes widen slightly. I release him, and the chill air of the academy crashes against me with the force of a bucket of ice. The mere mention of the king has my senses returning.

"They're here? In the academy?" I ask.

"Much to my dismay."

"Why?"

Kaelis steps away, tugging at his clothes. He seems to have reclaimed his wits as well. "I don't know why. My father has demanded we dine with them for the All Coins Day Feast. But knowing Ravin and my father, their reasoning certainly won't be good. So be prepared for anything."

CHAPTER 38

"I suppose we shouldn't keep them waiting any longer." I run a palm over my clothes as well. The remnants of Kaelis's needy hands are gone. But his scent still clings to the fabric. My heart still flutters. "Do I look all right?" I ask. But what I really mean is, *Do I look like I was ready to have you push me against the wall and fuck me senseless?*

The prince, to my surprise, answers sincerely. "Frustratingly immaculate, as always."

"Good to know my mere visage is enough to frustrate you."

"More than you know," he murmurs under his breath so quickly that I am left wondering if I heard him correctly at all.

The passageways blur as he leads me through abandoned halls and into lit ones. I stare at the now-familiar slope of his shoulders. At the silhouette he strikes against the light—as if rejecting its glow outright.

He's handsome. I've known that from the first moment I laid eyes on him. I've acknowledged as much before. Yet, there's something about him that draws the eye. Over and over again. He's more than simply pleasing to look at. He's unique. Otherworldly.

This is Kaelis, second-born and first hated! a voice in me screams the reminder. *But why?* is a softer question in response. He's the man who . . .

Killed a clan?

Yes, that is true. An odd thing to find myself able to stomach. But I've never carried much fondness for nobles. Wouldn't I have done the same if I had the power to level a clan?

Designed all my misfortune?

Is that true? He wasn't the one to put me in Halazar as I once thought. And he was the one to get me out . . . though only for his own benefit. Some kindness and a smoldering look through the shadow of his long, messy bangs should not—will not—undo everything he has been a part of. He has directly facilitated and benefited from a system that delights in torturing Arcanists and . . .

He's trying to dismantle that system.

If he can be believed.

Never before have I felt so conflicted about anything or anyone. Throughout my whole life, there has been a clear order to the world around me. *They—the Oricalis family and the high nobles who support them—are the enemy.* I can practically hear those words in my mother's voice. *They cannot be trusted. They are the orchestrators of our suffering. They would destroy the world, if given the chance.*

My stomach knots. Everything that I thought was so clear is now as shrouded as the academy was to me when I first stepped foot within it. The only thing that breaks through the murky vortex of my thoughts is the bright lights of the main hall as the doors open before Kaelis and me.

The main hall of the academy has been transformed for the All Coins Day celebrations. The scent of dozens of flowers assaults my nose the moment I step inside. They fill baskets supported by shepherd's hooks on the walls. Garlands of ivy and jewel-toned hanging moss are strung between them. The tables are all done in golds and greens. A forest floor of lichen covers the stone and pads our footsteps.

I'd be in awe of the beauty if I didn't feel like I were walking to the gallows. All eyes are on Kaelis and me. My hand rests lightly in the crook of his elbow as he escorts me past the initiates' tables. The faculty table has been split in two, with a new and separate seating area for the royals at its center in the front of the room.

King Naethor, Ravin, and Leigh are all present and already seated. The first two look at me with gleaming eyes. As if I am the main course they've been waiting for. Leigh is wearing a mild expression, but the way her eyes stare off into the distance and the muscles of her face seem pulled taut—as if fighting to keep her expression placid—tells me she'd probably rather be anywhere but here.

Same, I wish I could tell her. My heart races as I take my seat next to Kaelis, among the royals. It's an effort to keep my hands steady. The weight of everyone's undivided attention upon me has never been greater.

Despite all the japes and gossip, my engagement to Kaelis hasn't felt real until this moment. Not even during the soiree. But something about my peers and about the king seeing me in this way has made it real.

I swallow my worry and force a smile. The king stands as soon as Kaelis sits. He lifts a crystal chalice.

"To another successful All Coins Day. You are all truly the mark of excellence." King Naethor's eyes drift toward Kaelis and me. His slight smile looks anything but sincere. "And to my second-born son, your headmaster, and the woman he has seemingly chosen."

Hardly a glowing endorsement of me . . . But when he drinks, we all drink with him. There's not enough wine in the world to drown the sour taste in the back of my throat.

Dinner begins in earnest. The tables are filled to the brim with food laid out on ornate, heavy golden platters brought out by academy staff. I force myself to eat, even knowing that the food will taste little better than ash under these circumstances. I'm proved right.

"I must say that it is a truly unexpected *delight* to host so many from my family. Usually it is just Ravin visiting my domain and wearing out his welcome." Kaelis is the one to break the strained silence.

I resist stepping on his foot underneath the table. Must he instigate? As far as I was concerned, we could go the whole dinner without saying a word.

"Impossible! Visiting you is always my absolute favorite thing, brother. I know you secretly love when I surprise you with my affections." Ravin wears a shit-eating grin, and the brothers look more like boys about to resort to punches than the men they are.

I bite back a sigh. Royal or common-born, some things—like siblings—are ever the same. I wonder what Kaelis and Ravin's relationship is like with their youngest brother, the third-born prince. He's thirteen now, I think, so I suppose he'll be making more trips from the Oricalis Castle soon . . .

"It is a rare delight, indeed." The king's sentiment is oblivious to his sons' squabbling. In fact, it's almost . . . wistful? The king seems surprisingly sincere as he stares beyond my shoulders and into the vastness of the hall. If I didn't know better, I'd say it's the look of a man who genuinely cares for the Arcanists behind me. The hardness slips from his eyes, and his gaze softens to what I'd describe as longing. Then his attention shifts, and the cold and calculating ruler I've come to know is back with an almost menacing grin. "Especially now that I have another opportunity to sit with the woman my son has decided to surprise me with as a potential future family member."

"It is my honor to be in your collective presence." I keep my eyes on my food, using it as an excuse to feign deference.

"Twice in one day, even." The king leans back and stretches a hand on the table, tapping his finger in thought.

"I am truly blessed." I force a smile and take a drink.

"Indeed, especially as a common-born girl whom my son met— How did you meet?" His eyes dart between us.

I glance at Kaelis, grateful when he speaks. "I was doing work in Eclipse City—"

"I don't remember you doing work in Eclipse City in the past year at all," Ravin chimes in.

Kaelis narrows his eyes at his brother. "I don't tell you my every movement."

"But don't we have a deal that we respect each other's boundaries? If one goes to the other's domain, then it is clearly communicated?" Ravin leans back in his chair, swirling his wineglass. Leigh continues dutifully eating at his side, as if this is all very normal.

Four suits, I hope I don't ever actually *have to* marry into this family and get used to this. If I do, I'm taking her approach: silence.

"Maybe I'd respect the boundaries more if you did," Kaelis says.

"Enough." The king is solely focused on me. "I want to hear it from her."

"I . . ." I glance at Kaelis. We never discussed how we allegedly met.

"Don't be shy. Tell me of this love story for the ages."

"I was born in Eclipse City. My mother and father were deeply in love. Though his work kept him from staying in the city, as he was often called away." The truth surprises me. Fleeting glimpses of my early years drift through my mind. They almost condense into the face of the father that I've actively worked to forget. I can't share the whole truth, but that doesn't stop the painful details from softening my voice somewhat as I weave the fiction of what could've been. "We weren't anything special, my family. But we had enough and made our way."

"Where are your parents now?" the king asks.

"My father left when I was still toddling about. My mother died at the Descent." The words harden some. The king doesn't even have the decency to offer me condolences. So I'm shocked when Kaelis shifts and a knee slides against mine, pressing into me. Almost like encouragement. My eyes drift to him, lips parting slightly with questions I can't ask in this moment. *He knows what I'm saying is true,* I realize. He hears it in my voice. "There were enough funds left behind to help me sustain myself."

"Even though you were just a child?" Leigh interjects, genuine sympathy in her voice. Maybe she's not as bad as I first assumed.

"My mother had trusted family friends that I knew well. They helped look after me. Stepped in and managed things in her stead—until I was old enough to do it myself." I think of the cloaked figures that would always come around Rot Hollow. The people she worked with—the people I knew were always looking out for us, too. People like Bristara. "I didn't meet Kaelis until I was old enough to make my way to the Descent myself."

"Clara had recently discovered her arcane powers. I happened to be in town and, well, we got to know each other," Kaelis takes over. "It wasn't until I went to her home and saw some of the relics passed down on her mother's side of the family that I put together her unlikely lineage. After that, it was a matter of finding proof. Given her mother's untimely death, she's now the last living heiress."

"How lucky for you." Ravin's smile is more like a sneer.

"I've had a bit of luck, I think." I return his smile with one of my own.

"It does sound like quite the fated love story," Leigh says thoughtfully.

"A legendary love story or not . . . others have raised many questions about you both." The king speaks once more. "My court already buzzes like a field on a summer's day with talk of you two, when they aren't continuing to obsess over the Halazar escapee."

"Court gossips should find a hobby," Leigh murmurs under her breath with a note of disgust. She endears herself more to me by the second.

"I've heard those rumors—of the escapee." I seize the opportunity to shift the topic off Kaelis and myself and not appear to be intimidated by the mention of the escapee. "Is there merit to them?"

"Of course not." The king scoffs. "No one escapes Halazar."

"But, Father—" Ravin begins to interject.

The king silences his son. "*No one escapes Halazar.* And, were it to happen, the individual would not survive long." He speaks as though he's trying to bend reality to his will. But, for once, King Oricalis's preferred reality suits me, so I keep my mouth shut. "What I find far more dangerous is that my nobility doubts the sincerity of your arrangement."

So much for deterring him from Kaelis and me . . .

"Let them doubt." Kaelis waves the notion away dismissively. "I shall continue sending their clans skilled Arcanists, and that will still their tongues. They need not worry about me."

"You are second in line to the throne," he says sternly.

"Only until Leigh bears an heir." Kaelis tilts his head at his brother. "Which, how is that going? It's been, what? Two years already? Don't tell me you're not well equipped, brother."

Ravin's jaw bulges as he clenches his teeth.

"Heirs aside, there is also the matter of the possibility of a clan returning. It will shift the balance of power," the king says. There is little more frightening to all Oricalis than the idea of another Clan Culling. The last war between the clans tore the lands and its people apart. "Which is another source of doubt among the nobles. How could the last surviving heir of a clan actually love the man who slaughtered all her kin?"

"Father." Kaelis barely manages to say the word through a clenched jaw. His hand balls into a fist around his knife as if he has half a mind to stab it through his father's neck at the mere mention of Clan Hermit.

I step in before Kaelis can say or do something to make the situation worse. "What must I do to assure them that my love for the prince is sincere and that neither I, nor Clan Hermit, would ever be a threat to the other clans?"

"I think what my court shall need to calm their wagging tongues is further proof of this clandestine romance," King Naethor muses. "Proof that you are too focused on being a good wife to my son to be a threat to the balance of power."

"And how might we offer them that proof?" I deeply hope he doesn't suggest we rush to take our vows and seal them with the Four of Wands here and now.

"Many find it quite odd that you spend such little time together. For a couple *so* in love, and for a man as protective as my son, many would've expected you to already be a permanent fixture in his apartments."

"Well, then . . ." Kaelis turns to me with a warm smile. He rests his fingers lovingly on the back of my hand. His movements are relaxed, as if he hadn't been ready to stab someone seconds ago. "I suppose it's time we tell them." All I can do is smile and nod, hoping he knows what in the four suits he's doing. Kaelis focuses on his father. "Those arrangements have long been in process. It was merely taking some time to bring my rooms up to the standards of a lady like Clara. Most of my apartments were dusty and out of care from not being used. I would not want to introduce my future wife to anything less than perfection."

Ravin's expression shadows into a sullen glower; he's clearly not believing any of it.

"Is that so?" King Naethor arches his brows.

"Indeed," Kaelis insists. "She should be able to join me tonight."

"Excellent." The king looks to Ravin. "Don't you think?"

"Absolutely." Gloom clings to the firstborn prince, and the rest of the meal is eaten quickly and in relative silence.

When the king stands, the room pauses. There are respectful salutes and bows as he leaves, Ravin and Leigh in tow. Kaelis and I are left standing, alone, at the head table.

"I'm moving in with you?" I whisper the moment the king has left.

"It's this or Halazar," he says dully.

"You know, there are times I might actually choose Halazar," I murmur.

"You wound me."

"I like to keep you on your toes."

There's a spark of amusement in his eyes. But it quickly evaporates, as I can see it dawning on him as much as it is on me that we're going to have to live together.

"Go to your room and collect the essentials you want to carry yourself," Kaelis instructs. "I'll have the staff handle the rest."

Begrudgingly, I tear myself away and head for the dormitories. My steps are punctuated by my wondering what this will mean for me as an initiate. The limited freedoms I'd clawed back for myself are gone. I can't exactly be heading out most nights to see my friends if I'm right under Kaelis's nose . . . But I force myself to look elated—to look like a woman who has all but secured the blessing of the king and whose brow is destined for a crown.

So, with a sigh, I open the door to my bedroom—or what was once my bedroom.

I'd been expecting to be alone. I hadn't seen Alor leave the dinner. But, then again, I hadn't been paying close attention to anyone not at the high table. She lounges in her bed, on top of the blankets, and in her now-mended hand twirls a dagger—the same one she's slept with every night.

Her eyes are as sharp as its edge. "Tell me . . . How it is that you, as a first-year initiate, who should only be able to use the first five cards of a suit, were able to use a Ten card?"

CHAPTER 39

"I don't know what you're talking about." I give her an incredulous look before going to my wardrobe and grabbing my satchel. The staff can take my clothes—they're not really mine anyway. Most of what's precious to me is in the desk.

"I saw it." She stops all movement. "You destroyed my card before it could reverse."

I hum, *really* not wanting to deal with this right now. "I think I used two Aces and the Five of Coins."

"Do you think me stupid? I know what Coins magic looks like. I know the cadence of the cards." Alor's proper veneer is cracking. "And the Five, even combined with an Ace or two, isn't nearly strong enough to do what you did."

"I think you've had a long day. Which . . . sorry about your hand," I say gently and continue putting things from my desk into my satchel—though I remain poised to summon a card from the deck at my thigh. "It's easy to get—"

"Don't insult me!" The weapon quivers in her grip. Cards are scattered on the bed next to her. The woman is armed and ready. "I saw it. Just like I've tracked every night you have sneaked from this room."

"I didn't know I had a curfew," I say dryly.

"Tell me where you're going. Is it some kind of secret training? How can you do all that you're able to do?" she demands again.

"I didn't know you cared so much about me." I unlock the drawer of my desk and try to shove the very cards in question into my satchel without her noticing.

"I didn't, until you decided to involve yourself in my business."

"Is this because of the tokens?" She and Eza had made it clear the Swords spots were theirs. And since that's the only house I can now bid for . . . we're in direct contest. Three of us for two slots.

"It's because you clearly have some kind of advantage." She's now outright pointing the dagger at me. The only reason I haven't drawn a card is she has yet to leave her bed. "Is it because of the prince you can use more advanced magics? Did he take you back to the Chalice in secret?"

"I'd expect a noble of all people to know that the Chalice isn't the only way to access greater powers. It is difficult but possible to train oneself. Some Arcanists are simply more innately gifted—like how some can naturally run faster or jump higher." I keep my tone level.

She clearly takes it as me speaking down to her because a flush darkens her cheeks. "I know how magic works. I know Arcanists made the pilgrimage to the Chalice before this place was even a notion in Kaelis's mind."

"Good, then you know that some Arcanists never needed the Chalice at all. Glad we could have this talk." I know what the nobles are taught, what they believe. And it's hard not to, with the crown's laws stifling the natural growth of Arcanists and because the Chalice does work to expand an Arcanist's powers.

"How dare you—"

I sigh heavily, interrupting her. "Maybe I'm one of those extremely gifted Arcanists and I became the prince's consort *because* I'm that good."

With a snarl she stabs the dagger into her desk. It stands perfectly upright. Her eyes are ablaze, her forced nonchalance abandoned.

"Damn you, tell me how you do it!"

"There's really no trick, Alor. I can just use the cards I use. Despite what you've been told your whole life, there isn't just one way to use tarot, or gain its powers."

For a moment, she deflates. But then anger and disbelief win out. "No." Alor is on her feet. "No. I counted all the cards you used today. Others might have lost it in the chaos, but *I didn't*. I've watched you before then, even. Not even my sister can wield as many cards as you can in a single day. Not even the best of the third years the academy has ever seen." She thrusts a finger in my face, and only the fact that it's not the dagger keeps her alive. But she's really testing my nerves. "There's something you're not telling me. You have secrets you're keeping from everyone."

I open my mouth, but this isn't about what I have to say, not any longer.

"And then you give one of your tokens to *Luren*, of all people."

Defensiveness for my friend rises within me. "What I do with my resources, awards, and talents is none of your business."

"Is that so?" Her lips curl into an almost sardonic smile. "It is my business when you so clearly want to make me your enemy."

"I don't care about you!" I whirl on her, the exhaustion of the day finally snapping something in me. Alor seems stunned, and her shocked expression is worth repeating it again, just to make the words linger. "I. Don't. Care. About. *You*. I have so many other things that are so much more important than this petty academy and its stupid houses and tokens and tests."

"Take that back," she whispers.

"What?" What, there, out of everything, turned her rage to a frozen fury?

"Take it back!" Alor lunges for me. I dodge, but she expected me to and hooks my arm. We fall, landing hard.

Tumbling, I roll on top of her, pinning her down before she can strike me. "What in the Twenty is wrong with you tonight?"

The only thing stopping me from doing more—doing worse—is that if she wanted to really attack me, she would've. She could've grabbed her dagger. Could've cast a card. Still could. But she didn't... hasn't.

This isn't about me.

"This school is the only thing that matters," she almost shouts.

"*Why?*"

"Because it's the only way he's going to ever look my way."

"*He?*" I ease away. Even though her chest is heaving with ragged breaths and barely contained rage, I don't think she's going to lunge again. She's turning this pain back inward. "Eza?" I certainly hope it's not Kaelis she's pining for.

She barks laughter and sits as I slide off to the side. "Twenty, no. Eza is a means to an end. I promised him I'd help him get into House Swords in exchange for information."

"What kind of information?"

"It's personal." She draws her knees to her chest, wrapping her arms around them.

"Who is 'he,' then? Or is that 'personal,' too?"

"It is, but..." A sigh. She mutters a string of foul words under her breath that ultimately end in "My father. His attention has always been elsewhere. On people and things better than me—more important. My whole life, he's been gone." *I know how that feels...* "And when he's there, he might as well be a world away."

"Emilia's his favorite?" I venture, thinking of the man in plate leading the group of Clan Tower knights earlier today that Emilia joined. I didn't pay him too much mind in the chaos.

"Between her and me? Yes. But his true favorite is his duty. The secret agendas given to him by the king. Long missions and longer times away. There are always so many people and places vying for his attention that I've never been able to live up to." She looks away as her voice grows soft. "When Emilia began doing well here—when she became the King of Swords—it was as if she finally became worthy in his eyes. Every time she came home, he would talk with her about all his plans in his study. She was finally taken beyond his wall of silence.

"And I don't resent my sister for it," she adds hastily. Her panic at that possible misconception betrays her sincerity. "I'm happy she has his love and attention. She deserves it. I just want it, too. I want to earn it."

"But you know you'll be accepted into House Swords. Your sister has made that clear. As soon as the year is over, you'll return home triumphant."

"From what he saw in my showing today, nothing about me is triumphant." She wears a bitter smile underneath tired eyes. "And if you get into House Swords, too, *you* will become King in our third year. Not me."

I can't even argue. If it's a competition between us, I know I'd win. *But I have an unfair advantage,* I want to say. I want to tell her she's right. It's the secrecy of the Majors and my mission that keeps me silent.

Sympathy blooms in my chest. I piece together that, maybe, this was the source of her coldness toward me from the beginning. She probably heard from Emilia about my performance in the Arcanum Chalice. I can almost hear myself being described as "a natural" or "a gem in the rough." And now that she caught me using a Ten card . . .

"All right," I relent. "I'll help you as best I can." *How did I end up being the one to make sure all these other initiates do well?*

"What?" Her gaze had drifted out the window, but now it's back solely on me.

"I'll try to teach you what I can about inking and wielding—what I know beyond what they're teaching in classes. Don't ask me for a reading, though, I'm genuinely mediocre there."

"Can you do that? I thought you said it was innate talent."

"Talent is having your starting line placed closer to the finish. Sure, those with it get to the goal faster. But with hard work and diligence, you *can* cover the same distance. Even without the Chalice's rituals," I reassure her. I know the notion is oversimplified at best, and a bit naive to how the world works. But sometimes, we need reckless optimism to survive. It's what I always told Arina. And she shined. Every hope I would've ever held for my sister—the wishes I feel like I carried from before I could even say her name—came true.

Maybe they'll come true for Alor, too.

"You'd really do that? For me?" Her skepticism is understandable. This is the first time we've really talked to each other meaningfully, and I'm offering to help her in a major way.

"Yes," I say, as much to myself as to her.

"Why? I haven't exactly been nice to you."

"You haven't been *that* bad." Especially now that I know she and Eza aren't actually cozy. Thank goodness. Now that I'm looking back on all our interactions with a new lens, I realize that I'd been assuming a lot. "I know the importance of family. It's basically the only thing worth fighting for in this messed-up world."

She stills, eyes darting to the corner of the room. A sense of guilt clouds the air around her. "Is that where you've been sneaking off to at night? Your family?"

"Sometimes."

"Your parents?"

I shake my head and stand to finish clearing out my drawer. "Father didn't want anything to do with us. I only vaguely remember him before he walked out, can't even recall his face. I'd want nothing to do with him even if I knew who he was." Mother never had to say so, but I always knew that it was because of him leaving that the money dried up. We left the nice house that I can only vaguely remember and moved to Rot Hollow. There was a distance in her eyes when she spoke of him that only now that I'm older I can recognize as shame. "My mother died at the Descent. My sister . . ."

The words dry up in my throat, making it hard to swallow. I don't know what to say next. Am I prepared to admit to all this? To have Alor know so much about me? Do I trust her that much? I didn't even tell the king about Arina. But I didn't say outright I didn't have a sister. I painted my backstory with broad enough strokes that there shouldn't be suspicion if the truth ever got back to him.

For her part, Alor simply sits and waits patiently for me to continue.

"... my sister went missing."

"When?"

"This past year."

Alor considers this. "Then there's a chance she's still alive. I have access to some records in Clan Tower. I don't know how helpful they'll be. But if she landed in the care of Stellis, at any point, I should be able to find her. Maybe she'll seek them out now that she knows the truth of your lineage."

"I doubt it." *At least I hope not.* The records of the Stellis are the last place I want to see Arina's name. But, given the mysterious circumstances of her disappearance and the claim she ended up in a mill, which are overseen by the crown . . .

"Still, it can't hurt to look into it, and I'd like to offer *something* in exchange for your magical tutoring."

"You'd do that?" I turn to her, genuinely surprised by the sincerity of her offer.

"We're helping each other. It's fair." She nods. "Besides, I know the importance of family, too." It's because of that last bit that I believe her completely.

"All right, then." For the first time, I see Alor as more than an acquaintance, as a possible friend.

"What was her name?" The question is understandable, expected even. But I still freeze at it.

"Arina Daygar," I say finally. This is the first time I'm confirming my connection to Arina with another initiate, and I can't believe it's with Alor of all people.

"Arina Daygar?" she repeats with horrible recognition, confirming my worst fears. All I can manage is a nod. "Surely it's not the initiate from last year who ran away?"

"That's the story I've been told."

"Clara . . . they—she . . ." Alor sighs heavily.

I spare her from thinking she's going to break any news to me. "I've heard what's been said, that she 'ran away,' was caught, sent to a mill, and died. But I can't find any mills with a record of her." *The club looked.*

"So you want to know what mill she was sent to?"

"I want to know what *really* happened," I emphasize and level my eyes with Alor's. "We came from very little. This academy was the best we had to hope for; we had no idea there was a different family name we belonged to with a noble lineage waiting for us," I add at the end for the benefit of the illusion I must keep up. What I'm saying begins to dawn on Alor. "She made it through the Fire Festival. She *got in*. She wasn't a full-fledged student yet. But she still had a chance. Why would she run?"

Alor's brows knit as she considers this. I take the fact that she says nothing as a good indicator of her reaching the correct conclusion.

"She wouldn't," I continue, filling in the blank I know Alor has filled on her own. "At least, not without a really good reason—which I've not been able to find. Or, what they're saying is a lie." There are some who would consider me delusional for going against the official story from the enforcers. But it seems Alor isn't one of them. I like her more by the minute. "I knew my sister as well as I know you know yours. She wouldn't have run, not after getting in. *Something* happened to her."

"Well, I suppose that will make my investigation easier. If she was sent to a mill, those are under the purview of the Stellis, not the city enforcers. I should be able to find something."

"Thank you." I mean it, and Alor seems to pick up on my sincerity. For a moment, I almost see my sister's eyes in her—a determination unique to Arina.

"So, your extended family—the Daygars—that's where you're going now?" *"Extended family" is as good a way to refer to the Starcrossed Club as any.*

"Not this time." I stand and grip my satchel. "I'm moving in with the headmaster."

"What?" She lets out a scandalized gasp. "It's true, then? It really is? You're actually, for real, engaged?"

I nod and force a smile. "Deeply in love, too."

She snorts loudly. I blink at her. Alor blinks back. She blurts, "Oh, wait, was I supposed to believe that?"

I can't stop a grin. But it falls quickly. "It's . . . complicated. But I have my own deal with him. My safety is what's at stake, and we care about each other enough to want to help each other out."

"That sounds more like the Kaelis I've always known and heard of than a lovesick puppy." Alor nods and pushes off the floor. "Well, I can't complain about having the room to myself."

"No more sleeping with a dagger."

She shrugs. "I do that with or without you."

"You're an odd one."

"So are you."

I move for the door feeling like there's more to be said. I guess I'm not the only one.

"If you ever need to . . . you can come back," Alor adds the moment my hand lands on the door latch. I glance over my shoulder. She nods. "I mean it."

"Thanks."

"We have stories in Clan Tower about the second-born Prince of Oricalis." A shadow crosses over her features as if Kaelis himself has walked into the room. "Even if you have an understanding with him . . . be careful."

"Always am." I try to wear a bold smile as I leave.

But it quickly deserts my face the moment I'm alone in the halls once more. All too soon, I'm crossing the bridge. This time, I walk on top. I make sure the Stellis see me entering his chambers as though it is my home, too. I suppose it is now.

Kaelis waits for me in the entry, pacing a hole in the floor. He hardly looks my way when he gruffly says, "This way."

I follow him through the set of doors to the right—ones I haven't been through before. They connect to a narrow passage with even more doors. But through the one at the end is a stately bedroom. Only a fourth of the size of his grand chamber, but still larger than anything I've ever had before.

"Will this do?" The prince seems . . . awkward. I hate it.

"Yes."

"You know where to find me." Kaelis turns for the door.

I nearly stop him. But I have no reason to, and he leaves without another word. We both must sort through this new arrangement alone tonight, I think. Especially since the heat from earlier seems to have cooled into mortification that we were prepared to rip off each other's clothes.

With a soft sigh, I settle my satchel on the desk and then head for the bed, not bothering to change for the night . . . The thought of what happened between Kaelis and me earlier has sensations rushing back. I can still feel his hands on me, and that has me tossing and turning.

Just when I'm about to fall asleep, a soft scratching at the door jolts me awake. I look, waiting, listening. More scratching.

With my magic ready for whatever's out there, I pad lightly over to the door, easing it open. My eyes drop and meet a golden pair.

Priss lets out a loud meow that turns into a yawn before she prances into my room and settles herself at the foot of my bed.

Letting out an amused huff, I join her, reaching down to scratch between her ears and wondering if Kaelis is lying awake, now questioning where his usual companion has gone off to. *She does like me best.* I can't stop a soft laugh. Nothing is going to help me sleep better my first night here than the overwhelming, smug satisfaction of being chosen by his cat.

"I hadn't expected to share my bed the first night I was here," I whisper to Priss. "But, for you, I will gladly make an exception."

CHAPTER 40

Morning light filters through gauzy curtains, casting the space in cool, muted hues and the ornate bedpost in stark silhouette. I blink and, for a moment, a memory flashes—of being in Liam's bed, of his tousled hair and the warm, contented smile that would play on his lips before he kissed me. *I don't want you to go,* I said. *I know, but I have to, and I'll be back soon,* he replied.

We should've run away together.

All of us. Liam. Me. Arina. The whole club . . . Taken the mountain tunnels, endured past the desert, gone to somewhere that we could be free of Oricalis.

I close my eyes and force the memories away. I'm not sure why they're creeping back to me now. Perhaps it's because this is the only other time I've woken up in a man's room, more or less. Though, this time, I am alone. Not even Priss is with me any longer.

"You have a beautiful soon-to-be wife," I tell the specter of Liam that still lives on in me. The part that, somehow, even my sacrifice to the Chalice couldn't expunge. That night at Ravin's soiree . . . If I hadn't surrendered that future, would that have been the moment when we found ourselves coming back together? No, the details of the soiree didn't match what I saw in the Chalice's vision. But I rest the back of my hand on my forehead and tell myself the soiree was what I saw in the Chalice anyway.

I'm going to drive myself mad if I keep dwelling on a past that can't be undone. A past that, if I'm honest, I don't want. Liam was a closed chapter, even before the Chalice. I don't desire a future with him. I just want his memory to not hurt anymore.

Plus, I'm engaged now, after all. And I need to rise and face my first day here with Kaelis. Whatever that will mean.

The wardrobe in this room is empty. While I'm grateful no one was sneaking into my room during the night, I'm also mildly surprised that he didn't happen to have a dozen garments sitting around, just waiting for me. Knowing Kaelis, my clothes must be somewhere around here. I poke my nose out of the door.

It feels oddly like I'm sneaking around, even though, according to him, this is now my wing of his apartments. The hallway has five doors in total, and I emerge from the one at the very end. The one immediately to my right leads to a well-appointed but small bathroom—so there's at least one set of morning needs taken care of. The door to the left opens to a dressing room with clothes all in my size. There's even some new attire waiting for me. I knew I'd find it. I choose a supple but simple tunic and trousers that won't draw too much attention. I think I drew more than enough eyes to me last night.

The other two doors in the hallway pique my curiosity. The one to the left of the bathroom is a study that seems like it might share a wall with Kaelis's, if I'm guessing the layout of this place correctly. Although, given the labyrinthine nature of the academy, I could be far off. The shelves are barren, desk empty. I wonder if I'll settle in long enough to fill them, or if I'll always feel like a temporary guest in my new "home."

Vaguely, I wonder why he didn't put me in this study to work on my

Major Arcana card. I tell myself it's because, in his office, he could keep an eye on me. But... it doesn't ring true.

Across from the study is a narrow storeroom, crammed with boxes and dusty rolls of parchment that have my nose itching. The bindings on the books on the shelves are so moth-eaten that I worry they'd crumble under my touch. The gilding of the titles has flaked off so that they're no longer legible, and the gold flecks dot forgotten trinkets crammed between the boxes, collecting on a discarded wooden doll that perhaps once belonged to Kaelis. Though, imagining him as a boy seems... oddly unnatural. It's as if he had been born the severe man I've come to know.

In the very back are a series of cobweb-covered portraits. Each one looks older than the last. A particularly ornate frame catches my eye. Gently, I pull forward the other canvases that have been stacked atop it.

I fight an inhale so I don't go into a coughing fit.

A pair of sharp black eyes stares back at me. As intense as Kaelis's. But different. Older. Though not as old as when I saw them last night.

King Oricalis stands next to—not sits upon—a throne. In the center of the portrait is a queen with bright green eyes and equally dark hair, though hers has a unique sheen I recognize as Kaelis's—hair that's more of a deep shade of purple than black. She wears a five-pointed crown. Four points each bear a suit of the Minor Arcana. In the center, over her brow, is a massive sapphire.

I stare at the oddity, trying to make sense of it. I've never seen Queen Oricalis in person before. But I have seen portraits of the queen in clubs and pubs. I've heard tales of her pale hair and "moonlit beauty."

This is not her.

So if it is not Queen Oricalis... *Who is it?* And why is she the one in the dominating position on the throne, bearing the crown and holding—I lean forward to get a better look at what she delicately balances between her hands—*a blank card?* No... The gilding has flaked off here, too. The lines are barely visible. If I had better light, then maybe—

"Clara?" Rewina's voice startles me from my thoughts. I jump back, the canvases clacking into their place with a plume of dust. She stands in the doorway, her expression a mixture of disapproval and caution even though her words have a forced levity. "May I help you find something?"

"Oh, no, I was just . . . looking for the bathroom." The lie sounds bad, even to me.

"His highness would not approve of you being in here." She ushers me out.

"Why is that?"

"There's nothing in here of importance, just dust." Rewina coughs and waves away the cloud that follows me. She pats cobwebs off my shoulders. "Nothing a lady like you should be bothering herself with." She promptly locks the door behind me. None of that was a good answer for why Kaelis would not want me in there . . . "Now, if you would like to finish freshening up, breakfast is served."

I go to the bathroom and stand for a minute, picking cobwebs from my hair. A pop of magic crackles over my skin, and I suspect she's locking the door with more than the key I saw. Keeping my racing questions to myself for now, I follow her out of my apartments, across the central foyer, and into another hall that connects to a dining room I recognize from one of the dinners we shared here. Though the atmosphere this morning feels markedly different. Tenser.

The table is set with an array of dishes. Kaelis looks up as I enter. "Good morning." His tone betrays nothing. "I trust you slept well?"

"As well as can be expected." My tone is begrudging, though mostly out of habit rather than actual sincerity, if I'm forced to admit. I take the seat Rewina guides me to at his right hand. Though I would've gladly taken the opposite head of the table for the sake of keeping my distance from him.

"Given that you stole my cat—"

"I did not *steal* your cat." I roll my eyes and reach for my napkin.

"—I would hope that you slept quite well," he finishes, ignoring my objection.

"Are we expecting company?" The table is set for six, despite it being just the two of us.

"Based on my brother's annoying ability to enter the academy at his whim, one can never be sure."

The remark makes me think of Silas—he can magic someone in and out of the academy with no problem. And if he's Ravin's inside man . . . I keep the thoughts to myself. Just like I keep silent about the portrait. Knowledge is power, and I need to choose when I'm going to let those arrows loose from my quiver. Now is not the time.

Act when you're certain. Gather information first. Bristara's instructions are loud in my mind.

"While you're in class today, I'll see to it that your study is set up for you to start on your forgeries."

I nod. I suppose I wouldn't keep using the settee in his office, given that I now have my own. *But why not just give me that office in the first place?* The question from earlier returns. I look at Kaelis from the corner of my eye as I pick at my food, attention dropping to his mouth and the way it twists as he flips through the pages of a book he has open at his side.

Is the awkwardness because of what we said before the feast last night? Because of the lines we were so ready to cross but now . . . now that we're here it seems like we'd rather do anything but?

The silence is oppressive, and I finish my breakfast as quickly as possible.

"Come back in the afternoon so that we may begin work."

I pause, halfway to the door. I know a command when I hear one. "I'll do as I please."

Kaelis rests his chin in his palm. "Don't forget, Clara, they need to think you're madly in love with me. Not avoiding me. Otherwise, it could be back to Halazar for you."

Thousands of little pricks dance under my skin at the not-so-subtle threat. I cast him a disapproving frown, and, for a brief second, I see Kaelis's expression soften. As if he, too, is realizing the jab was unnecessary. But I don't give him a chance to say anything else and instead make my way to class.

The moment I catch up with the other initiates I am aware of their whispers rustling around me like autumn leaves. Many make no attempt to be subtle, eyes darting between me and their friends as they murmur about my eating at the head table and my sudden move to Kaelis's apartments and what they've heard about our relationship so far.

I keep my head high and smile bright. Doing so becomes easier when Luren quickly steps alongside me, with Sorza and Dristin on my left.

"You all right?" Luren asks, her voice tinged with concern.

"How could she not be when she's to become a princess?" Dristin says dryly. "One step closer to being royalty."

"Yeah, but it's by being engaged to *Kaelis,*" Sorza points out, and that silences him.

"I couldn't be better," I force myself to say. Threat or no, Kaelis is right about having to keep up appearances. I speak loudly enough for those around us to hear as well. "I'm glad that my quarters were finally prepared in his apartments. We'd spent far too long apart."

Sorza gives me a pointed look and slows her pace. I do the same, allowing Dristin and Luren to go ahead. The two quickly strike up a conversation. Dristin has been good to Luren in the months following Kel's death by always making sure she has someone by her side.

"Are you sure you're all right?" Sorza asks under her breath, drawing my attention back to her.

"Of course I am, I said I couldn't be—"

"I know what you said." Sorza studies me. "But you don't mean it."

"Yes, I do," I insist.

"Clara—"

I halt, stopping her with me. I lock eyes with Sorza. "I am right where I need to be, Sorza." *Please understand and drop this,* I beg without saying.

She must hear me because Sorza gives a slight nod and we carry on.

The classroom is a hive of activity as we all settle into our seats around the dueling ring. I rest my satchel on the floor at my side and shift to find a comfortable position, imagining I am that queen from the portrait. Serene. Meant to be perched on her throne.

"Today you will divide into threes to explore the different methodologies of dueling two opponents at once." Vaduin steps through the center arena, gaze sweeping over the initiates. "Because the circumstances we find ourselves in might not always be fair, but we persist . . ."

Time marches on as steadily as the chill that begins to creep deeper and deeper into the halls of the academy.

Classes have found their rhythm once more following All Coins Day, but the professors are beginning to emphasize the importance of *every, single, lesson,* as though each one were the very last before the Three of Swords Trials. Fortunately, I've begun to hit my stride now that I've truly learned what the professors are looking for. Even if what I am forced to do at the academy is not *my way* to ink, or wield, or read . . . it works.

At night, I focus on the hasty sketches Twino drew and passed to Jura via the parchment she slipped into my pocket on the march back from All Coins Day. I compare them against my initial, from-memory sketches, refine, compare again, sleep on it, then refine some more.

Even though I'm living in his apartments, I hardly see Kaelis. Which is unexpectedly odd. We have breakfast in the mornings but talk less than we used to when our paths would cross only rarely in the school itself. When we do speak, it's entirely about my forgeries.

"Promising." His voice is thick and deep when he's focused, especially before he's had his second cup of tea. He furrows his brow slightly as he examines my sketches in the morning light, meaning he's struggling to find problems. I'm starting to notice all these little things about him.

"You think so?"

"Yes, though I don't think this is quite right." Kaelis taps one of the lines. "Look at how awkward this is. Wouldn't something like this"—he reaches for a pen and sketches over my drawing—"be more natural?"

"'Natural' doesn't mean right, or accurate," I counter.

"It does when what feels natural to me is usually right and accurate."

"Funny, that's how it usually works with me, too."

We go back and forth drawing over each other's lines and debate until the bells toll and it's time for me to head off to classes.

Repeat. Repeat. *Repeat* . . .

I bundle up tightly in heavy wool coats whenever I set out in the evenings. Kaelis has agreed that for the sake of the likelihood of my being accepted into a house, I can't be a complete hermit in his apartments. But I'm not sure which atmosphere is more stifling: Kaelis's apartments, or the common areas where all the students and initiates look at me as if I have grown a second head.

The only breath of fresh air I find is with my unexpected group of friends in the hours we spend in the library or huddled in front of a fireplace practicing for the upcoming Three of Swords Trials. Or those rare moments when I return to my old room to train with Alor in secret. She's a fast learner, and she's sharp as the daggers she always has on her person. I even find myself picking up new techniques when I work with her.

I'm lost in my thoughts one night as I wander back to Kaelis's apartments later than intended. So I nearly jump from my skin when a voice I haven't heard in weeks says, "Clara, a moment?"

Silas leans against a stone archway.

"What is it?" I stop, but I don't approach him. He's still unfinished business. But I haven't dared to make any moves. I still don't have the proof I need to be sure of where I stand with him, one way or another.

"I wanted to tell you that the nobles are still talking about you and Kaelis. They're not convinced your love is real."

"And how would you know that if you never leave the academy?" I ask cautiously, calling back to his hesitation about leaving the first time we met.

"I hear things in these halls."

"As do I."

"Good, then you know you need to do more to convince them."

Irritation flares within me. "What would you propose? That I lie out on a table in the hall and spread my legs so Kaelis can take me then and there?" The words are laced with sarcasm, but there's an undercurrent of genuine curiosity. I can't help but wonder if Silas has actionable advice. Not that I'm sure I'd take it.

"Probably not that." His lips quirk in a half smile that he quickly abandons. "It's almost the recess before the Three of Swords Trials. Do something then to make them believe."

It's not an awful suggestion . . . "And do you have any ideas of what I might do?"

"Go to the court. Or, at the very least, the crown's solstice festivities. The Oricalis royals are always hosting something, somewhere. Show up, make a scene like you did at the soiree, but . . . more."

"I'll think about it." I turn to leave.

He catches my forearm. I didn't even hear him close the gap. "Clara—" Silas pauses, searching my face. "Have I . . . have I done something to offend you?"

"Of course not." I force a smile before my mask of composure can slip. "There's just a lot going on for me. Three of Swords Trials are coming up, after all, and I'm not as strong as I should be with reading. So I need to make sure I pass wielding and inking or else I'm headed for the mills."

"Right." He releases me.

I start to walk and then stop. Turning back to him and thinking better of every word, I ask before I can stop myself, "Silas, are you really on my side?"

But when I turn to face him once more, he's gone. As if he were never there to begin with. I stand, the chill in the air forgotten as I wait for an answer. But none comes.

Days condense into weeks. Fall surrenders its colors with one final, blustery day, and winter advances in earnest. The scattered leaves are like sand in an hourglass, reminding initiates that the Three of Swords Trials are right around the corner.

Reminding me that my time is running out.

I work in the Sanctum of the Majors. The change of pace brings new ideas to the forefront of my mind for my forgeries. Eza and I continue to circle each other like wolves, each nipping at the other's heels but never making a move. I help Sorza figure out how to ink her own card, and seeing how she paints her lines is how I ultimately make my final breakthrough, too.

That night, I work until the dawn. And the next day, as soon as I walk into the dining room for breakfast, I present Kaelis with the final designs for the forgeries.

He studies them in silence for an agonizingly long period of time. Finally, his eyes drift to mine.

"Yes." With just that one word, a rush tingles through my entire body. The glint in his eyes is like a spark on coal igniting. It's been weeks since he looked at me with anything more than ambivalence, and I'm shocked to find I missed that passion.

Love me, hate me, but only look at me like my existence sets you on fire . . . I bite the insides of my cheeks to keep myself from saying so and banish the thought.

"Now we'll begin the process of inking them."

"I've been thinking about that and—"

"These are special cards and will require special inks to make a believable forgery. My father won't be fooled by any normal ink or paper." Kaelis stands, clearly thinking his plan is the better of our two. Much the same had crossed my mind.

"The waters around the World statue?" I guess.

"Right line of thought, but no; the font of the World won't work. The color only changes to gold for a real card."

"Perhaps if I ink it with my blood?" Like I do for other cards.

"While you are astounding, for this we'll have to use something else as ancient and powerful as the font of the World."

"And what is that?" I ask, folding my arms. This had better be good, because he's not even entertaining what I had to say.

"Come to me promptly after classes. Give your best lovestruck excuse to the others who monopolize so much of your time." There's almost a note of . . . jealousy? Surely I'm imagining it, given that, if he wanted my time, he's known exactly where to find me for weeks. "For you will not be joining them for dinner tonight."

"What are we doing instead?" *And why is my heart starting to race?*

He opens his mouth but is interrupted by the bells ringing. He smirks. "Off you go, Clara. Come back soon. I promise it'll be worth your time."

CHAPTER 41

On a good day, it's hard for me to focus on what Professor Las has to say about reading in her breathy, dreamy tones. Today is even worse. As soon as the bells toll, I'm gathering my things.

When Luren asks about lunch together, I make it a point to say loudly that the headmaster—"I mean, my betrothed!"—needs me this afternoon. "*All* afternoon. Don't expect me for dinner." I throw in a wink for good measure.

More than one student in the halls makes some kind of noise, gesture, or expression of disgust. I pay them no mind. Silas's words—warnings—still burn in my ears. *They don't buy it*. I can't let up now by missing any opportunity to stress our deep "love" for each other.

Back in Kaelis's apartments, I ultimately find him in his study, hunched over his desk.

"You look like a woman with a purpose."

"You haven't even looked up." I put a hand on my hip.

"I can hear it in the way you walk. Your gait's different when you have a goal."

"I'm not sure how that's possible, since I always have a goal." I cross to Priss, who's curled up on the settee, and crouch down to give her my obligatory offering of chin scratches.

Kaelis's eyes dart our way, landing on his fuzzy companion. "Traitor."

Priss extends her chin out farther, as if to spite him. He rolls his eyes.

"Can we go to wherever this place where we can find our special supplies is?" I stand.

"Eager much?"

"Yes." And I am—there's no point in hiding it. I cross to his desk. "What're you working on?"

"How to get the Star." Kaelis closes the ledger he was inspecting before I can get a look at its contents. He puts it back in his desk and locks the drawer. "Since you're close to finishing your forgeries, it's about time I begin focusing on getting the last Major. Things should move quickly after. I need to secure the World before my father realizes what's happened."

"You said you knew where the Star is?" I recall his wording being something along the lines of *not to worry* and *leave it to him*.

"I do. But knowing where something—or someone—is and getting to that place are two vastly different puzzles to be solved."

"Where is it? Maybe I can help."

"Not with this one." He shakes his head and stands. "It's a problem for the future. For now, better to keep the Star in place than raise suspicion by moving too quickly and risk them being moved. Now, follow me."

I don't budge, even as he steps around me. "I can help."

"Clara—"

"You want me to trust you, right? You said we were in this together."

He sighs and runs a hand through his hair. Kaelis doesn't meet my eyes when he says, "I have reason to think the Star is either in or has been through Halazar. I don't know which yet. But I'm going to find out." He brings his attention to me now. Sincerity overflows from his gaze, flooding his words. "Either way, I swore you would not go back there, and I'm keeping that promise."

I swallow thickly.

He scrutinizes me, not missing a moment of my hesitation. "Unless you would want—"

"No, you're right, I've enough on my plate." Maybe I'm a coward. But . . . *I can't go back there.* Kaelis can figure this one out.

"If I think you can help, I will let you know." His gaze has softened as he stares down at me. I can't meet it for long. I don't want his pity . . . even if it's not misplaced.

"If the Star is in Halazar, you can't let them rot there." I force myself to hold his eyes. "Even if it means you ultimately need my help. You *must* get them out sooner over later."

"I will get them as soon as I'm able." He sounds serious enough. But . . .

"How long have they been there already?" I wonder if I would've sensed another Major during my time there. Though, the other Majors in the academy have felt much the same to me as any other Arcanist.

"I don't know."

"You sound so nonchalant." A harsh edge overtakes my words.

"Clara, if I cannot safely make a movement, then I risk myself, the Star, and our entire plan." *Our plan,* not just his. That stills me. "It's not always pretty, or nice, but I'm doing what must be done." Still, the sentiment is lacking the compassion I'd want when dealing with someone in Halazar. I glance away. Kaelis takes a half step closer. "Soon. Soon enough I'll retrieve the Star, the vessel, and we will summon the World. Once it is in my hands, everything will be better, I promise."

"Thank you." I leave it at that, for now, hoping he hears every layer of what I'm thanking him for. Kaelis nods and stretches out a hand. I take it.

He guides me from the study, through his bedroom, and into the passageway that connects to his closet. We descend, almost like we are heading to the World, and then we deviate onto a path that I've somehow not noticed before. The staircase narrows and becomes decrepit. The walls close in as if trying to squeeze us out.

This is the second time I've felt this unnatural sensation. Except, this time, I have a lifeline in our interlaced fingers. As if it is by his will alone that I am permitted to be here. With every step I take, an irrational fear roots in me that, were I to let go, the shadows would consume him. And me. And that I'd be lost in these depths forever.

All light vanishes. The chill in the air has the hairs on the back of my neck standing on end and my teeth chattering. But Kaelis has no hesitation. Even in complete darkness, he navigates at the same steady pace. He shows no signs of the frantic energy I had the first time I came here, or that I'm feeling now.

With a snap of his fingers, cold flames illuminate the forgotten torches that burn without scent or smoke. The light dances off the carved surface of a familiar door. I can't stop my attention from flicking to the floor where Silas originally dropped me after saving my life. The blood is gone. Did he clean it? Or did the magic of this place make it disappear?

"How are you managing?" Kaelis pauses to ask. "This whole place is warded to keep people out."

"That explains this uncomfortable feeling," I murmur, glancing back at the complete darkness that blots out the path we emerged from. Now that I'm out of it, warmth is returning to my toes. I wonder if the only reason I could make it through on my own the first time was because of my innate abilities as a Major.

"The Fool liked to work in solitude . . . and keep his discoveries to himself." Kaelis speaks with admiration.

"The Fool?" I repeat, certain I misheard.

He nods with a grin. "If only you could see your expression."

"You're telling me the Fool was . . . *here*?"

"The academy's foundations are that of the Fool's first castle."

"I thought the academy was in a fortress built by the Revisan Kingdom?" Now that I think about it, the structure has always looked quite good—far more modern than a kingdom that fell over a thousand years ago could have built. But the Fool existed well before even that. Something isn't adding up.

"Before it was theirs, it was his. Everything is built on the past. Renamed and reused. Rebuilt anew on long-forgotten histories..." Kaelis looks to the door. The light dancing off his face gives it an otherworldly quality. His cheeks seem more sunken, his nose sharper, his eyes... his eyes shine with a hunger that curls a strand of terror in my gut that I haven't felt around Kaelis in months. "Stay close, Clara. This path is treacherous... but if anyone else could learn it, it'd be you."

"And you'll show me?" I take a half step closer, aware that this is the closest we've been physically since that night following All Coins Day. My heart begins to gallop. *I can't let him know I was here before.* Something in me whispers that Kaelis wouldn't take kindly to the revelation... I barely resist the urge to massage my neck where the light last clipped me.

"Yes. You, and only ever you," he whispers.

Before the sentiment has a chance to linger long enough to elicit a response from me, he turns to face the door. Kaelis brings a hand to his chest and draws it away with a flourish. Three cards lift from the deck he keeps in the inner pocket of his coat and hover in the air. With a flick of his wrist, he slams the cards against the door. Light illuminates hidden patterns in the seeming chaos of all the symbols.

Just like before, the door silently swings inward, opening to yet more darkness.

"Follow *exactly* in my footsteps." Kaelis holds my hand even tighter.

"Understood." I take a deep breath, and we step through the living wall of shadow and into the dimly lit room with a floor of smooth sand. The same ten razor-thin beams line the walls. I can almost feel them sinking into my flesh, but I keep my face and movements steady.

Kaelis moves with his usual almost unnatural grace. But here, it's heightened even further as he sweeps his feet and arcs his body under and around the beams. I work to imitate his movements across the light-lined sand as best I'm able. Somehow, he knows exactly where every beam will be before it appears, always staying one step ahead. He manages to navigate himself and guide me effortlessly.

On the other side of the room, Kaelis lets out a slow exhale. His shoulders were so tense they were almost up to his ears.

"What was that room?" I carefully phrase my question so it's not obvious I've been here before.

"How fond are you of that coat?"

"What kind of question is that?"

"Not very fond of it, I hope?" He keeps ignoring my questions and holds a hand out expectantly.

"I assume you can get me a new one?" I shrug my coat off, already knowing what's about to happen but playing along.

"I'll get you any coat you could ever desire." Kaelis takes it. Once more, he moves on before there's an opportunity for me to decipher the deeper meaning of what he just said. "Now, watch."

Kaelis throws the coat into the room. It hardly has an opportunity to catch the air. The moment it opens, a beam of light blinks in and out of existence. The coat is cleaved in two. Like sharks in a frenzy, the quick flashing light cuts each piece a hundred times more before the pieces land on the sandy floor as barely visible scraps . . . little more than dust, or sand.

"*Oh.*" Had Silas not come to my aid, I would've been reduced to an unrecognizable pulp. No wonder why I saw the tiny shard of bone; there's nothing else left of the people who die here.

"That's why you had to follow me *exactly*."

"How did you know where the beams of light would appear?"

"It's a pattern," he says like it's obvious, but it certainly was not.

Resisting the sensation of feeling inept, I continue my inquiry. "I asked *what* that room was . . . How does it work? What cards made it? How does the magic sustain itself?"

"That is the power of the Fool." Kaelis turns, leading me through the tunnel. "Good job of keeping up, by the way."

"You sound impressed."

"Not really. I already knew how nimble you are." His voice is deep, and the glance he casts over his shoulder is borderline suggestive.

"Do you?"

"I've watched you closely for months. Made easier now that I share my apartments with you."

I pull us to a stop in the tunnel. Kaelis's eyes swing to mine, a dark brow arching. "Then why have you treated me like an unwelcome guest ever since I moved in?"

"I have not."

"You certainly have." I level my eyes with his, and he lets out a noise somewhere between a huff and a sigh that tells me he's giving in.

"Because . . ." His one word shivers up my spine. "Knowing I had you there, with me. It gives me ideas." The sentiment turns his voice deep and grave by the end.

"What sort of ideas?"

Kaelis's eyes shine in the low light. "You wouldn't want to know them."

"Bold of you to tell me what I do or do not, would or would not want."

"You've made your feelings—your *resentment*—toward me perfectly clear."

"And you feel the same about me," I say with confidence.

"Do I? Tell me how much hatred I have shown you. How much resentment." Kaelis waits. I open my mouth and slowly close it. The man has been withdrawn of late, but not resentful . . . In fact, it's been months since I last felt anything that might resemble animosity from him. I hate that I'm suddenly tongue-tied. Second-guessing half my thoughts and words. With a barely audible sigh, Kaelis pulls me along as if we're both running from the moment and headfirst into whatever else awaits us. "This way."

We round a corner. Heat and light pelt me. I blink, my eyes instantly watering. A wall of fire blocks our path.

Kaelis stops right in front of it. The swirling flames roar with such ferocity they create their own wind. It tangles embers in his hair, illuminating the black and purple with gold.

"Do you trust me?" He tightens his grip on my hand, looking back my way.

"What's with that question?"

"That's not an answer."

I know it's not. *Do I really trust Kaelis?* His dark eyes, now sparking with flames, bore holes into me. As if he thinks he can find the answer inside me before I can. Knowing him and his eternal arrogance, he probably *does* think so.

"Do you trust me?" he repeats, the question barely audible above the roar of the flames.

I suck in a breath. "Yes."

Fingers locked with mine in a viselike grip, he lunges forward into the fire. Shock steals a scream as I'm pulled through.

But the fire feels like nothing more than a whisper of cool air. Kaelis and I stand between two rows of flames lined by piles of ash that I suspect might have once been human. Still, even seeing as much, I can't help but wonder . . .

"Is any of it real?" Even as I ask, sweat rolls down the back of my neck.

"Most of what you see is real." Kaelis guides me down the next wall before pulling me through. "But there are gaps in the fire, filled with illusion. The places we're going are the only places that are safe."

We navigate to the other side, unharmed.

"How did you figure all this out?" I ask as we start down the next tunnel.

"Slow progression, testing, instinct." He shrugs, as if it's nothing.

"A dangerous game of trial and error." I really loathe when the prince is so impressive. It makes me want to work even harder.

"Isn't it always?" When he glances back at me, I can't help but feel like I'm the focus of that sentiment.

"What's next?" I move the topic to the task at hand and away from him and me.

"It's a room that can sense emotions—any negative or angry thoughts or feelings will trigger the room to fill with acid. Keep the room dry, for long enough, and the opposite door will open."

"Swords, Wands, Cups . . ." I reason. "The final room is something to do with Coins?"

He nods, and we come to a stop at the threshold of the next room. The walls are covered in crushed crystal dust, and they shimmer under the light of a central orb.

"This room will be easy enough to pass through. All you must do is be happy."

Before I can respond, Kaelis pulls me into the room. "Be happy"—the words drag across my mind as my feet stumble. How long has it been since I allowed myself to simply be happy? How long since I've had a reason for it?

Liquid from an unknown source seeps into the room and rises to my ankles. The leather of my shoes hisses softly. Tiny bubbles form. The acid is mild, but I've no doubt it won't take long for it to eat through.

"Clara," Kaelis says softly, drawing my eyes to him. The man isn't panicked in the slightest that we might drown and dissolve in a room of acid. He has that half-quirked smile that lets me know he really means it—that I'm seeing him truly. "Let go of it all, just for a little."

"Easier said than done." I laugh nervously. The acid rises again. As it reaches the tops of my shoes and begins to seep into my trousers, singeing my ankles, my heart begins to race. I want to let my pain and fears go—I'm trying to—but every time I try to not think about the trials of my life I think about them even more.

"Dance with me." The request is so unexpected that it stills all the emotions and insecurities swirling in me.

The acid halts its rise.

"What?"

"Surely you know how to dance?" He sounds the slightest bit skeptical as he holds out his hand.

I scoff and take it. "We had dancing most nights in the club."

The world spins as he turns me in place. A simple four-step. It's the sort of dance everyone learns as their very first, but with a few embellishments on his part, it becomes so much more. Enough to dull the increasing pain and make nothing else matter but him.

"You're very frustrating, you know that?" I say as his palm glides around the small of my back.

"Why so, this time?" His footwork is immaculate.

"Because you're so damn good at everything."

"Not everything." He still wears a smile, but it turns sadder.

"Name one thing you're bad at."

"Getting people to trust me." The words are heavy, as if they've been weighing on him for some time. "No, *earning* their trust."

"I just literally walked through fire for you, Kaelis. Five months ago, I was ready to slit your throat . . . I'd say you're not as bad at earning people's trust as you think."

He twirls us, pulling me closer in the process. His lips brush against my ear. "I've wanted to dance with you ever since the Arcanum Chalice. Ever since seeing *him* in the flesh at the soiree."

"You don't strike me as the jealous type," I say.

He straightens. "I'm usually not. But you are—you've always been—different."

"Why is that?" The question isn't a throwaway for conversation's sake. I want to know.

"Because . . ." A slight smile tugs at the edges of his mouth. "It's you."

"What does that mean?" I laugh.

"Every time I see you, I see what the world could be."

Without warning, the door opposite lights up and the acid recedes entirely. My boots and trousers are suddenly dry, fabric mended, as if the acid never existed. Whatever magics are at work here are extremely powerful indeed.

Through the tunnel that leads to the next room, I fantasize over what might be in this secret alleged workshop of the Fool. If this workshop is real—and maybe it is, given these barricades—what would the Fool protect with all his might? What is essential in there for me to ink these counterfeit cards?

In the next room, my wonder and joy vanish like the acid in the previous. Skeletons litter the floor. Most have been rotting for so long they have been reclaimed by the soil. But some look as polished as clean dishes. They are all, distinctly, human.

I knew people died here from the first time I stepped foot in this place and saw the bone shard—felt the light slice into me. But there's something different between that vague notion and . . . *this*. This isn't scraps of bone barely larger than the motes of dust slowly claiming them. Or piles of ash. I imagine the acid of the third room eats away its victims entirely. But these are the whole remnants of people left to rot. The brutality of these rooms comes into sharp focus.

"Are they . . . real?"

"Yes." His tone is grave.

"You just leave them here?" I look between him and the room of skeletons. "Have you no respect for the dead?" Kaelis couldn't do much about the remains in the first three rooms. But something could be done here.

"Firstly, they were trespassing."

"And you aren't?" I say quickly.

"It's my academy."

"Wasn't this *the Fool's* workshop? Which is why you're forced to sneak in here, too? Just like they did?"

Kaelis opens his mouth. Closes it. Purses his lips. Then opens his mouth again. "Well, if my bones were there, I'd expect them to be left as a warning, also."

I snort in disbelief at that.

"I would," he insists. "Moreover, even if I wanted to get the remains, it wouldn't be safe to."

"No?"

"This final test is fairly simple, it just leaves no room—or *very* little room—for error. Once we enter, you cannot make a sound louder than the rustling of leaves. No matter what you see, or what the plants do . . ." He points upward. The walls are covered with vines that creep down from the ceiling. Dozens of flowers, as bright red as a dancer's lips, hang from the vines.

"The final kiss," I murmur.

Kaelis's head swivels to me, surprise on his face. "You know of the Duskrose?"

"Surprised?"

"I didn't take you for a botanist."

"I'm not . . . but I've a good friend who is." Ren could make anything grow with a mere look. "Its pollen, when inhaled, causes total paralysis, including of the heart and lungs. When the pollen comes into contact with skin, it eats through flesh straight to bone." Little wonder the skeletons in here are so clean.

Kaelis nods. "Move forward as quietly as possible if you don't want to end up like one of these unwelcome guests. Are you ready?"

I nod.

He goes first, and I follow behind. There's no "right" path, but I end up placing my footsteps behind his anyway. I've had ample practice with sneaking around. But the empty gazes of the skeletons that litter the room are solidly unnerving, even for someone who lived in the horrors of Halazar.

We carefully scramble over large rocks in the center of the room, no doubt placed there to encourage someone to literally slip up and make a sound, given their surfaces are polished to a near-mirror finish. It's on the other side that a glint of silver catches my eye. I shift, swinging wide, my feet moving of their own accord to the skeletal wrist that still bears the metal around it.

It's a bracelet, delicate, with a circular emblem of sXc on it—the very same one I had gifted to Arina when she entered the academy. *So you don't forget all of us on the outside.* I rub wet earth off it, as if I could expunge the familiar marking.

"No." The word escapes me as a raw whisper, but in the silence, it sounds like a scream. My opposite hand flies to my mouth, as if I could take back the sound, but it's too late.

The flowers are opening. Their aroma is sickly sweet. The pollen is releasing. I scramble, and Kaelis reaches back. Survival instinct has me moving forward, one hand clutching the bracelet, the other clutching his. He throws his coat over my head, himself only half under it. I hear his sharp inhales—sounds he tries to muffle with the heavy fabric over us.

Somehow, we make it to the other side, tumbling to the floor as another rain of pollen cascades upon us. Kaelis curses and throws the coat back into the room as it begins to disintegrate. He turns to me with anger, but it evaporates the moment he takes in my tear-streaked face.

"It was her. Arina," I rasp. Kaelis's lips part slightly in slack-jawed shock. *I've a big break, one that will change everything. We'll have all the resources we can imagine and really stick it to the crown. They're keeping them locked tight because they're more powerful than anything we've found before,* Arina had said. I clutch the bracelet to my chest as everything I want to say but can't chokes me. Had she somehow discovered the World? *Change everything* . . . Did she think she could bring back Mother, too? "She shouldn't have been dead. I didn't believe. I—" I choke on a sob.

"Clara . . ."

"We're not leaving her here." With one look, I stop him in his tracks as he reaches out to, presumably, comfort me. Kaelis flinches almost imperceptibly. I might have missed it, if not for my wide eyes. "We're not."

His eyes drift back to the room—to the pile of bones that is all that remains of half of my heart. That is all I have left of her. There's a split second when it seems he's about to protest, to unnecessarily remind me of the danger once more, but he sensibly refrains.

Kaelis removes his long jacket as the flowers are retreating, becoming dormant once more. "I'll gather her."

"Thank you," I whisper. I should do it, I know I should. But my knees are still too weak. My heart can't beat strong enough to support me when it's in this many pieces.

Kaelis takes my hand. Even though he says nothing, there are a thousand words wrapped in his touch, behind his eyes. It is an apology, and a sign of a shared grief that assures me he, somehow, understands this pain.

Releasing me, he stands and goes back to collect Arina's remains.

CHAPTER 42

When Kaelis returns, Arina's bones are wrapped tightly in his jacket, knotted securely in the garment of a man whom I could blame for her death. I cradle her bones in my arms, clutching them to my chest so none come loose. I hold her one last time as we backtrack through the rooms the Fool designed to keep people out of his workshop. We're careful once more underneath the Duskrose. But the traps are disarmed heading from the opposite direction, so we pass through the first three rooms with ease. Though I don't have the energy or will to marvel at it.

I'm sorry, whispers every beat of my heart. *I'm sorry,* echoes every footstep through the academy's passageways as we emerge out from the warded depths. Reason fights against emotion. My sister was a force to be reckoned with. As raw and wild as magic itself. She deserved so much better than this.

Staggering, I lean against the wall, doubling over and burying my face into Kaelis's jacket. It smells of him, and of soil, and sweet, deadly pollen that makes me drowsy with the mere aroma. There's not a hint of the rosemary oil Arina would braid through her hair. Of the lavender lotions she'd begun using because they reminded her of Jura's cookies.

Kaelis stops, too. He rests a hand on my shoulder, like a breaker against the waves of grief. A pillar I can lean on until I collect enough strength to lift myself once more and carry on.

"We can stop," he whispers.

"No . . . I have to take her home." Not that I know where "home" is for us. It's not Rot Hollow. The club is gone. Arina might have never even been to the townhome before . . . but it's all we have. It will become her home now. "Please, keep leading us to the city."

With a solemn nod, the prince carries on, leading us on a path through the academy I've never cut before. The secret way out was behind a tapestry all along. It connects with another interior bridge tunnel—this time within the big bridge.

I found it. At long last, Arina, I found your passage out. We'll go across together.

The tunnel lets out into a small mausoleum in a graveyard at the edge of Eclipse City on the rise to the bridge that connects with the academy. The lock on the door is broken, something Kaelis clearly notes but says nothing about. I take the lead as we enter Eclipse City proper.

The walk to the townhome seems to take forever, and yet it also feels like it's over in an instant.

I'm standing on the doorstep, staring helplessly at the door. Silas always got us into the building . . . I don't even have a key. Kaelis knocks on my behalf. I can't bring myself to loosen my grip on the bundle.

After a long pause, Gregor opens the door. His eyes flick from me to Kaelis. Something between shock and anger and pure hate furrows his brow.

"You—"

"It's Arina," I interrupt his righteous indignation. Even if I told them my imprisonment wasn't Kaelis's fault, they will always be suspicious of him, and for good reason. They know the rumors about the prince. They will hold their grudges against the crown that he embodies. Perhaps even more so now because of the burden I am carrying.

"Arina? What about her?" Gregor says hastily, focus solely back on me.

"It's Arina." I lift the bundle a little higher. I can manage only those two words right now. Anything more and my voice will shatter.

Gregor's brow furrows, and it takes him an agonizingly long time to understand. I shift the fabric, exposing a pale bone. His hand flies to his mouth to muffle an immediate sob of grief. He looks like a mountain crumbling. But his hand cannot stop the tears that spill from his eyes. He stumbles, knocking into a wall so hard the foundation of the townhome trembles.

"I . . . She deserves a proper burial," I force myself to say.

Gregor moves aside, still unable to speak. Kaelis and I let ourselves inside.

"A star has fallen!" Gregor booms up, voice cracking with pain.

The Starcrossed Club. Each of us like little points in the sky, once so far apart, yet drawn together like constellations. And when one of us leaves for good, we fall from that sky. A life cut too short, a sparkling map that will never be the same. The design forever changed.

The others rush down, gathering on the stairs. They halt, enveloped in a stunned silence at the vision of me—with Kaelis.

"It's Arina," I say yet again, louder this time, though it's still just as painful to say it. Every time I repeat her name I'm ripped apart a little bit more.

"What . . . ?" Jura pushes past Twino and Gregor to get to me. I silently hold out the bundle, and she undoes the knot. The moment she uncovers an unseeing eye of the bony skull, she collapses, knees giving out. Jura lets out a wail that speaks for us all.

"She . . . She . . ." I struggle to find words. I'm losing my own composure—what little I'd scraped together.

"We will bury her." Bristara stands at the top of the stairs. Ever the rock of our club, she gives her orders.

It takes an hour to prepare for the burial, and we wander the townhome like ghosts. Arina's bones rest quietly before the crackling fire of the lounge on the bed of Kaelis's jacket. Jura has set out a pot of tea for her alongside the cookies Arina loved so well.

Gregor is in the small, walled backyard of the townhome, digging. Ren crosses through the hall with a large flowerpot in hand—a white lily. Twino is upstairs, preparing remarks.

As for me, I stay by her side. She's been alone for far too long already, and these are my final moments with her. So I stare at what's left of my sister as I keep my vigil.

It shouldn't have been you, I repeat over and over in my mind, *never you. I would've endured a thousand years of Halazar if it meant you'd keep living.*

Kaelis stands in the corner, a silent observer and sentry. A shadow that is not quite welcome in the throes of our grief but also has nowhere else to be.

"Second son of Oricalis," Bristara says briskly as she enters. "Make yourself comfortable in the front study."

It's odd to see Kaelis ordered around, and even stranger to see him heed the command without so much as a remark. But he does cast one last concerned glance my way. I don't have the energy to give him anything in return.

Bristara closes the doors behind him and crosses to the sofa opposite me, Arina between us on the table.

"It's my fault," I whisper.

"Death always feels that way." Bristara's voice is not overly warm. It never is. But it's sincere in her own manner.

"I was the one encouraging her . . . setting a horrible example by always taking on more jobs. We kept one-upping each other. Outdoing. Pushing each other to never give up." *Like the job that got me caught.* "She—"

"Wasn't a child, no matter how you saw her. Arina was a woman who made her own choices, just as you are. And we both know she was just as reckless as you, if not more so," Bristara interjects. I slump, knowing it's true. Hating that it is. Accepting all the blame for this would be easier. "Though I fear for where those choices are leading you. The Oricalis family is not to be trusted, no matter what they might tell you."

"*He* might tell me, you mean," I clarify, lacking the patience to dance around what she's actually saying.

Bristara purses her lips slightly.

"I know the dangers," I insist.

"I thought you did, but now . . ."

"Now *what*?" Agitation rips through me, rapidly riding the current of my grief.

"You brought him to our sanctuary. First Silas, now the second-born prince himself."

"I'll kill him myself before I let him become a danger to any of you." My hands ball into fists.

"Are you sure about that?"

"You don't think I'm capable?"

"Do you have the capacity? Yes. Do you have the will?" She shifts and leans back slightly. "I wonder." I swallow down a sharp retort. The assessment is fair. "Was he not the one to lead you to her bones?"

"We happened upon them." I can't help the defensive edge in my voice.

"In passageways I reason only he knew of? Since you did not find Arina on your own."

I know what Bristara is alluding to. "It wasn't him who killed her."

"Are you certain?"

I hang my head and rub my palms in my eyes. "He was just as surprised as I was."

"Can you be so sure?" Bristara lets the question hover. I have no answer. "That man owns the madhouse you're living in, top to bottom. He controls its teachings, its food, its entertainment, what is on- and off-limits, *everything*. If he wanted to lie or fabricate a story, would you be able to tell the difference in a place where his truth can become reality? Do you *really* believe him?"

"He..."

Bristara won't hear my objection. "Clara, *he* is the cause of all the pain we've experienced."

"He is as much one of his father's subjects as we are."

"Do you hear yourself?" She shakes her head with disgust.

"He is trying to rebuild something better." I can see that she doesn't believe me. Emphasizing it doesn't seem to help, but I do it anyway. "*He is.*"

"Forgive me if I cannot trust the man who benefits from the system saying he'll willingly tear it down." The statement sounds so much like my own months ago. How have I changed so much? "I know far more about the Oricalis family than you realize. More than you've been privy to, even while getting close to the prince." We share a hard stare. Neither of us moves. Bristara's gaze is the first to soften. There's an *almost* motherly look in it that serves only to agitate me more. "I hope you're right, Clara. I really, truly do. And I want to believe in you."

"Then believe in me."

"You make it hard when you inspire new doubts in me with every choice you make."

"I messed up with Griv, I know I did."

She isn't about to let me string too many words together. Bristara was never the sort to let much slide. "Even before then. Your obsession with avenging your mother's death drove you and your sister to risks you should have never taken, and now I see the same drive in you again—a drive that will lead you to danger. A drive that got your sister killed."

"Don't you dare." I'm on my feet, fists clenched.

Bristara doesn't even flinch. Instead, she locks eyes with me and issues a challenge. "Tell me I'm wrong with a straight face and I will retract my words."

I open my mouth, and the tiniest scrap of better sense has me shutting it. I fall back into the sofa again with a noise of disgust. Tears of pain, anger, and frustration prick at my eyes. "What would you have had us do? Let her killer walk free?"

"I would have you trust me when I have always told you I am looking out for you. That there are forces at play yet beyond your comprehension. That I want to know who killed her as much as you and Arina do, and if there is a way to find out, and bring them to justice, we will see it through together."

I very much doubt that. But I don't say so aloud.

"But throwing faith at the void-born prince is not the path to those truths," Bristara finishes.

"It's more than that," I murmur.

"Oh?" Something about the sound tells me Bristara knows what I'm about to say before I say it. But I speak anyway.

"I—*we*—have a chance to change the world." *To bring my family back from the dead and fix everything.* My wish for the World has doubled tonight. I'm already imagining how I might phrase my wish to ensure I get everything I want.

Bristara goes as still and cold as cast iron. "I said nothing last time, hoping these pursuits would be abandoned. But since they have not, hear and heed me now: *Never* seek the World." The words echo Mother's, and it stills me. "That is a force not meant for mortal hands."

"You believe in it, then?" I'm somewhat surprised. Bristara doesn't seem like the sort to believe in folktales, and she had no reaction to it the last time I told the group of the World.

Bristara doesn't hesitate in the slightest when she says, "It is real."

"Then we must—"

"Listen to me, Clara. There are things about the tarot you don't yet know."

"I know plenty."

"What the prince has told you of the Majors and the World is only a fraction of the picture."

"Then tell me everything!" I throw out my arms, pleading. "If you know something, say it, or be silent like before and leave me to do what I think is best."

"The World is a dangerous power that cannot fall into the wrong hands."

"Which is why I'm going to take it for myself. I have been to the font; I know what Kaelis will do and am already planning how I might take it from him. I just need to find this vessel before he does. Or be there when he summons the card."

Bristara goes completely still. A spectrum of emotions runs across her face. Shock, horror, anger, determination. Her voice drops to a hush. "You've seen the font."

"Yes. There I—"

"Then go no further. Do not, under any circumstances, allow the World to be summoned." There's a panic underneath her words that deepens my confusion and my curiosity.

"Tell me why I should give up an opportunity to make everything right because *you say so*."

"Because your mother would've wanted you to defend the World from that family at all costs."

Even though I have enough sense still to know she's right, I'm far too emotional to admit it. "Don't you dare tell me what my mother would or wouldn't have wanted."

Yet, Bristara does so anyway. "Your mother would rather stay dead than risk anyone in the Oricalis family having the means to summon the World."

I'm on my feet, seething, seeing red. "How dare you." The words are little more than a whisper. Anything louder and I will be screaming. "*How dare you.*"

"Clara, listen to me. Your mother had a reason behind all the warnings she gave. Laylis—"

"Keep her name out of your mouth," I snarl. "If you wouldn't do anything you can to bring her or my sister back, then you don't get to say their names in front of me."

Bristara sighs heavily and opens her mouth to speak again but is interrupted by the doors opening. Twino stands on the other side.

"We're ready," he says solemnly.

I make it a point to be the one to collect Arina's bones, casting one more harsh look Bristara's way. I'm not going to let her turn Arina's death into an opportunity to preach at me. To use the loss of my sister and my scattered mental state as an opportunity to twist my arm and force me to do something I don't want to. Perhaps she senses that I'm not going to be able to really hear her until the tide of grief has ebbed, because she stands up as well.

I leave the room before she can say anything more.

We all gather outside. The small garden is hardly large enough for all of us to stand shoulder to shoulder, but we cram in. Anger gives way once more to sorrow the moment I see the grave Gregor dug. My stomach is empty yet sick. A lump I can't swallow sticks in my throat.

Everyone turns their eyes to me, waiting. I grip the bones tighter, quivering. *It wasn't supposed to be like this.* I resist the urge to run. As if by not committing her remains to the earth I might be able to bring her back.

Finally, I kneel.

"You'll always be with us," Gregor whispers as I settle her bones into the hole. It's not very deep, though it doesn't have to be. There's no rotting flesh for scavengers to take.

"I know roses were her favorite, but all I have that I'm confident replanting is this lily," Ren says, somewhat apologetically. "I figured it'd be worse if the plant, well, you know . . ."

Died, we all think at the same time.

"It's beautiful, I'm sure she'd love it," I manage to reassure him around the lump in my throat. "She liked all flowers, really."

Ren settles the plant atop her and holds it in place while Gregor and I push earth around it. Every shovelful is a muted farewell. When we're finished, Jura approaches with the pot of tea—now cool—and pours it over the lily. It eagerly soaks into the ground, as if rushing to quench her thirst one last time.

Our silence is broken by a low, sorrowful note. It's been a long, long time since I last heard Twino sing. His voice is as beautiful as it is haunting. As deep as our sorrow. As uplifting as Arina's presence always was.

Jura's hand slips into mine, and I clutch it tightly. We stand together, hearts aching. One singular goodbye. Something unclenches deep within me. It's not relief, far from it . . .

But the coffin is no longer empty. I cover my mouth to catch a howl, hang my head, and finally weep.

CHAPTER 43

Kaelis and I are mostly silent on our way back to the academy. The night weighs heavy on me. My friends' tears, Bristara's words, the club's final farewells to Arina . . . My mind and heart are too full with it all to come up with any words for him. Before I know it, we're in his foyer, where I linger before the door to my hall. Kaelis sways, as if he wants to reach for me, but it's also as if he's holding himself back.

"Do you . . . Can I . . ." He abandons both thoughts with a heavy sigh and a hand running through his hair. *Do you want me to stay? Can I do anything for you?* he doesn't say.

But I hear the questions loud and clear all the same and shake my head. "I'd like to be alone." *Away from you,* I think he hears as clearly as I heard his unspoken questions.

"Yes. Understandable."

Yet neither of us moves.

"Thank you, Kaelis . . . for helping me bury her," I finally manage.

"Of course."

"I'll... see you in the morning." I turn and disappear into my hallway, leaning against the door as his footsteps disappear. I can feel him wanting to come back, wanting to hold me, in the same way I can feel power gathering right before an Arcanist draws a card.

I want it. I want that comfort. To be held. Loved. I want to weep into a warm chest until dawn rises. Sob until I vomit, as if I could physically expel this grief. Yet there's also nothing left to expel. There's a hole in my gut that's all-consuming. That threatens to suck in the rest of me until I blink out of existence.

Arina... My sister...

I whirl, open the door, and look out, half expecting to see him there. But he's not. Three options lie before me. His room. Mine. Out.

Bristara's words are as heavy in my heart as Arina's bones were in my hands.

I can't stay here.

The Stellis see me as I leave, but for once I let it be. This path is the fastest and doesn't involve going through Kaelis's room. Let them think what they will. Let the nobles talk about me leaving his room a wreck. I'm too tired to care.

The common area between the house dorms is completely empty. The hour is so late that even the night owls have taken to roost. But as soon as I slip into Alor's room, I'm welcomed by a flash of silver, followed by a dramatic yawn.

"I've no idea how you don't fall asleep in your classes," Alor mutters sleepily. "You are *always* out and about at night."

"Can I stay here tonight?" I blurt.

She shifts, sitting. Blinking. "What happened?"

"I don't want to talk about it." I start for my bed—what was once my bed.

Alor catches my wrist, locking eyes with me. "Are you all right?"

"Physically, yes."

"The prince." Her tone takes on a murderous edge. "Did he cross a line?"

"Twenty, no." I shake my head, clearly hearing what she's asking. "Nothing like that. It's something else."

Satisfied, she releases me. "Fine, though you should be gone by the dawn, lest people see you not emerging from his wing."

"Worried about me?" I crawl under my covers, already feeling far more at ease than I would have in his apartments. Something about Alor's ferocity toward Kaelis in my defense has me resting easier.

"I don't want things to go sideways for you and for me to lose my secret advantage." She yawns and rolls over.

"Right, sure, that's all it is."

"I don't like your tone." She makes it a point not to roll back over. I manage a slight smile, despite the circumstances. *She cares.*

"Alor, I've something I need you to do for me."

"What?" Her tone suggests she'd do anything if it meant not being kept awake for another minute longer.

"On the thirty-fifth day of Wands, last year"—the day I was captured—"a place called the Starcrossed Club was raided by Eclipse City enforcers and destroyed. I need you to find out who was behind the raid, if you can."

"I have access to Stellis records, not city enforcers."

"I know, but this was an illegally operated club. The crown would've been involved."

She makes a noise of comprehension. "It'll take a bit. I probably can't do it till after the break, but I'll do my best."

"Thanks." I roll over, putting my back to her. Within a minute, Alor's breathing is slow and even.

But my eyes still aren't tired. My mind is still moving. Guilt and worry fill the gulf of tears left behind by my sister.

What did I tell Luren? Live because she can't? But how do I keep living when my guiding star has fallen?

The World.

The thought returns. Damn Bristara's cautions. The World could fix everything. Bring back Mother, bring back Arina . . . and make our lives what they should have been. Kaelis might say he has noble reasons for hunting the World. But how can I be sure? All I know for certain is what I'd do if it were in my hands . . .

I'm going to have to steal it from him. There really is no other path for me now. Once, I might have been tempted to let him have his wish. But now? *Sorry, Prince, the World is mine.*

A week passes, then two. For a time, I live like a normal initiate of Arcana Academy. I go to my classes. I help train Alor in a forgotten room we found that now doubles as a small practice space. I spend hours poring over notes with Luren and Dristin.

Sorza goes to the sanctum . . . but I don't join her. It's possible Kaelis might be there.

Most nights, I escape his apartments and favor my own dorm room. People have noticed. Even Kaelis—if not from the rumors, then from my absence at breakfast. But he doesn't say anything.

Let them talk becomes my refrain. The will to care has escaped me.

It feels as if a rotten, wretched substance has replaced the blood in my body. I can still feel Arina's bones in my arms. Her bracelet around my wrist is comforting, but it's also as weighty as a prisoner's shackle from Halazar. *She should've been here to wear it . . .* The fact that she's not here has created a seed of loathing in me that I've no idea where to plant.

Luren catches me rotating the bracelet absentmindedly around my wrist late one evening in the library. Sorza and Dristin have long since gone to bed. But she insisted on staying. It doesn't occur to me that it might have been because of me until she asks, "What happened?"

"What?" I quickly stop the movement, tearing my attention from the lantern I'd been staring into and returning it to the book before me. As I'm blinking away the ghost of the light burned into my eyes, I realize just how long I was mentally elsewhere.

"You haven't been yourself lately."

"It's nothing," I murmur.

Luren's hand covers mine, fingers resting right by the bracelet. "You've helped me so much, if I can be of help to you . . ."

My eyes trail up her arm to meet her gentle gaze. Luren's dark brown hair cascades over her shoulders, half pulled up as she does to get it out of her face whenever she's reading books or tarot. I shouldn't say anything. But I'm back to the night following Kel's death in Luren's room . . . yet the roles are reversed.

"My sister died." As soon as I say it, relief floods me, riding on a fresh tide of grief. Saying it aloud to someone is like a breath of fresh air and drowning all at once. It's like I'm not alone, yet simultaneously still so far out of anyone's reach.

"Oh, Clara." Luren is out of her seat in a blur, arms wrapped tightly around my shoulders.

I brace myself for her pity. Her platitudes. All the things that one is supposed to say when they hear of another's grief.

But Luren says nothing. She holds me firmly. As if, for a moment, she's trying to offer me shelter against the storm.

I can't stop the tears. They come silently but are seemingly endless. The entire time, Luren stands there, clutching me. I'm not returning the embrace; I haven't even moved from my chair. She's just . . . there.

Because she understands. Just as I understood that night months ago. Luren gives me a space to silently shed tears I hadn't realized I'd still been keeping in.

At three and a half weeks since burying Arina, I find a letter tucked under my pillow—not in my room in Kaelis's apartments. But in the one I share—shared? *share*—with Alor in the dormitories. The note simply reads:

We need to speak.

I know we should. But I still ignore him. I'm not ready yet.

But Kaelis's patience with my avoidance finally runs out. It's just after inking class that I see him in a doorway down one of the halls—an open study room. I step aside before anyone else notices and the presence of the headmaster causes more of a commotion than either of us really want. Especially since we are, once more, everyone's favorite rumor, now that they believe we've had a "lover's quarrel." I never thought I'd miss the days of gossip about the Halazar escapee.

He shuts the door behind me as I slip inside. The lock clicks.

"Is that really necessary?" I eye it.

"I want a moment alone with you, and I don't want any zealous initiates nervous about their Three of Swords Trials barging in looking for a study room." Kaelis folds his arms and leans against the door. Clad head to toe in black and silver, he looks every inch the disapproving headmaster. By his standards, today's outfit is understated: An impeccably tailored shirt that looks more like black ink than silk. A vest of a light gray and trousers in a darker, matching color. Perhaps it's the light streaming through the window, but this ensemble looks almost cheerful compared to his usual attire.

"If you wanted to ensure we'd be alone, then perhaps you shouldn't try to meet where initiates and students frequent."

"I would've, gladly, had you ever decided to return to the apartments for more than a bath and a change of clothes . . . before not returning at all." When I open my mouth to speak, he continues. "Then I sent a note, and that was ignored. You've driven me to drastic measures."

"Amusing how walking among your student body is considered 'drastic.'" I lean against the center of a table, two chairs flanking me.

Kaelis furrows his brow. "Why have you been avoiding me?"

"I haven't been avoiding you." Now my arms are folded as well.

He snorts loudly. "You are usually an exceptional liar. Which goes to say that you know that claim is ridiculous as well."

I avoid his eyes, doubling down on my bad lies. "Things have been busy. I've been preparing for the Three of Swords Trials." The excuse worked on Silas, maybe it'll work on him . . .

"We both know that you have been preparing from the moment you got a hot meal and could train your body to recover from Halazar. You'll be fine in the Three of Swords Trials. Inking and wielding are second nature to you, and you only have to pass two of the three trials." His words are surprisingly warm, fond even. Gentle enough that I can't bring myself to look at him.

"It never hurts to be prepared," I say defensively. "Which, speaking of, I should meet my friends to study and train." I try to step around him, but Kaelis pushes off the door and blocks me.

"We both know what this is really about."

"Do we?"

He looks down at me. "You blame me for her death."

"Don't be ridiculous." I look away. The mention of Arina rakes against a part of me that is still too fresh, too raw. If only it were just her death clouding my thoughts when it came to him. But Bristara's words and warnings have stuck with me, too. She had more to say that night, I know it, but I wasn't ready to hear it. Am I now? I'm not sure. Part of why I've yet to return.

"Is it, though?" Kaelis takes a step toward me.

"Of course I know it's not your fault." My hands drop to my sides, and I grip the table, fingers trembling. *Do you* really *believe him?* I hear in Bristara's voice. I don't know if what I say is for myself or for him. It's all too murky still. But I know I might completely snap for good if he keeps bringing her up. "I know how she got there—she even told me herself she was pushing deeper into the academy, that she had 'something big.' She was the one who went there and took the risk."

Arina was a woman who made her own choices. Bristara's words, true or not, are of no comfort to me, no matter how many times I repeat them.

"She must've been miraculous to have made it even that far."

"Is that supposed to make me feel better?" My eyes swing back to his, and something in them makes Kaelis flinch.

"No." His tone relays that he knows how ridiculous that'd be. "Even with all that being true, I know . . . I am a part of the world—*this world*—that pushed her to her death."

I wonder if he managed to eavesdrop on Bristara's and my conversation.

"That's why I want to build a new world—a better one. I want to make things better for all those like Arina, like you and your Starcrossed Club," he continues, oblivious to my suspicions.

"Is Arina alive in your new world?" I whisper.

"Clara . . ."

I silence him with a ferocious glare. With all the hurt and pain I've carried for weeks. "Will you bring her back?"

"The world I want to build is bigger than the people we've lost."

"Nothing is bigger than them."

"There are countless others like you." His tone is torn between frustration and understanding. "We will have one wish. You cannot sacrifice the good of countless others for your own benefit."

"Of course you don't understand. It's not as if you have close family or friends," I mutter.

Kaelis doesn't flinch. Instead, emotion drains from him, as if he's retreating within himself for safety. I focus on the corner of the room rather than bringing myself to look at him.

When he speaks next, it's with forced calmness. "The World has the power to change everything, for everyone."

My chin jerks toward him. I meet his eyes with a silent challenge. "Then change it for me—bring them back."

"I can't."

"Then what good is it?" I snap. "Why have that power if we can't save the people we love?"

"Because the wish is complicated."

"It doesn't have to be!" *Don't make me your enemy again,* part of me begs. *Give me a reason to trust you, forever.*

"I know a lot more about this than you." Even though it's clear he tries to sound otherwise with his tone, he comes off as if he's speaking down to me. Kaelis continues hastily before my offense can grow. "The World gives *one* wish. You have one chance to speak your will, only one command. The more complicated it is, the less likely the outcome you hope for. Too vague and you run into the same problem. We must be *perfect*. Then, the deck is shuffled once more. Everything changes—including who the Majors are."

"I could lose my power?" I whisper, not realizing until this second how much I have come to appreciate it. Even if I've yet to use my Major again since Eza, there are so many other benefits to being the Wheel of Fortune.

"Nothing is guaranteed when everything is remade from the ground up," he says solemnly. "You might keep it, you might not. I might not be an Arcanist at all. It all depends on how the wish is phrased and how the World interprets it. Which is why I must be as careful as possible in crafting the wording, focusing on what will do the most good."

I. Not we. His wish. His world.

Maybe he's right; it probably is better to focus on the greatest good for the greatest number of people. More noble, at least. And who would've thought I would say that about Kaelis, ever?

But what has the "greatest good" ever given to me? I grip the table tighter and relax my fingers. This world, the next . . . it's not worth it without the people I love. Maybe I'm the horrible one between us now. This world has made me selfish and cruel.

"Kaelis, you don't have to convince me any more than you already have," I concede to keep the conversation moving—to avoid his suspicion. "I *know* we need to work. I know that the Three of Swords Trials are coming up and then it's merely seventy-five days until the Feast of Cups, where I must not only have my forgeries but also figure out how to get the cards from your father." The weight of it all, in this moment, is nearly crushing. "But my hands won't move. I've inked precious few cards as it is."

"Let me help you." He takes another step closer.

"I don't need help; I've lost people before and know this process," I say softly. "But it never gets easier. So let me ride the wave and I will find you when it passes. It will pass."

"I also know the ocean you're adrift in." The words seem almost painful for him to speak as he closes the gap between us. "I know these currents."

"How?" I don't think Kaelis would lie about something like this, not right now. But Bristara's cautions are stuck in my mind like barbs.

"My mother."

"The queen?" I've heard mention of her only as a reclusive individual—one who keeps mostly to her castle, doting on the youngest prince.

"*Not* the queen," he all but snarls. "That woman is not my mother." I blink at the revelation. I've never heard any mention of Kaelis being born of a union from anyone but the king and queen. The portrait I found flashes in my mind. "My father killed my blood mother."

"Kaelis . . ." I can't form any word but his name. Shock gives way to the dull ache of a sympathy I never expected to give him. And a shared understanding I never would have guessed I'd find with him: the pain of losing one's mother.

It's happened yet again: Just when I think I'm ready to hate him and pull away for good . . . he draws me back in. He does something I'm not expecting, and suddenly I'm not sure which way is up anymore. My heart is in knots.

Kaelis pulls out a chair, but rather than sit in it, he uses the space to lean on the table next to me. "I've spent my life as a prisoner in my own home. I spent my childhood enduring the madness of memories that carried no explanation—of a woman's smile in unfamiliar halls. I was told that the woman who I knew in my blood was my *real* mother did not exist. I've suffered a lifetime of knowing that I am only alive because of the power my father thinks I wield."

"That you can wield reversed cards?" I clarify.

"Exactly." Kaelis laughs darkly. "If I could, don't you think I would truly be a force to be reckoned with, and my father wouldn't be able to push me around? But, as it is, I am nothing more than a blade he can hold to the throats of those he hates. Sharp enough to be deadly to others, but not strong enough to be a threat to him.

"In his cruelty, he's had me kill and sacrifice. He took from me the only person who would have stood up for me—my mother. Every day,

I've had to endure his brutality. Had to look into the eyes of the man who would end me if it wouldn't be inconvenient for him to do so."

"Did you really destroy Clan Hermit?" The question is little more than a whisper.

The stories tell of a night when the clan was gathered—a night when a magic poison was introduced to the High Lord and through him flowed to everyone related to him by blood and by name, near and far. A magic so powerful and wicked that it even rotted the very ground the clan stood upon, causing the Archives of the Hermit to collapse into the earth.

"Clara." My name is a caution.

"Was it on your father's orders, as they say? Were they really plotting against the crown?"

"Clara." He pushes away from the table, shifting to face me.

"Will you use the World to bring them back?" I demand to know. "Will you bring back your mother?"

A shadow passes over his pained and haunted expression. The anger that the mere mention of Clan Hermit elicits simmers at the edges of his eyes. Kaelis draws a slow breath and exhales. "No."

"You . . ." I don't even have words. To have all that power and not seek to right those wrongs.

His throat tightens as he swallows hard. He forces himself to repeat, "No. I'm focused on the future, Clara, not the past. Oricalis destroyed my home, so I will destroy it. I'll dismantle everything, so that way there is an opportunity to begin anew and make something good. A world where King Naethor will never hurt anyone ever again."

The room goes still, the air heavy. For the first time since I've known him, I wonder if I'm seeing the real prince behind it all, behind the stories and the reputation. If I'm seeing the hidden hurt that defines everything about him, his goals, and the world he's trying to build.

However mistaken I still believe him to be.

"I'm sorry," I murmur, unsure of what else to say. "For your mother."

"I'm sorry, too. For everything you gave up—I gave up . . . for all of it."

I search his face and cannot find the hint of a lie. He means it.

Which . . . makes it worse that I still don't think I can forgive him for not being willing to bring them back.

My hand grips his, and I clutch his fingers tightly. "We're going to do it. We will get the World. We'll remake it all."

"Thank you," Kaelis whispers.

He means it . . . And that will make it all the harder for me to deceive him. His world means nothing to me if the people I love aren't in it.

CHAPTER 44

The Three of Swords Trials are a little more than twenty days away. Since next week will be the recess right before the trials, all the initiates are frantically cramming in as much preparation and study as possible. The nervous energy rattling the air has even found its way under my skin.

I wander the aisles of the library, searching for books on tarot iconography. The reading test is what I'm most worried about. I've managed to coax my inking and wielding style to fit the strict guidelines of the academy, but reading was always my weakest area. My hunt has taken me to one of the farthest back corners, where three shelving units come together to form a dead end. It's so secluded that even the lamplight is dimmer here.

Military records . . . History . . . Nothing particularly useful. I run my fingers along the shelves, skimming the titles just in case there's something on older reading practices. Perhaps tarot spreads I hadn't considered. Given how particular Professor Rothou is about reading, I've no doubt she'd place a lot of value in "how it was done ages ago."

My fingers brush over a set of letters carved into the side of one of the bookshelves. N+E. I can't stop a slight smile. I wonder if these lovers were from an earlier year of the academy, or if they haunted this secluded section for a moment alone ages ago.

"Clara?" Sorza stops me from formulating a whole love story in my head about two people who are probably long gone.

"Over here," I call.

She rounds one of the shelves, crossing quickly. Three books are heavy in her hands.

"Oh, good, you're alone. Luren and Dristin are holding the table. I offered to get what they needed so I could catch you alone since *someone* isn't coming around the sanctum very often these days." She slides up next to me, her voice falling to a hush.

"I'm focused on the Three of Swords Trials, as you should be, too."

"Yeah, so you say. But you know what you were also very focused on? Inking your card. And you know what I haven't seen you nearly as focused on lately?" She pauses.

The silence extends until I sigh. "What?"

"Inking your card. So I can only think that you figured out how to do it." She looks at me like Priss might a piece of fish on my plate.

How can I lie to that face? "Yes, I figured it out."

Sorza snatches both of my hands with a squeal. "Well done, you! Have you tried wielding it?"

"No." I'm not counting when Eza attacked me. That was hardly a controlled experiment.

"I haven't tried mine, either. Prince Kaelis said that we shouldn't explore them too deeply yet." *Did he now?* This is the first time I'm hearing either of them mention the other. "But I was thinking, maybe you and me sometime, we could . . ."

"Absolutely." I follow her logic with a slight grin.

"Excellent! After the Three of Swords Trials, maybe? Oh, has Prince Kaelis taken you to the—"

"Well, isn't this a lovely picture?"

Sorza pulls away, and we both look to the source of the voice. Cael, the Emperor and one of Eza's favorites, leans against the bookcase at the end of the row. His strip of hair down the center of his head has been teased and fixed upright today, instead of being its usual half-hearted mess.

"Cael, I'm surprised to see you here," Sorza says, collecting her books.

"And why is that?" He bites out the words.

"Because I didn't think you could read," she quips easily. He glowers. I fight a laugh.

"Go, Sorza. I'm not here for you," he commands gruffly.

"Oh? Here to keep doing Eza's dirty work for no good reason?" she snaps back. "Isn't it embarrassing as a second year to be ordered around by a first-year initiate?"

Cael closes the gap between them. He's an imposing force, with his sharp jaw and piercing violet eyes. His clothes are perpetually grungy, as if he doesn't want anyone to forget that he's one of the common-born students. It almost seems to invite a challenge.

"I've business with her." Cael nods in my direction.

"Then you have business with me, too." Sorza doesn't move.

Cael's eyes dart to me.

I shrug. "I'm not her keeper. She can do what she wants."

"Unlike how Eza treats you," Sorza adds.

"Just wait." Cael looms over Sorza. But she doesn't even flinch. "When you get your clan assignment next year, see how long you last before you realize you need to start making the right friends, and practicing the right skills. Not all of us have the luxury of a prince guarding them. And, given what I hear Justice is able to do, I suspect you'll be headed right to the royal court with me."

"I'm not afraid of that," Sorza says bravely.

"You should be." There's a glint of something damaged in Cael's eyes, like a door that's been ripped off its hinges. He's seen things he wishes he hadn't. Done things he probably wishes he hadn't.

"What do you want, Cael?" I try to refocus on the moment at hand. I've always been leery of Cael because of his proximity to Eza. But this is the first time that I've seen him as a danger in his own right. Something's hanging by a thread inside him, and I don't want to see it snap.

"There's something you should know about Eza."

"Eza's good little errand boy." Sorza just doesn't know when to quit, and part of me greatly appreciates her for it. The other part of me is pretty sure it's going to get her killed sooner rather than later.

Luckily, for now Cael ignores her. "Eza has asked Thornbrow to be your opponent in the wielding test, and Thornbrow agreed."

"Oh, lovely, even more to look forward to. Can't wait." I step to the side and go to move past him. "Now, if that's all . . ."

In a flash, Cael grabs my arm and pushes me against a bookcase. I have a card spinning midair by my hip in an instant. Sorza sets her books down so quickly that I'm amazed all the pages are still attached. Her own card is at the ready.

"You don't want to do this." I lock eyes with Cael, ensuring he knows that I'm not threatening him—I'm promising him what's about to come next if he keeps this up. "I'm not the half-starved, skin-and-bones woman you jumped months ago."

"You don't get it. They don't care what happens to initiates who don't pass. The wielding trial is the last one. And you'll be encouraged *not* to hold back."

"Good. I want Eza to come at me with all he's got . . . so I can beat him. *Again.*" Tension hangs in the air, thinning it.

Just when I think Cael has had enough, he leans forward, breath warm and frustratingly sweet smelling. It's almost like he's trying and failing to be unappealing.

"He knows *all* of your weaknesses."

"And I know all of his." My confidence startles him. Cael's grip loosens some. "As you said, I've the prince—and luck—on my side. What do you and Eza have?"

"Fail inking," he whispers, so soft that I barely hear it. Sorza is oblivious. Before I can react, he releases me with a slight noise of disgust. "Fine. Be ready; if you go into the arena with Eza, he's not going to fight fair. The king already has your card, it's not like he *needs* you anymore."

He strides away. My card returns to the holster on my thigh. Sorza gathers her books after returning her own cards. "What an ass. Don't pay him any mind. He's just trying to scare you."

I'd have to agree. *Fail inking?* Was that his way of trying to convince me to throw one of the other trials so if Eza beats me I'm out?

Yet, something about that interaction felt genuine . . . like he really was trying to warn me of something. But why would Cael, out of all people, try to help me?

Tonight is the first night I'm ready to return to the Fool's workshop. There's only so much I can do with the supplies we have in my or Kaelis's study. Kaelis is insistent that the only way we're making any kind of convincing forgery of a Major Arcana card is with the supplies from the Fool himself. And, I must admit, I'm curious about what these legendary items can do.

This time, knowing what's about to come, I pay even closer attention to Kaelis's actions. I count the steps between the openings in the walls of fire. I keep control of my thoughts in the water room.

But I can't stop a shuddering inhale when I see the final room . . . and not for the reason I'd been expecting.

"They're gone," I breathe. Every last bone has been removed from the soft earth. My attention spins to Kaelis.

"You were right, they deserved a proper burial." Kaelis shrugs. "Whatever paltry sentiments these hands could offer them was their final send-off."

"You . . ." I can't find the right words. "You did this?"

"No one else comes down here." The words sit uncomfortably on his tongue.

I look to Kaelis, and he holds my gaze for a long minute. I can imagine the prince coming down here, alone, during all the days I was avoiding him. Collecting the bones one by one, painstakingly slowly to avoid the Duskrose opening.

"I'm not a monster," he says softly. "Even if I must act like one sometimes."

"I know," I reply, just as soft.

"We should carry on, there's work to be done." Kaelis moves before I can say anything else, ready to abandon his discomfort and the topic entirely.

I don't press.

Past the final room, we now traverse deeper than I ever have before. The hall descends to a final antechamber with one last door. Kaelis reaches into his pocket with his right hand, pulling out a card. I don't see what it is before he rests it against my forearm. My fingers grip his left hand gently and he stretches out my arm.

"There's a trick to get through this final door—a barrier that will only open for individuals with certain magics." His eyes flick up to mine. "May I?"

"May you what?" I ask uncertainly, the card resting on my forearm, acting as the thinnest barrier between our skin.

"I'd like to give you a marking that shows you are friendly to the Fool—that will allow you to pass through his barriers."

"How do you know how to do this?" I ask uneasily.

"A lot of research, practice, and study." That I do believe. Kaelis is always poring over a book, or journal, or his own notes on various subjects. But this is also a magic greater than any even I have seen before, and Mother's powers were great and immeasurable. "I wasn't going to allow a door in my own domain to remain barred to me for long. It took a lot of trial and error. Mostly error, until something finally led to success." His eyes dart down to my arm and then back to my eyes. "It won't hurt."

Something in me tells me I shouldn't. But instead I say, "Go ahead."

Kaelis hesitates for a moment, vindicating that little worried part of me. Why is it that, in this moment, this feels like a point of no return? More than any other line I've crossed with him . . . *This* is different.

I suck in a breath, perhaps to object. He does the same. But a look of pure focus crosses his face, and the opportunity is gone.

The card explodes.

Light weaves and snakes around my forearm. It carves shapes across my skin, sinking underneath the layers of me. Kaelis was right, it doesn't hurt. I feel gentle pricks but no pain. A warmth that's almost like sunlight caresses me.

On my skin an image appears: thorny vines weave together, capped by silhouettes of white roses. The illustration glows and then settles into thin lines almost like faint scars before fading completely.

"White roses . . . the symbol of the Fool."

Kaelis nods. My hand still in his, he presses my palm to the door. The glyph on my arm illuminates once more, shining brightly. The door glows in tandem. When the light fades, the heavy barricade has vanished, as though it were never there to begin with.

"Good," Kaelis says proudly.

How . . . That one word launches a thousand questions that I keep to myself. How did he know how to do this? How did he master such magic? I've already asked him and doubt I'll get more clarity beyond "my prowess" even the next time around.

I stare at my palm, wondering just how deep this magic runs. And what he might not be telling me.

But Kaelis is oblivious to my worries; instead, he laces his fingers with mine and, with the giddiness of a schoolboy, hastily guides us into the hallway on the other side of the door. Lamps light themselves as we pass, burning with cold flames.

The workshop of the Fool is alive with magic. Shelves arc across the walls, laden with books and scrolls that exude the aroma of old parchment. Long tables are covered with vials and bulbs of multicolored liquid. Tiny, delicate machinery hums, performing its tasks without need of instruction. Magic sizzles through the air. The ceiling magically oscillates between night and day, as though it can never quite make up its mind.

One of the mechanical wonders steals my eye. It's a tiny version of the machine I saw on my very first night—a powder mill, with a hammer moving on its own, pounding a fractured shard of a crystal to dust. I cross the room to watch more closely how its gears turn. The larger version had extended into a hole in the ceiling, hiding half of it. Here I can see the whole machinery.

"It's the hammering itself," I breathe, realizing how it works. "The magic unleashed by the breaking of the crystal propels the hammer back upward, which resets the counterweights. That's how it knows how much force to use—it regulates itself based on how much magic is left in the crystal." And I had thought Kaelis secretly had servants, or even Marked, toiling away, working the mill. There's probably more to it than I'm guessing. But it doesn't require manpower, that much is apparent. "The Fool made the machine?"

I think about the etching I saw upon it, the one that was almost like a V and an E, unless it was an N and a 3? A different symbol for the Fool? Or, perhaps it was intended to be an F, but the etching was clumsy . . . I wish I could go back to see it, but I doubt Kaelis would take me if I asked.

"No, that—and this small prototype—were made by someone else." Kaelis's tone is utterly unreadable. "Someone who came after the Fool."

"Who?"

"Another nameless explorer between then and now. I don't know who."

I don't believe for a second that Kaelis doesn't know who it is. But I can tell by his tone that *if* he knows, he's not going to say. I can't blame him for his secrets. I keep my own. But that doesn't stop annoyance from fluttering through me at his constant avoidance of certain topics.

"Could we make more and replace the need for people to work the mills at all?" I ask.

"It's not that simple."

"Why?" I don't let the matter drop easily.

Kaelis's mouth tugs into a frown that doesn't last longer than a second. But something about the expression brings Bristara's voice to the fore. *Can you really trust him, Clara?*

Yet again, I don't know. Though, I want to . . . A part of me keeps hunting for a reason to believe in him.

"The metals required to channel the magic need specific smithies and refineries. Technologies lost to us along with the previous kingdom." Kaelis lovingly runs his hand along the shelves of books. "But that individual was inspired by the Fool's writings. If there is a way to uncover the secrets, or some kind of hint for how to do it in our time, we'll find it in here. I've dedicated years to compiling the history of the Fool's works and studying his brilliance. He had ways of doing things that we can only imagine. That if I have the opportunity to prove and share them with the world will only make all our lives better."

His eyes shine with such admiration and hope. He looks like a completely different man here. Kaelis is right, he's not wholly a monster. But he's not innocent, either. And I don't know, when all is said and done, which side of him will win out.

"Let's get to work," he announces and moves toward the jars in the back that contain shimmering powders not even I have seen before.

I can come to the workshop of the Fool on my own now. I remember the way I found on my second night and have learned the pathways through the trap rooms. One night I make use of my newfound ability. I know better than to think that Kaelis isn't aware. He was the one who gave me a key in, after all.

Alone, I take my time scouring the workshop of the Fool. In the back are the powders of the Fool's design—the ones Kaelis has insisted will make a card convincing enough to trick even the king. The powders are coarser than any I've ever seen. They almost look like they're made of shards of crystal, but it's unlike what we harvest from the Drowned Mines to ink Cups.

With a glance over my shoulder, I carefully tap some into a second jar I brought with me and place it into my satchel. Twino will have a delightful time analyzing this powder, and perhaps it's something I can use beyond making these forgeries. Kaelis has his secrets still . . . and so do I.

In the cold lamplight, I read through the journals, searching for what I couldn't find in the library or anywhere else in the academy. It takes an hour or two, but, eventually, I confirm my suspicions. I hunch over one of the long tables, shoulders up by my ears, and stare at the page.

The World can do anything. The words on the page whisper to me in Mother's voice. *Summoned by the twenty Majors, and imprinted upon a vessel card . . .* Vessel *card?* Kaelis had mentioned a vessel, but I can't recall anything about it being a card. Unfortunately, the book doesn't elaborate. Another thing to uncover, but it doesn't change my goals.

I can bring you both back, I don't dare to whisper aloud. I can remake the world into what it should be. Not just create another system that will no doubt rot and fester like all the ones before it, like Kaelis wants.

CHAPTER 45

The halls are empty, and the academy dormant. It's winter recess, one of only two breaks in the academic year. The summer recess between the Feast of Cups and the Fire Festival is nearly two months long, marking the transition from one academic year to the next. But winter recess is just one week, starting with the winter solstice. Not a lot of time, but enough time to rest and make final preparations before the Three of Swords Trials. For some initiates, this will be the last time they are out in the world free and Unmarked. For the rest, it's our final week before becoming full-fledged students.

Which has made me even more sour about my time being interrupted. I am not only being forced to go and spend time with Kaelis's family and some of the other High Lords and Ladies at a Swords Solstice banquet at the castle, but I am also missing out on time with my family from the Starcrossed Club. Jura makes the best winter solstice spread imaginable. And it's a tradition for us to swap stories over too much wine until we are red in the face and practically falling out of our chairs.

I'm dressed far more formally tonight than I would be if I were headed to the Starcrossed Club.

My reflection in the mirror is nothing short of a masterpiece, if I do say so myself. The gown is such a deep shade of midnight blue it's nearly purple, embroidered with delicate silver threads encrusted with gems. The silver embroidery supports a mesh that covers my arms and frames my hips like the border of a tarot card. The mesh also trails along the edge of a near-scandalous deep V in the bodice.

The dress somehow manages to both complement and contrast with my skin, now slightly more tanned from the sun than when I left Halazar, and a dusting of rouge on my cheeks brings out my faint freckles. In the low light and set against the blue and silver of the gown, my eyes seem to glow a bright crimson.

"At least I look the part." I finish hooking two diamond-encrusted earrings. *I look like a princess.*

A knock at the door pulls me from my thoughts. "Clara, are you ready?" Kaelis asks from the other side.

"Yes, just about, you may come in."

He opens the door, and my hands pause as I attempt to clasp the final piece—a black velvet choker bearing an ornate sword. Kaelis wears a jacket cut from a velvet identical to my dress. Silver embroidered swords dance along its trim. The vest he wears underneath is so thick with detail work that it looks almost like embossed metal and not thread and fabric. And everything contrasts with and brings out the deep purple of his hair—it's so much more than a flat black.

Kaelis crosses to me and takes the ends of the choker from my struggling fingers. He deftly closes the clasp. But then his fingertips trail along the necklace, landing on the sword at the base of my throat.

"You are stunning," he murmurs.

"As are you." The words escape me before I can second-guess them. But they're nothing more than the truth. The corner of his mouth quirks up in the slightest of smirks as if he, too, is well aware of this fact.

"I cannot tolerate being anything less than the best dressed. And as my future wife, you must be held to the same standard." He nearly purrs the words into my ear. His hand falls from my person, but his dark eyes continue to hold me with a steadying gaze, as if he can sense the nervousness I'm trying to conceal at the idea of walking into the Oricalis Castle. "The banquet is a smaller affair. Think of it as good practice for the Feast of Cups later."

"Except at this one I'm not trying to steal from your father."

"I know." He sighs dramatically, though his tone betrays amusement. "We can't have fun all the time, can we?" I give a slight laugh, and he beckons me to the door.

I follow him from my room and into the hallway. As we emerge into the foyer, I'm surprised to find we're not alone. Ravin and Leigh are dressed in their own matched set, done entirely in crimson and black. Leigh's dress splits to reveal tight trousers underneath and an ornate sword at her hip that is clearly more decorative than functional. Though I suspect she's just as lethal with it. I'm more than a little jealous at the mobility the trousers lend her. But at least my cards are safely tucked into a thigh holster under my skirts.

"Clara, this is Silas," Kaelis says, formally introducing me to a man I already know well. Silas is dressed in finery as well.

"Lovely to meet you," I say with a slight tilt of my head, hoping my instinct to keep our familiarity a secret is accurate.

"And you as well." Silas also plays the part of us not knowing each other. "Are we all ready, then?"

"Indeed." Ravin is eager to leave.

"Silas is the Chariot. He will be taking us to and from the castle tonight," Kaelis explains. The journey to Fate Hearth would be at least three days by carriage otherwise.

"That answers a few questions I had." I smile as Silas produces the Chariot.

With a swift movement, he activates the card, and a burst of silvery light engulfs the five of us. In an instant, we no longer stand in the academy, but in a small sitting room in the Oricalis Castle. I can already hear muted music and chatter through a nearby door.

"Impressive," I say with false wonder, as if it's the first time I've experienced the card. Then I genuinely ask, "How many people can you move at a time with the Chariot?"

"More people presents more opportunities for the magic to go awry," Silas says. "I prefer not to move more than five or six individuals, including myself, for safety."

So not an army. "Fascinating."

"The powers of the other Majors aren't something to concern yourself with," Ravin says with a smile. Despite this, there's a sinister undercurrent. "After all, only the crown is able to call upon the power of the Majors."

"Of course." I duck my chin in a display of deference, remembering what was said about the other clans needing to know that I pose no risk to them should Clan Hermit return. Little do they know that Clan Hermit isn't the threat.

"This way." Kaelis holds out his elbow. His eyes meet mine with a glint of something playful—something wicked. "*Darling.*"

A spark jolts up my fingers at the word as they wrap around his biceps.

I'm thrust into the thick of it as we step through the door, down a short stretch, and into a grand hall. Vaulted ceilings soar above us, adorned with frescoes that tell of the history of the Oricalis Kingdom. From the long, long-ago fall of the previous Revisan Kingdom, to the clan wars that followed, to the rise of the Oricalis family. Hundreds of years of history are rendered in brilliant colors and illuminated by crystal chandeliers.

There are about forty nobles milling about the hall, as sparkling and vivid as the paintings rendered above them. The music is loud enough to muffle conversations—and the readings that are taking place at tables set up throughout. Around the winter solstice is a traditional time to have one's future read for the entirety of the coming year, and it seems this party leans in to that aspect of the Season of Swords.

In the center of the room is one extraordinarily long banquet table with so much decor upon it that I wonder where the food is supposed to go. Kaelis's muscles tense as he ushers me farther into the throng of the court. His presence is an oddly reassuring anchor in the sea of nobility.

"We'll start with someone easy," he leans forward to whisper in my ear. The moment I realize he's guiding me to a friendly face, I can't help an audible sigh of relief. Kaelis lets out a low laugh of amusement, quickly composing himself. "High Lord Leva, please allow me to introduce you to my bride, Clara Redwin."

"A pleasure, my lord." I wear a warm smile. "Myrion, good to see you." The son is a spitting image of his father. They both have the same thick lashes, the same deep brown skin. The only difference is that Ixil wears his hair long, in a single thick braid that's adorned with crystals and silver discs.

"You as well, Clara."

"It is an honor to meet the woman who shall rebuild Clan Hermit." Ixil kisses the back of my hand. I can't tell if Kaelis glances away at the gesture or at the mention of Clan Hermit being rebuilt. "My son has told me much about you both. Notably how well suited you are. What was the phrasing you used? *Ah,* a 'destined match.'"

I must thank Myrion the next time we're alone for saying so even when he knows it's a lie. Especially since his father knows that, as the Lovers, he has a sense of these things. Yet again, he's looked out for me. All the fears I'd repressed, from my first day in the Sanctum of the Majors, that he'd see Kaelis and I are not in love evaporate.

"We seem to think so." I flash Kaelis a brilliant smile that seems to almost take him aback. He recovers quickly, but I didn't miss the startle.

"And a very happy birthday, my prince," Ixil says. My head whips to Kaelis. I can't stop my mouth from falling open with surprise. Ixil doesn't miss the shock. "Surely you knew?"

"It was not relevant." Kaelis's tone is cool. His pose stiff.

"Myrion, how are you feeling about the Three of Swords Trials?" I ask hastily, picking up on Kaelis's discomfort. "Third years take exams during the season as well, don't they?"

"We do . . ." Myrion, astute as ever, immediately launches into an explanation of the tests second and third years face.

We make small talk with the High Lord of Clan Lovers and his heir before moving on.

"It's your birthday?" I say softly when no one else is around.

Kaelis doesn't meet my eyes. "Unfortunately so."

"Why didn't you tell me?" It's clear he's not keen on the day. But I can't help the slightest ache at the idea that he'd kept something like this from me. "It's something that I should know as your blushing bride."

"You're right." He sighs heavily. "I simply loathe the day is all. The court whispers how my being born on the longest night of the year is further proof of being void-born." He sounds so dejected that I feel guilty for ever questioning if he could be.

"Ignore them." I slide my hand into his. "If there's one thing I've learned this year, it's that rumors take lives of their own."

Kaelis's voice drops to barely more than a murmur. "The day also reminds me of my mother."

He's not talking about the current queen of Oricalis. My stomach knots. I stroke his thumb with mine. The movement draws his attention to me and, for a breath, we're the only ones in the room.

"I'll make sure to move the topic along, then. Should it come up again," I say softly.

"Thank you." He means it. I can tell by the easing of the furrow in his brow. His shoulders relaxing.

It feels better than it should to help him.

I'm presented to the High Lady of Clan Magician next—a woman with a sharp gaze and sharper wit. I find I quite enjoy her company. But I have precious little time to savor it before we move along once more. Only two others bring up his birthday and I deftly maneuver around it.

Eventually, I find myself in front of Moreus Ventall, High Lord of Clan Tower. Unlike Lord Ixil, he's alone. His daughters are nowhere to be seen, despite most of the other high nobles having brought some, or all, of their immediate families. The things Alor has said about her family—specifically her father—return to me. I wonder if she was even invited to come. Or if she was relegated to staying at home.

Just as people could see blatant similarities between Arina and me and our mother, Moreus is obviously Alor and Emilia's sire. His hair is an identical shade to theirs, perfectly coiffed and held in place away from his face. His eyes are the honey brown of Alor's, but with the sharp gaze of Emilia's. He's a bit tanner than either of them in a way that suggests he spends a great deal of time in the sun. His appearance has clearly been honed to exude severity, as there's something about his very presence that feels like a threat.

"High Lord Ventall, a pleasure as always." Kaelis's tone is smooth, polite, and perfectly unreadable in how trained it is to sound innocuous. An odd approach to take with the man responsible for supplying the crown with their Stellis. I would've thought there'd be a warmer rapport between them.

"Prince Kaelis," he says somewhat briskly, turning from his previous conversation. His eyes dart to me and widen slightly. He must recognize me from All Coins Day as the one who saved Alor. "High Lady Redwin."

My name hovers in the air. Formal, yet soft. As if he wants to thank me for saving his daughter but can't bring himself to. I offer him a gentle smile and a slight dip of my chin as if to say, *You're welcome.*

"Still just Lady Redwin," Kaelis corrects with an almost pitying smile. "Though it's our hope that when my father accepts her, her status will be solidified . . . should the clans also be amenable to healing old wounds."

"Yes . . ." The High Lord's attention has yet to leave me. "You are common-born, correct?"

"I'm honored you know of my lineage." I smile politely.

"Quite lucky that the prince found you out of all the common-born women out there. The odds are . . . unlikely." His tone is impossible to read, so I'm left to assume there's doubt or suspicion there. Clan Tower *is* responsible for defending the crown. His eyes narrow slightly. "Especially given that, according to the best of our records, the full bloodline of Clan Hermit had been eradicated in a single, defining act."

Suspicion indeed.

"Your records are not always perfect." Kaelis's words are frigid. If there are two things that I know my prince doesn't appreciate, they are being questioned and the mere mention of Clan Hermit.

"But they so often are." The way High Lord Ventall looks at Kaelis makes me think of two birds of prey, feathers puffed, talons ready to strike. "I should like to inspect the evidence you found that verifies her lineage."

"I think you can take my word for it." Kaelis attempts to dismiss him. And fails.

"It's the duty of Clan Tower to protect the crown. I'm merely doing my job." He smiles, but it doesn't quite reach his eyes. His stare is still as hard as steel at my throat. "Especially with the rumors of an escapee from Halazar earlier this year."

"I believe my father said there wasn't one?" Kaelis arches a dark brow.

"Officially, no." Moreus shrugs slightly. "But one can never be too careful. There's always a nugget of truth in every rumor, don't you think, Lady Redwin?"

"Perhaps." I try to give away nothing.

"Wouldn't want anyone linking the rumors together, since it's quite an amusing coincidence that you showed up around the same time."

My palms are sweating now. *He knows.* He must. Why else would he be asking such pointed questions? *Fuck, Ravin.* I'm sure this is the firstborn prince's doing.

"If you have a point to make, High Lord Ventall, I suggest you get to it quickly." Kaelis's razor-sharp words are matched by a murderous glint in his eyes. His hand lands on the small of my back, featherlight yet stronger than armor.

Moreus opens his mouth to speak again but promptly shuts it when the lights of the room dim dramatically. Every candle on the chandeliers magically snuffs out all at once, guiding our attention to the far end of the room. King Naethor Oricalis stands atop a raised platform, three steps above the rest of us. The lighting, the platform, his opulent garb, and his sheer presence are enthralling.

Wordlessly, he holds up a tarot card. I catch a glint of silver. My eyes widen, and I am nearly blinded by the flash of fire that explodes from the card. The flames turn cold and ice blue and then become swirling water. Wind sweeps through the crowd, tangling skirts and drawing gasps from both lords and ladies. Light and shadow condense with the crackle of elements in Oricalis's fist as it closes around a magnificent scepter that writhes with living vines, burns with fire at one end, and emits frost at the other.

"Welcome, high nobles of my court, to the winter festivities." Naethor holds out his other hand, his voice carrying across the large room. "May your readings hold fortune, your cups be full, and your hearts find new allies among your fellow courtiers. May your years ahead be as balanced as the elements of the four suits. Dinner will be served within the hour."

The king steps back, and the lights across the room flicker to life again to the tune of respectful applause. While we were distracted, Lord Ventall appears to have stepped away. His absence allows me to focus on the question now burning on my tongue.

"How?" I whisper, looking to Kaelis. "I know of cards that can mend or modify objects. Cards that can conjure illusions. But I *felt* the heat and the wind." The scepter is passed on to a servant and looks as real as anything else.

"The Magician enables someone to craft something from nothing by calling upon the four elements."

"I thought only a Major Arcana could use a Major card?"

"The Hierophant is why. That card must be cast by a Major, but it can give an Arcanist the ability to use another Major Arcana *once*. Then the blessing fades, and it must be given again," Kaelis explains. It jars something in my memory of what Myrion said when I first arrived at the Sanctum of the Majors.

"Let me guess, the Hierophant is kept here in the royal court?"

"How did you know?" He smirks. But, without warning, Kaelis's eyes shift and his expression falls. Forehead creasing. "Clara, I need to step away a moment."

"What is it?" I ask. "Does it have to do with Ventall and his suspicions?"

"Perhaps." Kaelis is already moving away.

"Let me help."

"Not this time." He grabs my hand, silencing me with a light squeeze before I can object. "I'll be right back." There's urgency to his every movement.

"We're supposed to be . . ." My protest fades as he disappears into the crowd. "Together."

Curious and more than a little annoyed, I try to follow him through the crowd of nobles, weaving through the skirts and coattails to see if I can figure out just where—or who—he's heading toward. I lose him as people continue to mingle, blocking my view. I think I see him stepping aside with a man dressed in the colors of Clan Moon . . . *Glavstone?*

The crowd closes around them. I try to push through, but by the time I manage to emerge, they're gone once more. Just as I'm cursing under my breath for losing them, I spy Ravin pulling Silas through a side door with a wary scan of the room, clearly looking for any who might be watching. Their heads are bent in what seems to be intense conversation.

That's too suspicious not to explore . . . right? I give one last sweep for Kaelis but come up with nothing. Finding out what Silas and Ravin are up to is better than standing around waiting for Kaelis to reappear.

The men step through the door, attempting to be as inconspicuous as possible, and I trail behind them. I strain to hear their conversation over the music, but it quickly fades, and so I slip through the door myself. Their footsteps echo from down the hall, whispered words woven through them.

From a distance, I hear their voices through a door. Heart pounding, I creep up to it.

"Ravin, I've told you everything I know." Silas's voice is tense.

"I need more, Silas. If she is leaving Kaelis's watchful gaze . . ."

"I will let you know," Silas responds, a bit of defensiveness to his tone. "But I can't *force* her to leave without arousing suspicion."

"Perhaps it doesn't matter. You don't need a secret identity this time . . . We could just take her, rather than trying to maneuver her," Ravin muses.

Secret identity. This time. My suspicions are more deeply confirmed by the second.

"If I kidnap her from the protection of the academy, Kaelis will *know* it was me."

"She's a wild card. I'll make him think she ran away of her own accord." Ravin says it as if he knows me well enough to convince Kaelis of this.

"She wouldn't leave his side." Silas is convinced.

"Oh?" Even Ravin hears it in his voice. "Does she genuinely care for him? Is it really love?"

"I don't know. Everyone seems to think she does."

"I heard the opposite." Ravin hums. I hate the sound.

"Either way, Kaelis won't believe you that she ran. I'll be forced out of the academy and Kaelis's good graces, and you'll lose your easy path into your brother's domain." Silas dances with his words. An obvious, careful calculation.

"And we can't have that." Ravin sounds a touch frustrated. "Then perhaps, as another Major, you can lure her in."

"I can't get close to her without arousing the suspicions of your brother. I've *tried*. She ran from me the one time our paths crossed," Silas outright lies.

"Try. Harder." Ravin's words harden into a deadly edge. "You made her dance for you once, do it again. Make her slip up so we can be done with this charade once and for all. Why Father hasn't done it himself is beyond me . . ."

"I'll do my best," Silas says dutifully.

"Remember, Silas, what's at risk if you fail me."

Footsteps approach quickly. I dash behind a corner ahead. By my luck, Ravin doesn't see me as he departs. Silas doesn't follow. I know I should leave it be, but . . .

Frustration and anger get the better of me.

"You . . ." I push open the door slowly. He lowers his hands from his face. The man looks as if he collapsed into a chair and had yet to find his legs again. But I'll give them a reason to feel like jelly. "I *knew* there was something familiar about you when we first met. But it wasn't because of Arina's descriptions of you, was it?" My heels click as I cross the room. Silas doesn't move. "It's because of *you* that I was in Halazar, wasn't it?"

He doesn't say anything. He just keeps staring at me with those guilty eyes. I grab his collar, balling it in my fist. I can't hoist this mountain of a man, but he's also not resisting me, either.

"I rotted in there," I snarl, our noses nearly touching. "I almost lost everything and everyone I cared about, for good. Because of *you*."

"Yes, it was me." Resignation fills his voice.

"You let me tell you my history like you didn't know it. Were you just laughing inside the whole time? When you offered to help me the night we met, was it just the start of another betrayal?" I let him go with a noise of disgust, half throwing him back into the chair. He falls like a rag doll. "And Arina . . . when I was gone, she was a loose end for you in the academy. You sent her to the workshop of the Fool and got her killed."

"What?"

"No one knows the academy like you do, Silas. You knew of it—that's how you knew to find me. You told her to go there, didn't you?"

"Arina was sent to the mills. She escaped, right?" He seems genuinely confused, frantic. I hate him for it. How dare he look like he cares—like this wasn't all a ploy. I hate myself for still wanting to believe him.

How could I be so stupid?

"She wasn't at the mills; she went into the room you found me in and never came out. Just like you wanted." My voice trembles as I try not to scream.

"I warned her not to go too deep!" He repeats one of the first things he said to me. I believed it then, I don't know why.

"It's because of you she's dead." My words are daggers, and I see the moment they strike him in the chest.

Silas lets out a soft gasp. "Dead? No. She . . . she didn't escape? She's not at a mill?" I go still at his genuine horror and surprise. "Clara, I did the opposite. I warned her *not* to go too deep into the academy. I don't even know of a 'workshop of the Fool.' Honest! All I know is there are some dangerous things in the depths of that fortress, and saving you was the first time I have ever dared to venture beyond the door. But Arina, she's—she's . . ." His throat closes with a choking noise.

I look away, folding my arms. I'm not ready to give him comfort. Not over Arina or anything else.

"I'm so sorry," he whispers. "For Arina. For it all . . ."

"Spare me."

"I am." He hangs his head.

An icy silence passes. In this moment, I'm back to all the quiet hours we shared in each other's company as I was rebuilding my strength. The nights we ran into each other when I was out and about in the academy.

"Why didn't you tell Ravin about the townhome?" I ask softly. I have a thousand questions now for Silas. But that's the one I keep coming back to. "Why lie?"

"He'd kill them if he knew. Or use them to get to you again."

"That didn't stop you the first time."

"I didn't know you then," he admits. His words are laden with genuine remorse. "It wasn't until it was too late that I realized you . . . you're not . . . Your sister wasn't just biased; you're trying to help people."

"Obviously." Or, I was. Once. Now . . . Now I don't know what I am anymore. Trying to help others took everything from me. Now maybe I want to fight only for myself. "So you grew a conscience in the past year?"

"He has my family," Silas blurts.

"What?" That brings my attention back to him. "I thought you didn't know what happened to them. More lies?"

Silas flinches but continues, "Ravin, he's the one who has my family. He tortures them. Threatens to kill them, or worse, if I don't do as he says. I've seen them. He's made me watch." Silas's eyes glisten with tears. "I was going to tell you everything as soon as we had another moment alone."

"Why not tell me earlier? How can I believe you now?" I ask, despite wanting to. "After all you've done?"

"I knew you wouldn't trust me. Especially when I explained everything . . ."

"Accurate," I mutter.

"So I was waiting until I had something to prove myself to you—that I'm on your side." Silas produces a slip of folded parchment from the pocket of his coat.

I take it with two fingers, still regarding him warily as I unfold it. It's schematics, hastily drawn. "What is it?" I ask, even though I already recognize it.

"Drawings of the mechanics of the king's box—where he keeps the Major Arcana. I know this castle as well as I know the academy. While everyone was distracted with the event tonight, I snuck into the king's private study and picked the lock on his desk to get the schematics and made a copy. If you're going to get those cards, you'll need to unlock the box first, and you won't do it without knowing how it works."

It's impossible to conceal my surprise at the remark, even though I try. While my voice is level when I speak, I know my brows have shot up. I can't decide which catches me more off guard, that he managed to figure out my plot, or that he'd dare do something as risky as sneak into the king's personal quarters.

"What makes you think I'd try to steal them?" I ask.

"Ravin told me what happened when you met with the king on All Coins Day—to see the cards instead of asking for true nobility, or a guarantee of lands, or a pardon, or something else, when you could've had *anything*," Silas explains. "I can only fashion one explanation: you wanted to see where he kept them. And, knowing what I know of you, it's easy to imagine why that would be important to you."

I purse my lips. A denial would be insulting to his blatant intelligence, but I'm not quite ready to confirm. I ask, "Did you tell Ravin of this theory?"

"Of course not. I told him I had no idea why you'd ask for that when he inquired." Silas sways slightly, glancing away. He looks wounded and on the verge of defeat. Perhaps that's why the anger in me is beginning to ebb. "Clara, I never . . . I didn't—don't want to hurt you, or Arina, or any of your friends. It was never about you. I just want to keep my family safe. I don't want to let him control me anymore, but I . . . Please, help me keep them safe."

That's why. Once he truly learned about me, and the club . . . and realized maybe we could help. Maybe he'd even realized before, when he was pretending to be Griv, but was in too deep. This isn't about me, or him. He's doing this for his family, and that is the closest to trust I might give to anyone right now.

"Did you tell him our name?" I whisper, still staring at the drawings.

"What?"

"Arina's and my family name—our real one—did you ever tell Ravin?" Our eyes lock.

Silas shakes his head.

"If you're lying to me . . ."

"Arina swore me to secrecy. I kept my promises to her." He doesn't flinch. Doesn't waver. I sigh, and my shoulders ease away from my ears some.

"Where are they?" I finally ask, putting the schematics in my pocket. Twino's mind is much more suited to this sort of thing than my own. He'll be the one to validate Silas's offering—he saw the king's lockbox, too, after all.

"What?"

"Where does Ravin keep your family?"

"If I knew, I'd use my card to go there and take them."

"You said he made you watch." I'm wary about catching him in a lie.

"He knows my magic. He always moved them before, and after."

"Right." I tap my fingers on my biceps and give him a hard stare.

Silas holds it. There's a glint in his eye I don't like. "Remember, the first night we met? You said *anything* I wanted to repay me for helping you get out?"

I'm already cursing under my breath.

"I want this," Silas finishes.

I sigh heavily. "*Fine.* I'll help your family."

"Really?" Despite him calling on my offer, he seems as surprised to hear it as I am to say it. "You will?"

"Yes, but—"

"Clara?" Kaelis calls out, voice laced with a mix of concern and urgency.

"We'll talk more later. And if you step one foot out of line or even blink in a way I don't like . . ." I hastily whisper, pointing my finger at him.

Silas holds up both his hands. "I swear, I'm on your side now, forevermore."

With one more hard look and a whirl of skirts, I stride out the door. "I'm here."

"There you are." Kaelis breathes an audible sigh of relief. "Father is asking for us."

"Excuse me?" I blurt as Kaelis takes me by the hand. "Us? Specifically?"

"I don't know, either," he manages to say before we reemerge into the main hall.

It feels as if all eyes immediately swing to us. I stand a bit taller and try not to look suspicious. What else was back in those halls? Would there be an excuse for me to have been there? Or will Ravin automatically assume I was with Silas? Even as my thoughts spiral, I keep a placid smile on my face.

Kaelis guides me by one hand, and with the palm of his other on the small of my back, up to the very head of the table, where the king sits flanked by Ravin and a young man with nearly white hair who must be the third-born prince. The youngest brother keeps his head bowed, finger trailing along the edge of his goblet, almost bored.

King Naethor stands, commanding the room. We both bow as we come to a stop before him. With a hand on each of our shoulders, he turns us to face the nobles. Nearly everyone has taken their seats.

"Lords and ladies, my loyal subjects. I would like to formally present to you my son's intended. Lady Clara Redwin." Murmurs and some polite applause follow, a reaction I'm getting used to from the nobility. "Their love burns as brightly as the Ace of Wands. It is as overflowing as Cups. This union is as sharp as a Sword and roots as deeply as a Coin. Come the new year, we will welcome her into the Oricalis family. Before this time next year, we shall all lift our Four of Wands to a royal wedding!"

The clapping is more committed this time. I force myself to smile through my shock, glancing over at Kaelis. Surprise is mirrored in his eyes as well.

Our mission to solidify our relationship in the eyes of the court is no doubt accomplished. But now a bigger question looms.

Why is his father helping us?

CHAPTER 46

"I don't understand it." Kaelis paces in front of the fireplace of his room. I'm stretched out on the sofa—the same one I was on after Eza's second attack. Kaelis, or Rewina more likely, managed to get the bloodstains out. I suppose he really did like *this* particular piece of furniture after all to go through the trouble. Priss is in my lap, extending her chin so far for scratches that her ears have drifted back until they're plastered to her head.

"Why would he suddenly be for our union?" Kaelis brings his thumb to his lips and bites the nail. He does an exceptional job of keeping that particular habit hidden in public but has stopped caring when it's just the two of us.

"I suppose it's too much to think he just wants you to be happy?" Even I know that's definitely not the case. Especially now that I have proof Ravin knows who I am. But explaining that to Kaelis would involve explaining Silas . . . and there are some things instinct has me keeping to myself. Especially since I know Kaelis is still keeping things from me . . .

Kaelis stops and shoots me an incredulous look before he begins pacing again.

"He wouldn't, not with us," Kaelis says with absolute certainty. Then he adds, "He's never cared for my happiness before. Not unless he thought he was getting something out of it."

What I overheard between Ravin and Silas sticks in my mind. How eager Ravin seemed to be at the notion that I might care for Kaelis, or him for me. "Maybe . . . he believes it."

"Believes what?"

"That you love me." I lift my gaze from Priss, and our eyes lock. Kaelis goes completely still, as if he hasn't thought of the idea before and the concept is horrifying. "From his perspective: Either you genuinely love me, and he gains some control of you through me, or . . . he'll force us to give up the ruse by pushing us to the breaking point before we go through with our vows with the Four of Wands."

The prince remains a statue, his dark eyes boring holes through me. Finally, with a shake of his head and a noise of disgust, he drags his feet over to the sofa opposite me. Elbows heavy on his knees, he hunches over, runs a hand through his hair, bites his nails, and lets out another noise of disgust as he sinks back into the cushions looking positively incensed and yet somewhat defeated at the same time.

"You might be right," he finally says.

"At least he's wrong," I say with a shrug.

"About what?" Kaelis's expression is hard to read. I wish I knew what was going on in his head.

Let me in, part of me wants to say. The rest is afraid of what it would mean if he did.

"You don't love me," I say, looking back to Priss instead of him. "We're both just a means to an end for the other. None of this is real, no matter what dresses or formalities we put on display. Which means, he can't use me against you, or you against me. We still have the advantage."

Kaelis says nothing. The silence drags on long enough that even Priss turns his way, prompting me to do the same. The fire is alight in his eyes. It burns at the edges of his face. Once more, he looks like he's made of stone rather than flesh and blood.

"Right?" I press gently.

"Indeed," Kaelis says. But the word is noncommittal, and I fight the flush that tingles across my whole body—a heat that's part panic and part desire.

The rest of the winter break is spent working on my forgeries and preparing for the trials. Without the familiar pattern of the academy's bells, the days blur one into the next. I don't seek out Silas, not yet. Nor do I go to the townhome for leftovers from the solstice celebrations. I've decided to dedicate myself entirely to the trials and then focus on the Feast of Cups—first one thing, then the next. Kaelis and I still spend most of our hours apart, even though it feels like we're the only two living things in the entirety of the academy.

But the distance between us no longer feels cold. If I had to describe it, I'd say it's almost . . . fearful. As if we're both afraid of what it will mean should we break this fragile truce. Whether we'd break away from or into each other.

I see the way he glances at me when he doesn't think I'm looking. Just as I can't stop thinking about how his fingers glide over the inked lines of the draft cards I present to him for his feedback.

Why are we doing this? The thought crosses my mind more than once when I'm alone in my bed. If we're pretending to be lovers anyway, why not reap the benefits of it? I don't think either of us is particularly inexperienced. So it's unlikely that there are concerns over it being a "first time."

One night, my musings carry me to his doors, my hand against the cool wood. Ready to enter his bedroom. To have him enter *me* and be done with this agony.

But I don't do it.

I never can decide on the origin of my fear. Is it lingering anger and hate over Arina? Is it the skepticism I can never seem to move past when it comes to him? Or is it that even I don't know the answer to the question I asked him days ago?

You don't love me . . . right?

Of course not, I want to say. Yet, even in my own mind it rings hollow.

Before I can find my conviction, the students and other initiates return from their break. But there's no time for the school to return to normal.

Just a few days after everyone arrives, the Three of Swords Trials will begin.

The day of the Three of Swords Trials breaks with blustering winds. The all-black cliffs of Eclipse City and the farthest edge of the Oricalis Kingdom get their first dusting of snow.

Every time this season rolls around, I can smell the phantom aroma of Jura's mulled cider, threatening to bubble over because she filled her big pot to the brim and forgot to account for how much the cinnamon sticks would expand, or how much space a clove-speared orange would take up. Licking my lips, I stare out through the frost-coated glass, past the river and to the city. The winter solstice event, working with Kaelis, and preparing for the trials have consumed me.

Trials that I now face.

"Clara Redwin," Professor Rothou calls from the doorway, drawing my attention back to the stony walls of the academy.

"Good luck," Sorza offers from the opposite side of the hall, where she leans against the wall with Luren.

"You've got this!" Luren lays on the optimism a little too thick. We all know this is the trial I'm most likely to fail, even with her trying to help me at every study session we shared.

I merely smile and give them both a slight nod, feeling the eyes of the other initiates as I make my way to Professor Rothou. I'm called in the middle of the pack. Random draw.

The testing room is completely empty, save for two long tables that run parallel to each other. The nearest one stands alone, with no chairs surrounding it. On its surface are three decks of cards that mirror the position of the three department heads who are seated behind the table opposite.

Las Rothou takes her place at the end of the table where Vaduin Thornbrow and Raethana Duskflame sit as well. Rothou smiles warmly, as if we haven't clashed on many occasions in her classes on the very subject she's about to test me on.

"Welcome, Clara, to your reading trial," Professor Rothou says. "When you are ready, please begin."

I cross to the table with the decks of cards. The professors explained, in depth, every trial during their classes to better prepare us for what's to come. I start at the rightmost deck—the one that corresponds with Professor Rothou. Her eyes shine—she's amused, no doubt, that I'd pick her first.

To start this reading, I draw four cards, lay them out before me, and call out their names. As I do, the professors scribble notes. Save for Rothou—her eyes never leave me, even as I divert my gaze to the cards before me.

Early-morning light streams through the windows that line the room in vertical bars. Somehow, they make this place feel almost as cold and confining as Halazar itself.

They're just cards, Clara. I can't tell if it's my voice reminding me of that, or my sister's from beyond the grave. *They don't use you; you use them. Don't be so afraid.*

Sucking in a breath, I give my reading.

"Five of Cups: You're facing a challenge in your personal life, some kind of loss, a rift between"—I almost stumble over my words—"sisters." I touch the Six of Cups lightly, feeling its meaning as much as interpreting it with sight. It doesn't specifically mean sisters, just nostalgia for a time gone—childhood and early memories. But sisters feels . . . *right*. Maybe it's just the ache of mourning that's still so deeply ingrained within me . . . "A difference of opinion that is rooted in betrayal—Ten of Swords."

My eyes dart to her. The cards are a window, and through them I can see right into her soul. At least, I think I can. But her expression has yet to falter or flinch, leading me to second-guess myself.

"The subsequent Page of Swords would recommend that, to get to the heart of the matter, one—or both—of you will need to let go of the barriers that you've put up. To be open to exploring new ideas for how to bridge the gap between you."

Finally, she lowers her eyes and scribbles some notes. When none of them says anything, I move to the deck at the far end of the table: Vaduin's.

If Las's reading was as easy as looking through a window, his is as clear as a steel door. The cards make little sense to me, each as conflicting as the last: Five of Wands, Seven of Swords, Four of Coins, Eight of Cups.

I see a conflict in the Five of Wands that he is not sure if he knows how to overcome. Perhaps it is related to work, perhaps family; it's difficult to discern, as every Minor suit is represented, and the more I look at the cards the harder it is to make sense of their meaning. There are no clear images in my mind or gut feelings. In the end, the best I can offer him is an acknowledgment that he is in a difficult position from all angles, trapped between conflicting wishes—his own and those of others. The Four of Coins suggests he might be hoarding his resources, perhaps in preparation for the battle he sees ahead. I suggest that the only way out is to look at everything in its totality, but victory will come at a price.

The only card I struggle to work into the reading is the Seven of Swords. Every time my fingers land on it there's a sickening unease that shifts in my stomach. *Betrayal.* "There is deceit around you" is all I can say.

It's impossible to tell how accurate this is from his expression, so I move on to the last deck.

My confidence for Professor Duskflame's reading is somewhere between the other two. Not resounding, but also not a total loss.

They all take a moment, scratching notes on the papers in front of them. Raethana and Vaduin hand their papers to Las. The head professor of reading makes a few sharp strokes with her pen, her eyes flicking to me in equally pointed movements. She leans in to whisper to Vaduin, and they exchange a brief conversation that I can't hear.

Despite myself, I hold my breath.

"You pass," she says begrudgingly.

I'm in a state of utter shock as I leave the room.

Few of the initiates seem to want to discuss how they're doing between the trials. So we're all left staring at one another in hallways and holding rooms, silently sizing one another up. Of course, my friends and I have no problem sharing our outcomes. I'm not surprised by the rush of relief that courses through me at knowing Luren, Sorza, and Dristin all passed.

The second trial—inking—also takes place before lunch. It feels like it's over in an instant, and honestly, if someone told me that I'd actually slept through it, I wouldn't be surprised. They had us ink four different Minor Arcana cards, chosen at random. It was like another day with Glavstone, minus the beatings. Easy.

But when I go to hand in my cards, I hesitate, though for only a second. *Fail inking*, Cael had said. Professor Duskflame's hand waits expectantly as she asks, "Are you certain this is what you want to submit?"

"Yes." I place my cards into her palm, submitting them for review. *Fuck Cael and Eza and everyone else who wants to see me come up short.* I'm not failing anything.

I hand over my freshly inked cards and leave.

"I had been hoping for a bit of a challenge with inking," I say as my friends and I catch up over lunch.

"Brag much?" Sorza nudges me.

"It's good one of us feels confident." Luren is slumped over her food, picking at it listlessly. Despite all of our efforts and all the long nights spent in the common areas and the library going over inking, she still failed the inking test.

"You have one more trial. You only need two out of three to bid for a house." Dristin makes an attempt at cheering her up.

"I don't feel confident about it all coming down to wielding," she says with a sigh. The day her card reversed understandably still haunts her.

"Not eating your lunch isn't going to help you with what's to come." I lean across the table to nudge the plate a little closer in front of her. "You'll need your strength."

"What I need is a miracle."

"Maybe one will encourage the other. *Eat.*" If nothing else, food is a worthy distraction.

As Luren picks up her fork with more confidence, we're interrupted by the arrival of another initiate. Eza hovers at the edge of the table, attempting to embody pure contempt and malice. I meet his gaze and hold it for the sole reason of keeping his attention on me and not my friends. If he's focused on me, and me alone, then hopefully he won't get distracted by the notion of going after those close to me.

"The only person needing a miracle will be Clara," he announces.

I imagine he thinks himself quite sinister and intimidating. Especially since he seems annoyed when my expression doesn't change from bored and lackluster.

"I passed my first two trials." Even though I'm speaking to him, I allow my voice to be loud enough for others around me to hear. "I already have two out of three needed to pass the Three of Swords Trials. I don't *need* to win the duel. So beating you will purely be for fun."

Eza wedges himself between Dristin and Luren, leaning over the table with a sneer. "I'm going to wipe the floor with you and leave nothing but a pulp. There won't be anything left for any house to even consider."

"You're more than welcome to try." A thin smile breaks through my otherwise disengaged veneer. "But we both already know how it will end, don't we?"

The bells toll before he can say anything more. Eza pushes away from the table and casts me a final withering gaze. "I'll see you on the rooftop."

CHAPTER 47

The final trial is held on the same rooftop where Kel died. Now it's covered in a thin layer of snow that's partly melting in the afternoon sun. The moment we emerge, Luren's eyes instantly go to the spot where her best friend took her last breath. Mine follow, thinking of the hours of scrubbing—an act that could expunge the blood, but never her memory. Even though Vaduin had us running drills for the past season, it was always elsewhere. Neither of us have come up here since that day.

I rest a hand on Luren's shoulder and whisper, "You'll be fine."

"Do it for her," she repeats my words and renders me momentarily breathless. I'm back in her room, giving that advice. Back in the library as Luren repaid the favor, offering me comfort in a way no others had.

"We'll do it for them," I vow. I squeeze her shoulder tightly before releasing her. Luren nods. Never have I seen her more determined.

We continue moving with the other initiates, collecting at one end of the rooftop. The other students are permitted to watch this final trial—their own winter tests now complete—along with the full faculty.

And Kaelis.

My gaze snags on him. Emotions wage war in his eyes. There's the initial flash of worry, pride tempered with fear, with admiration, too. It's everything I've been wanting to see for weeks, that he kept me shut out of. Why can I see it only now? Why is he risking all of them seeing it, too?

It's part of the game. He looks like he cares only because other people are watching. *That's all it is,* I try to tell my racing heart. He wants them to see him be worried for me. All part of our never-ending ruse.

The announcement of our standings so far brings me back to the present, and I force Kaelis from my mind. I can't allow any distractions.

I'm pleased to learn that my overall scores put me toward the top of the class. Despite her despair, Luren is smack in the middle with Dristin. Which means, even though she failed one of the trials, she passed her reading trial with extraordinary marks, and that should say something to the students. Sorza continues to impress; she's right at the top, along with Alor. Even though Alor's hardly looked at me throughout the trials, I can only hope she considers my assistance invaluable in helping her pass and she'll continue looking into Clan Tower's records as I need. My sister is gone. But there are still so many mysteries: My mother's death. Silas. And so many more things for which I suspect Alor's resources will prove invaluable in the future.

One by one, initiates are paired off and take their stances on the dueling strip. We go three pairs at a time. No matter what, half the initiates will fail this trial. Only one person can win each duel. Whispers lap like waves against my ears. Somehow, even the snowfall seems loud as we collectively take a breath before Vaduin starts the first match.

Watching the other initiates gives me an opportunity to really assess everyone's skills. I've sparred enough with Sorza that there's no need for me to study her. But Dristin is fascinating: his manner of wielding is direct but almost delicate in its fluidity—no wasted energy.

Alor is as pointed as I would expect; she uses only a few cards but with lethal precision.

I'm not surprised that I am in the last group to step into the arena. Luren is with me off to the side, against Fyrn. And, just as he promised he would be, Eza's the one to move opposite me. On my way to my position, I catch another glimpse of Kaelis. His throat tightens with a hard swallow. I fight a knowing smile.

No need to worry, I have this, I try to say with a reassuring look.

Do you? his stare questions.

I'm somewhere between wanting to scold him for his worry and reassure him that it will all be all right. It's been a long time since someone new in my world looked at me with that much worry. My star-crossed family have been constants for so long in my life that I know they care. It's not a question. But everyone else has been a chasm away. I've never let anyone else get close enough to have worry for me alight in their eyes.

With one final reassuring smile thrown Kaelis's way, I shift my stance and turn to fully face Eza. The world begins and ends in our dueling ring. Everything else has been consumed by our mutual loathing, rendered inconsequential. My fingers itch at the sensation of my power building inside me. The deck is strapped to my thigh and feels three times heavier than usual.

"Are you ready?" Eza asks.

"More than you are, I suspect." I crack my knuckles. "How's your jaw?"

His arrogant smirk drops into a scowl. It only causes me to smile wider. The hate between us could ignite the snow. My breath catches and I hold it, every muscle taut.

Vaduin's voice rings out as if he's speaking to us and us alone. "Begin!"

We simultaneously spring into action.

Eza immediately goes for the Ace of Wands. A ball of fire shoots from the deck at his hip. Given his Major, I'd expected him to try to play some mental game. But I'm happy to meet him blow for blow. If

I didn't still have to hold myself back to keep up the ruse of being like any other initiate, I'd counter with the Seven of Wands—a shield.

Instead, I cast the Four of Coins. Four discs of golden light surround me, swirling upward. The snow turns to a rainstorm, soaking our arena and snuffing the flames before they can reach me.

Eza is as quick to respond as I knew he would be, casting the Ace of Cups to give him control over water. With a swing of his arm, the rain stops midair. What I wasn't expecting was for the raindrops to condense into spears of ice.

Shit.

He hurls the ice my way. The Three of Wands bursts from my thigh. I use the heat of the card igniting to block the initial wave, then try to levy the safety in travel that the card grants me to dance around the rest of his assault.

As I dodge, I use the Four of Cups. Fog condenses around his head, slowing his movements. Eza tries to shake it off but staggers. I crouch and press an Ace of Cups of my own into the ground. The rainwater crackles and freezes, creeping up his ankles.

Without pausing, I cast the Five of Swords, hand closing around the familiar grip of a blade that immediately cries out for blood. I lunge fast enough that even Eza seems surprised, given the widening of his eyes. The shock grants him enough clarity that another card launches from his deck.

It's the Ace of Coins—well played by him. Pointed columns of stone rise from the rooftop. I dance around them, but one catches my calf. I stumble and let out a shout.

The students shout and cheer. Just like at the Chalice ceremony, they want a show. They delight in pain and bloodshed.

Gritting my teeth, I push through the agony, closing the gap between me and Eza. Blood splatters the snow as I lunge. My blade hits its mark, but only as a glancing blow. Eza has summoned a sword of his own. Hilt to hilt, we struggle. It's now a battle both of magic and of physical strength.

"You really think you can beat me," he snarls, "trash like you?"

"I don't think, I *know*."

He frees one of his hands from the grip of his blade. This allows me to gain control. But as I go for another swing, I see the Five of Coins rise from his deck. There's barely time to register what's happening before my sword vanishes.

Eza twirls his sword through the air, and I dance back to the gasps and cheers of the students and faculty. I'm too distracted by dodging his swings to notice the next card until it's too late.

The Ace of Wands is a blast of fire, white-hot and blinding. He uses it as a shield. I can catch only a glimpse of what follows because of my proximity to him.

The Eight of Cups bursts with an unseen wave that crashes against me, as cold as the waters around Halazar. I stagger. He used the Ace of Wands to hide casting an upper card. *Damn it.* I hadn't been expecting him to dare use a card above a five. A grave oversight, especially since I hadn't thought of how I might be able to do the same.

What did he take from me? The Eight of Cups removes knowledge of something—like a fact, or a skill—for a short period of time.

I find out as Eza swings again. My steps are clumsy. My body refuses to respond as it once did. All thoughts of counterattacks are gone.

Bastard! It takes every bit of my control not to just give up on the ruse and use all the cards I've inked over the past seven and a half months. But I know the second I do, he'll call attention to it. He'll use any such action on my part to cast doubt on me.

His fist lands hard and I'm sent spinning. I think I hear him say, "Payback." Blood dribbles from my split lip as he charges in again, this time with his blade. I try to dodge. It's clumsy but successful. Another attack, another strike. I'm a mess in the dueling ring until this magic wears off or I can cast something to—

"Forfeit, Redwin." Vaduin interrupts my thoughts. "That's enough."

Bastard. I grit my teeth.

"Yes, forfeit!" Eza laughs with a crazed glint in his eyes as he lunges again. The sword clips my arm this time and I stagger back, gripping the wound. The whole crowd reacts with gasps and cheers as he stalks toward me once more.

"I'm not done yet." While I no longer have the knowledge of how to fight well in hand-to-hand combat, I can still use my cards. But what can I do that I haven't already? I cast the Four of Swords, stitching up the skin of my calf, then another for my arm. It's a pathetic mending compared to what the Queen of Cups can do, but it's a start.

"We'll see about that." Eza adjusts his stance. He's getting ready for another assault.

In a duel like this, I can't beat Eza with raw power, not while I'm limited in what cards I can use and he's not playing by the same rules. And I can't beat him with physical skill, since he took that from me.

So a brutal, chaotic, overwhelming assault is all that's left.

The Two of Coins allows an Arcanist to sustain the magic of two cards at once. It's an essential card for most Arcanists that I rarely need to use, given my innate skills. But I quickly let three copies of the Two of Coins fly, stacking the ability for the sake of those watching so that way they don't suspect any of my talents. Hopefully.

Eza is too committed to his attack to notice, or care.

Aces.

I cast *all* the Aces.

Vines shoot up from the ground, wrapping around his hands. The Five of Swords blade clatters from his grip. Ice freezes his ankles. Fire singes his arms, burns at his ears. Wind whips around his face, pulling tears from his eyes. Every element rages simultaneously.

Now I summon the Five of Wands, which sows confusion. I double down on the assault as exhaustion creeps into my bones.

Eza is helpless and trapped. One more summoned blade. One last Five of Swords in my deck.

I stalk over to him, keeping a firm grip on my power. Balling my hand into a fist, I pull it down, as if I'm grabbing him by the collar of his shirt and yanking him into a kneeling position. My exhaustion nearly has me collapsing as well. But I stay on my feet, looming over him.

"Yield," I demand.

"Never," he growls. Eza manages a twitch of his fingers, and that's all it takes for the Five of Cups to cloud my mind.

Thoughts of Arina dying alone, screaming in pain, overwhelm me. I hear my sister: *We're going to find Mother's killer together. We will get those royal bastards together; I'll be with you until the end.* The overwhelming grief I feel at all the promises unkept is followed by the memory of Bristara's worries about Kaelis: *He's deceiving you. Keeping secrets. He'll betray you.*

Even as my fears and doubts swirl, I hold fast to my sword. I keep my focus on maintaining the elements that hold him trapped in submission. I raise the blade.

Eza sees the movement. "You . . . How?"

I know what he's asking even as he can't finish the words. "I doubt the world around me. I fear what I can't control. But I do not doubt myself, and I do not fear the one thing I have power over: me." I bring the blade to his throat.

"But, *but* . . . I took away your ability to fight."

"I don't need to know how to fight to end you. It doesn't take skill to kill a man on his knees." I drag the tip of the weapon across his cheek. The Five of Swords won't vanish until it tastes blood. Now I can dismiss it at will. "Yield, or die."

"That's enough!" Vaduin's voice cuts through, begrudging and heavy. "Lady Clara Redwin is victorious."

CHAPTER 48

There are actual cheers—which surprises me—at the announcement. But they're distant. Unimportant. I continue to loom over Eza. My blade quivers.

"You going to kill me?" There's a small quirk in the corner of his lips. "Do it and risk the ire of Clan Moon."

"All initiates will have the next three hours to clean themselves up and compose themselves for the house placement ceremony, which will take place tonight in the main hall during dinner," Vaduin announces. I barely resist throwing him a withering glare.

I relax away from Eza and leave him to his defeat and humiliation. I can barely keep myself from stumbling and keeling over. But I need to hold my head high. Especially when a not-insignificant contingent of students is regarding me even more warily than before. I pulled out more cards than any other initiate during my duel, and I used them mercilessly.

I sweep my eyes across the crowd once more. Kaelis is gone. Did he even watch the whole fight? Did he care? Or had I misread him? I hardly hear my friends' congratulations as these thoughts weigh heavy on me.

But my answer comes in the form of a shadowed figure who occupies the hallway at the bottom of the spiral stair that leads from the rooftop. Kaelis finishes his conversation with a professor and looks to me. The latter departs and I don't even see what direction they go in. My entire focus is on the prince. My feet slow, unbidden. Time seems to drag.

"I'll see you all at the ceremonies tonight," I murmur, bidding my friends farewell. They all instantly know why. They can see Kaelis's hand on the small of my back as he ushers me away.

I practically collapse into him the moment we're out of sight. Kaelis's arm encircles my waist. Without a word, his other hand reaches up to my face, pushing sweat-slicked hair from my forehead and cheeks to get a better look at my eyes.

"May I carry you?"

"Please," I say without hesitation. I'm exhausted to my core, and no idea has ever been sweeter than allowing him to be my entire support.

Kaelis scoops me into his arms, like he's done before, and I sink into his sturdy form. "You were magnificent." His words sound like silk and feel just as good.

"Thank you," I murmur.

"But two times is too many for me to be carrying you to my chambers following Eza's foolishness. The next time, he will answer to me." There's a whisper of murder in his voice that's shamefully arousing.

"If there is a next time, I'll end him once and for all," I correct.

"Very well. If my lady demands it."

My lady . . . It sounds good on his lips.

We make it back to the apartments and he carries me not to my wing, but to his. Silently, I let it happen. Whatever "it" is about to be. He settles me on one of the chairs in his dressing room and murmurs, "I'll draw you a bath."

His bathroom is far more lavish than mine. Mine would more than suffice, yet I still don't object.

The sound of running water and ghostly curls of steam fill the air as he returns. Kaelis looks down at me. My heart threatens to beat out of my chest.

Slowly, he drops to a knee. His hands rise to the first clasp on my coat, up by my neck. The fastener comes undone. His fingers move to the next as our eyes lock.

My chest swells with a slow, quivering breath. My breasts press into his fingers as they undo another clasp. And another. Soon, he's sliding the coat off my shoulders. I shift so it comes off easily.

"Do you want me to leave?" he whispers.

"No" is the only reply that crosses my mind.

Kaelis's fingers dance down to the hem of my shirt. With slow, purposeful movements, he peels off the sweat-slicked garment and casts it aside. The air is icy against my bare skin, but I'm too enamored with his movements to complain. I don't want to move, or even breathe—I don't want to do anything that would even remotely risk him stopping.

Palms land on my hips and trail along the band of my tight-fitting trousers. I lean back, allowing him better access to the buttons. Before I know it, the fabric is pulled down my thighs.

"Do you want me to leave?" he asks again, as breathy as last time, with eyes threatening to devour me.

"No," I repeat, barely audible.

He undoes the front laces of the wrapping around my breasts. A few tugs and I'm exposed: Every scar that crosses my body. Every fold and sag and line of hardened muscle. Even as he sees me, pulling the last of my small clothes off, I do not shy away or try to hide.

"Magnificent," he whispers as his eyes return to mine. There's almost a trace of surprise there, as if he hadn't intended to speak at all. But the way he holds my gaze tells me he meant it. "Come."

With only his fingers curled around mine, I almost think I could right then and there. My knees are weak. Breath short. Body bare.

The bath is steaming hot and full nearly to the point of overflowing. He garnishes it with perfumes from the rainbow of crystalline bottles that line the wall. The perfumes have an aroma I've never smelled on him before and can only assume that it's a scent he's made for me. I sink into the water, the steam cleansing me from within as much as the water cleanses me from without.

Kaelis isn't finished with me yet. Kneeling at the side of the tub, he collects my hand from the water, holding it as though it were a fragile artifact, lathering each finger with the same slow precision that he uses for inking cards. His focus mirrors the way he studies his books in his office, or at breakfast.

I realize I've become a part of these little hallowed spaces he's allowed me into. The way he touches me makes me feel as sacred as the tools in the Fool's workshop. More invaluable than the golden cards I know he keeps hidden somewhere in these apartments.

His eyes flick to mine, and I hold his gaze. It feels as if we're both standing at the precipice of a cliff, daring each other to be the first to leap.

Will this be the moment? I ask him. I ask myself. There's no answer, not yet. The tension has been pulled taut to the point that it quivers.

This isn't collapsing into each other's arms. It's not fleeting moments of pleasure born of desperation and needs unfulfilled for too long. This is . . . something more. It's an intimacy that I have never known before. Might have never allowed myself to know, if it hadn't quietly sneaked up on me.

He stands and moves behind me, and even in the scalding water I fight a quiver at the closeness of his body. I sink deeper, dunk my hair, then rest my head against the curve of the tub. Tension eases from my muscles as his fingers sink into my scalp, lathering. My eyes fall shut, but not before catching a glimpse of his reflection in the water. A gaze that says a thousand things neither of us dares voice.

The silence is heavy but not uncomfortable, laden with longing. We won't call this fondness, or affection, or anything more. Because alongside all the admiration and appreciation . . . is skepticism and doubt.

Can you trust him? Even now doubt lingers in me. Everything about Silas, the workshop of the Fool, Kaelis running off during the winter solstice, and so much more . . .

I don't know is the honest answer.

But I do know that I want him. That singular thought lingers with me as he finally leaves to fetch me clothes. As I'm left wishing I'd asked him to stay.

When I finally emerge, mind made up, my clothes are neatly laid out and the chambers are empty.

The main hall of the academy has been transformed in a few short hours for the house placement ceremony. Strings of tiny lanterns have been suspended between the trees, zigzagging over the tables decorated in silks of the house colors, each table set with extra seats.

Notably, the two parallel tables in the center of the hall have been removed. On instinct, all initiates stand where they once were. In the back of the room, brands burn, ready for Marking the initiates who made it so close . . . but won't be able to call themselves students of the academy.

We will either sit among our new houses or leave for the mills. It's the last Marking of the academic year.

I smell of the perfumes from Kaelis's bath. I'm dressed in the leathers and heavy cottons he's tailored. And my eyes settle on him as he assumes his place at the front, looking as austere as always. He addresses the initiates as a group.

"The night of the Fire Festival, you committed yourselves to our teachings. You paid your way with your futures.

"At All Coins Day, you showed not only Eclipse City but your would-be peers what you were capable of through the practical application of your lessons.

"And, today, you proved to your teachers and, hopefully, fellow students just how much further you can go—how much more you are capable of." Kaelis gesticulates as he speaks. It's hard not to imagine those long fingers gliding over my wet, naked form. Teasing me without trying. Working a heat into my core that's still molten from his touch. "This will be your final hour as an initiate. You will declare your intention for a specific house, and, should that house deem you worthy, you will be counted among our ranks forevermore."

My breath catches, and I work to keep myself calm. I didn't realize how much this had come to mean to me until I was standing here now. Presented with the prospect that *maybe* I won't progress. I could pass all the trials in the top half of the class . . . and it still might not be good enough for a house to accept me.

The atmosphere shifts instantly as the first name is called. One by one, initiates approach the table of the house they are seeking to join. They place the coin down before the King of the house and, if accepted, take their seat among their ranks.

Dristin goes to Coins, a safe bet as it has the most slots. They're readily accepting the majority of the nobles, with Wands filling the gap. Sorza bids for Cups and is unsurprisingly accepted. Even though she's not a noble, she more than proved herself. Another guaranteed slot goes to Alor with House Swords.

With her coin quivering in her hand, Luren approaches Myrion. I hold my breath.

His eyes drift to mine, as if to say, *You vouched for her once, will you do it again?* Luren passed two of her three trials. Though she barely passed wielding. She is not the strongest initiate here by almost any measure, except for one skill. But it's one that I think everyone else is underestimating her astounding affinity for and that I desperately want to keep personal access to.

I dip my chin, ever so slightly. Barely perceptible to anyone else, but Myrion sees.

"I accept your application," Myrion says. "May your heart always guide you, and the well of your soul never run dry. Welcome to House Cups." He slips the medallion of the house around her neck, and Luren lets out a barely contained squeak as she eagerly takes her seat. There are a few sidelong glances from other members of House Cups.

The number of remaining seats is dwindling, and when my name is finally called, only one seat remains for two initiates: myself and Eza.

His eyes drift to mine again, and we share a long and hateful stare. Though his is twinged with smugness. He couldn't end me with his cards or his dueling. Couldn't spill my secrets for fear of Kaelis's retribution... So this is how he thinks he's going to win. Even still, even after what happened on All Coins Day. Even knowing I have Kaelis's protection. He still thinks he's guaranteed that last seat among Swords.

Unlike some of the other initiates who had their choice of house, I have one coin weighing down my palm, and I stride over to stand before the King of Swords, Emilia. She regards me with a stone-faced gaze. Cool and calculating, but not cruel. She exudes pure authority.

"I make my bid for House Swords," I say like I've no doubt that seat is mine. And not because I'm hoping Alor put in a good word... but because Emilia knows that I am the better initiate compared to Eza. Out of everyone, I *deserve* that seat, and I won't flinch under her scrutiny and questioning gaze.

"May your mind be as sharp as your blade and your will unyielding." Emilia's voice is somber and serious as she places the medallion around my neck. "Welcome to House Swords, Lady Clara Redwin."

Murmurs and gasps. It seems not everyone was as confident as I was.

"What?" Eza lets out something between a gasp and a yell. "I am of Clan Moon." A pause. Alor tenses slightly at Emilia's side as his eyes swing to hers. "You swore to me!"

"House Swords welcomes the swift in mind and body." Emilia isn't bothered by his outburst in the slightest; she carries on as if he hasn't spoken at all. "We have accepted the best among this year's initiates."

He storms over, eyes filled with wild, rabid, panic-fueled hate. He knows what's waiting for him and gives it voice. "I will *not* become a Marked. I am a noble. Nobles aren't sent to the mills!"

"Take your place, Eza," Kaelis commands. I don't think I imagine the slight glee in his voice.

But he won't listen. "You think this bitch is worthy to be among you? You have no idea who she really is."

"If you're truly a noble, then handle your failure with some decorum." I project calmness with my words. That I'm utterly unbothered by his outburst and not quietly panicking about what he's going to say next.

"She"—he thrusts a finger at me—"is not the noble you think."

"Silence," Kaelis snaps. "I will not have you tarnishing the good name of my future wife." The prince strides forward with purpose.

But Eza is nearly upon me. "You have them all fooled. But I know the truth, and they should, too, you *fucking liar*. She's the one who—"

My magic flares. An Ace of Swords flies from my deck as a burst of wind, toppling him. "Enough, Eza. I bested you once today, I will do it again." My threat is as empty as my deck. I'm exhausted and don't have the cards to make good on it. "Take your Mark with what little dignity you have left."

With a red-faced roar, Eza scrambles to his feet, charging for me. Kaelis begins to run—he's seen how empty my deck is; he was the one to remove the holster. I jump back on instinct, bracing myself.

Everything happens so fast that it doesn't register until after it's over.

A flash of silver. A sword appears in Eza's palm that is gladly fueled by his bloodlust. He lunges for me. Kaelis is too far. My powers sputter.

And then there's movement at my side that is little more than a blur.

Emilia is faster than any of us. She moves like the wind, leaping over the table. Eza falters, shocked by the woman who's suddenly before him. But he recovers, not backing down.

Why would he? He's a dead man either way.

Eza swings. Emilia dodges with ease, in the same movement drawing a dagger that mirrors the one I've seen Alor holding every night. I see the weapon, but Eza doesn't. He's still focused on me. I don't move. I don't even flinch, trusting in my luck—in Emilia.

The tip of Eza's sword quivers at my cheek, having just missed its mark and nicking my jaw.

Emilia's dagger dances across his throat.

He lets out a gurgling noise and collapses. *He was supposed to be mine.* The rogue thought is silenced by immediate horror. *What does this mean?*

"Let this be a reminder that House Swords will not tolerate attacks on its own." She nonchalantly wipes her dagger on her napkin before sheathing it again at her hip. "Our blades are sharp and always at the ready to come to the defense of our loved ones."

The other students hardly seem surprised by this turn of events. But something shifts in the initiates. We all, collectively, realize just how little we've seen of the other two years of academy life. The students have had their own classes in separate rooms. Their own dormitories. Their own schedules and culture that we only now realize are truly an utter mystery.

As I sit, I wonder just how many empty seats that the initiates are taking were vacated because students graduated—and how many were left empty for *other reasons.* Is the academy as safe as they would have us think? I doubt it . . . The sword medallion is heavy around my neck.

Throughout dinner, I search for regrets, or doubts, but find none. Kaelis barks orders, and Eza's body is cleared as unceremoniously as Kel's was and his blood is mopped up. It's as if he never existed at all. But what does stick with me, what's heavier than regret, is the knowledge that he was Glavstone's son. And what he said at the end of our duel.

You going to kill me? Do it and risk the ire of Clan Moon.

CHAPTER 49

When dinner ends, all students rise. It will be the first time the former initiates see the interior of the house dormitories—their new homes. Except for me. I linger awkwardly as the room begins to clear out, watching the other students leave.

"Clara." Kaelis approaches, this time making it all the way to my side.

"Kaelis, Eza . . ." My words fade, lost. I'm not sure what to say—what I dare say around all the other students.

"It's all right. I already got his card," he reassures me with a whisper, as if that were what I'm afraid of and not some kind of retaliation against me. "I'll answer whatever questions you have later."

Fine. I can push away my inquiries until we're alone again. After all, it shouldn't be long—

"You should go and see your new dormitory. The Bladehaven is a sight to behold."

Bladehaven . . . What a name for a dormitory. "Right, I'll be back after."

"No, stay there. Those will be your new chambers." He tugs at his jacket, adjusting unseen wrinkles. Not a thread is out of place.

"Are you sure?" I tilt my head slightly, giving him a look through which I try to encapsulate the question *What happened to pretending like we're a couple?*

"Of course." His hand twitches, as if he wants to reach over and grab mine. But the prince refrains. "We'll be wed within the year. So you should focus on getting to know your fellow house members."

Is that really it? There are too many people for me to ask here. Is it over between us now that we've had the blessing of the king?

As much as I wish we could communicate with our minds alone, we can't. I'm left staring him down, and he holds my gaze. But it doesn't lead anywhere.

"You're absolutely right." I force a smile and give his hand a squeeze. "I'll see you soon enough, of course."

Kaelis nods, and I leave the main hall; all the way back my insides are knotting.

I manage to catch up with the pack of other students from House Swords and follow them up the staircase. My first step into the lounge of House Sword's Bladehaven feels as though I've left Arcana Academy completely.

The room is sprawling, with soaring vaulted ceilings supported by columns of swords carved from stone. Chandeliers made of curved weapons hold troughs of all-white flames. The light makes every piece of stately black-and-white furniture cast long shadows. Instead of heavy drapes, layers upon layers of chiffon frame the windows. Cut in uneven lengths, they pick up the faintest breeze, giving the walls an oscillating, living feeling, as if the room itself were breathing.

In the center stands a large circular table made of a wood stained so dark it's nearly black. Its surface has been polished to a near-mirror finish in which I think I can almost see the reflections of students from throughout the years hunched over its surface, studying and debating. In the back, behind the table, are three training rings. Bookshelves dot the room, spacing off smaller sitting areas.

It isn't just a lounge, but a sanctuary for everything that House Swords holds sacred: knowledge, action, strength, and determination.

"Clara, Alor, come with me." Emilia leads us down one of the short hallways that jut out from the common area. The room is shaped like a wheel, and each hall is a spoke. The halls each end with two doors. "It's convenient you've roomed together previously, you shouldn't have any issue here. If you need anything, you may ask me or any of your other fellow house members."

"You knew I'd be here?" I ask.

"The headmaster requested we furnish you a room." Emilia nods. "I would've insisted anyway. You are a part of this house now. Your place should first and foremost be here with your academic family."

I simultaneously feel welcomed and adrift. The last person I expected to make me feel like I had a place was Emilia. But she just killed a man for me.

Meanwhile, the man who had begun to represent safety—my place here in the academy—has seemingly cast me out.

"Thank you," Alor says warmly.

Just as Emilia goes to leave, she thinks better of it. She steps to her younger sister and rests a hand on her shoulder.

"Well done." She offers a rare encouraging smile. "Father will be proud."

Before Alor can respond, Emilia leaves. She's left hovering in the wake of her sister's pride. Basking in a glow that I can understand all too well. "I'm proud of you" were four of the sweetest words that my mother or sister could say to me—and they were words I tried to share with Arina often. My chest aches as if with the force of a physical blow, of a thousand rocks crushing me. The hurt the mere thought of her brings will take years to lessen.

"You look good here," Alor appraises, bringing me back to the present. Grief is an ever-constant companion. Lingering in it will not help.

"As do you," I force myself to say, pushing thoughts of my sister aside.

She arches her brows, lips curving into a familiar smug grin. "*Obviously.*"

I let out a soft huff of amusement.

"I'm still looking into things, by the way. I managed to find a few leads over the break, but nothing material yet."

"Oh?"

"We'll see," she cautions, clearly not wanting to get my hopes up. "Perhaps a better way to say it is a *lack of* leads. I should have found more information than I have. It's as if someone intentionally scrubbed the details from the records."

I know all too well how that feels. But the thought brings me to another time I found a lack of leads. Perhaps it's all connected. The crown runs the mills, the pulping houses, the harvesting sites, and I always suspected them to be behind Mother's death . . .

"May I ask you to look into something—someone—else?"

"Needy much?" Alor huffs, but I can tell by her tone she's nevertheless open to my request.

"Laylis Daygar." Daygar was the name Mother went by when she died at the Descent. She wouldn't be recorded anywhere as Chevalyer, not when she swore it was to be kept a secret at all costs. Names upon names in our family, all to hide an identity that I'm only just now beginning to understand . . . There was always more to us than she let on.

"Laylis Daygar," Alor repeats, recognizing the name from Arina. "Your mother?"

I nod. "She died at the Descent in a way I always found suspicious. I'm wondering if, perhaps, her and Arina's deaths are connected."

"Someone really has it out for you if they are." Alor folds her arms, her sharp gaze missing nothing. There's an expectancy there—she wants me to elaborate why, since she already knows she's right.

But I'm not going to say anything more than "Apparently."

"All right, if I come across anything involving this Laylis, I'll make a note of it, too. So don't forget how nice I'm being."

"I'll be sure to repay the favor." I mean it.

"Now, if you'll excuse me, I think I will enjoy my room—free of your snoring." She opens her door, and I catch a glimpse of the refuge awaiting me.

"I do not snore." *Do I?*

"*Sure* you don't." Alor enters her room, and I do the same.

The room is done in similar colors as the common area and set up much the same as my first in the dorms—but with only one bed, desk, and armoire. Of course, I check the wardrobe first. It's full of my clothes.

He really was planning on kicking me out . . . Even as he undressed me. Bathed me. "I don't understand you," I whisper, hoping Kaelis feels those words deep in his bones. Why do we move a few steps closer together only to take several backward? But I'm too tired to deal with this now. I'll find him tomorrow.

I waste no time dressing for bed. It's early still. But despite that, and all the things that happened today, I'm exhausted, and sleep finds me easily.

But it flees when, hours later, I'm jolted awake by the sound of my door opening.

"Ka—" I start to say, stopping when I realize I'm not in his apartments and this shadow isn't the same height or build as the prince. A flash of silver would usually have me on high alert. But I've already recognized who it is. I'd know that dagger with its lightning-bolt hilt anywhere. "Alor? Is everything all right?"

Wordlessly, she closes the door behind herself. She pads across the rug. It's plush and black with swirls of mottled gray that dance like smoky tarot symbols, and as she sinks onto it, she stares at the equally intricate designs on the plaster ceiling. I wait for her to say something, as I know she will.

"Turns out, I couldn't sleep nearly as easily as I thought I could without your snoring," she says begrudgingly.

"I see." I'm fighting a smile. The last time someone creeped into my room was when Arina came after a particularly harrowing night where we weren't sure we were going to make it back through the tunnels and into the city alive. One of the last jobs she ever went on with me. "You been struggling to sleep ever since I left?"

"I'm not answering that." Alor continues not to look at me.

"May I ask you something else, then?"

Alor's head turns as I hold out one of the extra pillows from my bed. She regards it as skeptically as if I were handing her a vial of poison. She finally snatches it and situates it under her head. "Go ahead."

"Why do you sleep with the dagger?"

She yawns. "It's part of Clan Tower's training . . . There's always someone out to get you. Never know when they'll attack . . ."

"'They'?"

"Anyone else in our clan. In Clan Tower you're either strong or dead." She rolls onto her side. Putting her back to me signals that there's no more to be said on the matter. I don't pry.

Classes will feel odd now, to say the least. There's only about three months left until the Feast of Cups, and the main goal for the year—sorting us all into houses—has concluded. Judging from just one morning, the professors seem to be content for us to continue practicing the same fundamentals they've been teaching all year, but there's no urgency to it. And there's a sense of relief among the first-year students. Most can't stop twirling the medallions of their new houses around their necks.

We all made it.

But what awaits us next year remains a question. I had some idea of what the first year was like from Arina. Year two is a mystery that remains a problem for the future, one I'm hopeful Kaelis will help me tackle. If he'll even look at me, that is . . .

As soon as classes are over and lunch is finished—a lunch Kaelis was notably absent from—I head straight for the headmaster's apartments. I'm prepared to wait until he returns, until he lets me in. But I meet no resistance. The Stellis positioned at his doors still don't stop me. His chambers are unlocked, bedroom empty. But there's the sound of a pen scratching coming from the half-open door of his study. The soft hum of his focus.

I open the door the rest of the way and stand in its frame, waiting. He draws the silence out for a good minute before his eyes drift up to look at me. For a breath, neither of us speaks. The silence does little for my mood, and just the sight of him spurs my frustration.

"You seem like you have something you want to say." He looks back to the papers on his desk. "Well, then, out with it."

"What is wrong with you?"

His eyes flick up, but it's little more than a second of acknowledgment. "People would say 'many things.'"

"You sent me away."

Kaelis's quill scratches across the surface of the papers. "You made it clear from the very start that you were not particularly delighted by our living arrangement."

I suppose I did . . . "What happened to convincing people we're a legitimate couple? I'm *not* going back to Halazar."

"I don't think you're at risk of that anymore, thanks to my father's blessing. We could not have asked for a better endorsement. Nor could we have a better excuse than you joining a house to leave—it *is* important for you to connect with your new housemates." He doesn't sound like himself. It's almost like he repeated these words a dozen times over. He's not the cruel but driven prince I first met. Nor is he the soft-spoken and surprisingly kind man who tended to the wounds Eza inflicted across my body. He's emotionless. Void of everything.

"So, that's it, then?"

"What's it?" He sighs dramatically.

"You're not . . . We're not . . ."

"We're not *what*, Clara?"

"Would you look at me for one moment?" I snap. If I could just see his eyes, then I'd know. I'd know what this is—what we are. As if the thousands of other times he looked at me weren't enough already.

Kaelis leans back in his chair and drags his attention to me as if it's physically painful. There's a wall there. Cold and unfeeling. I'd be impressed he could erect such a thing in such a short period of time if it weren't designed to keep me out.

"What?" he presses when I don't immediately speak. Before I can respond, though, he stands. "What do you want from me, Clara?" Kaelis rounds the corner of his desk. "You have told me, in no uncertain terms, countless times, the depths of your hatred for me. You have run from me. Blamed me for the death of your sister. Doubted me and my intentions. There has been nothing I can say or do to make you think differently, and I have tried." With every bitterly true accusation, he takes a step closer to me. I don't move. An unseen hand holds me in place so tightly that my breathing shallows. "When I have finally given you what you wanted, you only resent me more for it. *What do you want from me?*"

The question repeats like a plea. His eyes search mine as he looms over me. The wall is cracking, my heart with it.

"I don't know." The confession is little more than a breath.

"Then set me free."

"What?"

"You consume my every waking moment. Devour my thoughts. You've poisoned my halls with your scent. Flooded my dreams to the point that I cannot tell if it is a delight or a nightmare to want to drown in you. If you hate me, *then hate me*, let us be eternal rivals. Let any future where you and I are more than enemies finally be done and gone.

"If you want something else from me, then take it. But, if it is neither, then set me free and let me be done with you once and for all."

"I can't." Those two words are the first thing to come to my mind. His eyes widen a fraction. His hands twitch, as if he's physically holding himself from reaching out and grabbing me. "Hate you. Love you. But I can't be nothing to you."

Once more, I'm the one to kiss him.

CHAPTER 50

The kiss encapsulates months of words unsaid, desires buried and abandoned, fears not quite conquered but now at last ignored. It is sweeter than the first taste of wine after Halazar and gives me just as much of a rush. I indulge a needy, shameless side of me that I've worked so hard to ignore because there was always work to be done. A part of me that he ignited at the soiree without even trying to.

But now he's here. I'm not even sure if I *want* it to be him. This is still Kaelis, the second-born prince of the kingdom, the man I've always seen as my enemy and orchestrator of my pains. The man I don't know if I can trust and, secretly, am still preparing my own moves against . . . But he's also become more than that. More than I want to admit. And if nothing else, he's tall and strong and capable of fulfilling all the needs that have been building relentlessly within me for years without release.

My lips part, and he takes full advantage, his tongue slipping into my mouth. I don't just let him—I match his fervor. My hands slide up and over his chest to grip the lapels of his tailored jacket closer to his neck.

His one hand trails along my jaw to grab my neck with purpose, tilting my head and further deepening the kiss. The other travels around my side, groping my ass, pulling our bodies so flush that I can feel his length, hard against me, eliciting a groan. My imagination runs wild with all the things he could do to me.

My back hits the doorframe, and he tilts my head to the side. Kaelis trails kisses down to my collar. I press my hips harder against his as a suggestion. A rumble of amusement rises from deep within his chest, the sound shivering across my skin and drawing goosebumps.

"Need something?" he almost purrs.

"*Fuck me*," I growl in reply, unable to think of anything else.

Kaelis pulls away just enough to look me in the eyes. Were it possible to take someone with a look, I'd be screaming with pleasure.

"Yes," he rasps against my lips, voice heavy and low with desperate need. "You have no idea how long I've waited to have you. Claim you. Make you mine beyond recognition."

His eyes search mine, as if looking for permission. Hand shifting, he drags his thumb against my wet lips. I can't stop myself from licking its tip. Eyes locked.

Kaelis groans, forehead pressing into mine. "I hate you for what you've done to me."

"That's fine. I never needed you to like me." My hands slide around his neck, fingers lacing with his hair. *Twenty, it's softer than silk.* When my nails dig into his scalp as I ball my hands into fists, Kaelis lets out a hiss. I rake my teeth against his neck. His hand is back on my ass, kneading, sending electric jolts up my spine. My whole body strains against every bit of fabric covering me, yearning for release. "I don't want to like you."

But I do. Damn it, I do. I'm just not ready to tell him so. I'll deny it with every angry part of me that he seems to adore about me despite himself.

He curses under his breath, as if in agreement. Then several times more with each undone button of his coat, and then his shirt, exposing the top of his chest and where his neck meets his shoulder. He's always so buttoned up. More guarded than the Stellis protecting him.

I wonder who was the last person to touch him. To expose him as that thing he so clearly fears being: A man of flesh and blood. A man who can have wants and needs . . . a man who can be broken.

Kaelis grabs my chin to look me in the eyes. The dark voids of his eyes are aflame. "If you give yourself to me, I will take it all. *Now.* Time and again. I will not be gentle."

"Good." Amusement, bitter and wry, tugs at my lips. "Do your worst, Prince."

That serpentine smile that I've come to adore crosses his mouth—something that is still as wicked as it once was but is also now familiar. Wanted, even. That smirk meets my own in a kiss deeper than all the others but now unhurried. Almost lazy in how he savors my taste and bites my lips.

Kaelis is going to take his time with me.

His hands move from my waist to the back of my neck, digging into my skin. I twist my fingers in his clothes. I can feel every ridge of muscle through his clothing, and I want to see it all, feel it all, run my tongue along every groove.

I shiver, and he yanks me closer. There's a breath where we both hang on every unspoken promise. Every indulgence. Without another word, he leads me to the bedroom.

Before I know it, we're at the edge of his bed. His fingers are running through my hair, and there's a glint in his eyes of an appetite that mirrors my own.

"What?" I ask, unable to handle his inspection a second longer.

"I can't decide what I want to do to you first."

"Make up your mind," I half demand, half beg. "Anything. *Everything.*"

As if to spite me, he unfastens my coat with dutiful slowness. After he slides it off, Kaelis licks down my throat. He bites my shoulder, sucking hard enough to leave a bruise. I return the favor, my fingers digging into his shoulder blades, nails leaving marks.

Next is my shirt, then my pants. He's so unhurried, as if this need isn't eating him alive. My hands are shaking.

Once more, he removes every scrap of fabric from my body, and Kaelis takes a moment to admire his work. I don't shrink in on myself or shy away. Instead, I put one hand on my hip, tilting my head.

"See something you like, Prince?"

He reaches out, and with the barest of touches, his hand outlines my shoulder and runs down my chest. He takes his time with the curve of my breast. Fingertips trace around my nipple, brushing it to attention with a caress that makes me shiver.

Kaelis pushes me onto the bed. I fall among the pillows and bolsters, cradled in velvet and fur. He crawls atop me with purpose.

The prince's hands are all over me now, exploring every inch of my body as though I am a land to be conquered. A card to be drawn. The touch grows demanding. He cups my breast and brings his mouth to it. Knees bending, toes curling, I exhale and arch my back into him, arcing my chest toward him. Kaelis grabs the opposite breast, fingertips leaving indents in my flesh—right to the point of pain but never leaving the realm of pleasure. His knee shifts, driving between my legs to apply a constant and needed pressure. I know he can feel how ready I am; I practically soak through his clothing.

Just when I think I can't take any more sensation, kisses, or nips, he releases my breast and growls in my ear, "I've wanted to fuck you for *ages*. Ever since I first laid eyes on you. Ever since I saw you dancing in that damned vision with another man. The audacity that fate would imagine that anyone else would ever touch the woman I'd claimed for my own."

I could split in two with the depth of his voice alone. The gravel that grinds under his jealous words is toe-curling. "If you've wanted to fuck me, then *get on with it*."

Slow explorations abandoned, he finds my lips again in an all-consuming kiss. I rip off his clothes, unable to take another second. The sound of stitches splitting fills the air. Buttons clatter across the floor.

"How dare you," he gasps. "I liked this shirt."

"I like it better ripped on the floor."

His pants are next, removed with equal haste. As naked as I am, Kaelis positions himself before me. The tip of him is at my entrance, rubbing. I'm already slick and ready.

"Tell me what you want," he demands, hand once more at my chin, nearly wrapping around my throat as if to remind me he's the one in control.

"I want you to fuck me," I say in no uncertain terms.

Kaelis leans forward, biting my earlobe and whispering, "More. I'm going to fuck you until you scream my name. Until the only shape your cunt knows is my cock. After me, no other man will ever satisfy—never come close." I shiver. The hand that isn't supporting him is back at my breast. "If you want to be spared from me, say so now, Clara. Or I will make you mine."

"You'd better be as good as you say after all this talk." I lock eyes with him as he pulls away. "And remember, you promised not to be gentle."

The prince lets out a low laugh that devolves into a growl. "Fine."

He closes the distance between us with a single thrust. Eyes pressing closed, I tilt my head back, and he once more takes advantage of my exposed neck. The room spins as I acclimate to his size. It's an explosion of sweet pain and the deepest pleasure.

Kaelis wastes no time setting a steady and forceful rhythm. His mouth is on my throat, on my breasts. Hands everywhere at the same time. They knot in my hair, pulling to guide me right where he wants me.

He leans back and brings one hand between us, thumb finding my clit. "Scream for me."

I can't not. Every muscle is taut to the point of trembling. My ragged breathing is about to betray my climax, and right when I am there, he stops without warning. I shoot him a glare, panting, and Kaelis wears a gloating smile.

"Yes," he murmurs. "Look at me with those deep crimson eyes. Look at me with all the hate you can manage and then some to hide the fact that you love me, and me alone."

"I could never love you," I pant.

"Go ahead and keep lying to yourself."

Without warning, he withdraws, flips me, and pulls up my hips with one hand. The other balls into my hair as he enters me again with a grunt. My back arches, and his fingers alternate between my nipples and my clit. Just when I'm about to reach my peak, he once more slows, pulling me back. Never leaving me.

"No, not yet. I'm not done yet." Kaelis sinks his teeth into my shoulder, my back arching against his chest. Never have I felt so exposed.

I give myself completely to him. Every errant thought is fucked from my body. I will ache tomorrow and want to thank him for it. He makes good on his promise to ensure that all my body will crave is him.

We keep reaching the edge and shying away. Keep torturing each other. Working up the frenzy of an all-consuming bliss. He maneuvers me, and I surrender to his will, turning again onto my back. The man looms over me. The pace is punishing now. Deliciously unbearable. I can barely breathe as I give everything to him.

All at once, the climax hits me. Kaelis finally brings me there, and a shout rips from my throat. He continues thrusting. Long and steady strokes. I grab his shoulders, nails leaving red lines across his skin. The second our eyes lock, he reaches his own orgasm and practically collapses upon me, his own moans a chorus in my ear.

Breathless, Kaelis twitches within me. His whole body shudders as I run my fingertips up his back. Eventually, he slides out and falls heavily beside me.

We lie in silence for a few moments. Our bodies cooling. The flush leaving our skin. A sweet satisfaction lingers deep within me, an itch *finally* scratched.

"I'm using the bathroom," I declare, getting up.

Kaelis makes a small noise in agreement. "I can get you a Five of Coins, if you need it."

"I have one in my room." Every Arcanist of age knows how the

Five can be used to prevent unwanted pregnancies before they take root.

"I'd rather see you use it."

I snort. "Trust me, Kaelis. The last thing I want right now is a baby. And the only thing I want less than that is to carry *your* child."

He sneers at me as I leave. I return the expression but lose it to a laugh. Even his own glare softens, and he huffs with amusement. We're such a fucked-up pair. But . . . I rather like it that way . . .

When I'm finished in the bathroom, I return to the bedside. He has yet to move and is quite the sight. The removal of his clothes was so hasty that I didn't get ample time to appreciate all his glory.

His frame is somewhere between that of a scholar and a warrior. Hard-honed muscle, but wiry, and lithe. Supporting a body that's naturally suited more for libraries than training grounds. Yet the way he carries himself exudes deadly power.

"You'll need to give me a bit longer before I can go again." He opens one eye, catching me staring.

"We're not going again . . . not today." I reach down, beginning to grab my clothes.

"Not *today*. So this wasn't a onetime thing?"

"We'll see." I still don't entirely know what this was, and I don't want to examine it too closely. It'd ruin the shock waves of pleasure still trembling through my body. I'd rather not think too deeply about the fact that I just let my worst enemy bring me to one of the best orgasms I've ever had in my life.

"You're already leaving?" he asks as I pull my shirt over my head.

"Did you expect gentle caresses and sweet nothings across the pillow like we're real lovers?" I pause, trousers around my thighs, to give him an incredulous look. "This isn't that kind of relationship, is it?"

"No, of course not."

"Good." I finish buttoning my pants. "It's better for us both if we don't confuse things."

"I couldn't agree more."

"Good," I repeat.

"Good," he echoes.

But, for a second, neither of us moves. The silence feels like an objection. A refusal.

"Thank you," I say with a soft note of sincerity. "That was . . . fun. I needed it."

"Me, too." His tone is earnest. I wonder just how long it's been for him. Maybe as long as me. Maybe longer.

For the first time, I wonder what kind of a lover Kaelis would be. Not just in bed; I know that now, and the answer is: very, *very* good. But as a partner. As someone to come home to at the end of a day. As someone to whisper tenderness to across a pillow. To hold me when the world becomes too much . . .

I try to push the notions from my mind as I make my way to the library, determined to keep my focus on what comes next in my preparations for the Feast of Cups, and what will be my greatest heist.

CHAPTER 51

I can't tell if things with Kaelis are better now, or worse. There's an unbearable, almost pulsating energy between us that's more palpable than ever. When I go to him to work, there are moments I want to kiss him—moments that I can tell he also wants to kiss me. Yet, somehow, neither of us crosses that line again. Maybe we're too unsure if it was really a onetime thing . . . or if it *should* be.

It probably should be. Yet I can't stop thinking about it. Can't stop from wondering if the memories and phantom hands consume his waking and sleeping hours, too . . . If he's imagining my mouth on him, his on me. Does the sound our hips make as he pounds into me fill his dreams, too?

I hate that I want it—want *him* exactly as he said I would. So, for now, I give off a frigid aura toward him, and Kaelis does the same. We're two combatants circling each other in the ring, separated after initial blows were thrown. Waiting to see who will make the next move. Who will break and close the gap for another round.

It's a tension that has me shifting uncomfortably around him and racing back to my room some nights, grateful that I have my own space. That I can lock the door and lean into the pillows as my hand slips between my thighs and my back arches off the bed. Sometimes I let myself very softly moan aloud, imagining him on the other side of the door, listening, stroking himself to my pleasure.

The release is the only thing that enables me to keep my distance and focus during the day.

We're making progress on the forgeries. My lines are more confident by the hour. But as the days slip by, I wonder if it's *enough* progress. I've begun to check them against not only Kaelis's memory, but Twino's as well. We're going to have only one shot at this, and that's begun to weigh on me.

Silas remains a reliable go-between. Even though I know the bridge route now, Silas's card is faster. Though, of course, the first time I take him back to the townhome, there's resistance as I reintroduce him and tell them the truth of Silas's identity.

"I still don't trust him," Gregor announces vehemently, not caring in the slightest that Silas is standing right next to me by the hearth. "Never gonna. It's because of *him* we lost the club."

"That's . . . understandable." Silas rubs the back of his neck.

I touch his forearm gently and look to the rest of them. "We lost the club because of Ravin, not Silas. And, frankly, if Ravin wanted to get to me, or destroy the club—which he obviously did—he was going to do that with or without Silas's help. Silas is as much a victim of the crown's cruelty as any of us or any of those we fight for."

Gregor folds his arms and sinks back into his chair. Twino shifts his grip on his cane, eyes alight but silent. He's said precious little, and, for once, I can't read if that's a good or a bad thing.

"How do we know that he's not playing both sides?" It's never a good sign when even Jura doesn't mince words. "He could be trying to earn our trust to let Ravin in."

"If he was going to lead Ravin here, he would've by now. I overheard them talking; the prince was pressing for information on us, but Silas didn't budge. He risked lying to protect us."

"Maybe it was a show for you." Gregor huffs.

"They didn't know I was there. I swear it." Of that much, I'm confident.

Jura purses her lips and takes a long sip of her tea, crossing her legs and leaning back into the sofa in a position similar to how Bristara is sitting. The founder and matron of the club has been alarmingly silent. But that doesn't stop me from feeling her disapproval. Yet again. It seems that's all I can manage since getting out of Halazar.

"He could be the one who killed Arina," Gregor adds with a low growl.

"I would never," Silas says hastily.

"We're going to need proof of your loyalty, I think," Bristara muses, finally speaking. "If we're ever going to be able to trust you enough to work with you, that is."

"I would've said the same, had he not already come with it in hand." I hold up the schematics he acquired for us.

"What is that?" Twino asks.

"They're sketches—copies of the workings of the box the king keeps strapped to his chest that he keeps the cards inside of." I pass the paper to Twino, who unfolds it. His eyes widen slightly. Brow furrows.

"What is it?" Ren leans over to ask.

"Nothing like I've seen before," Twino murmurs. "But it does look like the box I saw on the king."

"Could you use it to open the box?" I ask.

"If it's real, yes."

Bristara taps her fingers on the arms of her chair—a sign she's agitated. She speaks directly to Silas. "Whenever you're here, you will stay in the garden—where we can keep an eye on you—and go nowhere else," she declares. "Until we can determine the validity of this information, this is how it shall be."

Silas nods. I don't dare speak against the decree. For the rest of the night, Silas stays alone in the garden, sitting and sketching on the pages he brought with him in his satchel. He's not inking cards, but what has him so focused escapes me.

I take it as a good sign when Jura brings him a mug of tea and a small plate of scones after a few hours. Even if she doesn't speak to him while doing so.

The next time we go to the townhome is much the same.

Silas never objects. He never protests or tries to argue his way out of being forced to sit in the garden. Even on the coldest of nights, when his breath curls in the air as puffs of white that match the snow that drifts from the sky above. He's heartbreakingly familiar with solitude.

All the while, the club and I work and plan. Getting the cards from the king isn't something I'm going to be able to do alone. I've told Kaelis as much as well. After how they all helped with All Coins Day, the prince has the good sense not to object.

That's how an unlikely plan is devised . . . and how Silas is finally given another chance to prove himself.

"Your bag stinks," Silas says the moment the door to his apartments swings open.

"Is that any way to greet a lady?" I step inside.

He closes the entry and steps behind me. "What is it?"

I adjust my grip on the satchel, debating whether I should tell him. It was hard enough to come to the conclusion of doing this at all. And, even if my star-crossed family knows what I'm bringing . . . being presented with the thing that killed Arina is going to evoke a lot of feelings. Unsure what drives me to the conclusion that it's for the best to share, I open the flap.

"Duskrose," I say. Silas takes two whole steps back. "Don't worry, I trimmed it before it bloomed. The pollen is safely contained."

"You could trim it while staying quiet enough that it didn't open?" He's understandably impressed.

"I had someone who knows *a lot* about plants that told me how."

That person is Ren. Who is probably the only one of the club who looks more fascinated than horrified when the flower is later plopped onto the kitchen counter after Silas takes us back to the townhome. Jura is utterly aghast at its presence in her kitchen. Twino leans against the wall, surveying. Gregor didn't come downstairs. I'd suspected it might be too much for him to face.

Ren takes the lead, carefully slicing into the plant with the precision and steady hand to rival a surgeon. He walks Jura through how to make a tincture from the pollen. I remain out of the way, next to Twino, both of us watching with fascination and holding our breath at parts.

When all is settled, we finally emerge. All except Jura. She's probably going to be scrubbing her counters and muttering to herself for the next few hours.

Silas's attention drifts to me as Twino and I emerge into the garden, still quietly finalizing the last of our plans.

"I've come to a conclusion." Silas stands and adjusts his coat. The weather has been oscillating wildly recently as winter refuses with every last gasp to give way to spring.

"And what is that?" I ask for both myself and Twino.

"You're going to poison the king." Silas's bluntness betrays his confidence.

"And how have you arrived at such a conclusion?" Twino asks, as cool and collected as if the topic were mundane . . . and Silas wasn't right.

"I've been thinking about how all this fits together." Silas's eyes drift to me and stay there. I'm reminded of his expression when he first explained his theories at the winter solstice gala in the castle. "I thought, at first, you were only trying to steal the cards. But I think it's more than that. With how close Kaelis has kept you and from what I've learned of your other innate abilities as Fortune to ink cards . . . you're going to make forgeries so the king won't suspect anything, buying you—and Kaelis—more time to get the final Major, the Star.

"Why else would you go deep into the academy after clearly having Kaelis and me on your side? You must've been looking for something to help you with the forgeries. That's how you found Arina's body." He doesn't mention the workshop of the Fool outright, and for that I'm grateful. He'd said he didn't know of it when I mentioned it during the gala. But he's clearly sharp enough to have drawn conclusions about what it might be.

"You more or less had these theories before; it's why you gave us the puzzle box schematics."

He nods. "But then there was the Duskrose. Knowing how to open the box alone won't be enough. To get the cards off the king, you'll need to incapacitate him. How else will you even give yourselves the opportunity to get the box? I suspect"—he stands a little taller as he reaches his ultimate conclusion—"that you're going to use a watered-down variant of the Duskrose's pollen to put him out long enough to get the cards you need and swap for the forgeries you made."

A breeze passes through the garden, the only sound rustling leaves.

"You have a lot of theories, but I'm not seeing your point." There's a hint of challenge in Twino's words.

"I've been in the palm of the crown for years. Between Kaelis, Ravin . . . even the king himself—I've seen things they refuse to allow anyone else to see because they no longer even seem to acknowledge I'm there." Silas doesn't sound proud of the information he wields. If anything, he's . . . detached. But determined. "Things like the king's hobby of tinkering with gears and metal. Where the royals keep certain secrets, like the schematics. Or how the king is afflicted by debilitating headaches. There's a medicine the king keeps on hand—prepared only by his royal physician—to alleviate the symptoms. I know where the medicine is kept, and the tea he prefers to drink it in to make it more palatable."

Twino and I share a look. I remember seeing the king rubbing his temples on more than one occasion. How the king's tea was different at Ravin's manor, something I'm sure Twino noted as well. There's enough anecdotal evidence to support Silas's claim.

"You'll give us all this information?" Twino clarifies after a long moment.

"If it's enough to earn your trust once and for all." Silas looks between us. "I want to help you rescue my family. Not just stand to the side." His eyes settle on me. "You told me once the world was too big for me to stay confined. But I can't go anywhere without them. Once they're free, though, I'm going to leave and never come back. You won't have to worry about me being a risk to your group because I will be long, long gone."

Another stretch of silence. Finally, I look to Twino, who meets my gaze and holds it. I give a slight nod to his unspoken question.

"Come inside," Twino says finally. "We've much to discuss, and Bristara should be a part of it."

Priss is settled next to me, her furry head resting as heavily on my thigh as Kaelis's is on his desk. The prince dozed off somewhere between the Six and Seven of Coins, mid-inking. I'd get up to stopper his inkpot, but laws of the cat deem that I am trapped until Priss moves.

Even though it's quite late, I'm focused intently on my work. Kaelis managed an incredible blend of inks from the Fool's workshop this time, and my pen is alive, dancing across the page. Winter is already thawing, giving way to spring. The Feast of Cups is growing ever closer.

And tonight is the night I complete the forgeries.

I move as if I'm possessed. Nearly a year of work comes together. I ignore the cramps in my hands, the pain in my back from hunching.

Every line must be right. Perfect.

And, as dawn breaks, they are. I set down my pen and lean back, resting my head and my eyes. I don't realize I've dozed off until the smell of hot tea and warm biscuits dappled with cheeses and pork wakes me. For a second, before my eyes open, I almost thank Jura. But I'm quickly reminded of where I am.

There's a tray waiting on Kaelis's desk. The man himself stands opposite the small table he had made just for me to be the perfect height for the settee. At some point, Priss wandered off, and it's just the two of us.

Kaelis lifts each of the cards, one by one. I feel as exposed as if I'm naked under him. After the last one, his inspection turns to me.

"You've outdone yourself."

"Can't make good cards without good ink."

The prince holds out his hand with a slight smile. "Let's discuss the final plans for how we're going to literally steal from underneath my father's nose over breakfast."

The package arrives without a name, letter, or word. Following my afternoon classes, it's there on my bed. Black silk ribbon skewered with a silver dagger to hold it shut.

"Really, you're so dramatic." Even though I sigh, a smile creeps onto my lips. *He truly is, though* . . . Pulling out the dagger and unwrapping the ribbon, I lift the top and stop with a gasp.

I can't get naked fast enough.

I stand before my floor-length mirror, and the heavy satin of my gown whispers against the plush carpet as I turn right and left, studying every pleat. In the low light, it looks almost black due to the heavy saturation of color. But every shift of the satin highlights the deep, rusty red that's almost like blood. It's a stunning complement to the shade of my eyes. A lace-up front allows the dress to hug every one of my curves from my hips upward. The heart-shaped top arcs over my breasts. Covering their swell is lace that looks almost like silver leaves falling down my torso. The lace runs up my neck, where it fastens with a silver clasp and then runs down over my arms.

I thought the last gown Kaelis had sent me was stunning. But this is *everything*.

A low whistle distracts me. Alor leans against the doorframe. We've adopted the habit of leaving our doors cracked when we don't want privacy, since there are no other rooms on the hall but ours. No one else has ever come down this way. If there's one thing I've gathered, it's that Swords appreciate their discretion. Yet another reason for me to love the house.

"Don't you look like you could sit among the royals at the ball?"

"Is it too much?" I run my hand down the front of the gown, fingers trailing along lace and ribbon.

"It's fitting for the prince's betrothed. After your showing at the Swords Solstice celebrations, they'll all be watching you for what comes next."

I nod. Alor seems to know all about my appearance at the solstice celebrations despite not being there herself. I wonder what her father said, but I haven't asked out of fear that it could lead to more focus and scrutiny on me. "Will anyone from Clan Moon be there?"

"Worried about Eza's family?" She's followed my thoughts. This is the first time I'll be publicly leaving the academy following his death.

"I'd like to have the night go smoothly." The last thing I need is for someone to come at me in a fit of righteous vengeance. Fortunately, things in the academy have gone smoothly. No other students have stepped forward to avenge Eza. Cael and Nidus have made themselves scarce around me.

"You can take them."

"I don't want to have to."

"Clan Moon are the spymasters of Oricalis. They're not ones to start trouble overtly. Instead, they'll maneuver their revenge from the shadows."

"So you're saying I should watch my back?" I'm now wondering how many nobles of Clan Moon are in the academy . . . in House Swords, even.

"I'd hope you were already doing that." I give her a tired look at the remark. Her arms drop to her sides. "But, if they're going after anyone, it'll be my sister."

"I don't want Emilia fighting my battles for me."

"That's her duty. The second the medallion fell around your neck, it became her responsibility to guard and defend you as she would her own family. And when she graduates this year, it will fall to the next King. Swords are defensive and offensive, but the one thing they're not is passive." Alor's tone shifts, becoming lighter. "And, much like you, she can handle herself."

"That I don't doubt." Something that had been nagging me bubbles to the surface. "I'm sorry about Eza."

"My sister really isn't at risk."

"Not that." I shake my head. "You said you were entertaining Eza earlier in the year for information. I'm sorry you lost that resource."

She shrugs. "I got what I needed from him."

"Which was?"

"It's personal. You're not the only one with secrets." Alor's smile tells me my asking didn't offend. "I'm going to start sorting myself for the feast and begin packing." She goes to leave. Students will be departing the academy for the end-of-year break following the feast.

"Would you like to share a carriage?" I ask, stopping her. The Feast of Cups will take place outside of the academy in Eclipse City so the nobles can also be in attendance. It's a grand introduction of all the initiates who have progressed to being students—the Arcanists who will be assigned to noble clans next year. The final lists of second-years' clan postings are made public at the feast. And, it is a celebration of those graduating.

"Not this time. I've some other matters to attend to before and during," she answers cryptically. Given her tone, I think I'm supposed to understand what she's referencing, but all I can think of is the records I asked her to search for.

"Good luck" is all I can say, unsure if I'm ready for whatever she might have found.

She nods. "You, too."

I'm left to wonder if Alor knows how badly I'll need it. I shut the door and tug on the laces of the dress. As I go to return the garment to its box, I notice another scrap of fabric I overlooked. It must've bunched into the corner as I pulled out the dress.

Hooking a finger through a lacy strap, I lift a whisper of silk that claims to be a slip of a dress. Pinned to it is a note:

Wear this. Dinner tonight.

CHAPTER 52

I leave the dormitories with a thick coat pulled tightly over the tiny dress. The chill creeps underneath, caressing my bare legs. With every shift of hidden silk, I'm aware of how little I wear. Of the implications he sent with a few pieces of fabric and lace and a single short note.

I emerge into his closet, knocking softly on the door to his bedroom. Silence is my response. Cracking the door, I'd almost been hoping to catch him mid-dressing. But the room is empty. One of the side doors is invitingly ajar, and I step into a long sitting room that adjoins the dining room.

Kaelis is mid-movement as I enter, and he finishes setting out the silverware he was placing as I shut the heavy door behind me. The clicking of my heels fills the silence that, somehow, isn't oppressive. There's a familiar warmth to our solitude now, especially here.

"Did you do all this yourself?" I ask as I approach the chair opposite where Kaelis set out his place. For once, he's not at the head of the table.

"I did."

"Is Rewina taking the night off?"

"I gave it to her." He crosses to me and holds out his hands for my coat. "I do hope what I told you to wear is underneath this."

"Keep demanding things and I might not be inclined to give them to you." I keep my arms folded, arching my brows.

Amusement rumbles up his chest. It makes my toes curl. Kaelis leans forward slightly, tilting his head, messy waves of dark hair shadowing his eyes. "I accept the challenge."

My throat has gone dry, and it only gets worse as he slides the heavy velvet off my shoulders. I'm aware of how alone we are. My nipples perk to attention, and I know they're visible through the silk. I intentionally wore nothing underneath . . . a fact that Kaelis seems to take a moment to appreciate.

"There is no light or shadow that doesn't complement your form," he murmurs softly, pulling out my seat. I take the hint and slip into it, the chair meeting the backs of my knees.

Kaelis serves both of us from dome-topped platters. I suspect the kitchen didn't get the night off as well. The food is good, as always, but I only pick at it. My focus is elsewhere. Like how his fingers close around the bottle of wine. How sharp his eyes still are—parts of him that are abrasive and cutting—even when his smile can be so gentle.

"Are you ready for the Feast of Cups?" he asks.

"I think so. I'll go to my crew tomorrow night to make sure everything is as it should be." The Feast of Cups is the night after.

"Good." We each take a long sip of wine, the implication of what the celebration will bring giving weight to the moment.

"Clara . . . if something goes wrong at the feast—"

"Don't weep for an empty coffin," I interrupt him.

He's understandably confused. "What?"

"It's something we—the club says. Don't give in to despair until you know the coffin is full. Yes, it applies to literal life-and-death situations. But it is more than that. Don't exhaust yourself over something that might not come to pass." I run my finger along the edge of the wineglass, eyes darting to him. "Tonight, I don't want to worry about what the day after tomorrow will bring. I didn't come here to plot, or plan. We've done all that. And, frankly, if it's not good enough by now, it never will be."

"Then what did you come here for?" His voice is heavy. He nearly consumes me with a look that makes my heart stutter.

"Don't you know? After all, I wore the dress and nothing underneath." I slowly uncross and recross my legs.

"I want to hear you say it."

"So demanding." My voice has dropped to little more than a whisper.

"You like me that way." Kaelis rests his elbow on the table, chin on the back of his hand, leaning forward slightly. "Tell me, what did you come here for?"

Those eyes . . . I could spend forever being lost in them and thank him for the time.

"You."

Kaelis stands, rounding the table. I shift myself and my chair to face him. Kaelis holds my stare, and the air is electrified. It's not the wine that's buzzing under our skin. His presence alone steals my senses.

He leans forward, his face stopping a breath from mine. I can feel the heat of his body. The warmth of his lips that begs to be met.

He's so frustratingly, achingly attractive. Even when my mind says, *Don't do this.* My senses abandon me. I want to be putty in his hands. Even though I fancy myself a logical, capable woman . . . sometimes I just want to be fucked by someone who's very, very good at it.

"There is no world in which you do not consume my very being." His voice is low and husky. My body clenches with anticipation.

This time, I wait for him to close the gap, and the immediate, skin-tingling sensation of his lips on mine nearly has me whimpering into his mouth. With a thumb, he presses gently on the side of my face. I open to him, and he readily deepens the kiss.

Kaelis straightens away, and I rise rather than breaking the kiss.

Shifting his body, he guides me over to the other half of the table without food or dishes. Its surface meets my back, and I'm pinned between him and it. Kaelis leans forward, hands gliding down my body, grabbing my ass underneath the dress and pulling me up.

I move to his whims and my own needs. Leaning back. Half seated on the table.

"You . . . you really do have nothing on underneath," he rasps against my ear as his hands glide up the hem of the slip.

"I thought it'd be easier access."

I tilt my head as an invitation. With a low growl in the back of his throat, Kaelis kisses down my neck. His hand slides all the way up my dress to grab my breast. He continues moving. The heat of his mouth draws a moan from me as his lips encircle my nipple over the silk.

His other hand glides along my left thigh. The world narrows onto my core as his fingers dance at the edges. Teasing me. Eliciting soft, short moans. I grip his shoulder as if in a silent plea, trying to convey the urgency for him to *move*. One finger slips in. Then another. I clutch him tighter.

His fingers move in and out of me at the same time as his thumb traces circles around my clit. Waves of pleasure that border on euphoria shiver across my bare skin. I tilt my head back with a gasp and Kaelis sucks, skillfully using his teeth, before he moves to the next breast. I want him to leave marks all over me. I want him to go slow and be gentle and I want him to annihilate me.

"Come for me," he demands with a growl, moving faster. The man knows—has learned so quickly *exactly* what to do. My insides clench, obeying him.

Kaelis once more has full control of my body. Slow, timed movements have me shuddering uncontrollably but not yet over the edge. He has me at a never-ending peak, and just when I'm about to push him away, he stops. I inhale a deep gasp. As I'm finally about to catch my breath, he claims my mouth again and enters me, meeting no resistance.

A low moan rises in the back of his throat. I hardly recall him opening his pants. There's something mind-numbingly erotic about being fucked while he's still completely dressed and I'm naked, save for a whisper of silk that's pushed up over my chest. It's primal. A bit filthy. And I fucking love it.

Already overly sensitive, every nerve in my body explodes as he sets an aggressive pace. My moans fill the air, echoing off every edge of the room. Never has the candlelight been so gorgeous than when it is gilding the edges of his face.

"You're so fucking perfect. It's infuriating," he rasps, every word punctuated by a thrust or a kiss so hungry that it's as if he's trying to consume me whole. His hand covers the bruises he left, wrapping around my throat for only a second. The motion feels more dangerous than it ever was as his voice takes on an angry edge.

I grin wildly, nails digging into his shoulders as I hold on. I want to frustrate him. To drive him mad in every way possible with my existence.

Without warning, he pulls himself from me and steps back. Without his counterbalance, I slide off the table and onto my feet. Kaelis turns me, hands gripping my hips so hard they leave indents. He pushes me down, and I brace myself against the tabletop. Another moan escapes my mouth as he enters me again.

"Why . . ." he growls as he slams into me.

The question is never finished with words. But every slap of his hips against my ass asks everything that's unsaid between us:

Why can I not stop thinking of you? Why do I want you so badly? Why does everything with you straddle the line of pleasure and pain? Why is it that it's never enough?

I want to dissolve into him. My mind goes blank. Every thought is hammered from it. There's nothing but ecstasy. Nothing but him and me and the line between us blurring. Melting into each other until he releases himself into me. The sound of his moan, cut short with a shuddering gasp, nearly sends me over the edge once more.

We're left breathless in the aftermath. Sweetly aching and sweat-slicked. Eventually, he pulls himself from me, and I push myself upright. My muscles tremble, and I'm forced to lean against the table—half sitting on it once more—for support. A weary and *oh-so-satisfied* smile eases its way onto my mouth.

But the bliss evaporates as I see my satisfaction isn't quite shared.

Kaelis's brow is furrowed. Eyes conflicted.

"What?" I ask. The look has alarm bells ringing.

He places his hands on either side of me, leaning in. His forehead presses against mine and his eyes close, as if he's wincing. Desire has been replaced with desperation. With a need for more than the carnal.

"Stay with me tonight," he whispers.

"What are you afraid of?" My hands glide up his chest to wrap around the back of his neck.

"Stay with me?" he repeats.

"Yes." It's easier to agree than I'd ever imagined it would be. "But tell me what you're afraid of; I see it."

"Our doomed future."

"The future will be what we make it," I remind him.

Kaelis opens his eyes to meet mine. There's so much unsaid there . . . enough that I'm afraid to ask. "Yes, so long as we have the World, we have a future."

Though, the real question remains: Which one of us will be the one to use it?

The townhome is quiet.

I didn't announce I'd be coming, so most people have retreated to their rooms. Asleep, probably. Silas makes himself at home, heading to the kitchen before he'll settle himself in the front study. Now that he's more welcome, he's been given some unspoken liberties that he takes.

The doors to the lounge in the back are cracked open, a strip of light inviting me in. Bristara sits before the fire in her usual chair, staring into the dying flames. She doesn't even acknowledge me as I slide the doors shut.

"You wanted to speak before tomorrow?" I round her chair, settling into the end of the sofa closest to her.

Her eyes drift to mine. Their purple is offset by the orange firelight. Fearsome without even trying. But every muscle in her body is relaxed, almost weighted down. Her attention drifts back to the flames.

"We need to talk about your mother."

Not even so much as a hello. The words douse me like a bucket of ice water, drenching me from head to toe.

In my panic, I reach for dry sarcasm. "It only took you, what—four, five years?"

Bristara huffs and shakes her head, returning her attention to me. "She and I weren't particularly close. Acquaintances whose paths overlapped once or twice, briefly, nothing more." Sure, that's what Bristara says, but I know Mother wouldn't have shared our name with just a mere acquaintance. "I didn't find out about what happened at the Descent until months after, and, by then, you and Arina had slipped away. She taught you well . . . you were able to evade us for so long."

"*Us?* The Starcrossed Club?" I ask, even though I suspect she isn't talking about the club.

"No."

"Who, then?" My voice has dropped to a whisper. *Why tell me this now?* I want to ask. She's had years to tell me. But I want whatever information she's going to impart much, much more.

"Your mother should have been the one to tell you this." Bristara runs her fingers in a circle over her temple, then along her brow.

"Tell me; I can handle whatever it is." I'm glad my voice is level despite the cold, sinking feeling that is threatening to drown me.

"What do you know of the Worldkeepers?"

"The name means nothing to me."

"Oh, Laylis . . ." She sighs. "The Worldkeepers are the guardians of the Majors. And, first and foremost, of the World itself. It is an ancient order that has existed across time and time anew. We are the ones who will always remember the worlds we walked should it be scrubbed from memory if, or when, it is rebuilt. And we guard the secret of the vessel upon which the World is imprinted."

As she speaks, Bristara rolls up her sleeve and rests a small, circular card on her forearm—a shape I've never seen a card cut before. It bears a delicate inking that reminds me of something Mother would make, but the lines mean nothing to me. The moment the paper touches her flesh the card melts away and a symbol illuminates just above it. It's like a tattoo cast in a metallic, almost rusty ink. The design is simple: a diamond with a starburst in its center. I'm certain I've never seen it before. Just as quickly as it appears, it fades away.

My mouth nearly drops open in shock. Here I was, hunting through the library, scouring the workshop of the Fool, trying for months to see if I could get Kaelis to drop a clearer explanation about the vessel he'd mentioned. And all the while, Bristara had the information I needed.

"What is the vessel?" I try not to sound too eager.

"A card, just like any other. Yet it's also unlike any other card. It is created by a sacred and secret inking process passed down through generations in the Worldkeepers' bloodline." She grips and relaxes her hands on her chair.

"And all the Worldkeepers know it?"

"At one time, worlds away. But not any longer. The Worldkeepers, in the last days of the previous world—before it was changed to its current state—were ruthlessly hunted. Only a handful survived, and only to be pursued with equal violence in this world. Among those who persisted was your mother. And she was the last remaining Worldkeeper who knew how to ink the vessel."

I open and close my mouth. Shock has me easing back into the cushions. I run a hand through my hair.

"Everything she taught me . . ." Every inking process. Every night we stayed up drawing, her teaching me how to ink in our own way— how to *feel* the cards and let that guide me. *This, Clara, is our special card*, I can hear her whisper, as if she wants to be a part of this moment here and now. Her rigorous instruction wasn't because I was a Major—or not *only* because I was a Major.

"You, Clara, are the last person alive who knows how to ink the vessel. A fact I am sure the crown is not far from uncovering, if they haven't already." Bristara shifts in her seat to face me more evenly. "And you will soon have a choice to make: Will you give that knowledge to the family that has been our enemy for generations? Or will you protect it as your mother did?"

"Kaelis isn't like the rest of his family."

"He is worse." Her eyes darken. "He is the last of the Revisan bloodline."

The portrait of the mystery queen and King Naethor. A woman whom I had never once heard mention of—who seemed like she'd never existed.

"The Revisan Kingdom was thousands of years ago..." I say weakly, already knowing things aren't quite adding up for it to be true: the age of the fortress the academy occupies, modern yet supposedly ancient; the machines within from centuries ago, yet still in good working order.

"You know better than that," she calls me on the obvious truth. I do.

Kaelis's mentions that now suddenly have so many more layers. He said his father had killed his mother—that his memories of her were scattered. Kaelis's disdain for his family and wanting to destroy Oricalis. *Did King Naethor use the World to kill Kaelis's mother and, if so, why?*

"Why are you telling me all this now? You've had years." Panic wars with anger between my words. A mystery that was once thrilling is now terrifying.

"The Worldkeepers' induction is usually at twenty-one as an homage to the World we protect." It's not lost on me that they apply similar logic as the academy when it comes to age of induction. The irony is stunning. "But, when you were taken to Halazar, we all agreed waiting any longer was foolish. If—*when* you managed to get out, or we managed to break you out, we would immediately induct you."

"Why haven't you, then? I've been out for almost a year."

"Given your recent *associations* . . . we wanted to be sure that we could trust your instincts." A flash of the disapproval I've been seeing for weeks is back in her eyes.

"You kept me in the dark because you were testing me?" My anger is as searing as a red-hot branding iron.

"Oricalis already knows too much. Before giving you more information, there were those among the Worldkeepers who wanted to be sure you wouldn't funnel even more to them."

Those among the Worldkeepers, not all. Still, I get the sense Bristara is going a bit rogue. Not that I'm complaining. "But *you* don't doubt me?"

"I think, when the time comes, you'll make the right choice. That it is too dangerous to keep you unaware of the greater forces at play. Who knows how you would've acted had you known all of this from the start?" The answer soothes my annoyance slightly. But I try not to let any of it show. The information is too valuable to possibly lose out on because of an outburst.

"How many of you are there?" I focus on her heavy use of "we."

"Now a few dozen, minus the ones we lost attacking King Naethor on All Coins Day." She adds, with a somewhat disgusted uttering, "Fools."

That was how the assassin knew my real name on All Coins Day. How she recognized me. I wonder if she could've been one of Mother's "friends" who came by from time to time in Rot Hollow. Had I seen her before? Or did she just know who I was through this organization?

"The tunnels in the mountains—"

"Our pathways."

"And my sister—"

"The academy is as much of a blind spot to us as it is to everyone else." She stops me. "You know as much as I do when it comes to her, likely more."

"But you knew she didn't make it out of the academy," I realize. Bristara's expression hardens. "Because if Arina had been sent to a mill, you would've followed her. You let the rest of the club think there was a chance Arina was out there." My voice drops to a whisper. "Would you have ever told them?"

A long stretch of silence.

"We do what we must." Bristara is unapologetic and unflinching.

"Do you even care about us?" I whisper.

"Of course I do. You and your sister have *always* had people looking out for you, even if you never noticed. You still do." She's genuinely offended, shifting in her chair. "And me? I care about this star-crossed family I've built more than anything else in the world. The club never had anything to do with the Worldkeepers."

"Yet you'd lie to us."

"I was protecting everyone, you included." Bristara sighs softly and looks out the window at the courtyard where Arina now rests. "The more you all knew, the greater the risk. You and your sister weren't the only ones with the proclivity to recklessly run off." I think about how Gregor was out patrolling the streets for me after hearing of the escapee.

"What about my mother's death?" What she's saying still isn't sitting right with me in the slightest. "Do you have information you haven't shared about that, too?"

"You have always been right in suspecting that it was a murder."

"Sanctioned by the crown?" Even as I ask, Kaelis flashes before my eyes, over me, in me. But I must know if the man I've fallen into bed with is behind her death once and for all. If I am a traitor to the memory of the people I loved most.

Bristara purses her lips, as if she doesn't want to say. "While we have every reason to believe that the crown sanctioned the attack—given King Naethor's desire to purge all of us—we have not found anything concrete."

I sigh heavily, sinking so far into the sofa that my head tips back and I stare at the ceiling. Dead ends on dead ends. *What good is a secret society if even they don't have the information I need?* I barely keep from asking aloud.

"We did uncover involvement on the part of Clan Tower, however." At that I straighten. Alor might be able to find something, then. Perhaps I'd asked her to investigate the wrong person all those months ago. "Not surprising, given it involves resources for the mills and Clan Tower is under orders of the crown."

"Yet something about it did surprise you." I can't help but pick it up in her voice.

"All our information points to Prince Ravin"—*Twenty, I hate that man*—"as being the one charged with hunting Worldkeepers. Yet, strangely enough, for your mother's death, we can't find evidence of his direct involvement."

"What can I do to find evidence?" I work to put aside the idea of Bristara having information on Mother's death that she kept from me. It doesn't sound like it was much.

"The best thing you can do is what you are already doing—focus on the World. Steal the cards from the king, but *do not* give them to Kaelis. Keep them for yourself. No one else. Secret and safe."

My eyes drift over to her. Bristara knows me all too well. I wonder if she suspects that I've been siphoning just enough resources from the workshop of the Fool to make an extra card, but not enough for Kaelis to realize the materials have depleted a little bit faster than they should. One forgery to give to Kaelis . . . and an original card to keep for myself.

"Is this part of the test to see if I'm worthy to join your group?" I ask.

"The fate of our world hinges on what you choose to do. It is much more than the approval of anyone in our organization." She exudes confidence in me that I'm not sure is well placed. "During your recess following the Feast of Cups, we will properly induct you into the order of your ancestors. Then, all the questions you no doubt have will be answered when you meet everyone else. I am not the lore keeper among us; most of your questions are better asked elsewhere."

I'm silent the entire way back to the academy. Silas clearly knows something has changed, but he doesn't pry. He takes me back to the academy—close to Kaelis's chambers, as I ask. I'm just about to leave when he stops me.

"Clara." Silas's hand closes around mine. I glance over my shoulder, easing into a more relaxed stance when I see the severity of his expression. The conflict that's wrought across his features. "Tomorrow is the Feast of Cups."

"I know."

"Your heist . . ." He trails off, struggling to find his words. I give him time to work up the courage. "It could go wrong."

"I know," I repeat gently. Silas is new to all this. He's spent his life under the thumb of the crown. Of course he's nervous about going against them. "That's a risk we're going to take."

Silas releases me, eyes on the floor. He rubs the back of his neck uncertainly. "I . . . You see . . . *Fuck.*" The man curses under his breath, and I lean back in surprise. I don't think I've ever heard him say any sort of harsh language before. Silas reaches into his pocket and thrusts a silver card into my hand. "Take it."

I blink, eyes darting from the card to his face. When it's clear he's not about to look at me, I focus on the card—the Chariot. The ink is slightly raised and cool to the touch, as if wrought in actual silver. I've seen Silas draw this card a dozen times, yet I've never inspected it so closely. The details of the horses' manes as they tug an intricate chariot through swirling mist.

"You're . . . giving me a card?" Awe drops my words to a whisper.

"If things go bad, use it."

"You're trusting me with this?"

Silas nods.

Months ago, he wouldn't give me the card even to use once. I couldn't promise or beg him into it. Now he's handing it over to try to help protect me. He's entrusting me with what amounts to treason, given that this card is intended only for the crown.

I throw my arms around his shoulders. Silas tenses instantly. I wonder how long it's been since someone last held him—last showed him any kindness.

"Thank you," I whisper. Out of everyone, Silas was the last person I expected to be able to trust. But after all the revelations, maybe he's one of the few. "I won't let you down."

"Good luck." Silas returns the tight embrace, and we stand there for a breath. When he releases me, he promptly heads in the opposite direction, leaving with the swiftness of a necessary retreat.

I pocket his card and head for Kaelis's apartments, my thoughts swirling even more.

On silent feet, I emerge into the prince's room.

Kaelis is sleeping. The indentation of my body is next to his on the bed from where I got up earlier to sneak out. The same spot where I stayed last night. Where I thought I might return to tonight. He trusts me enough to let his guard down and sleep deeply.

It'd be so easy to kill him right now. The rogue thought is said in a voice I no longer recognize. It's my own, but from a year ago. Bristara said the Worldkeepers were hunted—that Oricalis is our sworn enemy. I knew the crown was behind Mother's death, and now I have more proof than ever.

Kill him, the voice urges. Perhaps it is the echo of my Worldkeeper bloodline. But the notion has my stomach churning. I turn away from the sleeping prince and silently make my way to my room.

There, I lay out all my inking supplies—that which Kaelis gifted me, and that which I quietly stole—and take a breath, facing my choice.

Do I believe Bristara? Do I believe the woman who took me in off the streets, has always defended me, and knows enough truths that I do not suspect her of lying? But she's also the same woman who has had years to tell me everything and didn't. If I put my faith in her, then it would mean I throw my lot in with these Worldkeepers. People I've never known. Who've only ever existed as shadowed, hooded figures and mysteries. But who did look after my family—people whom my mother trusted.

Or...

Do I put my trust in the man of flesh and blood who has claimed my body and my heart? The man who has a vendetta against his father as much as I do. Who wants to remake the world and make it better for Arcanists so that none will ever have to sacrifice themselves in body or magic to the crown again. *If* he's to be believed...

My pen quivers as I pick it up.

There is a third option: Myself. What I've thought all along. I take the World and I make my own wish. *Damn everyone else.* The only person I can ever depend on to take care of the ones I love is me.

"Kaelis..." His name is wrenched from my lips. Pained. It cuts the silence like the first line of my inking cuts the unblemished surface of the paper.

We were born enemies. Made to be enemies.

How could we have ever thought there was a different path for us?

CHAPTER 53

Students are taken by gilded carriage to the venue for this year's Feast of Cups: the Fatefinders Club. To this day, it's the largest social venue in Eclipse City. The Starcrossed Club spent years competing with—and trying to steal clientele from—the Fatefinders Club, which has turned out to be a boon. The Starcrossed Club already had knowledge of the establishment and its people well before tonight. But that doesn't stop my nerves from making my stomach flip.

When the carriage door swings open, I am the first to step out. Some second years from House Swords whose names I've only just learned shared the ride with me. Alor went on ahead with her sister—business to attend to, as she'd said. The marbled façade of the venue glitters brightly in the magical glow of lamplight. A black carpet with the Major Arcana as constellations dancing across it guides us into the grand entrance.

Positioned on either side of the doors are rows of footmen, all of impressive build. Some break away to offer to take coats and capes to a cloakroom. Others remain poised like statues. I'm sure most of the nobles see them as little more than staff. But I see the Fatefinders Club's security gathered in force . . . including a familiar face.

Gregor does a good job of not acknowledging me as I pass. Not even a flick of the eyes. He's such a lovable oaf around the house that I forget just how good he is whenever he's given a job.

The main room is a feast for the senses: crystal chandeliers, the overwhelming aroma from the fresh flowers that drape between every column intermingling with the intoxicating scents of spiced liquors and a spread of mouthwatering food, and a full band that serenades all those gathered. Most of the individuals initially pay me no mind. I'm just another in a long string of students making their way into the banquet hall. Even if I might be one of the most fabulously dressed people here.

But the most valuable things in all my satin and lace are the cards that are hidden in the pockets of my dress. A deck, complete with two silver Majors—the Chariot, and my own. Though I've never ventured to use it since my fight with Eza. The card seems far too unpredictable and unclear for my liking—all Kaelis could find in his texts about Fortune is that it shifts fate. Hardly reliable. Next to my deck there are five forgeries to exchange for the king's cards. And one additional forgery, possibly for Kaelis. But that's a decision I don't think I'll fully make until the moment.

The main area stretches out beyond the banquet tables. Music booms off the tall ceilings. I recognize many of the nobles dancing. Lord Ventall catches my eye. A woman with hair a similar silky straight texture as her daughters is wrapped in his arms, gracefully spinning across the dance floor. But I don't see those daughters anywhere.

Nor do I see any of the royals. But the crowd is dense. It seems like every clan has turned out tonight to meet the new students they will soon lay claim to. Just as I'm about to hunt for Kaelis, my path is unexpectedly blocked by a familiar figure.

"Oh! *Oh.* Clara." Liam barely stops himself from bumping into me. "It's good to see you again."

He always was an awful liar. Instead, I say, "And you as well."

"Congratulations on making it through the first year of the academy. I hear you were a triumph all the way through. Minus a few scandals." He smirks, and I wonder which of my many scandals he's referring to.

"Thank you." Etiquette and not wanting to make a scene are the only things that stop me from moving away as quickly as possible. "Where's your wife?"

The moment I ask, I realize this situation is familiar. The words aren't the same. Nor is the way he's looking at me. But there's a striking sensation of similarity. Was this what was meant to be the moment I discarded in the Arcanum Chalice? Is what's happening now a twisted alteration due to my sacrifice? My stomach goes from flipping to knotting in an instant.

"Listen, I should've—"

I hold up a hand, stopping him. "I've heard it before. It's fine."

"Heard it before? You mean in the Arcanum Chalice?" It seems my mind wasn't the only one to venture there. I expected him to find out about what happened on the day of the Fire Festival, but I was content never having to confront him with it.

"Must we talk about it?" I glance around him, hoping to see Kaelis.

"I wanted—want to. I tried to the night of the soiree. But . . ." He trails off. That brings my eyes back to him. "I suppose it's all the same."

"The same as what?"

"When I went off to the academy." He shrugs. "You didn't want to talk then, either."

"What are you talking about?" I phrase the question partly as a demand for him to speak plainly.

There's a flash of hurt in his eyes. Of old wounds that I know all too well but didn't expect to see mirrored in him. "I assumed you wanted nothing to do with me after you never responded to my letters."

"What letters?" My voice has dropped to a hush. My lips don't even close all the way as shock settles on him as well.

"I . . . I wrote to you, multiple times throughout my first year. I admit, not right away, you know how chaotic it is those first few months." He rubs the back of his neck. "I should have. I'm sorry if they arrived too late and—"

"*Nothing* arrived." My heart is pounding. "I never got a single letter from you."

We stare at each other in a silence that's loud with the ringing ears of disbelief.

What could've been? The question I'd wholly let go of returns with a vengeance.

"I don't know what happened to them . . ." He's somewhere between stunned and horrified.

Something the Chalice version of Liam said returns to me: *I was identified by Clan Star early in my first year.* If they identified him, if he was already chosen as a potential mate for someone . . .

My stomach churns, and two things dawn on me: The first is that I don't love him, not anymore. Maybe I'll live forever wondering about what could have been. But that doesn't change the flow of time that has created a gulf between us.

The second is horror at the realization of what he might have put in those letters . . . If they were intercepted, who took them, and do they still exist?

"See if you can find out," I say.

"I think it's a bit late for that." He laughs softly, somewhat sadly. He's not following, and I can't make up my mind about how much I want to say.

"I'm engaged to the prince now, Liam. I'd rather not have old love letters come back to haunt me, if you catch my drift." I force a little smile, trying to simultaneously express severity while also not seeming *too* bothered. I don't know how much I can trust this man as he is now.

"*Ah*, of course. Well, I doubt there's anything I'll find, but I'll take a look."

"With the utmost discretion, please."

"I'll do my best." He hovers, and I can feel all the words left unsaid drifting around us. "I'll let you know if I find anything."

"Thank you." I nod.

He takes two steps backward, eyes holding mine, before turning and leaving. Liam strides over to his wife and engages in a brief conversation. Her attention darts my way, and I offer a warm smile—anything else would probably come off as more suspicious. She hooks her arm with Liam's and ushers him away. I feel like I have my answer already about the letters . . .

Don't worry, I wish I could tell her as it dawns on me that this, without doubt, was the moment the Chalice showed me. *I don't want him. He's yours. Just don't come after me . . .*

Kaelis slides in beside me, seemingly out of nowhere. The noise and music and crowd—it all vanishes with his presence. A bubble of easy silence envelops us.

"What did he do?" Kaelis asks, misreading the concern on my face, eyes darting toward Liam.

"Nothing."

"It doesn't look like nothing." A frown tugs on his lips. "I would love a reason to end him; give me one."

Instead, I give him an almost contented smile. "Liam and I have been ended for a long time . . . No need to dig up the grave."

"Good," he says, though I suspect part of him still wishes I'd given him a reason to go after Liam and end it in a different way. "Then, in that case, may I have this dance, my love?"

My love. The words strike me. He's never called me that before. I try to tell myself it's just for the benefit of the crowd around us, but . . .

"Clara?" My name on his lips feels like a lover's caress. I've heard him say it a thousand times, and yet it sounds different tonight.

"Kaelis?" I should show him the proper respect, if not as the headmaster, then as a prince. But I can't bring myself to do it. *You're not above me,* I remind him with the name. Doing so only makes him smile.

"Dance with me?" He offers me his arm.

"Always." I take it, fingers brushing over the soft wool of his coat.

His clothing is understated tonight. Of all the times I would've expected him to lean in to his inclinations toward luxury and excess, this would be it. But he's dressed in a black suit—as impeccably tailored as ever. A vest of the same material is underneath, over a pale gray shirt. As he leads me to the floor, I notice the faint silver embroidery on the shoulders and lapels of his jacket that mirrors the designs in the lace of my dress. The red stitching done in the same nearly blood-red shade. A color that almost matches my eyes.

It feels like the band plays just for us. That there's no one else on the floor. Only the press of his hand at the small of my back, the all-too-familiar warmth of his body, the firm grip of his fingers on mine that pulls on the tension that stretches between us, tighter and tighter, like a trip wire we're dancing across without a care in the world . . . As if there isn't an abyss beneath us, threatening oblivion with one misstep.

"You're beautiful tonight. As always."

"You don't look so bad yourself."

"Are you ready?" he whispers, lips so close to my ear that the warmth of his breath sends shivers down my arms.

"Yes."

"Your co-conspirators?" He extends his arm, and I spin underneath. Kaelis pulls me back with force.

"Professionals," I say quickly, barely moving my lips. "They're all here, ready."

"Good. You'll have one shot."

I tilt my head back enough to look him in the eyes. "You think I don't know that?"

Kaelis's expression hardens. I can feel his worry. I've intentionally kept him in the dark on a few of the details, at Twino's request.

"I'll get the cards," I reassure him.

"That's not what I'm worried about." His gaze sharpens with something akin to desperation.

"What, then?" Another turn. The music swells as he draws me closer, tighter this time. My breaths are short, breasts straining against the corset. Against his chest. Fingers pierce the lace between my shoulder blades and find skin. He clings to me as though the moment he lets me go, he'll lose me forever.

"I'm worried about *you*," he chokes out. The room goes silent, and all I hear is him. I can feel the fear that furrowed his brow the other night at dinner. That had him holding me tightly throughout the night. "If this fails, if it doesn't go according to plan, I don't know if I can protect you this time. As pathetic as my last attempt was . . ."

There is nothing but raw sincerity exposed by the fear that so obviously gnaws at him. The last emotions I expected to ever see from him, for me. Emotions I'd willfully ignored. Outright told myself couldn't exist.

"This was supposed to be simple," I whisper, anger tugging on my words. I'm angry with him—with myself. How dare he draw me in like this, body and soul.

"Nothing about us will ever be simple." The timbre of his voice is so low it causes me to shiver. "Clara, you are—"

The melody transitions, and a new figure comes into view. It is another man who carries himself like a force of nature. The one Kaelis gets it from.

King Oricalis, regal in red and gold, seems to materialize instantly at our side.

We break apart like two children caught sneaking behind the hedges to steal a first kiss. The room floods back around us like the blood rushing to my head. *Pull yourself together*, I scold myself. I was just telling Kaelis how he didn't have to worry. Time to show him I have these matters in hand.

I sink into a curtsy as Kaelis gives his father a begrudgingly respectful nod.

"May I cut in?" The king's tone suggests it's a command more than a question.

"You honor me, your majesty," I say as I stand.

Kaelis's gaze meets mine for a heartbeat before he steps back. My hand is passed from one Oricalis to another. Without a word, the prince leaves me feeling as though I've been abandoned to a monster's den. But my plastered-on smile doesn't leave my face as the king takes me into his arms, and I remind myself to breathe, or else I might seize up from the sheer terror that tries to grip me by the throat at this man's mere proximity.

"He dresses you well." The king's eyes miss nothing. "Once more, he has you looking like the part."

"I am honored by his highness's affections." I'm not sure what else to say, so I defer to platitudes. This is the first time I've ever spoken to the king alone.

"As you should be."

The music shifts, and we turn. I take the opportunity to subtly brush against the king's chest, feeling for the contours of the mechanical box. It's in the same place as last time. Simultaneously, I scan the room, looking across all the serving men and women for a familiar face.

Jura stands with a platter of flutes filled to the brim with sparkling wine. We share a purposeful look that lasts only for a second.

"Take his kindness, and his infatuation." The king seems none the wiser to my movements. But he stares at me with renewed purpose that draws my focus back to him, and him alone. "But discourage my son from his bold ambitions."

My heart pounds. *He knows?* He can't. But his eyes suggest otherwise.

"Kaelis has grand dreams for the academy; I doubt anyone could discourage him from that." I try to plaster on the most oblivious smile I can muster.

The king's grip on me tightens. "I know what my son is," he says solemnly. "And that is precisely why I think you, of all people, are the only one who can be with him. Tame him. Temper him. Though it will never be in the way he has promised you."

There's something wild, almost feral in the shadows of the man's hardened gaze. For a moment, he's unrecognizable as being related to Kaelis at all. The intensity I've seen in the prince is nothing like this, and my words almost catch in my throat.

"What do you mean?" I dare to whisper.

Before he can answer, the song ends, and polite applause fills the room. The king smiles and steps away, readily discarding me after issuing his cryptic warnings and partial commands. There's only a second's worth of time for me to doubt the plan. If he knows Kaelis will move against him . . .

I watch helplessly as Jura hands the king a specific flute. The wine is spiked with clear liquor—enough to set off a headache, according to Silas.

Whatever doubts I might have, whatever the king does or doesn't know and what it might mean, the plan is in motion.

There's no going back.

CHAPTER 54

It takes about ten minutes, but the king finally excuses himself from the ballroom. His hand rises to his temple as he makes his way to a side door. I wait five minutes before following. Kaelis is working the room and keeping his brother occupied. Ravin is the only one, out of everyone, that I'm worried about.

No one pays me any mind as I slip out of the ballroom. I've studied the layout of this club enough times to know where the toilets are to make my departure look believable enough, and where the staff accesses connect. A door marked as PRIVATE has been left unlocked, just as it should be. The guts of the building are stark in comparison to the public areas. That makes them easy to navigate.

My heels click lightly on the marble floor as I emerge into a back passage. I slow my pace. This area is usually set aside for the high rollers and nobles. Tonight, it's reserved for the Oricalis family. I see a familiar set of broad shoulders positioned at the corner of an upcoming intersection. I slow to a stop.

"He just came through. Ren was shortly behind," Gregor whispers. He knows me by my gait.

"Good. We'll give it another minute, then." I keep my voice equally soft. "Any others come through?"

"No. Bristara's done a good job of giving us a window where there'll be no guards."

"Twino?" As I ask, he emerges from a door opposite me with Jura at his side.

"The tea was prepared," Twino says carefully. Even though we appear to be alone, it's best not to take any chances.

We all share another set of nervous glances and look to the stately door at the far end of the hall where Ren is. We'd debated if it was better for Twino to serve the king or Ren. But, in the end, we didn't want to risk the same person being in such close proximity to the king twice in a row. Ren is the least known among us.

Twino leans against the wall, heavier than just taking a load off his leg. His eyes are fixated on the door. I shift over to him, grabbing his fingers and holding them tightly. *Ren will be all right,* the motion says. We've been planning and practicing for months.

My other hand slips into the concealed pocket in the billowing skirt of my dress, gliding over the cards hidden there, waiting to be used. I still haven't made up my mind. Bristara's warnings and truths ring louder in my ears than the rushing of my blood. Yet, all her own secrets remind me of Kaelis's. Can anyone be trusted?

The door at the end of the hall cracks open. We move.

A grand salon has been converted into the king's private chambers for the evening. The room is opulent in a detached way. Finery for its own sake lines the walls and floors as intricately embroidered drapes and brilliantly patterned rugs. But it lacks personality, warmth. Much like the sovereign himself.

The king is laid out on a daybed. His chest rises and falls with breaths so shallow they're barely there. The movement is slight enough that I worry Ren overdid the tincture . . . But Ren looks confident, so I keep my faith in him.

Twino is at the king's side in an instant, carefully unfastening his jacket and shirt. No doubt remembering just how every button and medallion was placed in the process.

"Did he suspect anything?" My voice is hushed from tension.

"Not that I could tell," Ren says. "If he did, I suppose he wouldn't have drunk the tea."

Twino finishes the last button of the king's shirt and goes right for the exposed box. Jura shifts around to the other side of the daybed. She approaches the box with the same detail-oriented care as when she decorates her winter solstice cookies. Her nimble little fingers are critical to getting the mechanism open.

Even though it's the two of them who have been practicing, based on Silas's drawings, I'm leaning over, watching every movement. As the box shifts between them, its edge catches the light. I squint, narrowing my focus.

A symbol has been etched there. It looks like the last vertical line of an N has been used to write an E, making it a single symbol. My breath catches. It's the same mark I saw on the mechanical mill on my first night in the academy, I'd thought it was a V then, but I'm certain this is the same. The mill prototype in the workshop of the Fool . . . whose creator Kaelis said was long gone, who belonged to the Revisan Kingdom. Once more, the portrait I saw is in the forefront of my mind . . .

Bristara's words return to me. The doubts I had about what she said are evaporating. King Naethor was part of the world before this one. The world that was rebuilt by the twenty-first tarot. A world I would bet my life on that he was the one to destroy, given that he now holds all the power here.

Kaelis knows this, too. He must. The mechanism . . . it could've been used to help—if they'd wanted. King Oricalis chose to make this world as horrible as it is and keep it that way. I feel dizzy and try to calm my racing thoughts and heart. *Focus on the moment; the rest can wait.*

The metal box on the king's chest opens, and we all take a collective inhale.

I grab the cards, carefully sliding them out. One by one, I compare my forgeries to the real deal. Ren and Jura's concoction works its magic and the king stays asleep while I go through every card. Gregor goes to check the door. No one says anything, and the silence is deafening.

My fakes are perfect.

The moment I settle the forgeries in their slot, Twino snaps the box shut, locking it once more. Closing it is far easier and faster than opening it. I ease away, hand in my pocket. There's no marked difference in how the cards feel to the touch, which is reassuring. But my dress feels heavier on the side. My palm is scorching from the power I know they carry.

"Keep it tidy, everyone," I say solemnly. Jura nods and leaves quickly to resume her duties as a server; she'll be among the last to leave but will be dismissed from her position soon. Ren follows a few steps behind, turning in the opposite direction to where I assume the kitchens are. Gregor stays by the door, keeping watch.

Twino and I emerge into the hall together, Gregor shutting the door behind us.

"Stay safe getting out of here," I whisper.

"I'll make sure he does," Gregor answers, ever confident in his own abilities.

Twino's face relaxes into an easy smile that says, *Don't worry*, without him having to say a word.

I do worry. I always have. It's worse ever since Halazar and that night. I can't bear the idea of losing them all again. But no matter the cost, we keep moving forward.

Which for them is through another side door. For me it's the opposite direction. I emerge into the grand hallway and wipe a thin sheen of sweat from my brow. I can't go back looking as guilty as I am. After taking a moment to collect myself, I move through the hallways on a different route than before. Bristara might not be physically present for our missions, but her organizing and coordinating of them never fails. As long as we're all where we're supposed to be, it's as if we walk with invisible shields. She maneuvers security and staff by changing delivery times, schedules, and turnovers with a hand that always extended far beyond her reach.

I round the corner with all the confidence in the world and find myself face-to-face with a group of Stellis.

Not staff. Not security. Not even city enforcers.

Stellis. The one group that would be the hardest for Bristara to have control over.

Fuck.

They all face me as if I'd actually said the word and not just thought it loudly. The world freezes as they assess me—my flushed cheeks, the sweat I was wiping from my palms. I *look* guilty, and I can't have that. Not appearing guilty is the majority of innocence.

"Evening, gentlemen." I force myself to incline my head slightly. I hope I give them enough respect that I don't come off as rude, but not so much that it would suggest deference to them.

"What do you think you're doing here?" the man in the middle asks. He has an extra set of feathers coming from his helmet and a badge pinned to his breast. A captain, I believe.

"I was looking for Prince Kaelis." I keep an air of authority about me.

"Prince Kaelis hasn't left his brother's side for the past hour," the one to the right says skeptically.

Well, damn him for doing exactly what we'd agreed on. "Oh, really? I thought we'd agreed on him meeting me in private to . . ." I stop myself with fingertips on my lips and hope my flush looks like a blush. "Never you mind. I'll head back to the ballroom, then."

Just as I turn, the leader catches my wrist, his grip firmer than I'd like. I plaster on a confused, borderline annoyed look.

"Excuse me?"

"The king told us to look out for you."

"Did he now?" I ease my expression into a coy smile. "Did it occur to you that perhaps he said that so you could properly welcome me into these chambers, since I am Kaelis's betrothed?"

They share an uncertain look, affirming that the king didn't elaborate. Which could work to my advantage. Or . . . no.

"We're going to need you to come with us. Better to check."

Bile is right at the top of my throat. I swallow it down. Flashes of the night I was caught race through my mind, attacking me from every direction. *Don't panic,* I command myself.

"The prince might have something to say about that," I say.

"The prince answers to his father as much as we do."

I suppose that's true. My fingers twitch, resisting the urge to call upon the deck at my hip. I still have the Chariot card Silas gave me, but I don't want to use it except in desperation.

"Very—" *well,* I'm about to say, but I'm interrupted.

"Clara." Alor's voice is flat. She stands in a doorframe, as surprised to see me as I am to see her. "There you are." She hastily closes the gap. Her eyes dart from the hand around my wrist to the man clutching it. "Is there a problem, Ilvan?"

"The king had asked us to watch for this one. We were going to bring her to him—"

"That is a future princess of Oricalis you are holding like she is some street urchin," Alor interrupts with a tone that is part scandalized and part chiding. I take note of how she's not in a gown or suit like the rest of the students, but rather in a more practical set of leathers under a sparser version of the plate the Stellis wear. She's dressed like a Stellis in training. "We of Clan Tower are in service to the crown."

"And the crown itself has asked us to bring her to him." Ilvan is sounding more uncertain by the second. I happily let Alor take the lead.

Alor shakes her head with a sigh, as if she can't believe she has to deal with this. "Probably not by tugging her like a mule on a lead. Unhand her. I'll take her to the king myself."

There's another second where it looks like Ilvan is going to object. But he doesn't. His fingers begrudgingly unfurl from my wrist.

"Good." Alor handles herself as if she's the one these Stellis report to, despite them clearly outranking her. I'd expect nothing less from the daughter of the High Lord of Clan Tower. "Clara, if you'll follow me, please."

I step around the Stellis, holding my head high even though my heart is galloping. Their eyes are pinned to me as I follow Alor away. I add a swish of my skirts for good measure as she escorts me into a nearby room.

"What do you think you're doing?" Alor whispers the moment the door is shut. "You're not supposed to be— You know what? I don't want to know what you're doing back here." She rubs the bridge of her nose with a sigh. "Go through that door, then to the right; it's a straight shot to the ballroom from there. Go before someone else takes an interest in you. If anyone asks, we tried to find the king and couldn't."

"Thank you." The words are tinged with an emotion deeper than relief.

"Don't thank me yet. You're not in the clear, and most people I can't save you from."

I step away. I'm not going to waste her kindness, or the opportunity. But, just as I'm about to open the door, she stops me by calling my name. I pause, and Alor crosses to me as she pulls a slip of paper from her pocket. I regard it warily, remembering the information I tasked her with finding on Arina . . . and my mother.

"I couldn't find much on your sister, which made me curious. So I dug deeper. The name Laylis helped, so thanks for that tip." She takes my right wrist with one hand, placing the paper into my palm with the other. But her grip holds on both, as if she's unsure whether to release the information to me.

Her eyes flick to mine and stick. Something in her stare makes my heart pound faster than when the Stellis confronted me minutes ago. It's fear. Apprehension. The only thing that has her releasing me is a determined grit of her teeth.

"This isn't just about you any longer."

"What did you find?"

"Not enough, yet." Alor gives a nod to the door she mentioned earlier. "We need to talk after the gala."

With a wordless nod, I depart, following the path just as she outlined. But before I reach the door to the ballroom, I pause and unfold the paper she thrust into my palm. I suck in a sharp breath.

What I'd thought was one slip of paper is three folded up on each other. The first has a date that corresponds with about two months after the Fire Festival nearing two years ago—only a few weeks after I was captured. It reads:

> Arina Daygar, captured by Eclipse City enforcers.
> According to head enforcer, taken to Mill No. 23.
> No record of receipt of Arina Daygar at mill.

None of this is a surprise to me, though it does fill my mouth with a sour taste corresponding with the churning of my stomach. I swap out to the next slip of paper. More of Alor's notes:

> Record of Ravin's involvement. Request *specifically* for her? Hunting her? Why her?

I flip to the last paper and my heart stops. This page is unlike the others. It's worn and yellowed with time. Torn on one edge.

Somehow, even after all these years, I'd recognize that tear anywhere. I'd bet my life that if I were to sneak back into the enforcer headquarters I'd managed to get into, right now, and pull their logbook, it would link up with the tear on the missing page from the day Mother died at the Descent. The page I had been hunting for. The page that has proof of her murder, and who killed her.

It reads:

> Laylis Daygar
> Killed on the command of High Lady Helena Ventall.
> Two children are said to survive her: Clara and Arina Daygar. They are to be apprehended immediately on sight.

My palm covers my mouth, though I don't think I could make a sound if I tried. I have my answer. I finally have a name to lay the blame of all my family's misfortune upon:

Alor's mother.

CHAPTER 55

Shock rings through me like the low toll of a distant bell. I'm not sure how much time I spend standing there in a dumbstruck state; in total disbelief that she would give this to me. Her mother is here. Right now.

Does she think I wouldn't target her? Does Alor put that much faith in our friendship and the shared debts to each other that she thinks I won't hunt her mother? That I'm so honorable?

The paper crumples in my trembling fist.

When Mother died, everything changed. Arina and I lost our safety and our home. Our lives became a never-ending loop of survival and vengeance. Arina's drive to find the truth led her deeper into the academy than ever before. Perhaps even to find the World to bring Mother back, just as I want to.

I pocket the papers, and my hand brushes against the cards. Six of them. Five real—Death, the Hierophant, Judgment, Temperance, and Fortune. Plus one forgery.

Slowly, I take them out and flip through them. I hold two seemingly identical copies of Death. It mocks me. Of all the cards, I found it the easiest to make as my other forgery.

The king having previously used the World. The fall of the past kingdom. Worldkeepers. Mother's death. Ravin knowing more than he let on while playing his own game. *Kaelis* . . .

Don't trust Oricalis, Mother whispers from beyond. Then I hear her, as gentle as a lullaby, *The World can do anything* . . . And if I have it, I'm changing everything. I'm fixing it all. My mind is made up.

I swap the two Death cards. The forgery goes with the stack of four back into my pocket. I twist and pry at the top of my corset, gaining enough space to wedge the real card around my ribs.

As subtly as possible, I reenter the ballroom. My hands are still shaking. Ears still ringing. Especially when my eyes instantly find Lady Ventall among the crowd. I slowly move on the edge of the room, finding a spot from which to observe her for a while. She's a tall, wiry woman with skin like her daughters' but hair in a more golden shade. The Death card burns against my side. Even though, as a gold card, it can't be used, I fantasize about trying to cast it her way. I might not know what it does, but I'd bet it's not good, and I'm ready to unleash all the pain I've been forced to carry for a lifetime.

Keep it together, I command myself. Head high, I tear my eyes away and fall into the flow of the room.

Lady Ventall might have been the one to order Mother's death, but did someone command her? She's the High Lady of Clan Tower—the closest clan to the crown. No doubt her hand moves at the king's whispers. Even Bristara said that they had proof of Clan Tower's involvement, but that Prince Ravin is the one charged with hunting the Worldkeepers. It could have been his command in an effort to obfuscate his involvement. If I kill her here and now, I risk not only never finding out the full story of who killed my mother and why, but also the World itself.

The latter is more important.

"While I appreciate how murderous intent lights your eyes, I do think you might want to control it before too many people take notice." Kaelis's voice and movements are as smooth as the silk lining of his coat.

"Murderous intent?" I'm sure my smile is positively sinister. "I've no idea what you're talking about."

"I take it your work went well?" His voice drops especially deep as he struggles to keep it from rising with anticipation.

Rather than answering, I close the gap between us and reach into my skirts. I transfer the five cards from my pocket to his, slipping them inside his jacket with a pat. Letting my knuckles drag across his chest. Looking up at him through my lashes, I inhale deeply, feeling the real Death card press against my ribs. So long as I have one of the true Major Arcana, no one in the Oricalis family can summon the World. I keep control over it and reserve the chance of using that legendary card for myself.

"It went perfectly. He should be none the wiser." And neither is Kaelis about my true intentions. I'll see where he puts the cards, then make more forgeries as I'm able to subtly collect more supplies. I'll steal them from under his nose, just like I did his father. If Bristara spoke true, Kaelis isn't summoning the World without the vessel card that only *I* know how to make. But I don't know enough about it to feel confident relying solely on that.

"Clara." He catches my hand, eyes searching mine. They narrow slightly. "What is it?"

"What is what?" I pull away a little; he holds fast. It's like he sees right through me. Like he knows every thought without me saying a word.

"There's something more."

"I couldn't be more excited for what's to come." I smile earnestly and mean every word. For a second, I think I've shaken his suspicion. But Kaelis continues to study me. It feels like his gaze is peeling the fabric from my body, that I'm exposed before him. It has me fighting a shiver.

"No . . . There's something more here." His other hand reaches for my face, cupping my cheek. It's somewhere between tender and commanding. "Tell me."

My lips part, but no words come. I must get away from him. Just being in his presence, I'm torn in two. Torn between all I know and feel and fear, and the want to trust him once more as I was starting to. To believe in him the way I wanted to believe.

"If you need me to kill someone, say the word and it shall be done." He gives me a slight smile: arrogant, wicked, and frustratingly appealing all at once. "The world is ours to design or destroy."

Before I can muster the words to say something, a commotion interrupts me. A group stands at the entrance of the ballroom, causing those gathered to fall to a hush. The crowd parts as they make their way through.

If I thought I was cold before, I'm completely numb now.

These are not Stellis, adorned with their raven and dove feathers. Nor are they the city enforcers that line the walls with their silver and green. These men and women are dressed in a drab gray-brown color that is imprinted in my worst nightmares.

At the center of the Halazar guards is Glavstone. A waking nightmare who has come back to haunt me with his now twisted and scarred face, remnants of Kaelis's abuse.

Kaelis wraps an arm around my waist, pulling me closer.

"My apologies for interrupting your soiree," Glavstone announces. The music halts, the band catching on to the abnormality. "But there is an escaped fugitive in your midst."

Whispers and gasps rip through the crowd. I try to move away. Kaelis holds fast.

"Don't run," he whispers harshly. "It'll only look worse. Stay by my side; I will protect you. I swear it to you, Clara."

I know running will look horrible. But it's all I can think of. *I won't go back there.* I can't.

"Don't let them take me." No sooner have I uttered those words than Glavstone's eyes swing to me.

"There she is." His face is filled with a hatred deeper than any I've ever beheld. With a lift of his finger, the guards move for me. It's like my first night in the academy all over again, but this time so much worse.

Kaelis positions himself between us but remains close at hand, no more than a step away. "Warden Glavstone, I will not have you sullying the good name of my bride-to-be."

The guards clearly don't know who to listen to, and they freeze mid-step. The whole room is as still and silent as they are. Waiting to see what will come next.

"Her 'good name' is not what you think." Glavstone thrusts a hand in my direction while addressing the room. "This woman has deceived you all. Her name is not Clara Redwin, but Clara Graysword."

Technically not that, either, I would've japed, if I weren't locked up with panic.

"She is the fugitive who escaped Halazar nearly a year ago, hiding in plain sight, and making a mockery of our royal family with her deception."

More gasps. Somehow, in the crowd, I find Luren. Her eyes are wide, mouth agape. I pull my attention from her before her shock can fill me with guilt I can't conceal.

"You would dare call into question my word?" Kaelis's voice has dropped to a deadly hush.

"Only to protect the sovereign I love so well."

"My brother is right." Ravin emerges from the crowd to our left, a good twenty paces away. The mere sight of him has rage igniting in me once more. "You make a bold and dangerous claim against a woman who is set to be the High Lady of the new Clan Hermit. I hope you wouldn't say such things without proof?" He's defending me? As if he weren't the person to put me in Halazar last time . . . But I don't let my guard down for a second.

"Your royal highness"—Glavstone approaches and bows, holding out a small envelope—"I present my evidence."

Do something, Kaelis, I beg with every beat of my heart. But he doesn't move. Why won't he move?

Ravin opens the envelope. What's inside is more than enough for the world to crack underneath my feet. Two sets of cards. One inked on the pitiful scraps of paper Glavstone would acquire off cutting room floors for me to ink his illegal cards upon. The other set inked with the pristine inks of the academy, the cards I'd worked so hard on for the Three of Swords Trials.

"I previously uncovered her illegally inking, even within Halazar. How she got the materials, I don't know," Glavstone says, like he wasn't the one telling me to ink. "I confiscated the cards she made in prison. The similarities to the cards she submitted during her Three of Swords Trials are apparent."

"Liar," I breathe. My inking completely changed during my time in the academy . . . didn't it? Was it enough? Does it even matter?

No . . . they'll use whatever proof—or lack thereof—they want.

"Quiet," Kaelis hisses.

Glavstone continues, "Forgive me, I thought I could yet reform her." He gives a dramatic sigh. "But perhaps we should be glad of her ways. How else could we have uncovered the truth?"

"This is, indeed, irrefutable evidence," Ravin says finally, passing on the cards to his father, who comes to a stop at his side. But he seems irate. *Does he know?* My heart beats in my throat, drawing nausea.

"I would like to see these cards for myself." Kaelis moves, leaving me and crossing toward his family. "I am the one who oversees the Arcanists of Oricalis. I should be the judge of their similarities."

"Brother, would you not be biased?" Ravin smirks.

"Seize her," Glavstone commands the guards, taking the opportunity of my protector no longer blocking their path.

The guards heed his command, led by none other than Savan. His eyes shine with a cruel delight that says, *Finally I have you.* Ravin steps around Kaelis at the same time, positioning himself to keep Kaelis from getting to me, if he should try.

I take a step backward. Their hands reach for me. Suddenly there are hundreds of hands lurching from a prison cell that's been overcome by a grime and filth that I, somehow, have yet to be able to wash off my skin. Off my very soul.

"Clara—" My name is so full of warning. Kaelis's voice is the only thing that could cut through the swelling panic. But it's too late.

"It's time to come home, wretch," Savan snarls. Glavstone looks on with uncontainable glee.

Turning on my heel, I run. I almost make it to the door that I entered from. But the guards are faster. They grab me, and a scream rips from my throat.

The Ten of Wands rises from my deck. I don't even remember calling it, but it bursts into ten tongues of fire that slam into the men and women holding me. They tumble backward. Fabric rips as they try to hang on to me. My skin is a constellation of bruises and scratches.

"Was that the Ten of Wands?"

"Couldn't be."

"Isn't she just a first year?"

Whispers sting like bees. Never have I felt so exposed. They all see me. They know who I am—what I am. They'll find out everything if I stay.

I keep trying to move forward for the door as if it opens to another world for me to slip into. Somewhere I can be safe, and not just a back hall where there's probably already a dozen Stellis waiting.

Ravin moves into my field of view, a card in hand. Silver flashes before my eyes. It's a Major, but I can't tell what. "Enough."

"No." I barely have time to say it. My body and magic move on instinct. A silvered card rises from my deck. The whinny of a distant horse echoes throughout the hall and weaves among the crowd's gasps and murmurs.

Our cards explode into a shower of sparks and glowing dust at the same time. Ravin's face twists, mouth opening, but whatever he was about to say or do is lost to me. Light shimmers around me, and the Chariot whisks me away.

CHAPTER 56

I land on the packed earth of the townhome's courtyard with as much grace as if I had fallen from the sky. The wind is knocked from me. My head reels. Silas made using his card look seamless, but now I know there's a learning curve to it. I double over, retching. Not sure if it's from the teleportation or from the feeling of the guards' hands on me, trying to force me back to Halazar.

I'll die before I go back there, I think as I wipe my lips with the back of my hand, heart still pounding but mouth set in a determined line.

"Everyone. Lounge. Now!" I throw open the back door and shout, praying they're back. That they didn't encounter any issues.

Feet pound the stairs. The floor above me rattles. I'm pacing in front of the now-dark fireplace as they enter.

"Clara?" Jura gasps softly, taking in my haggard form. I heave a sigh of relief, my hard exterior momentarily cracking as they all appear, still with makeup crusted on their faces from our deception at the ball.

"How did you—" Gregor begins to say.

"What?" Ren speaks at the same time.

"What happened?" Bristara cuts through the rest of them much like her sharp eyes piercing the night. There's worry and fear in that stare. But enough compassion that I almost crumple like a child, desperately searching for the embrace of a mother long gone. For someone to hold me and tell me it'll all be all right. But there's no time to fall into selfish comfort. Not when time is running out for all of us.

"They know." So much is encompassed in those two words: *They know I'm a Major. They know I'm the one who escaped Halazar. They know I'm done being their puppet on strings.* Judging from the horror that creeps across Bristara's face, relaxing all the small muscles and smoothing out the hard lines at the corners of her mouth, she understands.

"We're leaving through the mountains tonight," she announces. "Gather what you can."

Everyone springs into motion. Not one question is asked. Save for Jura's: "Fresh clothes?"

"Please." My feet move on their own while my mind is a city away, back in the dark halls of Arcana Academy.

Kaelis . . . He told me not to run. He was right, I knew he was. But what else could I have done? *It's over now, isn't it?* Our sham of an engagement. My time at the academy. Probably us working together— what we had . . . whatever it really was. Kaelis and my indulgences should be the last of my worries right now, but my mind returns to them with every step. I press my hand into my corset as we begin to ascend the stairs, feeling the Death card where it's still safe against my ribs. He won't uncover my treachery until I'm long gone. Then we will truly be enemies.

I halt, mid-step.

There's someone else in those dark halls of the academy. Someone who Ravin now knows has been helping me.

"Silas," I whisper. Jura turns. I look over my own shoulder, back to Bristara. "I escaped because of him; Ravin and Kaelis both know it." I don't know what Ravin will do to him, but I know it won't be good.

"Clara—"

"I can't leave him behind," I interrupt, already hearing the mix of warning and scolding in her tone. "Not after all he did to help us." I promised I wouldn't let harm come to him.

"You can't go back there." Bristara takes another step and, with her height, we're eye to eye even though I'm higher on the stairs. "If you do, they will never let you leave again."

"They'll have to find and catch me first, and I've had a year to learn the hidden and forgotten passages of the fortress. I only need to make it in and to Silas. He'll get us out."

Bristara opens her mouth to speak, but I watch the determination evaporate from her face and turn into frustration. "Your mind is set, isn't it?"

"Unequivocally."

"Go, then. As fast as your feet can carry you. There's no time to waste on argument."

"You'll move faster in trousers." Jura stops me before I can bolt down the stairs. I'm forced to agree.

I don't waste time fully changing out of my dress. There are too many laces to bother, and I don't want to risk the Death card leaving my person. I slide on a sleek pair of black trousers and then take a knife to the skirts just underneath where they seam into the corset, cutting and ripping them loose. I tear free the remnants of my lace sleeves right before Jura hands me a loose shirt and slips a hooded cloak over my shoulders. She fastens it at my neck, and I slip my arms through the slits to keep it on me during what I know will be a sprint.

"We lost you once, Clara." Her eyes meet mine. "Don't let us lose you again."

"I won't," I vow.

Her fingers tremble. I catch them before they fall and yank her to me. Our arms tighten around each other in a breathless embrace.

"Lavender scones," I whisper into her ear. "That's what I want when we're all in whatever safe place is next."

"Be there to eat them."

"I will. Till then, don't weep for an empty coffin."

She says the last part in time with me as I release her. I don't waste another second. I'm down the stairs, nearly out the door, when Bristara stops me by calling my name. She stands by the wall of the stairs, a secret door unhinged. I hadn't even noticed the seams in the paneling of the wood under the stairs.

"You'll have an hour, no more. Then this whole place is going down." There's a spark in her eyes that promises to become flames that will soon engulf the townhome. For a second, the errant notion that *she* might have been the one to destroy the club races through my mind. But I banish it. Bristara wouldn't have had a reason then. At least, not one that I can think of . . . "We can't risk being found, not when this passage directly connects to the tunnels underneath and out of the city."

I've seen this before. A woman, standing by a secret door underneath the stairs. The notion almost has me staggering. It's not Bristara, but Mother. Arina, just a babe, is in her arms. *We must go,* she whispers, *your father will come soon. We can't let him find us.* I was small, barely more than a toddler. *Be strong for me, Clara. This is all nothing more than a bad dream.*

"Was this my old home?" I whisper.

Bristara's eyes go wide.

The papers that were in the pocket of the skirts I just cut off—papers I entrusted to Jura. The High Lady of Clan Tower was the one to request my mother's death. The symbol of Clan Tower in the room Twino had made into his workshop. *You don't know of any other homes abandoned by noble clans we can take over, do you?* Jura had said of this place.

No . . . no, it can't be. An image begins to form in my mind. A history from before my memories. The money was gone. Mother had left the comfort of it. Father "abandoned" us. But, what if it was the other way around? What if it wasn't because my father didn't care, but because of the people around him?

"My name, the one Mother told us never to say, Cheval—"

"Never, *never* say your real name," Bristara cuts me off with a growl, evoking all the force Mother wielded whenever she impressed upon us the importance of secrecy about our name. Now that secrecy takes on new meaning. A reason why she'd fight so hard to hide it.

"Am I a Clan Tower bastard?" The horrible question slips out without a thought.

Bristara closes the gap between us, grabbing my arm. "Don't ask questions that you don't want to know the answers to."

But I want the answers. I want all of them. Mother never spoke of Father; is this why? Bristara said she was never that close to Mother, but did she know my father and that's how she got this place? Was it because of him—because of my mother's association with him, and his with Arina's and my existence—that she was murdered? I've a hundred more questions, but they lodge in my throat, refusing to release. Because . . .

"I don't fucking have time for this." I wrench my arm from Bristara's grasp, shooting her a glare. The anger might be misplaced. I don't know. But it's overflowing. "When I'm back—when we're all safe—tell me *everything*. Worldkeepers. Mother. My bloodline. Everything you know. No more secrets."

"No more secrets." Bristara means it when she says it. With a noise of frustration, I start for the front door. "An hour, Clara."

"I won't even need that long." I shut the door behind me, adjust my hood, and begin to run through the city.

I run like the enforcers are on my tail. Like all of Halazar's guards are a pack of wolves that have my scent. I run through the streets that I've known since I was a girl. All too familiar. Painfully so now.

Was this my home?

What would've been my life, were it not for the machinations of Clan Tower and the crown they serve? My nails dig crescents into my palms, and I run faster, nothing more than a blur in the night. I follow in Arina's footsteps, in my mother's . . . in the footsteps of countless people who I'm sure came before me. People who also wanted to scream at the cruelty of it all. At how the whole world feels like a powder mill and we are the ingredients, hammered constantly into dust by an unseen hand that perpetually looms above us.

I run until I reach the ruined entry to the passageway at the end of the bridge. One hand on my side, the other supporting me on a piece of rubble, I hunch over, nearly retching for a second time. I'm burning from the inside out. Everything in me is screaming. But I'm silent other than my ragged breaths. I stare at the academy looming on the horizon, a blackened silhouette against a dark sky. Underneath my palm, the Death card remains. Like a promise and a threat.

Through the gate, I descend one more time into the shadow-filled tunnels of this forsaken place. Across the bridge and into the den of the man who lifted me to nobility . . . not knowing the blood of nobles might already be in my veins. *Will I see Kaelis again? Do I even want to?* A part of me aches for what could have been had the fates smiled more kindly upon us. But I'm not sure if that part would ever—could ever—win out.

Fate puts that theory to the test.

Kaelis stands in my path. I stop in my tracks, blinking, as if he's some specter I've summoned with a thought. He doesn't vanish. Merely stares.

Perhaps he knew I would come here. But even if he did . . . the likelihood of him finding the path I'd take in this vast monstrosity of a structure is next to none. But here we are, bathed in moonlight through cobweb-laced windows, at opposite ends of a short hall. His dark eyes meet the embers of mine.

My fingers twitch with magic. But no cards rise from my deck. He doesn't move either. The air is still, and time itself holds its breath.

I should have admired him more when I had the chance. I should have taken in every delicate detail of the crimson stitching. Of the silvered thread that holds fast the buttons of his jacket. The way his hair, now an oil-slicked purple in the crystalline light, shadows his eyes. I should have, shamelessly, enjoyed him with reckless abandon more often while I still could. Should have damned all my morals and qualms and given in to wickedness and indulgence before knowing too much ruined whatever chance we would have.

He curses under his breath, looking away. The trance is broken. It's almost like permission.

I go to leave. Kaelis moves simultaneously. I freeze in place. He halts as well. *Run,* part of me whispers. *Stay,* a treacherous little voice implores.

"I'm not going back with you." I break the silence.

"You can't now." Kaelis moves once more. The wide strides of his steps swiftly eat away at the distance between us. "You made sure of that."

"I'm not letting you take me to Halazar."

He comes to a stop before me. The air between us is instantly charged. I stare up at him, searching the anger that furrows his brow. The pain that's alight in his eyes.

"I swore to you, time and again, that I never would," Kaelis says softly. He truly means it.

I inhale slowly, wishing my chest would brush against his. Fighting the urge to grab him, I say, "You really are going to let me leave?"

"If I must."

"You know I can't stay . . . not with you." My voice has dropped to a whisper. Though the conviction doesn't leave it.

"I know." Yet, he reaches for me, and I don't move away. Kaelis's hand hovers just off my face. His knuckles brush my cheek, and his attention falls to my mouth. Fingertips glide down, pushing back the wide neck of the shirt to expose the swell of my breasts still straining against the ragged corset top. I can't stop an inhale and the slight arch of my back that accompanies his motion. Even as the world around me crumbles, my body betrays me. I lean in to him.

His fingers glide around my waist, and, for a second, my breath hitches not from his touch but from fear that he felt the card. But Kaelis's focus remains on me. The way he looks at me is as if I am the most magnificent thing he's ever beheld. As if the world begins and ends here.

"You have everything you need from me. We're over." I don't know if I'm talking more for myself or for him.

"I know," he repeats. But this time he doesn't sound convinced. I open my mouth to emphasize it, but he speaks before I can. "We never were anything to begin with. Never could be anything . . . not in this lifetime. But give me one last time."

"What?"

"Let me kiss you one last time when you know me as I am. When you see the man beneath the cards and the names, the crowns and the power." Even as he's asking, Kaelis is leaning in.

I do nothing to stop it.

The kiss is agonizingly slow. Our bodies finally meet not with a crash, but with a defeated sigh. His other hand comes to rest on my face, holding me in place with a featherlight touch when the rest of the world couldn't even with threats and chains.

I take what fate has offered and indulge in this final moment. I savor the taste of him as his tongue slips into my mouth. His scent envelops me like his arm around my waist. The fire within me collapses into ash. The moon blinks out of existence and, for a moment, there's nothing but darkness. Cold, unending, glorious darkness. A place to hide from everything I know and everything that has yet to be.

My hands glide over him, seeking purchase on his lapels. I hold him tighter. The fire returns. It isn't until he pulls away that I realize my fingers have wrapped themselves around his throat, the pads digging in lightly.

Kaelis tilts his head to the side, amusement alight in his eyes. "Do it."

I could. He'd let me. There's a madness to that glint.

"I'm a relic of a bygone era," he continues. "A cursed man with no future who shouldn't have existed in the first place. If anyone will be my downfall, it's you."

How many times did I swear to be as much? My fingers tremble but don't move. They're little more than a caress on his ghostly pale skin.

"No, I won't kill you yet." My fingers uncurl, one by one. I release him, even though I don't know why. I ease away.

"If not now, then when?" A slight smirk tugs on his lips. I hate how much I love it.

"When I'm done with you." I turn on my heel, beginning to walk away.

"You'll never be done with me," Kaelis says with all the arrogance in the world. "I will haunt you from this world into the next."

I don't answer. I don't even look over my shoulder. The echo of his words emphasizes their point. Once I'm out of view, I rest my hand on my side over Death. He won't have control over any world, so long as I carry this.

CHAPTER 57

The way to Silas is second nature to me by now. I push Kaelis from my thoughts; I've wasted enough time on him. The notion that he might have been intentionally stalling me has my feet moving even faster. He'd know that Silas had given me the Chariot, too. What if Kaelis was on his way back from punishing Silas?

"Silas!" I throw open his door. The man in question nearly levitates with surprise. I don't bother hiding my sigh of relief. "Good, you're still here."

"Where else would I be?"

"Not here, shortly." I cross to his desk and begin to take the liberty of packing his inking supplies. I've seen him do it enough times that I know what goes into the bag. "We're leaving."

"Leaving? What? Clara"—he grabs my hands, stopping me—"what's happened?"

I can't look him in the eyes, so I stare at my hands instead. "I'm sorry." The silence that follows is unbearable.

"You used it, didn't you?"

I nod.

"Ravin saw."

Another nod.

"He knows you're helping me." I manage to pull my chin up. "The club is moving tonight. We're all leaving through the mountains. Come with us and—"

"I can't," Silas says gently, taking both my hands in his and squeezing them. "You know I can't."

"Your family?" I suspect. He affirms with a nod. "Silas, we'll find them. But you won't be reunited at all if you're dead."

"Nor will I be if Ravin kills them." He wears a sad smile, one of defeat. "If I go with you, he'll kill them. If I stay, then I can claim you stole the card from me and beg forgiveness."

My knuckles are white, hands shaking. "He will never set them free no matter what you do. Silas, please. We can find your family together and save them. If you leave, you'll keep them safer. He's not going to kill them as long as you're alive because he wants you—needs you. Your card is too powerful."

"He'll find the next Chariot if I die." Silas is so bloody resigned it makes me want to fight even harder.

"It takes time that he won't want to spend."

"They have the Hierophant in their service; his innate ability can help locate Majors."

"Do you want to die?" The question comes out harsh, but I mean it.

"Of course not." He seems taken aback that I'd ask.

"Then come with me." I'm not going to have Silas's blood on my hands. I'm not going to risk it. "He'll use your family as leverage to force you to come back, and that'll be his error. That will be how we find them."

Silas seems to brace himself, his attention leaving me and sweeping across the room. I wonder what he sees in this small place. Is it all the hours he was forced to spend here? How much he committed to this place when, all along, he could've left?

I see in him the same man I saw when we first met. Nothing has changed. He still fears the outside world. He's still trapped in stasis by Ravin's cruelty. I can't leave him like this. I couldn't from the day I first met him; I won't start now.

"Trust me, please." My words seem to finally make it through to him. Silas swallows his fear and nods. "Good. The club is leaving soon; I need you to get us to the townhome."

He packs quickly and lightly. When he's done, the room has been turned over. Clothes are scattered. Drawers have been emptied. I assist with the inking supplies I'd started gathering, shoving them all into the bag.

"Are you ready?" I ask, holding out a hand.

"As I'll ever be." All the apprehension in the world is in his eyes. "You're certain you'll be able to help my family?"

"I swear it on my life."

"Right, then."

A silver-inked card rises into the air between us. The whinny of a horse reverberates through the air. The world flashes, light and then dark once more. As always, Silas teleports us with a deft hand, and I've none of the dizziness that I'd experienced when I used the card.

We're in the garden of the townhome, not far from where Arina was laid to rest. *I'm going to have to say goodbye to her again,* I realize. Just as I go to cross over to the flowers that mark her grave, a commotion rises from within the house.

Silas and I both turn toward the shouting.

Right as we do, the windows explode.

CHAPTER 58

Glass turns nearly to dust, and we are thrown back. We land in the garden that Ren tended to so dutifully. The force scatters a rain of leaves from the lone tree that shades the courtyard. Fire and ice dance within the hollow windowpanes, a battle unfolding inside.

A deep ache sears my side. Ears ringing, I pry myself from the wet ground. A tugging in my abdomen is followed by a sickening *pop*. My hand moves on instinct and comes away stained crimson. I was thrown onto one of the small iron fences that line the flower beds.

More magic flares within the house. I blink, trying to get my eyes to focus as my head spins. *Heal yourself. Queen of Cups.* I cast the card with a thought, and my flesh knits.

"Silas." I work my way to standing, tugging on his elbow. He's in even more of a daze than I was. Judging from the trail of blood running down the side of his face, he struck his head on the pavers. The physical wound is small, and the Queen of Cups can't do anything for ailments of the mind. He's barely able to sit before he doubles over and empties the contents of his stomach.

Not good.

The back door to the courtyard being thrown open draws my attention from Silas. At the same time, there's movement in the window frame that leads to the lounge. Drab brown combines with flashes of silver on green. Now I'm the one about to throw up. Halazar guards and city enforcers. *Here.* No doubt hunting me. Brought to my friends' doorstep because of me.

I release Silas and step forward. Cards fly from my deck. My assailants' eyes turn to me and there are no words. Only magic.

One of my cards disintegrates midair. I don't see who used the Ten of Swords, but it tells me there are powerful Arcanists among my enemies. I let other cards fly with reckless abandon. A fiery explosion bursts from my Ace of Wands. I follow it up with the Seven of Wands—the card splits into seven tongues of flame that surround me. Another twitch of my fingers, and a brief moment of second-guessing myself.

The Nine of Wands disintegrates into glowing stardust that coats my skin. I'm now on a timer. For nine minutes, I won't feel pain or fatigue . . . but that doesn't mean it's not there.

I launch myself forward.

"She's here!" one of the enforcers shouts.

The Eight of Wands falls from my deck, sparking around my boots. My speed is enhanced for the next eight minutes. With a flick of my wrist at the same time, I summon a trusty blade with the Five of Swords. The enforcer barely has time to look at me before I skewer him on the weapon, clean through the chest.

Fire pops at my side. One of the seven tongues of flame fizzles out, blocking a spear of ice lobbed at me by a guard. I twist, shifting my focus to the next, dispatching him with the aid of the Four of Cups.

I cast aside all caution and reason. My body will feel like it's been torn apart after this much card work. But there won't be anything left of my enemies at that point—it won't matter how exhausted I am.

Another burst of flame—another protective shield disappears from the air around me. I shift, faster than the next enforcer can follow. My blade glides across his throat. I spin, instantly slaying the next through the door.

There's a seemingly endless stream of guards and enforcers. But the layout of the townhome funnels them, preventing too many from getting outside at a time. That doesn't stop one guard from jumping through the remnants of a window in an attempt to flank me.

As soon as he does, ten tongues of cold flame descend on him and he falls to the ground with an audible *slam,* as if an invisible box of bricks were dropped on his head. The man twitches, eyes rolling back in his head. He doesn't get up again.

My attention darts back to Silas. He leans against the tree for support. One hand clutches his head, as if the exertion of using the Ten of Wands nearly tore him in two.

"Clara!" Bristara shouts from within. There's a flare of magic that simultaneously draws my attention back. She's at the far end of the hall, by the front door, fending off others trying to get inside. "Go!"

The hidden door she opened earlier is currently being held by Jura. She's assisting Bristara in trying to keep additional enforcers from getting in without leaving her post. When Jura catches my eye, she makes a beckoning motion.

I look back to Bristara. "But—"

"Go!" she repeats. No sooner has Bristara said it than an enforcer nearly overruns her, getting in a solid attack that leaves Bristara burned and staggering.

I turn around and rush to Silas, grabbing him by the wrist. His eyes still lack focus, his movements jerky. "We have to run."

"It's too late," Silas murmurs as he hobbles alongside me, a far cry from the run I'd been hoping for. "He knows . . . he knows . . ."

"We have a way out. They won't catch us."

"Too late," he whispers over and over. "My name . . . my name . . ."

I ignore him. Fear, panic, and head trauma aren't the best mix for confidence. I'm going to get him out of here. I pass Silas to Jura.

"Take him and go."

"Clara—" Jura starts to object.

"I'm getting Bristara and will be right behind you." The shadows of the rest of them are deeper in the passageway. Jura is about to object, but another burst of magic has her flinching. I give a confident nod.

She wraps an arm around Silas and pulls him inside.

"Wait, no. What about Clara?" Silas looks over his shoulder as Jura pulls him farther into the darkness of the stairwell.

"She'll catch up," Jura says.

"No. Clara." Silas twists. "You don't understand. It doesn't matter. Ravin will kill me now!"

Gregor emerges from down the stairs, physically manhandling Silas away.

Holding out my hand, I look at the faint sheen still covering it. The magic from the Nine of Wands is nearly faded. But I have a few minutes left. It'll be enough time.

Every movement is purposeful. No wasted energy. Cards rise from my ever-thinning deck, fanning out around me and the last two remaining shields from the Seven of Wands that hover over my shoulders, illuminating my face. I imagine myself to be some winged creature of fire and shadow—destruction wrought from magic and given the form of a woman.

Luck is on my side. It always has been. It always will be.

I launch myself into the fray.

"What're you doing?" Bristara barks.

"I'm not leaving you." I drop the sword I'd summoned in the courtyard and immediately call upon another. It's my last Five of Swords in my deck. Two short daggers appear in my hands, much better suited for close-quarters combat. I swipe for an enforcer. He blocks me with his forearm, casting a Four of Cups. One of my remaining two shields of flame consumes the haze before it draws me to slumber. I take the opportunity to swipe with my other blade, catching his chest. He tries for another card. I follow up with a stab, and that does it.

Bristara grabs my arm as I round for the next one. She jerks me toward her. "*You* are far more important than me. With Arina gone, you are the last one who knows the ancient inking. You must—"

"Is that so?" A voice, cold and cruel, cuts through the chaos. For a second, everyone stills. Ravin stands beyond the open door, flanked by Stellis. I vaguely recognize one from earlier tonight in the back halls. "Excellent. I suspected you were the last loose end, but the confirmation is much appreciated."

"Go." Bristara pushes me back.

Everything happens in a second.

It feels like an eternity.

I stumble, recovering quickly. But Ravin is too fast. Eight blades of swirling light and shadow pin Bristara in place. Ravin's eyes are alight with something that I can only describe as pure evil. Another card rises. Bristara strains against the magic, her own deck shuddering in its holster—the cards refuse to move; they're just as pinned by Ravin's magic as she is.

He's going to kill her.

But then his attention shifts to me. The card hovering in the air over Ravin's shoulder is silver. Bristara screams. She can see what it is better than I can since she's closer. But even from where I've stumbled, I make out the card's design. I know it all too well.

Because it's identical to the card pressed against my side.

A knight stands among a field of white roses. Half coated in armor. The other half is nothing but exposed bone. On his flesh and blood, the roses wither. But they thrive on the opposite side—vining up the femur and trellising through the exposed rib cage.

Death.

I let out a shout and the only card I can think of that might help. A Major against a Major. *Turn the wheel,* I beg fate and fortune. The last time I called upon this power, it destroyed another Major card. *Let it happen again.*

"Clara Daygar." His card bursts with a flash of light, radiant and terrible. At the same time, my own card spins, faster and faster. Time itself seems to sputter. A strange, mechanical ticking sound resonates in the back of my mind. The world blurs at its edges, and it feels as if the ground moves underneath me, just enough that I'm forced to take a step to stabilize myself.

The light fades, exposing Ravin's scowl. I destroyed his card. Kaelis told me that non-Majors can use Major cards only once with the blessing of the Hierophant. Ravin wasted his use.

This is my chance.

I reach for Bristara, and, right as I do, she falls back into my arms. I catch her clumsily, staggering. We tumble to the ground. Her body in my arms. Limp. Deadweight.

"No . . ." I whisper. "No, this wasn't . . . Bristara." I shake her. "Bristara!"

The world is still, save for my shuddering breath. The Stellis at Ravin's sides are poised. Unflinching. The reinforcements clamor to a stop behind him.

"Bristara," I croak. The woman who took me in. The woman who never tried to mother me yet had become a guardian and a mentor. My chest is hollowed out to make room for the screams of rage that are burning up my throat. The fire is present in my eyes when I jerk my chin up at the sound of Ravin's footsteps drawing near.

He *tsks* with his tongue. "Such an unpredictable power. So helpful at times. Useless at others. Spin the wheel of fate and one never knows where things will land."

I release Bristara. As much as I want to cling to her and weep, it won't do any good. She's gone. But Ravin has used his greatest weapon.

Fuck finding out the truth and every last detail of my mother's death, *I'm killing him now.*

I stand.

Ravin chuckles and tilts his head to the side, pausing to assess me as if I'm little more than an amusement. "You think you can fight me? As you are?"

"I will kill you if it's the last thing I do," I swear.

"Doubtful." Another card rises from the deck strapped to Ravin's biceps. "We won. You lost. The world is as it is, and nothing will ever change that. Not you, and certainly not my accursed brother."

Just as I go to summon a card from my deck, I realize what card he's called upon. It turns, exposing the inking. *Silver.*

Another Death card.

"You . . ." Only Majors can use other Majors' cards without the blessing of the Hierophant. Which means Ravin is a Major. But not just any Major . . . the one who I'd always assumed was left behind at court. Hidden away. *No, King Oricalis hid him in plain sight.* I whisper, "You're Death."

Ravin merely smiles. "Clara Daygar," he repeats the name again.

The card bursts, a thousand howls of spirits long gone tearing through my mind. But they're distant. The magic washes over me, leaving nothing but a clammy chill on my skin akin to walking through a graveyard at night.

The crown prince stares at me. Shock instantly crumbles beneath the weight of rage. Without warning, he grabs me by the throat. I clutch at his forearms. The last of my cards rise from my deck, instantly destroyed by Ravin and the Stellis behind him.

"Which name is fake? Clara? Daygar? Both?" Ravin snarls as he squeezes. I gasp for air. I claw and scratch, but the Nine of Wands has worn off, and all the exhaustion I'd dulled hits me with the same force as Silas's Ten of Wands on the enforcer's head earlier. "What is your name?" I wheeze. He shakes me. "Tell me your name!"

I wheeze again, trying to form words as my face grows hot from the lack of air. Ravin eases some. I move my lips slightly. The prince leans forward, as if trying to hear better.

"My real name is . . ." I rasp. He leans closer still. "Lady Go-fuck-yourself." I bring a knee up into his groin, *hard.*

Ravin drops me, and I stumble. I scramble for Bristara's deck. She still has cards. If I touch them, I can know them, and if I know them, I can call upon them.

But the prince recovers quickly. He slams into me, sending me tumbling. His boot meets my side, and, for a second, I fear he'll know I have his gold card. But he seems none the wiser.

"It's fine. It's fine." He laughs wildly, smoothing his hair from his face. "I can kill you the old-fashioned way."

He needs to know my true name to kill me, I realize. It must be a rule of the Death card. *Guard your name at all costs,* Mother whispers from beyond the grave. Protecting me to this day.

Any sense of triumph is short-lived as Ravin kicks me again. And again. Each time with more force than the last. I gasp for air as his toes sink into my stomach.

Instinct has me curling into a ball to shield myself. But I'm utterly at his mercy. All I can do is endure. And he's enjoying himself far too much to stop anytime soon . . .

He stomps on my side, heel digging into my already bruised ribs. There's a distinct crunch and a pop that has me screaming. His eyes shine with perverse pleasure.

The prince does it again. Then rolls me over to do the same to the other side.

I'm wheezing, gasping. Fighting bile out of fear I'll choke myself if I throw up now because I won't have the strength to get the vomit out of my mouth. My whole abdomen is torn from the inside. I clench my teeth for every hit. Bracing.

Make it stop, I plead silently. But I'm no stranger to pain, and I will push through it rather than giving him the satisfaction of seeing me begging for mercy. *Kaelis . . .* The second-born prince appears only in my mind, as if I could will him into the present. *Save me, please.*

Without warning, Ravin stops and staggers back. Heavy, ragged breaths mirror my own. Involuntary trembles rip through me. I'm cold all over. Cold enough that I wonder just how much blood I've lost . . .

I blink, trying to see what made him stop. A figure looms, and, for a quivering, hopeful breath, I think maybe Kaelis did come. Maybe even after what felt like goodbye, he found me. *He came for me.* A sob almost escapes me. But then my vision sharpens just enough to bring the shining, silver-plated boots of a heavily armored Stellis into focus. I try to turn my head to see who it is, but my body doesn't respond.

The world fades in and out, more the latter with each passing second. It's distant.

". . . think you're doing?" Ravin snarls.

"My prince . . . more valuable alive?" The voice is masculine. Vaguely familiar. But it's not Kaelis. My heart sinks. Why would he come for me after our goodbye? "After . . . force her to ink her card . . . nothing else . . . draw out Kaelis." I can't place who's speaking. My ears are ringing too loudly. Head swimming in its own fluid.

Who would stand up for me? Though keeping me alive now might be more of a cruelty than a kindness . . .

There are a few more words exchanged. I strain to listen but miss almost all of them.

"Very well." Ravin doesn't sound pleased. "Take her."

Clanking plate surrounds me. My battered form is hoisted upright. I'm completely suspended between two Stellis. Blood and bile drip from my slack jaw.

Another silver Death card hovers in Ravin's palm. "No loose ends," he murmurs. "Silas Erentu." The card flashes, and when the light fades, a ghostly outline of Silas runs above Ravin's outstretched hand. The projection of Silas looks over his shoulder, talking to unseen figures. *The rest of the club*, I realize; they're still with him. None of them knows that the eyes of Death itself are set on Silas.

I try to open my mouth to object. To beg, if that's what it takes. But no sound escapes me. Silas . . . he was loyal until the end. He knew my name and never gave it to Ravin. He put all his faith in me, and what did it get him?

Ravin clenches his fist, and the specter of Silas seizes and collapses just as Bristara did.

Dead. Because of me.

The last of any fight leaves me. I'm too weak. Too unarmed. Too broken. I spun the wheel, and now I've no choice but to surrender to whatever future awaits me.

My luck has finally abandoned me, and I am truly alone.

Or so I thought . . . But then Ravin turns and addresses the Stellis carrying me. Halting them. I barely have the strength to lift my head to watch his lips sound the words:

"This time, she goes into the dungeons of Halazar. Somewhere *deep*. Somewhere no one, but especially not my brother, will ever find her." A smile slithers across his lips, so cruel it transforms Ravin's face into something inhuman. "Put her with her sister."

THE STORY WILL CONTINUE
IN BOOK TWO OF
THE ARCANA ACADEMY SERIES

GLOSSARY

Cards listed as they have appeared so far.

WANDS SPELLS

- Ace of Wands: Channels the elemental magic of fire for small to moderate magical acts.
- Two of Wands: If the caster is lost, the Two of Wands creates a tongue of flame that sparks in the direction of where the caster wants to go. After offering the direction, the flame disappears.
- Three of Wands: Safety in travel. Blessing of ships and temporary protection when traveling.
- Four of Wands: Blessing unions between people—the card that is used for engagements and marriages.
- Five of Wands: Sparks anger/agitation/confusion/mental discord in another person.
- Seven of Wands: A "shield" of wands—summons seven spectral flames that surround the individual and guard them from seven attacks/blows that would otherwise hit them.
- Eight of Wands: Enhanced movement and speed for eight minutes.

- Nine of Wands: For nine minutes, the individual does not feel pain or fatigue. However, they are still exerting energy and are still capable of being harmed.
- Ten of Wands: Creates a weight that crashes down upon an individual.

CUPS SPELLS

- Ace of Cups: Channels the elemental magic of water for small to moderate magical acts.
- Four of Cups: Casts sleep/sluggishness upon a person.
- Five of Cups: Fills a person's mind with their greatest doubts.
- Eight of Cups: Removal of a skill for eight minutes. For example, taking away the knowledge of how to effectively fight with a sword.
- Nine of Cups: Fulfillment of a minor wish, such as not getting a stain on a dress at an event.
- Queen of Cups: Can heal/cure any physical wound/ailment—except fatal ones.

COINS SPELLS

- Ace of Coins: Channels the elemental magic of earth for small to moderate magical acts.
- Two of Coins: The ability to cast and maintain two spells simultaneously.
- Three of Coins: Construction of small and simple structures or modification of items. All requisite material must be present.
- Four of Coins: Momentary and minor control of the weather.
- Five of Coins: Removal of something tangible.
- Page of Coins: Grants an individual of the caster's choosing expertise in a skill for a day.

SWORDS SPELLS

- Ace of Swords: Channels the elemental magic of air for small to moderate magical acts.
- Two of Swords: Creates confusion.

- Four of Swords: Minor mending of physical objects and small healing (scratches, bruises, etc.).
- Five of Swords: Summons a magic weapon that will not disappear and must be wielded until it has drawn blood, or if another card is cast that would destroy the blade.
- Six of Swords: Helps an individual emotionally overcome a challenge or mental block.
- Eight of Swords: Calls upon eight spectral swords that will trap a person in place.
- Nine of Swords: Once contact is made with the target, nine spears of light will pin the individual in place, allowing the casting Arcanist to ask them nine questions of their choosing. Any lies the target tries to speak will elicit pain, becoming more painful over time.
- Ten of Swords: Destruction of another card (but not a Major).
- Knight of Swords: Inflicts pain on another by way of magic blades.

MAJOR SPELLS

- The Magician (I): Calls upon and combines all the elements to manifest an object into existence from nothing.
- The High Priestess (II): Peers into someone's mind and learns their innermost thoughts, secrets, and truths.
- The Hierophant (V): Can "bless" a regular Arcanist with the ability to use a Major Arcana card once. The blessing lasts an indefinite length of time but disappears after the regular Arcanist uses a Major. Can be recast after the blessing is gone.
- The Lovers (VI): Can make two people fall in love if their true names are known.
- The Chariot (VII): Teleportation between two locations that are known to the caster.
- Wheel of Fortune (X): A manipulation of luck. A turn of fate. The caster can ask for something to happen, but ultimately fate decides what's given and how.
- The Hanged Man (XII): Traps a target in a mental prison of the Hanged Man's design. The target can experience pain but cannot die.
- Death (XIII): Kills anyone, anywhere, if the caster knows their target's true name and face.

- The Sun (XIX): Removal of pain from an individual—physical or mental.
- Judgment (XX): Can revive someone from the dead within five minutes of dying.

The World (XXI): The ultimate wish. Can utter a single request that can change anything, or everything, about the world to fit the caster's desires.

ACKNOWLEDGMENTS

Where do I even begin? This book began as nothing more than a little seed of a notion in my mind ages ago. It's been quietly growing year by year, with each errant thought and idea. I never knew when it would take root and bloom, but I certainly never expected it'd be like this.

So many people have touched this book at every stage, helping to bring it to life. I'm sure I will forget to mention someone who impacted this story along the way, and that thought breaks my heart. Let me apologize in advance for that, and then start at the beginning . . .

Jenny, my gratitude for you is boundless. You didn't just believe in this story; you believed in me as an author. In an industry full of "no"s, you were the one big "yes" that changed the course of not just my career but my entire life. Zoë, Emma, Victoria, and everyone at The Bent Agency, I am forever in awe of the expertise and grace you brought to the entire process of bringing this book to life. I would've been lost without you all.

Speaking of "big yeses," Tricia and Molly, I am still staggered by the faith you put in me and this story. This dark, glittering world exists because of both of you. From endless brainstorming sessions to months of back-and-forth edits, you both stood by me every step of the way. I must also thank your incredible teams at Del Rey and Hodderscape for all the effort, expertise, and heart everyone put into this story.

But it's not just the teams behind the English language I need to acknowledge—my publishing partners around the globe, you are all astounding in your own right. This book is a testament to all your efforts, and I'm deeply grateful for everything you've done.

Leo, I must single you out because you were such a huge part of making this happen. Thank you for believing in me, for introducing me to Jenny, and for all you've done for me and all my books.

Every book I write benefits from the collective support of friends and family. Michelle, I cherished every moment we spent talking about this world. Thank you for your excitement, your friendship, and, of course, all the tarot practice! Bailey, Amy, Gideon, and Katie, your insights were invaluable. From helping me realize I needed to up the stakes (thank you, Bailey), to what did and didn't land about the romance (thank you, Amy), to what was and wasn't working about the world (thank you, Gideon), and helping ensure broad appeal (thank you, Katie). You each helped check my gut and enabled me to proceed through my various edits and changes with confidence.

Danielle, my dear friend, how do I even begin to express what you mean to me? Thank you for pushing me to explore the traditional side of the industry . . . and for your comically large card that will forever hang in my office, humbling and inspiring me every day.

My darling writerly friends and fellow turtles—Angela, Emma, Helen, Janice, Jenny, Jessica, Meg, Melinda, Melissa, Sarah, Sara, and Sylvia—you are the best community a woman could hope for. Every hour of the day, all the memes, shop talk, and brainstorming—I would be lost without the safe space we've cultivated.

Dear Family, what would I do without you? Meredith, you're the best sister I could've ever dreamed of. Our story may (thankfully) have far less trauma than Clara and Arina's, but you inspired me to write about siblings who always have each other's back—who would move the world for the other. Mom and Dad, sharing each edition of my books with you fills me with pride. Thank you. And thank you to Bob and Stephanie as well, for all your help as I juggled writing and editing this ambitious project while navigating the early stages of first-time motherhood.

Robert, my lifeline, my cornerstone, my North Star . . . as with all my books, this wouldn't have happened without your love and support. For every hour you took the lead on caring for the baby, for all the mornings you let me sleep after long nights of work, for keeping me grounded when I felt like I was unraveling—you made this book possible by holding me together. My little dragon, thank you for the baby snuggles, the best distraction when writing became too stressful.

And, of course, my patrons on Patreon: Shaeli S., Zachary F., Michelle, Madalyn W., Francesca, Anika M., Kelci S., Jessica G., Emi C., Lauren B., Winter M., Courtney, Maryalyce B., Allie, Sharon B., Karin, Amanda H., Christine P., Ayragon, Pippa S., Tiffany H., Zoe B., Brooke R., Carolyn H., Courtney, Moa E., Aly N., Adrienne A., Kristýna, Elizabeth H., Dyani S., Pauline, Chloe F., Jade, Amanda C., Imzadi, Vixie, Caitlyn P., MasterR50, Rebecca R., Steffi, Aniyue, Anne, Laura R., Sarah T., Nancy S., Laura B., Mandi S., Melinda H., Taylour D., Stephanie H., Nichole M., Sarah M., Gemma, Rose G., Karolína N. B., Laura Henman, Dani W., C Sharp, M Knight, Jamie B., Jennifer G., Marissa C., Monique R., Ru-Doragon, Claribel V., Sarah L., Lisa, Sorcha A., Tea Cup, Caitlin P., Bridget W., Kristen M., Kelly M., Audrey C W., Allison S., Ashton Morgan, Mackenzie S., Kaitlin B., Amanda T., Kayleigh K., Alisha L., Esther R., Kaylie, Heather F., Andra P., Melisa K., Serenity87HUN, Chelsea S., Alli H., Catarina G., Stephanie T., Mani R., Elise G., Traci F., Samantha C., Lindsay B., Sara E., Karin B., Eri W., Ashley D., Stengelberry, Dana A., Michael P., Alexis P., Jennifer B., Kay Z., Lauren V., Sarah Ruth H., Sheyl K B., Lindsay Shurtliff, NaiculS, Justine B., Lindsay W., MotherofMagic, Charles B., Kira M., Charis, Kassie P., Angela G., Elly M., Amy B., Meagan R., Axel R., Ambermoon86, Tarryn G., Cassidy T., Kathleen M., Alexa A., Rhianne, Cassondra A., Emmie S., Emily R., Tamashi T., Amy H., Michelle, Ashley J., Heather K., Anastasiya Z., Christina B., Amy & Trevor—thank you for all your support!

Finally . . . last, but certainly not least (more like saving the best for last) . . .

I want to thank YOU, the reader. *You* are the reason I write. This book, these words, are nothing without you. Every recommendation, every review, every post, like, and share mean the world to me. I see you. I appreciate you with every fiber of my being. I wish I could thank each one of you personally, but please know this: With my whole heart, thank you for being on this journey and for being a part of my worlds. I couldn't do what I do without readers like you.

ABOUT THE AUTHOR

Elise Kova is a *USA Today* and internationally bestselling author. She enjoys telling stories of fantasy worlds filled with magic and deep emotions. She lives in Florida and, when not writing, can be found playing video games, drawing, chatting with readers on social media, or daydreaming about her next story.

elisekova.com

ABOUT THE TYPE

This book was set in Caslon, a typeface first designed in 1722 by William Caslon (1692–1766). Its widespread use by most English printers in the early eighteenth century soon supplanted the Dutch typefaces that had formerly prevailed. The roman is considered a "workhorse" typeface due to its pleasant, open appearance, while the italic is exceedingly decorative.